BOOK ENDINGS

LOSS, PAIN, AND REVELATIONS

SYNTELL SMITH

ISBN:0-692-03698-9 ISBN-13: 978-0-692-03698-3

Copyright © 2020 Syntell Smith Publishing Published By Syntell Smith

To obtain permission to excerpt portions of the text, please contact the author at syntellsmith@gmail.com

Chapter graphic courtesy of the Boston Public Library, used with permission.

Library of Congress Cataloging-in-Publication Number: 2020912519

Cover design by Aidana WillowRaven of WillowRaven Illustration & Cover Creation

For John Leslie Smith, with love. I did it, granddaddy...you would have been proud of me.

ACKNOWLEDGMENTS

CHARACTER INDEX

The staff of the 58th Street Branch Library

Robin Walker – Idealistic, intelligent, opinionated, full-time college student and part-time library clerk. Transfers to 58th Street from his neighborhood branch Fort Washington, in upper Manhattan. Under the mentorship of Barbara Schemanske, Robin has been trained to take his position extremely seriously, following the Procedures of Conduct to the letter.

Sonyai Yi – Branch Senior Clerk in charge of supervising and mentoring the library clerks and pages. Traditional and just, respectful to her clerks and overprotective of the four female library pages, Sonyai values the integrity of the branch above everything and is constantly at odds with Augustus Chavez over policies to serve the public.

Augustus Chavez – Head Librarian, determined to bring the branch to its fullest potential and to serve the public by any means necessary. Favoring those who privately contribute charitable donations, Augustus' politician-like mentality brings him close to breaking the rules and putting the library at extreme risk.

Zelda Clein – Branch Librarian and Augustus Chavez's assistant, long-time friend, mentor, and confidant. She does whatever it takes to protect all staff members of the branch, playing the dangerous game of keeping the balance when it comes to all the existing conflicts within its hostile work environment.

Heywood Learner – Information Assistant and Librarian-in-training. With a conservative outlook and an inclination for clean and wholesome family values, Heywood challenges Augustus' liberal agenda as the two constantly argue over the smallest aspects of branch politics.

Angie Trueblood – Information Assistant who is attending evening classes at Queens College to earn her Associates in Library Science. Isolated and neutral in terms of the workplace conflicts that plague the branch, Angie strives hard to prove her worth and be a credit to her native indigenous people.

Tommy Carmichael – Library clerk with light experience who is learning everything he can from Sonyai Yi as her protégé. While friends with his other two clerical co-workers, he sees Robin Walker as an outsider and is more than eager to antagonize him.

Gerry Coltraine – Library clerk with enough experience, he believes he should be 58th Street's Senior Clerk instead of Sonyai Yi and makes that point loud and clear by questioning, challenging and undermining her authority every chance he can. Ill-tempered, Gerry tends to engage in heated exchanges with patrons which are triggered sometimes due to racial tensions.

Ethel Jenkins – Experienced Library clerk who views 58th Street as her final stop in a long, illustrious career. With retirement within her sights, she wants no part in any of the drama in the workplace and the rest of the staff have obliged her out of respect...and fear.

Janelle Simms – High school senior approaching graduation and the oldest of Sonyai Yi's four library pages. She was next in line for 58th Street's part-time clerical position before Robin Walker arrived. The inconvenience of losing the position is ill-timed since she has recently learned she is pregnant.

Alex Stevens – Library page who becomes a strong opponent against Robin Walker's arrival due to her close friendship with fellow page, Janelle Simms. Like Tommy Carmichael, she goes above and beyond to alienate and annoy the new hire once she discovers a self-conscious and sensitive frailty he has.

Tanya Brown – Library page who is impartial to Robin Walker working at the branch when he arrives, staying out of the intense drama that unfolds. She unfortunately gets tangled in a love triangle unknowingly at school, which brings hostiles looking to do her bodily harm.

Lakeshia Seabrooke – The youngest Library page, very meek and naïve. While concerned for her co-worker Janelle Simms' predicament, Robin Walker's arrival will test her loyalties and trigger emotional feelings she has never felt before.

Supporting Characters

Eugene Iscaro – Branch security guard re-hired from a brief hiatus to keep the peace after several tense incidents occur upon Robin Walker's arrival. Has a history with the S.I.U., a department that deals with library investigations of everything from book theft to accusations of corruption.

Jon Walker – Robin Walker's grandfather and guardian. Lost his hearing after working on the tracks in the tunnels of the New York Subway. Jon attempts to hide his declining health from Robin as he prepares for the inevitable.

Franklin – Robin Walker's best friend, a former Library page himself, who worked at Fort Washington. Not taking his career too seriously, he left and is currently working at a boutique in midtown while attempting to find himself.

Barbara Schemanske – Head librarian of the Fort Washington branch library and mentor to Robin Walker. With a formidable reputation known throughout the New York Public Library, she is all-knowing, all-seeing, and a force to be reckoned with.

Sarah Carmichael – Tommy's wife, who is pregnant with their first child. With their interracial marriage challenged by her parents over cultural differences, Sarah struggles to keep her explosive temper from endangering her health.

Cervantes – Immigrant taxi driver who is indebted to Robin Walker for saving his life during an attempted carjacking. While serving as an occasional provider of sage advice, Cervantes also offers Robin free rides around the city.

LIBRARY TERMINOLOGY GLOSSARY

Call Number – Combination of letters and numbers used to classify the specific location of library items by subject. Alternatively known as Dewey Decimal Numbers.

The System – A term known among dedicated library employees for the New York Public Library network of branches among the three boroughs of The Bronx, Manhattan and Staten Island.

Procedures of Conduct (or P.o.C.) – Rules and guidelines on how a library employee carries themselves. Proper etiquette on introducing themselves (identifying the previous branches worked), how to address others, how to present themselves to the public and how to behave when working in a branch.

Patron – Men, women, and children of the public who frequently visit libraries for the use of their services.

IA – Abbreviated term for Information Assistant, title for library employees acquiring or recently acquired college accreditation from American Library Association mandated schools.

Page – Entry-level part-time library position for adolescents attending high school. Duties include shelving returned books among other shelf maintenance tasks. Pages are expected to become clerks upon graduation from school.

Collapsible Security Periodical Baton (or CPB) – Adjustable plastic sticks which newspapers and periodicals are kept in for public access by patrons. These replaced the extended wooden sticks used previously by libraries.

Shelving Cart (or Truck) – Use by pages to place returned items in their proper locations among the shelves.

Clustering – Temporary relocation or exchange of branch clerks between libraries, usually done on Saturdays or emergencies in which a location is short-staffed.

PREVIOUSLY ON CALL NUMBERS

Robin Walker has transferred downtown to the 58th Street Branch library. But his position was promised by his new supervisor, Sonyai Yi to Janelle Simms, because she was next in succession, and she's pregnant. Sonyai plans to antagonize Robin upon his arrival in hopes he'll transfer someplace else before Janelle's secret is discovered.

The branch is in a feud between clerical supervisor Sonyai Yi and head librarian Augustus Chavez. The two constantly disagree on several policies on how to serve the public. Augustus believes in favoritism, rewarding exclusive access and occasionally bending the rules to those who contribute charitable donations to support the branch individually.

Both sides deal with usurpers of their leadership. Gerry Coltraine confides to Ethel Jenkins his doubts in Sonyai's plan and is conflicted when Ethel and fellow clerk, Tommy Carmichael, participate in the hazing of the young arrival. Challenging Augustus among his camp is Information Assistant Heywood Learner, whose conservative views clash with his supervisor's liberal thinking. Heywood receives occasional assistance when opposing Augustus. Unbeknownst to either side, the elderly puppet master and assistant librarian Zelda Clein, manipulated all the pieces on the chessboard to provide a certain balance in the conflict.

Neutral from both the clerks and librarians is Information Assistant-in training, Angie Trueblood. Like Robin, she attends college at night to acquire her associate degree in Library Science and climb the ranks to become a head librarian in her own branch one day.

Working the shelves with Janelle are the rest of the branch pages, Alex Stevens, Tanya Brown, and Lakeshia Seabrooke. Alex joins Janelle in her hatred for Robin, while Tanya discovers Lakeshia has developed a crush on him.

Robin struggles to prove himself while being tested on the job as he attends school and faces the reality of his grandfather's failing health. He also endures social misadventures involving his college friends, including several missed opportunities with an elusive, mysterious Asian student he keeps engaging. After several hostile incidents, a fistfight with Tommy and a racially insensitive practical joke by Alex, Robin finally finds himself in Sonyai's favor when standing up to Augustus in the face of his applied favoritism.

Lakeshia's infatuation with Robin results in her sexual awakening. She fantasizes about being with him but is unsure how to proceed with these new feelings and emotions. The young page confides in Tanya, who uses the surrounding resources to teach her about human sexuality. Tanya deals with pressure in school from a bully after getting caught inadvertently in a love triangle. Lakeshia gets involved after some near-miss harmful encounters and pleads for Robin's assistance. He takes care of Tanya's situation and then wins the respect of the other pages (including Alex and Janelle) by offering advice in a routine group reassignment.

Gerry is approached by Eugene Iscaro, a newly hired security guard assigned to the library who warns that Sonyai is being investigated for mishandling funds by the Special Investigation Unit. Gerry agrees to prove her innocent by secretly getting copies of the branch ledger, which is locked in a safe. With Tommy's help, Gerry succeeds only to find out Eugene was working with Sonyai to test how far he would go find evidence of her misdeeds. He justifies his intentions once again, saying he was trying to prove her innocence, but she knows where his loyalties lie.

Heywood meets a female nightclub singer and they begin to have a relationship. It is drastically affected by the death of her childhood friend who turns out to be Kurt Cobain, the pioneer lead singer of Nirvana. She moves in with Heywood after an emotional performance dedicated to Cobain which resulted in her losing her job. Pushing his agenda, Heywood misrepresents Augustus while preparing for one of the branch's events and his deception is discovered. The head librarian unleashes a tirade to set him straight and warns Heywood to never undermine him again.

Augustus executes a campaign to improve public circulation statistics with a recommended promotion that is approved but then fabricates false paperwork that gives 58th Street an unfair advantage. Sonyai suspects that Augustus has the tools and the means to produce fraudulent documentation, but must have proof to confirm her suspicions. Others suspect Augustus of foul play, including officials from nearby neighborhood branches in their cluster.

Robin and Lakeshia attend a sports event with the rest of his college friends. They agree to keep their friendship strictly platonic due to their age difference, for the sake of not drawing attention to themselves. She's hurt, but he leaves the door open to explore the possibilities when she graduates from high school. Meanwhile, Angie accidentally discovers a box with the materials Augustus uses to make fake memorandums that support his campaigns. She meets Sonyai outside the branch and reveals what she discovered. The two plan to work together with Angie attempting to prove what she couldn't believe about Augustus, and Sonyai getting what she needs to bring him down.

Upon returning home, Robin discovers in horror, his grandfather collapsed on the living room floor...

PROLOGUE

November 1992

"There I was, about to sneak out of the lunchroom and head to the computer lab to play some Prince of Persia..." Robin Walker began.

There was a light dusting of snow outside George Washington High School as secretary Sally McIntire rolled her eyes and listened to the current yarn of the senior student and repeat offender. Robin was summoned to the guidance counselor's office by Sally's boss and she was in no mood to hear a recap of the upstart's latest act of mischief.

Staring out the window, near a row of chairs in the waiting area, Robin continued. "When I see Marcellus Castleberry teasing Diedre Anderson by putting a slice of cheese in her hair!"

Of course, Sally thought. *It would have to do something with that Anderson girl.* It was no secret that the two were dating during the three-and-a-half years they'd attended the school. While their relationship had its ups and downs, Robin always protected the special education student like a rabid pit bull protecting a kitten.

"So I sit back down and grab three meatballs from Hannah Vega's lunch tray, right? Mash them up into a softball sized mass. Then I kicked off the lunch table, turned and hurled that sucker across the room, like maybe 20-30 feet, with some smoke and serious spin...Velarde to Mattingly, easy! And it hits him square in the throat, right under his double chin!"

"Oh dear!" Sally gasped.

Robin let out a series of high-pitched cackles as a silhouette appeared in the office doorway. A woman slowly walked in, wearing a lavender dress suit with Doc Martens snow boots. She had a solid build that would challenge the starting linebacker on the Trojans (the school's football team). Despite a short stature, there was something about her presence that one would find intimidating.

"And he starts turning blue!" Robin continued, not noticing the visitor. "It's hilarious! He's grabbing his throat, flopping around like when Macho Man Randy Savage dropped the ring bell on Ricky The Dragon Steamboat!"

The woman listened on while studying the teenager, then turned to McIntire, her face stoic with dark eyes and her gray hair cut in a close bob.

"Is this him?" she asked.

The gravelly voice nearly startled Robin as he turned from the window. "Huh? You the new behavioral specialist Mister Ramirez wanted me to speak to? Boy are *you* a spooky character!"

Taken aback by the response, she tilted her head and squinted. The mysterious woman was not used to being addressed in such a manner.

Robin took a seat and looked up with wide, doe-like eyes. "Shall I tell you about living in the orphanage, where the old man chased me around with his shoe when I was younger?"

"So, you know your literary classics...that's *Oliver Twist*," she replied with an arched eyebrow.

"Or, how my sister Amy had to sell her hair to feed us that harsh winter," Robin continued without missing a beat.

"It was Jo who sold her hair in *Little Women*, you're getting your classics mixed up."

"Ah," he replied with a nod.

"What else do you know?" the visitor challenged as she folded her arms in front of her chest.

"Um, I know two plus two is four, the square root of 16 is also four, there are 16 ounces in a pound, and there are also 16 pawns in a chess set. What I *don't* know is what happened to Jon's roommate and Odie's original owner, Lyman? They just wrote him off the strip..."

The woman appeared unfazed by Robin's sense of humor. He stood and sized her up with a questioning glance. "You're not a guidance counselor..." he asked slowly, his eyes darting around wildly. "Are you?"

"No young man, I'm not...my name is Barbara Schemanske. And I would like to talk to you about the New York Public Library."

CHAPTER ONE

TIME WAS OF THE ESSENCE. ROBIN KNEELED AND TURNED JON OVER. HIS face was blue, and he was not breathing. Robin tried to feel a pulse on his wrist, then his neck. He shook his shoulders, frantic.

"Granddaddy!? Granddaddy!?" he called out.

HE CAN'T FUCKING HEAR, YOU IDIOT! A voice screamed in his head.

He jumped up and ran to the secretary's desk, then picked up the phone, dialing 9-1-1. Seconds ticked away in slow motion like hours as he waited while the receiver rang.

"911. What's your emergency?" an operator asked.

"My grandfather's collapsed on the floor. Send an ambulance! 111 Wadsworth Avenue, the high-rise bridge apartments between 179th and 178th on Wadsworth! Apartment 16D, D as in David! Hurry goddamnit!"

"Paramedics are on their way sir, please remain calm. Is he awake? Can you check if he's breathing? Check for a pulse, does he have a history of heart problems?"

"He had a congestive heart failure scare back in 1987, I think he's breathing, I'm not sure..." his eyes watered as panic registered in his voice.

"Okay, stay on the line with me. Don't try to move him."

Robin cupped the receiver to prevent the operator from hearing him as he moved to the apartment intercom. He pressed the TALK button.

"Hey security! Paramedics are coming! Hold an elevator in the lobby for them!"

He released the button and pressed on the LISTEN button for a reply from the guard stationed downstairs. "Okay, they're already here. They're coming up!" came from the speaker.

Robin turned the knob on the metal door, pulled it open, and then turned the lock tumbler to stick out and hold the door ajar. He then rushed back to Jon just as two EMT's entered the apartment.

"Help him, please!" Robin cried.

"Step back, Son!" one of them ordered.

Robin gave way as the technicians examined his grandfather.

"Got a pulse, pass me the O2 and get the stretcher!"

Please God, don't take him now, please, Robin prayed.

Please not now...

An hour later Robin was in the waiting area of the Intensive Care Unit at Columbia Presbyterian Hospital. Every moment when someone wearing a white jacket or scrubs walked by, he would tense up expecting the worst.

"Don't die, please don't die...not now, please..." he whispered.

A short middle-aged white man with thinning black hair walked down from the hallway and called out, "Mister Walker?"

Robin stood up. "Yes?"

The physician approached him. "I'm Doctor Hale Kelsloan. Your grandfather is in stable condition..."

"Oh thank you, Jesus!" Robin interrupted.

"...but he's not out of the woods yet, young man," Kelsloan finished.

"When can I see him?"

"Soon. He's been placed in a room for observation, but his condition..."

"Go on, I need to hear it, Doctor," Robin said, taking a deep breath.

"He's suffering from Pulmonary Edema, which means that fluid is building in his lungs. The oxygen in his blood is at an extremely low rate. We took out 10 ounces of liquid. That's a little more than a soda can. I have no other way to tell you this, but...he doesn't have much time left."

Robin let what was just said sink in. "H...how much time are we talking here?"

"Depending on his strength, no more than four to six weeks at the most."

"Is there anything you can do?"

He shook his head. "At his age, in his condition, not even a transplant would help. I'm afraid the only thing to do is make good with the time he has left."

Robin turned away and closed his eyes as the doctor walked back up the hallway. Another hour went by and around midnight Jon was admitted to a room on the third floor. Robin tried to see him, but he was sleeping with no sign of waking up soon, so he went back home.

Walking back in the apartment, Robin was beginning to grapple with the possibility of living alone. His stomach was doing flip-flops. He thanked his lucky stars he didn't eat any concessions at the Knicks game. It was time to call someone he was in no mood to speak to.

"Um, hey, it's...it's me, Mom. I don't know if you even listen to these messages. It's been months since I've heard from you or Raven. It's probably due to her busy schedule, but um, the reason why I'm calling is..."

Robin cupped the receiver, took a breath, then sighed.

"...th...there was an incident with granddaddy. He's fine, for now, but he's been admitted to the hospital and will be there for a few days. The...the doctors are saying, that...that he doesn't have much time left. We've had some scares before, I know, but I...I..I think this could be it, Mom. So please, give me a call when you get this. I think you might need to fly home from wherever you are at this moment, okay? So, bye."

He hung up the phone. Using a calling card for long-distance rates just to leave a message was so annoying to him. His mother used an automated answering service, and rarely returned his calls. The last time he physically spoke to her was a five-minute conversation around Thanksgiving.

Robin looked at the clock. It was two fifteen in the morning. He had no idea how he was going to function while going to class and work on four hours of sleep. After a night like tonight, sleep wasn't even an option.

Lakeshia was still walking on air despite lying in bed with her eyes closed. She kept reliving the moment in her head, the warm embrace they shared. How strong his arms were. The souvenir t-shirt was draped down her bare chest. Her mind began to slip away into a dreamlike state, fantasizing about Robin lying next to her.

His fingers traced up and down her entire body, giving her the chills. It felt so real to her. She started to moan, becoming aroused. The cloth of the shirt brushed against her nipples as they suddenly perked to life. Her thighs began to rub together and after a moment she began to spasm and jerk violently. She opened her eyes as her body went limp. She had no idea what just happened, but something felt...wrong.

Lakeshia sat up and gasped as she looked down and noticed her sheets were damp. She turned on the lights and leaped out of her bed, still grasping the shirt. After examining the bed, she took off the sheets and went out of her room to the linen closet.

At eight o'clock in the morning, the door to Augustus' office opened. The intruder crept inside and went to the supply closet. Gloved hands carefully opened the closet and slowly removed the box with the fake memo supplies. Without making another sound, the intruder left the branch and locked the door.

Sonyai was working the returns side of the circulation desk when Robin walked in. He appeared to be distraught about something. She followed him inside the clerical office.

"Walker, what's wrong?" she asked.

He debated about disclosing his personal crisis. "Um, it's nothing. Just didn't get that much sleep last night."

She turned and closed the door behind her, then looked back at him. "Look," she began, "we haven't known each other long enough to share anything personal, but something is obviously troubling you."

He looked at his supervisor for a moment, then rolled his eyes and sighed. "My grandfather went to the hospital last night. He's sick."

"I'm sorry to hear that. You have my condolences."

Yeah, right, he thought. "Um, thanks," he said instead. "I was wondering if I could work a straight shift with no break...so I can leave early and check on him?"

She raised an eyebrow. "To work without a break, even for part-time clerks would be against the law..."

Robin just stared back at her. She could see how exhausted he was.

"However, I'm willing to, ahem, make an exception this one time."

He nodded. "Thank you, Miss...Thank you, Sonyai."

She reached up and extended her hand to his shoulder. "My, I never noticed how tall you are."

That brought a smile to his face. "I'm not tall, you're just short," he joked.

She scoffed as they both returned to the circulation desk.

Tanya was working the shelves at four o'clock when Lakeshia shuffled quickly toward her. "Um, can I talk to you for a sec?" she asked with a shaky voice.

"What's wrong?"

Lakeshia pulled her arm as they went upstairs to the auditorium. When they arrived, she turned and looked at Tanya frantically...

"Something happened last night!"

"Geez, what? Another wet dream? What is with you?"

"I...I...was sleeping last night, th...thinking about Robin and he gave me this Knicks shirt as a souvenir and...and...and I was holding it while I was asleep, and it reminded me of him...and..."

"Knicks shirt? Souvenir?! When was this? Nevermind, what happened next?"

"I felt something...something...*funny*."

Tanya narrowed her eyes. "Between your..." she whispered.

She nodded.

"And your bed got..."

She nodded faster.

They said in unison, "*IT*."

Tanya sighed. "What did you do?"

"I changed the sheets in the middle of the night and slept on the floor." She started to cry and grabbed Tanya. "Oh my God, I was so scared! I didn't know what to do. I didn't know what was happening, I thought I was..."

"Bleeding?"

Lakeshia wiped her nose and mumbled, "Mmmhmm..."

Tanya sighed. "It's okay, Leelee, it's a perfectly normal reaction for your body...we'll get to that chapter in the book. But you gotta tell me how you got that Knicks shirt."

"Well..." Lakeshia began as she remembered promising Robin to keep their "date-that-was-not-a-date" a secret. "You can't tell anyone, not even Miss Yi...but I went to a Knicks game with Robin...and his friends. He had an extra ticket and we went just as friends."

Tanya arched an eyebrow. "Uh-huh."

Lakeshia looked down sheepishly. "Thank you for...helping me with this, Tee."

"Don't thank me yet because...speaking of the book..."

She wiped her face and looked up at her.

"Did you know it's overdue and they sent ME a notice in the mail?" she asked.

"What? I thought I had a few more days."

"No, and what's worse, my mom opened it and she's furious!"

"What?"

At that same moment, miles north at the Seabrooke home, nine-year-old Quinton Seabrooke was playing with his remote control car, buzzing it around the living room. He then turned it toward the hallway and it bounced off the wall into Lakeshia's room.

"Aaaack!" he cried out. If his sister found his car in her room again she would get their parents to take it away from him. He quickly ducked inside and searched for his toy. After checking the closet and the dresser, he looked under her bed and found the car. It was next to a book that he pulled out and read the cover.

His eyes went wide as he screamed out, "MOOOMMMMMMMM!"

It was nearly closing time and Robin was holding his own against a line of patrons checking out materials when Sonyai approached him.

"I've closed the cash register. Go ahead, give your grandfather my best," she ordered.

"You sure?"

She nodded and they switched places. Robin retrieved his book bag and rushed out the door. Across the floor, Angie Trueblood stood up from the information desk and joined the senior clerk checking out books.

"We should look for the box," she whispered.

Sonyai nodded. "Once the pages leave."

The room fell silent as the last of the patrons departed, with Alex and Tanya leaving behind them. Sonyai turned out the lights in the clerical office, then walked over to join Angie in front of Augustus' office. Sonyai looked at Angie as she slipped on a pair of gloves.

"Aren't you being a bit TOO paranoid?" she asked. "We've touched his door several times already."

The information assistant didn't reply as she slowly opened the door.

They walked in and Sonyai turned on the desk lamp so they could see. Angie walked to the supply closet, opened the door and felt around inside where she left the box previously. While she searched, Sonyai looked on the desk and remembered the friendly discussions she'd had with the head librarian's predecessor.

"Shit!" Angie hissed.

"What? What is it?" Sonyai asked, snapping back from her memory.

"It's gone!"

"What do you MEAN it's gone?"

She stepped back. "I mean, it's not here!"

Sonyai stepped forward and opened both doors, searching the closet. "Where did you see it?"

"It was right here on the fourth shelf next to the reserve post-cards," Angie replied, pointing. "I put it back and left it right here."

She stepped back and slammed her fist on the desk in disgust, then turned back to Angie. "Do you think someone tipped him off?"

"No, I placed it there carefully. There's no way he would know it was disturbed."

"He must have moved it somewhere else, look around..."

They searched the room and his desk carefully. When they didn't find anything Angie said, "Maybe it's upstairs? The staff room? Or even..."

"Forget it!" Sonyai interrupted. "This was just a waste of time..." she stepped from around the desk and headed to the door.

Angie was a step behind when Sonyai opened the door and froze after stepping outside. She was about to say something while almost bumping into her, but then gasped as Zelda stood in the middle of the floor staring back at them. All three looked like a deer in headlights, obviously not expecting to see each other at this hour.

"I...accidentally left my purse in my desk..."

"Uhhh..." Sonyai uttered as her eyes darted in every direction.

"What were you two doing in there?" Zelda asked.

"I...I...I, um..." Angie stammered.

"Miss Trueblood was just...showing me the uh, new pencils Augustus ordered!"

Angie nodded and exclaimed, "Yes! Th...those pencils were nice, weren't they?"

"Yes, yes they were. He did an excellent job with those supply acquisitions...well, we were just closing for the evening. I'll leave you to it, then. Have a...nice evening." Sonyai quickly walked past Zelda to the exit as Angie looked at Zelda sheepishly.

"Um, I guess *you* can lock up now...after you get...um, your purse."

"Yes, I suppose I can," Zelda said skeptically.

Without another word, Angie also walked past the librarian and left the branch.

Robin made it back to Presbyterian by seven. He got off the elevator on the third floor and signed in. Jon was sitting up slurping on chicken broth in bed when Robin stepped through the doorway. The sight of his grandfather still alive and eating brought him to tears. Then he remembered what the doctor said and put on a brave face.

"*Hey,*" he signed with his right hand while wiping a tear on his glove.

Jon greeted him with a weak smile. "Too tired to sign..." he said, his voice hoarse.

Robin took his hand and slowly said, "It's okay," so he could read his lips.

"W...what did they say?" Jon asked.

Robin changed the subject. "I um, called Mom...left a message,"

Jon shook his head. "She won't come. Call your aunt instead." He looked down in defeat.

Robin didn't even think of Aunt Regina. He nodded and made a mental note to call her when he got home. Jon's hand felt cold and clammy. "Look, fuck what these doctors said. Put it out of your head right now, we...Granddaddy, hey, look at me..." Robin barked and clapped his hands.

He lifted his head as they faced each other.

"...We will get through this...okay?" There was a fierce look of determination in his eyes as the young man assured the elder.

Jon looked down again and simply nodded.

A nurse came in to check on Jon.

Robin stood up and asked her, "When can he go home?"

She looked at him. "I know he looks fine, but we just want to watch him for two or three more days at the most."

Robin clenched his jaw. "Fine, but he is NOT dying here, okay? When that time comes, he will be home surrounded by his family and loved ones."

He stepped out of the room for some air while the nurse resumed her examination. Out of sight in the hallway, he leaned against the wall and lightly hit the back of his head against it.

"I heard what you said back there."

Robin turned to see Doctor Kelsloan standing next to him.

"Sorry, don't mean to sound ungrateful..." Robin said with a sigh.

"It's alright, we hear it all the time. You're at stage one, now."

Robin frowned. "Um, video games have taught me that the first stage is usually the tutorial and the easiest stage. THIS does not feel easy!"

"I'm talking about the five stages...of dealing with the death of a loved one."

He stared at him quietly, waiting for him to continue.

"Denial is the first stage. We have a natural fear of dying so when we are faced with it up close we refuse to accept it or we just don't believe it...until it's too late."

"I am at peace with what will happen, but I know my grandfather, and he's a fighter, okay? There have been times when he's knocked on death's door, but he's still here. When he's strong enough, he will *walk* out of here. That's a promise."

He went back inside as Kelsloan shook his head.

"Sex!? The joy of Sex!?...What in the hell is Lakeshia doing reading books about the *joy* of sex!?" Rudy Seabrooke yelled.

"Calm down," Jennifer Seabrooke pleaded. "I suspected this would happen. We should have had 'The Talk' with her, but you kept putting it off. And then pulling her out of that class in school."

"So you saying this is *my* fault, Jen? Is that what you're saying?"

"No, I'm not saying that. It's just that we have to deal with this now."

The phone rang and Jennifer answered it. "Hello?"

"Yes, my name is Cynthia Brown. My daughter Tanya works with your daughter after school in the library. I found her name and number in my daughter's address book. Am I speaking to Lakeshia's parents?"

"Good evening, Mrs. Brown, I'm Jennifer Seabrooke, Lakeshia's mother. You've called at a pretty convenient time. I believe we need to get our two children together...and have ourselves a conversation."

Tanya was at the Webster Branch again Tuesday after school watching Andrew working the floor. He was checking on the pages, briefing each one. When he was done, the senior clerk walked straight to where she was sitting with her face behind a newspaper.

"Tanya?" he said as he stood in front of her.

She lowered the paper and looked up at him.

"I wanted to tell you, but you didn't give me a chance."

"I...I trusted you, Andy...I..." she rolled her eyes and held in the tears. "I *loved* you...and you broke my heart."

He looked down. "I'm sorry."

She stood up. "Yeah, you damn sure are!" She grabbed her book bag and stormed out of the branch. It was her day off so she took the train home. When she walked in, her mother was waiting for her.

"Mama?"

"Drop your books. We're going downtown," she ordered.

Janelle knocked on the door and Evelyn opened it. She walked into the apartment and took a seat on the couch.

"Avery went around the corner to the store. He'll be right back. Would you like some water?" Evelyn offered.

"Yes, thank you."

She came back with two glasses. "It's hot as hell today and it ain't even the summer yet."

They sat quietly, sipping their drinks.

"We barely spoke last time because I was upset..."

"More like you were *angry*," Janelle interjected.

Evelyn paused at the child's interruption. She blinked hard and then put on a tight smile. "Yes, I suppose I was...as I was saying, we barely spoke, but now that this is happening I would like some details."

Janelle smiled back. "Of course. What would you like to know?"

"Why aren't you in school now?"

"I finished early, earning my 40 credits as of February. I'm just waiting for the graduation ceremony as a formality."

"So, you *could* start college now if you wanted to, possibly in May?" Evelyn asked.

"That...is possible, but I haven't applied to any schools yet. I'm taking a year off to be there for the baby."

Avery's mother nodded. "I see." She took another sip. "Um, when are you due?"

"I'm four months along, due the second week of October," Janelle replied.

"Have you thought of any names?"

"I want to be surprised, so I don't know the sex yet. I haven't discussed it with Avery."

The door unlocked and opened with Avery stepping inside. The two women turned to face him. A smile grew across his face. "Janelle!" he greeted. She stood up and the youngsters embraced.

"School hasn't been the same without you...everyone's wondering why you left. They haven't figured out you got all your credits. They don't think you're...you know, but rumors are all over the place."

She sighed. "Great, wait till they see me in June with my stomach sticking out."

"Well, don't worry about them. How are you? How's the baby?" he asked.

She smiled. "I have a treat for you." She reached into her back pocket and pulled out the sonogram printout.

His hands began to tremble as she gave it to him. From the couch Evelyn stared with a wild wide-eyed glance.

"I...I can't..." he squinted. "Wha..."

She moved closer to help him. "I know it's weird, but here's the head..." she pointed. "That's the body, and the legs..."

"Wow, is it a boy or girl?" he asked with a grin.

"I...don't know. I want it to be a surprise."

He looked at the printout quietly. "Our baby..." he whispered. He looked up. "I...I wanna see...I wanna go to one of your appointments." He turned to his mother who looked back and nodded.

"Okay," Evelyn agreed.

"I'll...talk to Miss Yi and give you the address."

They hugged again and he kissed her on her forehead. "I love you," he whispered.

"I love you, too," she whispered back.

Evelyn cleared her throat, then took a sip of her water. The teens broke their embrace. She looked down while he scratched the back of his head.

"Um, I should go," Janelle said.

"Yeah."

Janelle craned her head toward Evelyn. "Thank you for the water, Miss Brooks."

"Take care, child. Take care."

Avery walked her to the door. "I'll be there," he whispered to her before she left.

Lakeshia and Derrick arrived in front of their building at six thirty. After parking the car the siblings exited the vehicle and walked up the steps to their apartment. She jogged down the hallway on their floor and Derrick tossed her the house keys. She unlocked the door and walked in...to see her parents and her brother Quinton, who were joined by Tanya and her mother, whom she'd met only once.

All eyes were on her as she stood frozen in the doorway. Only Quinton was smiling, and her mother was holding up the *Joy of Sex* book in front of her.

"Sorry," Tanya mouthed to her with a frightened look.

Derrick closed the door and walked past her. He then grabbed Quinton by the wrist, dragging him to their bedroom as he protested furiously.

"Wha...wh...what is going on?" she stammered.

"Have a seat," Rudy ordered. "And we'll all find out."

She swallowed hard and stepped forward.

The group dispersed as Lakeshia and Tanya sat next to each other on the couch. The parents all sat on chairs from the dining room table. Jennifer placed the book down on the coffee table between them.

"Explain yourself, young lady," Lakeshia's mother said coldly.

She didn't know where to begin. She dared not look to Tanya for help because her mother looked just as furious as hers.

"I...I've been having these...feelings..." she began. "And I didn't know what to do, so I asked Tanya for help..."

Cynthia Brown flinched at the mention of her daughter while Rudy stole a quick glance at her.

"Why didn't you come to us?" Jennifer asked.

Lakeshia shrugged her shoulders and looked down embarrassed.

"Tanya," Cynthia started. "Why did you use your card to check out the book?"

"I can answer that, Miss Brown," Jennifer explained.

"We have restrictions on her library card," Rudy interrupted. "We tried to prevent this exact thing from happening."

"Then what about school?" Cynthia asked. "I mean, I know she just turned 15, but I remember having sex-ed my freshman year in high school."

Jennifer turned to Rudy, who thought for a moment and then nodded. "We...pulled Lakeshia out of her sexual education class..."

"MOM!" Lakeshia stood up and yelled.

"...for religious reasons," she finished.

Lakeshia sat back down on the couch and covered her face with her hands. Tanya finally moved, turned to give her a questionable look.

Cynthia grimaced. "Huh?"

"My wife and I are practicing Jehovah's Witnesses."

Lakeshia sighed as Tanya whispered, "Whoa."

Rudy continued. "We raise our children to respect the ideas of others, but when it comes to certain subjects, we shelter them from several aspects of life that public education could possibly misconstrue."

Jennifer approached Lakeshia and kneeled to look at her face-to-face. "Honey, you know to ask us about anything...your father and I are always available to talk."

"I'm...sorry, Mom."

Rudy pulled out his wallet. "How many days overdue is this...book?" he asked.

Cynthia looked at Tanya who looked up at Rudy. "If returned tomorrow the fine will be .45, Mr. Seabrooke, sir."

He put his wallet back and took out some change. After counting two quarters, he handed them to Tanya. "Please return this book tomorrow, and we would appreciate it if you not borrow any other books on my daughter's behalf."

Cynthia stood up and stepped in front of Rudy, taking the coins out of his hands. "I'll see to it that she doesn't, *sir!*" She turned to her daughter and tilted her head to leave. Tanya stood up and grabbed the book, then walked to her side. The two girls exchanged looks, then Cynthia led Tanya to the door. Without a word, they let themselves out.

"Did you have to tell them, Mom?" Lakeshia whined. "She was my only..."

Rudy pointed to her. "You stay the hell away from her at that library, you hear?" he scolded. "Go to your room! Now!"

She quickly ran down the hallway and into her room.

Downstairs after exiting the building Cynthia said, "Fucking weirdos with their pamphlets, handing out shit! Tanya, you stay the fuck away from her or you will NOT be working at that library anymore!" She threw the quarters out into the street. "You pay for that fine yourself! You hear me?"

"Yes, Mama!" she answered.

"This is all because of that damn date she had with that boy!" Rudy barked. He pointed and Jennifer. "I told you she was too young, reading sex books, we have to nip this in the bud, Jen!"

"Did it ever occur to you that she reached out to this girl because she knew you'd react like this? She's not six-years-old anymore!"

"She's not 16, either! The boys were right. When Derrick was her age we made sure he didn't fall into temptation..."

"This is different, Rudy. We have to accept that she is going to discover herself. Remember the incident with her stuffing her bra with tissue paper?"

"Oh geez, Jen..." he cringed. "Must we go over *that* again?"

"All I'm saying is we can't keep her locked in her room like

Rapunzel in a tower. We have to talk to her about everything, from condoms to STD's..."

"Jennifer!" he gasped.

"Rudy it's the 90's....things are a lot different than it was for us back in the day."

He shook his head. "I can't believe this is happening."

"Well, let's hope it's for the last time."

"Hope? We ain't having any more kids, woman. Three is enough."

She smiled and traced her finger down his nose. "I dunno sweetie. Four has a nice round number feel to it."

Rudy chuckled. "There you go, getting my blood pressure up!"

CHAPTER TWO

"It's been over a week since I caught Angie and Sonyai coming out of your office, Gus," Zelda said. It was the first week of May on a Thursday morning. Augustus sat at his desk studying some reports while Zelda was pacing in front of his desk.

"Calm down. You're making me dizzy, and probably yourself as well," he said calmly.

"You're not a bit curious to know what they were doing?" she asked.

"I have my theories...but it's all taken care of."

"Really?"

"Yes, and I will be happy to discuss them with you when I come back from my trip."

"I figured you were going to Mexico for the holiday this year. Making up for missing it last year, I suppose."

"Yes, you and I know I couldn't go then due to what transpired here."

"I remember. Fine. If all is taken care of, I won't worry then." She turned to leave. *I'll just find out for myself!* she thought.

Ethel and Tommy were working the desk at eleven o'clock, when Gerry emerged from the clerical office to relieve Ethel. She went inside and Tommy asked, "What'cha doing tonight?"

"Probably what half the city will be doing. Drinking themselves silly, why?"

"Figured you'd like to roll with me and Heywood after work."

"Where ya going? The Pig N' Whistle as always?"

"It's Cinco de Mayo, Gerry! We go to the Pig all the time. Nah, we're going someplace else."

"Well alright, I'm down...luckily Ethel and Sonyai are closing tonight."

"Right, Angie too, so all three of us can leave after five."

Gerry nodded. "Cool."

"Man I hate Cinco de Mayo!" Tanya said.

"Don't let Mister Chavez hear you say that," Alex said. "He'll think you have a problem with Mexicans."

The pair were in the staff room finishing off some pizza Alex brought in.

"It's got nothing to do with them and you know this."

"Tee, you're far too young to be a grinch around your birthday." She took a bite of her slice. "Besides, you're turning 17. That's awesome!"

"Not when you have no boyfriend to celebrate it with."

Alex sighed. "You and Andrew?"

Tanya shook her head. "Got himself a white chick, some IA..."

"Damn, he just can't help dating a co-worker, huh?"

"He played me, Alex. I need to bust him in the balls..."

"What good would that do? The best thing to do is to forget about him and move on."

"Yeah, I guess you're right. It's just...when he left last year, he told me when I turned 17 we could get back together. I thought maybe I could follow him to Webster and be a clerk there when I graduate in two years."

"Now, you know that's not gonna happen."

"Yeah, he's going to pay, though. Someday, I'll be a senior clerk too, running my own branch!"

"That's the spirit, Tee! Yeah!"

"Yeah, he ain't seen the last of me! Can't toss me away like some candy bar wrapper, Andrew Friedman! Tanya Brown don't play that!"

Alex high-fived her and Tanya did a fist pump. "Someday," she whispered.

Robin finished his hour doing checkouts at four o'clock. He left the circulation desk and headed to the door leading upstairs.

"Excuse me, sir? Could you tell me where the books on Prima Nocta are?"

He turned to see Franklin walking up behind him. "Wha? You idiot!" he greeted him and laughed. "How long you been here hiding?"

"I was here earlier, but left and came back 'bout a half-hour ago. Walked all the way over." he looked around. "Nice little branch you got here...It's *cozy*."

"Uh huh," Robin grunted. "This whole branch could fit in Fort Washington's Children's Room."

Robin noticed Lakeshia watching from across the room. He waved her and the other two pages over. Franklin cocked an eyebrow, sizing up the trio.

"Ladies, I'd like you to meet Franklin, my best friend. Franklin, these are the pages of 58th Street, Alex, Lakeshia, and Tanya."

"Ahhh yessss...Good Morning, Angels," Franklin purred.

He looked at Alex and said, "Hmmm, this porridge is too hot," then turned to Lakeshia and said, "This porridge is too cold."

The two exchanged shocked glances as he stood in front of Tanya. "But this porridge is...just right."

Tanya blinked hard as Franklin flashed her a smile. "You got a number I can call for you? Or do I have to search the white pages under *FINE*?"

She blushed as Robin pulled him back by the arm. "Anyway," he said, "Why don't we get a slice outside?" Robin nodded. "Tell Sonyai I went on break," he called back to the girls. Franklin looked back at Tanya and winked. When they got outside he said to Robin, "You know, the one in the middle kind of reminds me of Ros..."

"Don't go there," Robin interrupted.

Tucked away near the edge of the East Side on First Avenue and 58th Street, Rosa Mexicano was a Mexican restaurant known for festive Cinco de Mayo celebrations. Tommy, Heywood, and Gerry walked in at five-thirty. They were greeted by the hostess who escorted them to a table with four chairs.

The atmosphere was sparse. There were more people at the bar than the dining area. The majority of the customers were similar to the patrons from the library, the after-work office crowd. Gerry was puzzled by the additional fourth seat while Tommy and Heywood looked around.

"I hope this place was worth the hike, Tommy," Heywood said.

"How'd you hear about it?" Gerry asked.

"Sarah. Her father knows the head chef, they go way back," Tommy explained. "Half-priced drinks and 25% off the bill."

There were nods and affirmations all around as a waiter approached the table.

"Hi, we're friends of Josefina. Lorenzo says '*¡hola!*'" Tommy said.

"¡Si, senor!" the waiter replied with a smile, then took the trio's order.

As they waited for their food they helped themselves to some bottles of Heineken from the bar. Engaging in idle conversation for several minutes, the place began to fill up with more people. After six, the restaurant was getting more festive.

Heywood was sharing a funny story about Jackie when to Gerry's surprise, Eugene arrived at their table and took a seat.

"Hey guys," he greeted. "Next round's on me."

"Alright! Hope you can catch up!" Tommy said. He grunted as Gerry elbowed him in the ribs.

Eugene waved for the waiter and Tommy whispered to Gerry, "What gives?"

"You didn't tell me *he* was coming!" he hissed.

He shrugged. "What does it matter?"

Gerry glared back at Tommy then leaned back in his chair and picked up his bottle.

Another hour went by. The crowd noise and the music were reaching deafening levels. Tommy went to use the bathroom and Heywood was eating a taco platter. Eugene and Gerry stared at each other from opposite ends.

"You've been eyeballing me for ten minutes," Eugene yelled across the table. "You still pissed over that shit with Sonyai?"

Gerry cocked his head. "You fucking played me, man!" he replied. "Not. Cool."

"She came to me. She doesn't trust you...take it up with her."

After another moment of staring, Eugene nodded. "C'mon...shit ain't worth holding a grudge..." he held up his bottle. "We good?"

Gerry chuckled and shook his head, then lifted his bottle. "Yeah man...we good, fuck it!"

They clinked their bottles and drained them down.

Across town, Robin and Franklin walked into TGI Friday's on the corner of 50th Street and Broadway. Up the block, the Winter Garden Theater had a huge banner display for the musical *Cats*. At the bar the two grabbed barstools and the bartender, a tall blond whose uniform looked painted on, greeted Franklin.

"Lucky Lindy, long time, sweetie. What can I get ya?"

He held up two fingers. "Two Michelob Golds..."

"For *him*," Robin interrupted. "I'll take a screwdriver." Franklin rolled his eyes.

"Coming right up," the bartender said.

"She didn't card us?" Robin whispered.

"Elizabeth's good people. Shops at Bolton's all the time."

"She thinks you're gay too?"

He grinned. "She *does* look good in a pair of matching bra and panties."

Robin laughed. "You're gonna get caught in the lie one day..."

"Not if I keep hanging around with you for appearances."

"Very fuckin' funny."

Once their drinks arrived they went upstairs and got a table.

"How's Jon holding up?" Franklin asked.

"He's finally coming home Sunday...but it's not looking good."

"I know you're scared, but you need to face reality, man. I lost my grandfather when I was 10. He was 83. Lived a good long life. In the end, he was in so much pain everyone felt his passing was a blessing. But I didn't."

"I just wish I heard something from Mom. Despite their estranged relationship she needs to be here to help. I can't do all this alone."

"Yeaaaah, let's change the subject...what's the story with that Tanya chick?"

"Dude, she's 16!" Robin lied, knowing that today was actually Tanya's seventeenth birthday.

"Okay, I'm willing to wait. She diggin' me, though...you saw it."

Robin snickered.

Franklin leaned in. "And you'd be blind not to see that lil miss 'cold porridge' has eyes for you!"

Robin rolled his eyes and scoffed.

"Oh, c'mon, it's all over her face. She probably follows you around like a little lamb."

"Will you shut the hell up?!" Robin snarled. "We're not going there, alright?"

Their orders arrived as they stared each other down. Franklin acknowledged he touched a nerve and decided to drop it...for now.

Tommy was on the restaurant's payphone next to the bathrooms talking to Sarah. Behind him, several Hispanic gentlemen were losing their patience waiting for the phone to get free.

"I'll be home around 10, Hon...just hanging out with the guys..."

"HEY! Hurry up, will ya?!" someone yelled behind him.

"You want me to bring anything in?" he asked.

"Yo!"

He nodded and ended the call. After hanging up, he turned around and said, "We got a problem here, Fuckface?"

The three youngsters balked at the challenge and remained silent.

"Didn't think so..." he said and walked back to his table. As he passed the group he intentionally bumped the shoulder of one of them. They all exchanged glances while one of them went to use the phone.

Tommy came back to see Heywood laughing with Eugene and Gerry, who appeared to have buried the hatchet. He punched Gerry in the shoulder playfully. "Ain't this great?" he asked and took his seat.

"So, who's buying the next round?" Tommy asked.

A beer bottle crashed on the top of his head, swung down by an unknown assailant.

Eugene reacted first as he stood up and assessed the three attackers. *Young, Hispanic, possibly Mexican, mid-to-late-20s, unarmed, no serious threat.* He moved to cut off their path to the exit sensing a cheap-shot-and-run scenario. Tommy slid off his chair, clutching his forehead. Heywood attended to Tommy, kneeling down to check on him as Gerry socked the nearest of the three in the jaw.

There were screams from women as chaos erupted in the dining area. Eugene pushed the man who hit Tommy and his friend against the bar, then raised his knee to the attacker's stomach. Gerry moved to back up Eugene as he grabbed the arm of the second guy at the bar before he brought another beer bottle down on his head.

More and more people joined the fight. Heywood and Tommy got up and defended their friends. There were punches and blows landed between at least ten men. Glasses and bottles were thrown. People were getting cut and bloodied. The door flew open as uniformed police officers entered and identified themselves.

"POLICE! Everybody put their hands up, now!"

Anyone involved in the altercation stopped instantly at the threat of guns drawn and surrendered with their hands in the air. The officers proceeded to handcuff and arrest Eugene and the guys as Gerry turned to Tommy and said, "Damn, maybe we should have gone to the Pig N' Whistle."

Franklin and Robin took the 1-train uptown heading home. Robin got up as the train arrived at 168th Street so he could check on Jon at the hospital.

"Hey!" Franklin called out. Robin turned to him. "Sorry for being a dick."

He shrugged. "It's cool, you'll do it again."

"I know," he grinned.

They slapped hands and Robin stepped off the train.

It was one o'clock Friday morning at the 18th Precinct. Inside the holding cells with over twenty arrested suspects picked up throughout the night, Gerry, Heywood, Eugene, and Tommy sat in a corner. Most of the people from the restaurant fight were also in the cell staring down the group. Tommy had a bandage on his head, Heywood was nursing a swollen jaw and Gerry's hand was wrapped up after receiving a serious cut from glass.

Eugene was asleep, snoring loudly while leaning against a wall.

Gerry nudged him awake and the security guard gasped, flailing his arms wildly.

"Oh, what the hell?" he asked, turning to Gerry.

"How can you sleep at a time like this?"

"Shit, I've slept through worse. One time I slept through a shootout in the hallway outside my apartment!"

"Damn."

"I know. Woke up with bullet holes six inches above my head. Cops came by asking me what happened. I told them hell if I know!"

"You're a crazy motherfucker, man."

Eugene giggled. "You don't know the half of it."

Gerry shook his head. "Well, thanks for having my back."

"Thank *you* for grabbing that guy who nearly got the drop on me."

They nodded to each other as a mutual sign of respect. Eugene leaned back and dozed off again.

"THOMAS CONNELLY CARMICHAEL!!!" A woman's voice boomed throughout the floor. Everyone behind bars became shaken to the core. "You get your pale white Irish, potato eating, U2 listening to, leaving the toilet seat up all the goddamn time ass out here RIGHT NOW!"

"Awwww, shit," Tommy whispered. "You think you can just leave me here and lock the cell, please?" he called out to the nearest guard.

Eugene woke up and noticed Tommy and the others were waiting near the cell door as Sarah walked in the holding area looking at her husband behind bars.

"Do you have any idea how many phone calls I had to make in the last three hours?"

"Uh," he began.

"SHUT UP! I called my father who convinced the owner not to press charges! I had to call your stuck-up parents from Long Island and *beg* them to wire me the $300.00 it took to get the four of you stooges out!"

Eugene stepped up and yelled, "Hey which one of us is Shemp? I don't wanna be Shemp!"

Heywood pulled Eugene away from the bars as he giggled uncontrollably. Sarah was not laughing.

"It was a $75.00 fine for each of us?!" Tommy asked. "Christ! I'm never gonna hear the end of it!"

A uniformed officer approached the cells. "Alright, Carmichael, Coltraine, Iscaro, and Learner! You're free to go. Step forward."

Sarah stepped aside as the officer unlocked the cell.

"You think you're in pain now, púta madré, wait till you..."

"Take it easy, Big Bird, chew 'em out when you get home!" the officer barked.

Sarah turned her head. Tommy reached out to restrain her, but it was too late.

"Who the fuck are you calling 'Big Bird' you donut inhaling, pig in a blanket..."

"One more word and I'll lock you up, pregnant or not!" the cop warned, pointing a finger at her.

Tommy pulled her away gently. "We'll be going now, sir... sorry to be any trouble." He turned her around and carefully pushed her toward the hallway she emerged from, with Gerry and Heywood following. Eugene was still groggy on his feet. "Hey! Wait for me!" he called out behind them.

Tanya was in class Friday morning. She was glad another birthday had come and gone. Her thoughts wandered, thinking of that smooth white boy that was with Robin. *What was his name?*

"Miss Brown?" her math teacher called out.

"Huh?" she grunted.

All eyes were on her as the teacher asked again, "How would you calculate the length of each leg of this isosceles right triangle?"

She thought for a moment. "Uh, the square of the hypotenuse is equal to the sum of the squares of the other two sides."

The teacher blinked. "That's...correct, I apologize for thinking you weren't paying attention." He turned around and continued writing on the chalkboard.

Tanya sighed, then smiled. "Franklin..." she whispered.

Angie was on the train proofing her paper for her evening class. A lot of the passengers in the car looked hungover after partying last night. When she arrived at the branch a few minutes before ten, she noticed Gerry and Tommy were also recovering from a wild night. She sat at the information desk and tucked her book bag underneath her chair.

She turned to the right and saw Heywood sitting on a stool between shelves nodding off.

"Heywood?" she whispered. She couldn't believe her eyes.

He stammered and shot up from the stool. He looked more frazzled than both the clerks she saw when she walked in.

"What on earth happened? You look like Popeye with your face all swollen..."

"Shhhh..." He put his finger on his lips and then sat back down.

"They're all out of it," a voice said, approaching her.

Angie turned to see Sonyai walking from across the floor. "Apparently the *boys* got drunk and were in a jail cell most of the night as the result of a bar fight."

She turned back to Heywood, who was nodding off again.

"Good thing Chavez decided to take a trip to Mexico for the long weekend," Sonyai finished.

"He's not here? Good, that gives us another chance to look..."

"I'm done looking for the box," Sonyai interrupted.

"What? Why?" Angie asked.

"He obviously found out you discovered it and moved it someplace else. We'll never find it now."

"No, I put it back perfectly. He doesn't know. We can still..."

"Drop it, Trueblood. If he's faking these memos we'll get him another way."

"But..."

"As far as I'm concerned, this wild goose chase is done. Thanks for your help. At least you confirmed my suspicions. I can wait as long as it takes before he goes down."

The senior clerk turned and walked away. Angie sighed and looked at Heywood again, sitting lifeless and surrounded by books.

Alex arrived at the branch at two-thirty with Tanya right behind her. "You had a short day at school, too?" Alex asked.

"Yep, most of the teachers were drunk off their asses they just wanted to get the weekend started quickly."

They shared a chuckle and went inside. "Hey, let's sit over here for a second." Alex nodded toward the tables near the New Books in the front of the circulation desk. Ethel and Gerry were at their stations with Ethel on checkouts.

The girls took a seat. Alex reached into a bag and pulled out a wrapped gift box. "Here. Happy birthday."

Tanya looked down at the box and then at Alex, dumbfounded. "Lexi! I can't take this..."

"Ah, ah, ah...I insist. C'mon, open it!"

Behind them, Ethel narrowed her eyes.

Tanya ripped open the gift to reveal a sneaker box. She gasped. "Air Jordan 9's? These are off the chain!" She looked at her. "I...I can't. My mom will freak out, plus they're killing people in my school for sneakers these nice!"

"Then wear them around here. I don't care, just...enjoy, okay?" She stood up. "17, girl...be happy." She walked away as Tanya began to lace up her new shoes.

Alex walked across the floor feeling good about surprising Tanya with the gift. From the circulation desk, Ethel's eyes followed the teen as she headed to the staff room.

"Gerry?" Ethel called out.

"Hmmm, yeah?" he replied, still tired and groggy.

"Cover for me will ya? I'm taking a quick break."

Ethel rarely went upstairs to the staff room. The two flights of steps leading there always tired her out. She was sweating profusely after eight steps and by the time she was at the door, she was out of breath. She knew it was because of her weight and other contributing health issues that she ignored in the past catching up with her, but she was determined to talk to the page alone.

Alex was reading *The Rules of Attraction* by Bret Easton Ellis when Ethel opened the door and walked in. She lowered the book and tilted her head at the clerk's haggard appearance.

"Wow, Miss Jenkins," she began.

"Hush up, girl, and let me catch my breath!" she panted.

She grabbed the back of one of the kitchen chairs, dug her elbows into the table for support and sat down. After using a napkin from the dispenser to wipe the sweat from her brow, she took in a gasp of air and relaxed.

"Now then, I couldn't help but notice those expensive tennis shoes you gave Tanya."

Alex chuckled. "Sneakers, Miss Jenkins. No one calls them tennis shoes. Tee definitely doesn't play," she shrugged. "I thought she could use a pick-me-up after getting in trouble with Leelee's parents. Besides, have you *seen* what she's been wearing on her feet these days?"

"Do your parents know about that purchase?" Ethel asked.

Alex snapped her head in Ethel's direction. "That's none of their business," she said with a sneer.

"Watch that tone with me, girl," Ethel warned. "You ain't old enough I can't snatch that smart mouth off your face!"

Alex looked down and whispered, "Sorry, Miss Jenkins."

The elder rolled her eyes. "All I'm saying is ease up on the spending..."

"It's *my* money and I'll spend it how I want!" Alex protested. "Just because you and Mister Chavez are cool with Mom and Dad doesn't mean you can tell me what to do!"

"Hey!" Ethel held up her index finger. "One phone call and you will be a distant memory in this branch, Alexandra Stevens!" She then pounded the table. The page jumped in her seat. "You nearly got me in trouble after that stunt you pulled sneaking in here with *that* key and now you think you can fucking talk to me like you grown?!"

Alex shuddered, squirming in her chair as Ethel pointed directly at her face across the table. "Chavez and I aren't your parents, but they entrusted us to watch over you and that is what we will do!"

She stood up. "You listen to your elders, girl. This ain't up for debate." She walked to the door and gave her one last look. "You watch what you're doing and leave that boy Robin alone. Sonyai Yi won't be enough to protect you from me, ya hear?!"

She left with the door slammed behind her. Alex huffed and went back to her book. Outside in the hall, Ethel felt her heart palpitating. Her blood pressure was probably through the roof. She made a mental note to make another doctor's appointment in the near future.

CHAPTER THREE

A FEW MINUTES AFTER FOUR, ROBIN WAS TAKING A QUICK NAP ON THE couch in the staff room, when a very faint noise caught his attention. He opened his eyes and put his hand down on the tile floor. After craning his head and sticking an ear up, he stood.

In the auditorium, Lakeshia was playing a scale on a Steinway grand piano when Robin opened the door and walked in.

She stopped playing and gasped as Robin smiled. "Oh wow, a piano!" he exclaimed.

"How did you know I was in here?" she asked.

"I heard you playing from the staff room."

She shook her head. "That's impossible. This room is soundproof with reinforced fiberglass. That's how we show movies and have concerts without disturbing the people reading downstairs."

"Okay, then maybe I have super-hearing," he joked and approached her. "How did they get this in here?" He marveled at the sight of the instrument.

She pointed to the only other door in the opposite corner. "It's taken apart and stored in the closet. We take it out the first week of May for performances. You play?"

"Hell yeah, had a Casio keyboard since I was 12." He took a seat next to her on the piano bench.

Lakeshia resumed playing the scale as he listened. "So, what's on your mind, kiddo? I used to play the piano before music class whenever me and my girlfriend had a fight in school."

She stopped playing and looked at him. "Y-you had a girlfriend?" she asked.

Boy, walked right into that one, didn't I? Robin thought. "Uh, yeah...we um, broke up senior year, though. She went off to college in New Jersey." He felt weird about lying to Lakeshia, but it spared him the trouble of revealing what really happened.

"Oh, well, Tanya got in trouble with her mother for doing me a favor...and my parents also found out, so all three want us to stay away from each other."

"Hmm," he didn't pry, knowing whatever it was, it had to be something serious. "That's kind of hard to do now since y'all work together, but I have noticed all four of you have been keeping your distances from each other lately."

Lakeshia sucked her teeth. "It's like we each got our separate dramas. Alex with her suspension, me and Tanya with this, Janelle with..."

Robin looked on as she stopped herself from almost revealing the pregnancy. She darted her eyes. "Um, Nevermind," She resumed playing the tune on the piano.

"Pretty good, there." Robin nodded. He then joined in, playing further down the scale. The pair were in sync with each other perfectly, matching key to key.

"Hey, try this..." he challenged and proceeded to play the beginning of "Simple Gifts from Appalachian Spring" by Copland.

"Oh, I know that one." She played the next arrangement. They went back and forth for the entire song and finished with a flourish. She was starting to feel better as they both smiled.

Robin started to hum the beginning notes for "What Can You Lose" from the Dick Tracy movie soundtrack and began to play. Her face lit up as she started to sing the duet and play along.

After the song, he whispered, "I didn't know you were a fan."

"I saw the movie three times that summer."

He looked at her. "At the age of 10?"

"11!" she corrected.

They were both quietly staring at each other for over a minute, then Robin broke the trance. "Well um..." He cleared his throat and stood up. "It was nice, playing with you." He blushed as soon as he said that. "On the um, on the piano, I mean."

She nodded rapidly. "Yes, um, the, uh...you were very good...playing your organ...I MEAN PIANO! The piano, you, you know." She couldn't stop blushing either.

"Yeah, well...I, I gotta..." He jerked his thumb to the door. "Yeah."

"Okay!" she exclaimed nervously. "Thanks!"

"Ye-yeah, sure, no problem, uh, see ya!" He opened the door and stepped out.

When the door closed, she dropped her forehead on the keys and whimpered, "Sooner or later, I'll get my...man."

After a long and slow Saturday afternoon, Janelle and Tanya walked out of the branch. Behind them, Sonyai locked the door from the inside. The girls parted ways, heading to opposite ends of the sidewalk, then looked back to each other.

"Have a good weekend Tee," Janelle said. "What's left of it." She giggled.

"You too, Nellie."

Janelle walked up toward Park Avenue as Tanya stood in place, waiting while someone approached her from across the street.

He had a rose in his hand and a smile on his face.

"I guess you didn't feel like looking me up in the phone book," Tanya said with a smile.

"I'm more of a direct approach type of guy," Franklin replied. He handed her the rose and she accepted.

"Wanna take a walk?" he asked, sticking out his forearm and elbow.

She sniffed the rose and hooked her arm into his. "Yeah."

"Hi Aunt Gina, it's Robin in New York," he began recording the message on her answering machine. "I'm calling to let you know that Granddaddy's coming home from the hospital tomorrow and um, it would be nice if you, Sid, and Marcus could come by and visit because," he sighed, "Uh, he, he's like in his...final stages of, you know...life. Um, please just call me back when you get this okay? It's Robin again, um, okay, bye." He hung up the phone.

Sitting alone in the apartment, he worried about the possibility of taking care of Jon by himself during his last days. Juggling school, work and him? It would be too much. Something would have to give. He couldn't figure out why the rest of the family was freezing him out? They may be living down south, but when the time came, Robin hoped his cousins and the rest of the family would put whatever grievances aside and do the right thing.

Franklin walked Tanya all the way home after treating her to dinner at a restaurant in her neighborhood. They stood in front of her building looking at each other.

"You sure you wanna do this? Robin's my co-worker and your best friend. He probably wouldn't want us mixing it up."

"Well, he's heavy, but he ain't my brother."

She smiled, "That's not how that line goes."

"It does for me." He leaned forward and surprised her with a kiss on the lips.

Taken aback, she pushed off from him. "Take it easy, Vanilla Ice. You're gonna have to earn a bite at *this* cookie!"

He looked down for a second and chuckled. "Well, I don't mind the work, for that *Brown Sugar*."

She gave him a coy look. "Did...did Robin tell you my last name?" she asked.

"Huh? No, why?"

"Because 'Brown Sugar'...does have a nice ring to it."

She leaned in and they kissed again, for a longer moment this time.

The doorbell rang in Robin's apartment Tuesday morning. He answered the door and Pepsi walked in. "Thanks for stopping by," he greeted his cousin.

"How's he been?"

Robin was about to reply when a bell rang out from the bedroom.

"He's getting better...and crankier."

When Jon came home from the hospital Sunday in a wheelchair, Robin brought him a bell the elder could ring when he needed to call him. He regretted the decision after the first two hours. Until they could get a regular home aide, Pepsi offered his services to watch over Jon while Robin went to school.

Jon was ringing the handbell while sitting up in bed when Robin and Pepsi entered his bedroom. Jon lowered his arm and signed with one hand, "What took you so long?" and pointed to the visitor.

"How did you know he was here?" Robin signed back to him.

"I felt the walls vibrate from you closing the door."

Robin turned to Pepsi. "He's all yours."

"Before you go, a word outside?" Pepsi said with a nod.

Robin waved to Jon and the two stepped out to the hallway.

"Have you spoken to...your mother?" Pepsi asked.

Robin sighed and shook his head. "I left a message, she hasn't called back."

"What about Regina?"

"Called her too. No answer."

"You might have to try her sons, but to be honest, I'm not surprised."

"Meaning?" Robin asked.

Pepsi was quiet for a moment.

"Hey, it's no secret they weren't on good terms with Granddaddy, but they need to make peace with him before..." he trailed off. "Before it's too late."

He saw a worried look cross Pepsi's face. "You better go. I'll keep an eye on him here."

Robin looked on as Pepsi walked past him back inside, taking a seat next to Jon in the bedroom. He pondered for a moment what could make Jon's only two children despise him so much that they wouldn't care he was at death's door.

"I hear this is your *second* check-up this year, Ms. Jenkins," Doctor Shania Bond said. "May I ask what was wrong with my colleague Doctor Chan?" Doctor Bond was possibly fifteen years older than Ethel and practiced from a private office rather than Morris Heights Health.

"I just wanted a second opinion."

"Yes, I see...well, based on these results I'm going to sound like a broken record."

Ethel stared blankly.

"You've been borderline for a while now, but I'm afraid you've crossed the threshold for a positive diagnosis of..."

"Wait! Don't say it! Let me take another..." she blurted out.

"This is not a mistake and you don't get any second or third chances. YOU. HAVE. DIABETES, Ethel," Doctor Bond stated flatly.

Ethel sighed and looked down. "So...what now? Insulin shots in the stomach?" She was completely aware of the treatment expected to deal with the disease that had haunted her family for years.

"This is not the end of the world. You're only Type 2 at the moment." The physician opened a drawer in her desk and pulled out a small orange pill bottle. "Canada has identified a certain drug that has been effective in preventing Diabetes. It's worked for them since the 70's, but the FDA is just getting around to approving it here by the end of this year. It should be available to the public within 18 months. I only have a limited supply to give out as samples." She pushed the pill bottle across the desk to Ethel.

She picked it up and noticed there was no label with at least thirty pills inside. "What is it?"

"It's called Glucophage. Take one a day after breakfast. You need to consult a nutritionist and start an exercise regimen. Drugs are not going to do it alone."

"Exercise?!" she exclaimed, wide-eyed. "I'm 46-years-old!"

"You don't do something, you won't see 50."

She gasped. "I'm starting to see why you're in private practice! Your bedside manner stinks!"

"Well, with what they pay me, I can be brutally honest. Believe it or not, I'm doing you a favor with those pills. Don't take this for granted."

A few hours later she was at the branch fifteen minutes before opening. Browsing in the 600's, Ethel searched the shelves for a particular subject. Zelda appeared by her side with the stealth of a specter. "Missed you coming in this morning." she greeted.

"I took some comp time. You got something on your mind?"

"Have you seen Sonyai talking to Angie when we're not around?"

Ethel didn't flinch. "Land O' Lakes may be gray matter, but she got no reason to hang with us."

Zelda looked around to make sure they were alone. "I saw them leaving Augustus' office after closing. They looked like they were snooping around for something."

"Like what?"

"That's what I'm trying to find out. Work with me, here, Ethel!" she exclaimed.

Ethel reached out and traced her finger around call number 616. She pulled out a copy of *The Joslin Diabetes Gourmet Cookbook* by Bonnie Sanders Polin and opened it to read a few recipes. Zelda noticed the book and looked concerned.

"Ethel? Are you okay?"

She sighed. "No, no I'm not." She turned to her. "And I haven't seen Angie and Sonyai say nothing more than "Hi", "Bye", "Good morning" and "Good night" to each other. I have other things to worry about."

Zelda stammered, "I..I'm sorry, Ethel. You need anything, you know we go way back. I'm here for you."

"Yeah," she said. "I know." Behind that hard exterior, the clerk's eyes softened in a rare moment of weakness.

As quickly as the librarian appeared next to her, she was gone a moment later.

Robin left class at ten-thirty in the morning and searched the campus for Walt. He didn't want to deal with Jacques at his place again, so he asked around until someone said they saw him in Union Square Park. It was a bit of a hike, so he took the scenic route on the M101 bus down 3rd Avenue, then walked east on 15th Street.

Near the statue of Marquis de Lafayette, Robin found Walt laying on a blanket in the grass next to a girl reading a book. They appeared to be studying, but their conversation would stop for a few minutes and they would just look at each other quietly. He smiled, watching from across the street in front of the Toys R' Us.

The mysterious woman checked her watch and stood up. Walt packed his blanket in his book bag and they parted with a quick embrace. He watched her leave the park into the Subway hub for the 4,5,6 lines. Robin put his index finger and thumb in the edges of his mouth as whistled. Walt snapped his head to his right, and Robin waved at him.

Walt waited for Robin to cross the street and enter the park. He couldn't resist grinning as he approached. "Is this why you bailed on that Knicks game two weeks ago?"

Walt looked down sheepishly. "Guilty. Her name's Sherry..."

"A black girl named Sherry. Holy shit! She wear a red dress too? Like the song?"

"Huh?"

Robin rolled his eyes. "Nevermind. So how'd you two meet?"

"You'll never guess. I saw her on the train!"

"Really?" Robin feigned surprise and was taken aback by the irony.

"Yeah, we just locked eyes, and I sat next to her and we started talking...I think this is it, man."

"Hmmm." Robin had heard this all before.

"Now I know you've heard this before, but I'm making it work this time. I've cut down on the drinking, I'm going to class...hell I'm *actually* learning shit!"

"Wow," he chuckled. "Well, here's rooting for you two, alright? Don't fuck it up!"

"I won't, I won't. Hey man, wanna go to Barnes and Noble and read the *Garfield* books?"

Robin thought about it. "There's a McDonald's across the park. Let's stop there first."

Derrick pulled up in front of the library to drop off Lakeshia at three fifteen. "I'll see ya after work, okay?" he called out while she exited the car. Once he pulled off and turned the corner, Lakeshia saw Tanya and Alex step out and approach her. She stiffened and looked down, increasing her pace.

"Leelee, wait," Alex said.

"I got nothing to say!" Lakeshia yelled. "Let me pass!"

Alex cut in front of her as Tanya kept her distance. "C'mon, don't be like that. Give us a second to talk."

She grimaced. "What's the point, huh?" She looked over her

shoulder. "I already know how she feels about me now, just like everyone else who finds out!"

Alex looked confused and turned to look back at Tanya.

"I didn't say anything, Leelee. It's just...my mom was pissed, and I..." she trailed off.

"Look," Alex said. "We need to squash this, okay? Both y'all parents may not want you two to talk, but they're not here watching us all the time. We need each other's back more than ever now, so can't we be good like it was before this?"

Tanya stepped forward. "I don't think you're a freak, Lakeshia. I...I think differently when it comes to religion, too," she confided.

Alex's confused look returned, but she remained silent.

"I...I don't believe...in God," Tanya whispered. "I'm an atheist."

Lakeshia looked at her stunned.

"I know what it's like, and I don't think any different of you. My mom doesn't know. Nobody knows but you two."

Lakeshia nodded. "Okay." She then looked at Alex. "If we're going to be cool again Alex, there's something you should know."

"Huh?"

"My family and I are practicing Jehovah's Witnesses. We don't celebrate Christmas, Easter, or birthdays. Whenever people find out at school, they treat me differently."

Alex shrugged. "Okay, so?" she smiled. "You wouldn't think WE would do that, would you?"

Lakeshia smiled, and the trio started to laugh. They came together for a group hug. "I missed hanging with y'all! I never want anything to come between us again!" Lakeshia squealed.

"Hey! There room for one more in there?" a voice yelled.

The girls turned around to see Janelle standing behind them.

"Come here, you!" Alex waved her over.

The four pages all hugged each other. "Okay, we have to make sure nothing like this happens again, and keep the parents out of the loop, okay?"

Tanya and Lakeshia looked at each other and nodded.

"Alright, now let's get to work. Books need shelving!" Alex cheered.

"Yeah!" they all agreed.

Robin and Gerry were working the last hour at the circulation desk. Robin surveyed the floor and noticed the pages were interacting with each other again. Tanya and Lakeshia actually exchanged a few words. Whatever discretions they had been experiencing appeared to have been worked out. He couldn't help but smile.

Gerry checked in a few books, then asked, "Hey, Robin?"

"Yeah?"

"Me and my twin sister are celebrating our birthday Saturday, you wanna join us?"

"You never mentioned having a twin sister before."

"Well, I'm mentioning now. We're going bowling at Ball Park Lanes near Yankee Stadium then up to The Newsroom after."

"I'm up for bowling, but there's no way that old folk's spot will let me in."

"Let me worry about that. You in?"

Robin thought for a moment. "Can my homie tag along? He's good people."

"Alright, sure," Gerry said with a shrug.

"Cool. Count us in."

Gerry nodded and tensed up as a woman approached Robin at the checkout side. Robin saw his reaction and turned around in time to formally greet her. "May I help you?"

"I would like to speak to whoever's in charge."

Augustus was off today, and both Zelda and Sonyai had left at five. All indicators would suggest that Heywood at the information desk would be the one to handle the angry patron. But Robin decided on a diplomatic approach.

"What seems to be the problem?" he asked with a friendly smile.

The woman reached into her handbag and pulled out a copy of

Sex by Madonna and dropped it in front of him. "I caught my son reading this filth that he was able to borrow from this branch! I demand an explanation of how something like this can happen."

Robin cocked an eyebrow and kept his composure. "Ma'am, please be calm and keep your voice down. People are trying to read. With that said, how old is your son?"

"He's 16."

"Well, since he's over 13, his library card grants him the ability to borrow adult books, such as art books like this." He gestured toward the item in front of him.

"This is NOT art. This is smut!"

"That is a matter of your opinion, ma'am. The publishers thought differently, as well as the thousands of people who contributed to it becoming a bestseller."

"This garbage does not belong in the hands of teenagers and you'd think as librarians you would know this!"

Gerry stepped forward to Robin's left and whispered, "What are you doing? Learner should be talking to this loon!"

He ignored Gerry and continued to address the patron. "Miss, the New York Public Library does not believe in censorship. All materials available here provide information and knowledge for the purpose to expand one's mind. Would you allow your son to go inside a museum and observe the nude statue of David by Michelangelo?"

"I want to speak to your supervisor! Now!" she yelled.

That gained the attention of several people who were reading.

Robin tilted his head toward Eugene and then extended his hand toward the information desk. "Very well, the gentleman at the desk in the middle of the floor can help you."

She picked up the book and stormed across the floor, where a nervous Heywood stood up to receive her.

Eugene walked up to Robin as he and Gerry looked on at the confrontation.

"Why do you engage them when they come to you?" Eugene asked.

"Yeah, man! If Augustus catches that, he'll freak out!"

"Fort Washington taught us how to deal with irate patrons. I like to stay on my toes," Robin answered with a grin.

Heywood was trying his best to de-escalate the tirade, but the woman was furious.

"I better get in there," Eugene said with concern.

Robin reached out and pulled at the guard's shoulder. "Wait! Two more minutes," he said with a chuckle. Eugene looked down at the hand and Robin quickly pulled it back. After staring at him for a long minute, he turned and headed to the information desk.

"Testy," Robin said to Gerry.

The clerk rolled his eyes.

They went back to their stations. Eugene issued a warning to the woman, then she left the book with Heywood, yelled a few curses and left the branch with the security guard close behind her. Once things calmed down, Robin waved at Gerry.

"Hey, I've been meaning to bring this up. You think Saturday you could, I dunno, spruce up your hair a little bit?"

"Huh?"

"The afro, man...it's a little out of style."

Robin had no idea how he would react to the suggestion, but he had to try.

Gerry scowled, then grinned. "Think so?"

"Yeah man. I mean, you talk like it's the 70's, dress like it's the 80's, yet you're smart enough for a conscious brother in the 90's."

He snickered at the statement. "Okay, I'll consider it."

Heywood announced that the branch would be closing, and the clerks straightened up, preparing for the final minutes of the hour.

Heywood Learner was feeling like the luckiest man on Earth. His relationship with Jackie Daisy was so comfortable now she had no qualms about walking around his apartment nude. He was pretending to read the Thursday morning Daily News as she was frantically looking for her high-heeled shoes. He tried to remember what happened to them himself. Last night they were very adventurous.

"You know, you could be helping me look instead of staring at my ass," she playfully joked.

He chuckled. "We were all over each other last night. I remember them flying across the room."

She opened a closet and checked several shelves, then pulled out a curious looking box. She turned and held it up. "Hey, what's this?"

Heywood looked at the box of supplies he took from the branch. "Um, nothing. Just some stuff from the job I was asked to hold here for a while."

"Oh, okay." Jackie put the box back inside the closet. "There they are!" she exclaimed. A part of the heel was sticking out from under the laundry basket. After retrieving her shoes, she picked a few articles of clothing and reached over for her purse on the nightstand. Wearing stockings and a leather vest on top of a blouse, she took a seat next to Heywood and handed him a wad of money.

"Here."

"What's this?" he asked, accepting the money. He unrolled several twenties and a hundred-dollar bill.

"I don't like to live off someone without contributing. I'm replacing one of the opening acts for a concert next Friday, the 20th . Got some extra tickets if you wanna invite some friends."

Heywood thought for a moment. "Okay, I'd like for you to swing by before I invite anyone. Get acquainted and all that."

"Sure, I got another audition today. Wish me luck." She leaned over and gave him a kiss.

Hours later, Heywood was with Augustus in his office for the daily briefing. The pair agreed on selections for June's film presentations with no problems.

"Now that the piano is upstairs we'll need musicians for

Wednesday night performances. Eight weeks starting in June," Augustus commented.

"I'll reach out to some contacts," Heywood replied.

The librarian concluded the briefing with a nod, and Heywood stood up and left.

Zelda waited a moment in her corner and then turned to Augustus. "How was Mexico?" she asked.

"They're opening a museum at the university finally in October. It may take a while, but my photos will get the recognition they deserve."

She nodded. "That's great."

Augustus sensed there was something troubling her. "Zee? What is it?"

She sighed. "What are Sonyai and Angie looking for, Gus? You have to tell me, just in case."

"Damn it, Zelda. You need to drop this!"

"I won't!" she barked back. "I respect you too much to have this house of cards fall over your...arrogance!"

He raised his eyebrows.

"We've known each other for over a decade and I've played your conscience too long for you to shut me out. You're going to tell me what the hell is going on and you're going to tell me now!"

He had never seen this side of her. The outburst took him completely off guard. "Alright, damnit, I'll tell you." He got up and locked his door so there would be no interruptions, then walked over to the supply closet. "By revealing this, I trust you more than I have since we met."

"You have my word, Augustus. This will stay between us."

He sighed. "Angie came in here to retrieve some reserve postcards." He opened the closet to show her the neatly placed boxes of office supplies. "There was a box...of confidential materials that she discovered." He reached into his pocket and pulled out a penlight. "Using resources from my photography career, I covered the box in question with a dye that will only show when shined on with ultraviolet light." He turned on the light in a demonstration and flashed one of the shelves inside. Several spots lit up in a fluorescent color mixture of yellow and orange. He moved the light to the floor where more spots were revealed.

Zelda looked on in awe. Augustus turned off the light and closed the closet. "I believe Miss Trueblood accidentally knocked over the box and discovered its contents, then quickly put it back the way it was making sure it wasn't disturbed. But as you can see, I have taken precautions to make sure it isn't found again. *That* is what Sonyai was looking for, with Trueblood's assistance. The situation is well in hand," he concluded with a slight nod.

"I see," she nodded back. "Two questions: what is inside the box? And where is it, now?"

"You know all you need to know. I'm not telling you anything else."

She smiled. "You don't need to."

He blinked as a trickle of sweat slid down the side of his forehead.

"Sonyai is going to find that box, and when she does, I'll make sure she doesn't bury you with your own shovel."

She stood up and unlocked the door. "By the way, that's a neat trick with the invisible ink. You would have been a great spy."

Robin was working the circulation desk with Sonyai when she turned and asked, "How is your grandfather recovering, Walker?"

He looked back at her and smiled. "He's okay, thanks for asking."

"That's good to hear. I have to admit, you are finally finding your place here after your turbulent arrival." She stole a glance inside the clerical office. "You haven't gotten into any mischievous antics lately, unlike several others." She was referring to Gerry, who was still tending to his bandaged hand, and Tommy, who was using his hair to cover the bandage on his forehead.

"Even the pages are getting into trouble, yet keeping together their bond of solidarity."

"The advantages of a part-time hire dedicated to his college studies," he said, outstretching his arms.

"Indeed."

While the youngster was proving to be quite an asset to the branch, Sonyai was still looking for a position for Janelle. After reaching out to all her connections, she had still not received any possible leads. She was so deep in thought she didn't notice a remarkable looking patron walk in. A woman dressed all in leather with a tall mohawk of white hair.

She drew in glances from the entire floor as she walked to the information desk and was greeted by Heywood. Robin gestured to his co-workers, trying to get Tommy, Ethel, and Gerry to step out for a peek. Out on the floor, the pages were also trying to figure out the connection between the visitor and the usually conservative information assistant.

Heywood sat down as Jackie took the seat next to the desk facing him. She crossed her legs, seeming to revel in all the attention she was receiving. No one made a sound. Whoever wasn't staring directly, was attempting to be polite and concentrate on their tasks at hand...but not succeeding.

"So this is where you work, huh?" she remarked nonchalantly.

"Yep," he replied with a nervous chuckle.

He looked around as she sat quietly smiling.

Back at the circulation desk, Sonyai was taken from her personal thoughts by the sudden eerie silence that came over the room. She looked around and noticed that no one was moving, and that all eyes were on the information desk.

"What the...?" she whispered. She snapped out of whatever trance that took over the floor and nudged Robin.

"Ow, hey?"

She then turned to the doorway where the other clerks stood. "What's the matter with you? Quit staring and do something inside!" she ordered. The trio dispersed, and she turned to look at Robin. He shrugged, then stood back at attention in front of the terminal.

Time passed and the final hour of the day arrived. Sonyai and Ethel left for the day while Gerry and Tommy worked the desk. Robin decided to stick around and use a few books in the branch to work on a paper. Jackie waited for Heywood, sitting at a nearby reading desk with a newspaper. At closing time, once the public left, Heywood made proper introductions to the rest of the staff.

"Everyone, this is Jacqueline Daisy. She also goes by "Stormin' Jackie Daze".

"I bring the rain!" she exclaimed with a flourish.

The staff laughed at the joke, then introduced themselves one by one.

"I love your outfit!" Alex said with a smile. "Your whole style is off the chain!"

"Thanks," she replied.

"What is it you actually do?" Tommy asked.

"I'm a singer, been performing on stages for as long as I can remember."

"Really? I figured you for a weather personality... Stormy Daze, forecasts at 11!" Angie said sarcastically.

Heywood scratched his head, confused by her snide remark.

"Okay, Pat Benatar, rock on!" Robin yelled.

"I sing Grunge, which is an *alternative* to rock."

"And I'm not a doctor, but I play one on tv, Miss road warrior," Robin said with a wink.

She gave the young clerk an icy stare. Heywood then cleared his throat. "Well, Jackie's opening for a big show next week at the Roseland Ballroom."

"Yes, and you're all invited!" she cheered.

Angie looked less than impressed as she stood folding her arms. The pages cheered with excitement.

"Oh, except the girls. Sorry, it's 18 and older."

The pages groaned.

"While I'd love to go, me and Sarah have a...baby-thing to do," Tommy admitted with embarrassment.

"I too must decline, I'm afraid," Gerry added.

"I could go," Robin began. "But unlike these two I actually have the balls to tell you that it's not my scene, no offense!" He waved as everyone gave him hard glances. "Nice meeting ya, Stormy!" He then caught himself. "Wow, you DO look like that comic book character now that I think of it!" He laughed and left.

"That's Stormin' NOT Stormy!...What a dick," Jackie scoffed.

Alex laughed. "Yes!" she agreed.

"Guess that leaves you, Angie. Wanna check out the show?" Heywood asked.

"Sure," she said dryly.

"Alright! Well, we have to get going!" Jackie pointed to the four girls. "Stay in school, don't do drugs, and learn an instrument in music class, ladies! It's all about the arts!"

She locked an arm with one of Heywood's and they walked out of the branch. The pages and clerks waved them goodbye...but Angie didn't.

CHAPTER FOUR

"MAN, I HAVEN'T BOWLED SINCE MY MOM TOOK ME, LASANDRA AND Lenny to Shell Lanes out in Brooklyn," Franklin said. He was sitting on the couch in Robin's apartment. It was Saturday afternoon, and they were both waiting for Gerry to pick them up. After checking on Jon earlier, Robin was adjusting his glove in front of a mirror on the living room wall.

"How are big brother and baby sister?" he asked.

"The prodigal son is all A's at NYU, and little princess is keeping Auntie busy out in Queens."

"Hmm."

"We all can't have famous supermodels for siblings, can we?"

Robin glared at him for a moment, then turned as the intercom buzzed. He walked up and hit TALK. "Who?" he asked.

"It's Gerry."

"Okay." He answered and hit the DOOR button to let him in the lobby.

"Hey, this guy's a bit...out there, okay? So don't try to fuck with him. He may not find your shtick amusing."

"Hey, whatever, I'll be on my best behavior," Franklin said, crossing his fingers behind his back.

The doorbell rang. Robin walked to the door as Franklin stood up. When he opened the door, his jaw dropped immediately, and Franklin cupped his mouth with a gasp.

"What the hell?!"

Gerry stood in front of Robin wearing jeans and a light blue striped nylon polo shirt. His trademark afro was nowhere to be seen. Instead, Gerry's hair was permed in a Jheri curl, glistening and dripping on his shoulders. He saw the stunned look on Robin's face and asked, "What's wrong?"

"No, no, nooooo! What the hell is this?! What is with the hair, man?"

"You said you didn't dig my 70's look. You told me to spruce it up."

"So you turn the dial 10 years to the 80's? You look like Turbo from Breakin' or that rapper Ice Cube!"

Franklin took this moment to get a closer look. Robin sensed him over his shoulder. "Gerry, this is Franklin. He used to work at Fort Washington."

Franklin waved. "Hey man, fuck the police!" he yelled with a laugh, referencing the N.W.A. song.

Robin looked up to the ceiling exasperated as Gerry stared at both of them. "You're embarrassed by me and you hanging out with a white boy? I don't see a problem."

"Hey, Franklin has more soul than you and I put together. What do you think, man?" Robin asked his friend.

"I think there's only one place that can salvage this crime against humanity..."

They looked at each other and nodded. "Hair-o-Matics!"

"C'mon guys, my sister and friends are meeting us at 2 pm!" Gerry protested.

Robin and Franklin were walking him down Audubon Avenue, approaching 181st Street.

"It's 1:15 pm now. They'll understand if we're fashionably late,"

Robin said. He looked over to Franklin. "You think Xerx will take us?" he asked.

"It's a 50-50 shot."

Hair-Matics (or Hair-o-Matics, depending on who you ask) was a salon and barbershop where Greek hairstylists and Dominican barbers converged to attend the needs of all of Washington Heights residents who needed a new hairstyle. It was located on the second floor of a commercial building on the corner of 182nd Street. The guys climbed the flight of stairs and entered the establishment.

"Xerxes! We got ourselves an emergency, here. Can you squeeze us in?"

There were eight salon chairs, four on each side with benches and folding chairs where customers would wait for their professional of choice. At the corner seat next to the window, a short white man wearing a smock turned to greet the arrivals with a smug look.

"You come to me on a Saturday afternoon with no call ahead or anything, not even a 'hello'?"

Robin, Franklin, and Gerry all exchanged concerned looks as the rest of the shop held their breath.

Xerxes smiled. "Of course I can squeeze you in, sweetie!" He waved them over. "C'mon and have a seat here, let's see what we're working with!"

Franklin sighed, and they walked across the floor. Gerry leaned in. "Uh, who the hell is he calling 'sweetie'?"

Robin waved. "Just go with it, man. The guy's a genius."

"You're lucky I had a cancellation," the flamboyant hairstylist explained while gesturing toward his chair.

Gerry took a seat while Xerxes looked him over. "Hmm, I've seen worse."

"Can you hook him up?" Robin asked.

"Did Prince purify himself in the waters of Lake Minnetonka?"

"No, Apollonia did."

"Shut up!" he yelled with a dismissive wave, then turned to Gerry. "Do YOU trust me?" he asked.

"Yeah."

"Do you LOVE me?" he asked quickly.

"Whaaat?!" Gerry yelled.

"Oh, I'm sorry, I was lost in your eyes for a second." He waved dismissively again. "Nevermind. Let's get to work."

Franklin slapped Robin on the shoulder. "Hey, wanna go across the street to 143's courtyard and play Suicide?"

Robin looked out the window. Adjacent to the salon was I.S. 143, the local Junior High School named after Eleanor Roosevelt.

"You got a ball?"

Franklin pulled out a blue rubber ball from his pocket.

"We'll be right back," Robin nodded to Gerry and Xerxes.

"Hey!" Gerry called out as the two left. "How you gonna leave me here?!"

"Relax sweetie, you're in good hands," Xerxes cooed.

He tensed up with a concerned look on his face.

A half-hour later, the pair came back as Xerxes was applying the finishing touches. His back was to the door as Gerry and the stylist were engaged in friendlier conversation.

"It's pretty ironic where your name comes from considering your heritage," Gerry was explaining.

"I know, I know, tell me about it...oh hey! Y'all back!" he said, catching Robin and Franklin from the corner of his eye. He pulled the chair around to reveal Gerry's new look. With his hair straightened, fluffed and moussed up, it was definitely an improvement that received nods of approval.

Xerxes handed him a mirror, and he was surprised. "My God, I look like Morris Day!"

Robin laughed. "Which is funny because people say Franklin looks like an even lighter version of Prince!"

Franklin scowled as Xerxes shared a chuckle of his own. "He does!"

Gerry nodded to Franklin as they both said, "Which makes YOU Jerome!"

Robin grimaced. "Alright, good one...let's go, we got a party to get to!"

"What do I owe you?" Gerry asked, standing up out of the chair.

"I'll settle it up with these two. Don't worry about it." Xerxes waved, "It's your birthday after all. Go out and have some fun!"

They all said their thanks and left out into the street.

In the shadow of Yankee Stadium, underneath the elevated subway tracks for the 4-train, Ball Park Lanes was on River Avenue across the street from the stadium bleachers entrance. The team was out in Milwaukee that afternoon, so the neighborhood was quiet.

Gerry, Robin, and Franklin got off the Bx13 bus at the last stop and walked inside the bowling alley at two-thirty. The two-story facility was loud with the sounds of music and crashing pins. "Return to Innocence" by Enigma was playing as they approached the front desk.

"Denise and Gerry Coltraine Party?" Gerry told the manager.

"Y'all are upstairs, Lanes 22-25. It's $1.50 for shoe rentals. What sizes?"

"I'm a 9," Franklin said as he took off his shoes.

"Me too," Robin added.

"Two 9's and a size 11, please."

"$4.50," demanded the clerk.

Robin passed Gerry a five-dollar bill. Once the trio got their bowling shoes on, they headed upstairs.

The second floor was reserved for leagues and private parties. There was a bar with a television hanging overhead playing sports. A dining area was selling pizza, hot dogs, hamburgers and fries. On each floor there were twenty-five lanes with twelve on the right and thirteen on the left.

Gerry led Robin and Franklin past the lanes, counting and looking for number twenty-two. At the far end of the left side, more than ten of Gerry and Denise's friends were taking turns bowling strikes. He spotted his sister and waved. She waved back and walked up to meet them halfway to the group.

"What took you so long? We've already played two games—" Denise stopped mid-sentence once she saw him up close. "What is with the hair?"

"You like it?" he asked.

"It's...different."

Franklin's eyes went extremely wide at the sight of the woman. He drifted past Robin, who reached out and pulled him back. "What are you doing?" Robin whispered.

"Oh, where are my manners? Denise, meet Robin Walker and his friend, Franklin."

Robin waved. "Wow, Gerry, you didn't tell me you were the brother of the Statue of Liberty!" he joked. "She's even taller than you. What is she? 7'3? 7'4?"

Franklin smiled a goofy grin and stepped forward again. "Man, it doesn't matter." He reached out and took her hand. "Hello, gorgeous. How are you besides *stunning* this fair afternoon?"

Denise raised an eyebrow at how forward the youth was. "How old are you, little boy?" she asked.

"How old do you *need* me to be?" he let out a lusty laugh from his throat.

She giggled and looked at Gerry. "Come on, let's say hi to everyone." She gestured for them to follow her.

Cheers greeted Gerry as everyone said their birthday wishes and complimented his hair.

"Looking good, man! You sugar sharp!"

"Thanks, Blue!" Gerry extended his arm toward Robin. "Everybody, meet Robin and Franklin."

Robin waved and greeted everyone with a smile. Franklin was still checking out Denise.

"This is Blue, Johnny, Betsy, Gianna, Wendy, Shannon, Kathy, Alonzo, Deon, and Elizabeth."

The group all said their hello's, and Robin couldn't help noticing something.

Denise stepped forward. "Okay, now that big brother's here, I can start playing! I had to play scorekeeper to even the teams. Now it's 7-on-7."

"Okay then, birthday twins are the captains," Gerry announced. "Who do I got?"

"I gotcha Gerry!" Robin volunteered.

"I'm on Denise's team!" Franklin yelled.

Robin and Franklin started looking for balls while the others started.

"What is going on here?" Franklin asked. "This dude's gone from Morris Day to Rick James surrounded by all these go-go chicks! Remind me to thank you again for bringing me along!"

"I did *not* expect all this!" Robin replied. It was peculiar to him. Aside from Kathy (and Denise, of course), all the other women were *white*.

There was only one on Franklin's mind. "I want to *climb* that woman, like King Kong climbing the Empire State Building!" he said, referring to Denise.

"Calm down, you horny toad," Robin joked. "She's got at least 10 years on you."

"Five dollars says I get her number."

"You know I don't like betting for money."

"A couple of slices then...from Tony's."

"Tony's on Broadway?" Robin licked his lips, anticipating the pizza meal. "You're on! She shoots you down, I want two slices and an orange soda!"

"Bet!" Franklin agreed.

They shook hands, sealing the deal.

Gerry's team consisted of Blue, Alonzo, Robin, Betsy, Elizabeth, and Shannon. Denise had Franklin, Johnny, Deon, Gianna, Kathy, and Wendy. Robin was up and took his ball to the approach area. Behind him, Alonzo leaned over and whispered something to Blue. Robin squared up and hurled a centered ball down the lane for a strike.

After a quick celebration, he turned in time to see Blue hand Alonzo a bill of currency.

Robin walked over to Gerry as Elizabeth took her turn. "Hey man, what's with Huggy Bear and Dolemite over there?"

"Huh? Oh Blue? He likes to place small bets. Makes things more fun, no big deal." Gerry held his finger up looking seriously at Robin. "Chill with the nicknames. These people are my close personal friends, but they're also your elders. Respect your elders."

Betsy stepped up to the two gentlemen. She was the woman from Mid-Manhattan that shared a hot dog with Gerry back at the end of March.

"Well, aren't you a plump 'lil sugar cookie? How ya doin' Husky Jim?" she asked playfully. She had a bubbly personality that would have went well with a career as a Playboy Bunny.

"What?" Robin spat. *And he was just telling ME about nicknames?* he thought.

Gerry laughed. "Hey Betts. Robin, this is..."

"Tell me, Starshine," he interrupted. "How much fun was it doing lines in the bathroom stall of Studio 54 with Farrah Fawcett and Ryan O'Neil?"

"Hey! How rude!" she yelled with a look of disgust.

Gerry pushed him a step away from her. "What did I *JUST* say? Don't be disrespectful!"

"She started with me with the fat jokes. *'Plump lil sugar cookie'? 'Husky Jim'?* I don't stand for that shit!"

"She's just being friendly, that's how she talks!"

Robin scoffed. "Whatever."

Across the lane, Denise's team observed the exchange of words with raised eyebrows. Deon stepped up and prepared to take a turn.

"Your friend's a bit of a hothead, there," Denise said to Franklin.

"He's just sensitive," Franklin dismissed with a wave. "So, um, which one of you was born first?"

She smiled. "He was, I came out seven minutes later."

"Wow, I envy those seven minutes."

"Why?"

"They must have felt like a lifetime as you descended from heaven."

She smiled at the flirtatious line. "Well ain't you something?" She couldn't help but blush.

"You want anything from the bar? I could use a drink."

She walked up to him. "Then how 'bout *I* get us one...you might have a hard time, Babyface." She gestured with her finger. "Follow me."

"To hell and back, baby...to hell and back," he whispered.

They both walked to the bar.

After alienating and being bothered by his teammates, Robin decided to wander across the lane and talk to the only other black woman around. While Johnny played a turn, Robin greeted Kathy with a friendly smile.

"Hi."

"Hi."

"Where do you know Gerry from?"

"I don't actually. I'm Dee's friend. We've known each other since high school."

"Oh, okay."

She leaned in close. "I saw what happened, and I know what you're thinking," she whispered. "Gerry and Dee have always had some eccentric friends. Gerry knows more loan sharks and gamblers than I've ever seen."

"Hmmm."

She leaned back and said in a normal volume, "If you ever wanna hear a funny story, ask them where they got their names from."

He frowned. "What's so funny about Gerry and Denise?"

"You'll see, oh! Excuse me, it's my go. Nice talking to you." She stepped away and grabbed her bowling ball.

"Thanks, you too!" he called out.

Robin was holding his own with a score of seventy-nine after five frames, but Denise's team was winning overall. Alcohol seemed to be a contributing factor as the atmosphere became more relaxed. Most of the women were fawning over Gerry and complementing his hair.

Soon the contest wasn't important anymore as people started substituting for others and the music was getting everyone dancing. Robin picked up the spare on his second roll and took a seat. Franklin was sitting next to Denise with his hand on her leg, and Gerry was sandwiched between Elizabeth and Shannon. No one was bowling on either lane.

"So Gerry!" Robin called out, getting his attention over the loud conversations and music. "Tell me this joke about your names, man! I heard it was funny."

He stopped his conversations with the ladies as encouragement came from the group to recall the story. Everyone became quiet as he started. "Okay, Mom and Dad were big fans of variety tv. Carol Burnett Show, Dick Cavett, Johnny Carson, and the sort. But they love them some Flip Wilson."

"Okay."

"Originally, if Mom had a boy, they were gonna name him "Flip", and "Geraldine" if it was a girl."

"They had no plans in the event of twins!" Denise chimed in.

"Right, so they decided to get clever. They broke "Geraldine" in half."

"And so," Denise explained, "On that special day, May 14th, 1962 they named their firstborn boy twin, "Gerrald Clarence Coltraine"."

Franklin laughed out loud. "Clarence!" Denise shared a giggle as well.

Gerry stared hard at him. "And the second-born twin girl, "Denise Estelle Coltraine"...Gerrald and Dee, Geraldine!"

"To a year older..." Denise started.

"...but not any wiser!" Gerry finished.

The twins raised their glasses to each other for a toast, and the group erupted in applause and cheers.

"You're right, that is a funny story!" Robin agreed.

"Hey, let's get back to the game. I got some money to make!" Blue yelled.

The group snapped back to attention, checked the scoreboard, and resumed playing. Gerry slid over next to Robin. "Thanks for coming, and hooking up my hair. They love it! You having fun?"

"Yeah, man, and you're welcome." They gave each other a high-five. Gerry looked on as Robin chuckled to himself. "You know what? You kill me, man," he said playfully.

"What?" Gerry asked.

"All that talk 'bout *"Supporting the sisters"* and you got more Snow White rabbits here with you than Walt Disney!"

"What'cha talking about? *YOU* the one hanging with the funky white boy who's macking my sister kinda hard there," he said, pointing at Denise. "What's the deal with him? Ain't he ever seen a tall black woman before? You said he was good people!"

"He is. Relax man, Franklin's just...friendly."

"You better warn him or something." Gerry's eyes went wide. "I will break his goddamn legs!" He stormed past him and Franklin gave him a questionable glance.

They finished at five-thirty, playing a total of four games. Two before and after Gerry arrived. Downstairs at the shoe return, Robin chucked his thumb as a signal to leave and Franklin nodded.

"Hey Gerry, it's been fun, but me and Franklin are gonna bounce."

"What? We're goin' up to Gerrard Avenue to the..."

"It's cool man, y'all have fun. I got a ride outside to take us home. I'll see ya Monday, alright?"

Before Gerry could react, the pair waved and quickly ran out the door. Gerry was highly upset. Outside, Robin and Franklin darted across the street where a taxi cab was waiting for them. Franklin went around while Robin took the seat behind the driver.

"Go, go! Before they come out!"

The cabbie took off down River Avenue toward 158th Street.

Franklin was laughing hysterically. "What the hell? That guy has the *weirdest* group of friends I have ever seen! All he needs is

Cleopatra Jones and the Shogun of Harlem to start a funk band the world has never seen!"

"Damn, you think you know a nigga," Robin sighed. "Now I know why he stays rocking the afro!" He looked over at his friend. "So, I believe we had a wager...hey! Don't take Macombs Dam Bridge. Get on the Major Deegan back to 178th and take that across!" he instructed his cab driver friend he nicknamed Cervantes.

"You got it," Cervantes answered.

"Well," Franklin started. "I didn't get her number."

"Uh-huh," Robin nodded with a grin.

"But...she took *mine!*" he cheered.

"She was being nice. She won't call. I'm pretty sure it's in a trash can somewhere."

"We'll see."

"Yeah, in the meantime, I'll be collecting those slices after work Monday."

"What?!"

"You said it yourself, if you didn't get her number..."

"But she got mine. She'll call and then I'll have it!"

"If she doesn't call by Sunday at midnight, a deal's a deal."

Franklin groaned. "It's a technicality!"

After thinking to himself he nodded. "Yea, it is, but I still get my slices."

"Oh c'mon! Technicalities are only supposed to work for white people. Y'all don't know anything about that!"

Robin arrived at home and immediately felt that someone else was in the apartment. He went to Jon's room and found Esme finishing a private conversation with her brother. She turned to face Robin.

"Where the hell were you?!" she demanded. "How could you leave him by himself here?!"

"I was gone for only a few hours. I left Pepsi's number for him to call in case of an emergency."

"Pepsi has his OWN job and a life. You should be at his side as much as possible!"

"Hey, I'm going to school, work and I have a life of my own, too!"

"Will you two settle down?!" Jon barked. "I can't even hear and I can sense y'all carrying on like a pair of hyenas!"

She stormed off. As Robin stepped aside to let her by, he stepped forward and checked on Jon. "You're alright, right?"

Jon sighed. "She fusses so much, damn drama queen." He waved his hand. "Don't worry about it."

Alex was working Saturday and had Wednesday off, so she took the A-train after school and headed to Brooklyn. She lied to her parents and told them she was going to the A&S Mall on 34th Street with her friends. Getting off in the heart of Downtown Brooklyn at Jay Street-Borough Hall she came to street level, then walked north toward Tillary Street to the campus of The New York City College of Technology.

She pulled out the card Mr. Karl Kani gave her and read the instructions again. There was a park on the other side of Tillary. She was to enter and take a seat on a certain bench. Children were playing on the swings and monkey bars while Alex walked by. She took a seat at the bench near the slides. *This is stupid!* she thought. *I feel like I'm waiting to hire the A-Team!*

A teenager riding a dirt-bike stopped in front of her. He was wearing a windbreaker and sweatpants. "You looking for something?" he asked.

She looked at the youngster and showed him the card. "Yeah."

"Alright, follow me."

The kid with the bike led her to a brownstone several blocks away from the park. "He's inside," he said with a nod. She started up the steps, then looked back, and the kid was gone without a trace. Once inside, she followed a long hallway to a door on the end. After knocking first, she turned the doorknob and walked in.

The room was a huge photography studio. There were lights, a white backdrop and other walls of backgrounds, video equipment, and cameras. A lone occupant was adjusting lights to point to a stool in front of the white background.

"Hello?" Alex called out.

"Be with ya in a sec," he replied.

She thought about turning around and leaving, but stood waiting. After two minutes the tall, obese man stepped forward. He towered over her, looking like Frankenstein. Upon closer examination, she noticed the stranger was Asian, wearing glasses and a blue buttoned-up shirt complete with a pocket protector holding three pens and two pencils. Wearing black slacks and Chinese slippers, he extended his hand in a friendly greeting. She noticed a calculator watch on his wrist.

"I'm Steven. You here for an ID?"

She shook his hand gently and nodded. "Yeah."

"You got the money?" Steven asked, lowering his arm.

"The guy who sent me said it would be free." She handed him the second card, confirming the statement.

"Alright, cool." He nodded at the stool. "Take a seat over there."

She sat on the stool as he walked to a table and picked up a Polaroid camera. "Before we start you need to know, you get caught with this ID and tell them where you got it, someone's breaking your legs, got it?"

"Hey, I ain't saying nothing! You kinda freak me out, honestly."

"Aww, I'm just a big ol' teddy bear," Steven taunted with a sinister smile.

She swallowed hard while sitting and looking forward.

"Okay, next, my ID's are as good as the real thing, but it's important to remember, it's all about *confidence*. You have to whip it out of your purse or bag and show it like its nothing. If your hands shake or you show fear, even hesitation, game over."

"Gotcha."

"Okay, straighten your shoulders, look up and don't smile. This isn't picture day or a yearbook photo. You're 18, ready to vote and die for your country but can't fucking drink. Look bleak."

She posed, and the camera flashed. Steven took several pictures, then walked over to a huge machine in the corner of the room. "This is going to take around 30 minutes. You want anything to drink, there's a fridge over there."

"You got any chairs anywhere?"

"Just the stool," he replied.

It was *forty-five* minutes later before they stood in front of his table of photo development equipment, where she saw other fake IDs and Passports from different states and countries.

"Why do you do this?" she asked.

"To perfect my craft. I want to be an artist one day." He showed her three separate New York State Identification Cards with her picture on them.

She looked at the array. "None of these have my real name on them."

"That's the point. New name, address and date of birth. I'll let you pick one and practice."

"Okay, how about this one." She picked up the card in the middle. "Traci Britt, 14 Sylvan Terrace."

"Nice, near the Jumel Mansion, the oldest home in Manhattan. George Washington slept there," Steven explained. "Okay, get your mind right and show me how you'd hand over your ID."

She put the card in her purse, then walked up and presented it to him. He stared deep into her eyes and she faltered. "That was terrible. Try again."

"You're fucking scaring the shit outta me, guy!" she yelled.

"You think I'm scary, imagine a white cop with a semi-automatic nine-millimeter pistol on their hip just waiting for you to flinch. Look, I don't know what you're using this for and I don't care, but your nerves have to be on point before you leave. Now try again. Remember, it's all about..."

"Yeah, yeah, yeah, confidence, I got it."

Another hour later, Steven was satisfied, and she was about to leave. "All the pictures and materials I didn't use are going to be destroyed. You lose that one and come back it's $130. No exceptions."

"Damn," she gasped. "I won't lose this one, and it'll be a couple of years before…"

"Don't wanna know and don't care," he interrupted. "There's the door. Peace!"

She turned and headed straight for the door. "Yeah, peace!" she called back to him.

After the door slammed, Steven swiped all the contents of the table into a metal trash bin, lit a match and dropped it in. He didn't even notice that there was only *one* other ID remaining.

Tommy was working the circulation desk with Gerry when Robin entered the branch. The young clerk and Gerry exchanged icy stares as he walked inside the office. He closed the door behind him once inside.

Tommy nodded. "You've been hostile toward him since Monday. What happened?"

"Nothing. You were right. He's got a chip on his shoulder the size of the moon. Serves me right, thinking I could reach him."

Tommy thought about taking the discussion further, but didn't.

Inside the clerical office, Robin was confiding to Ethel about what happened Saturday.

"All I was doing was defending myself," he explained, handing her a can of diet sprite. She finally relented and embraced the ritual she started to give him a hard time. Opening the can, she continued to listen.

"His friends were condescending assholes, so I decided to bail." He nodded to Ethel, "No offense, but I'm surprised you weren't there. Why didn't he invite you?"

"Because I'm not *stupid* enough to socialize with the people who work here outside in the real world!"

He scowled at her.

"Okay, "stupid" is a harsh term. Let's just say "foolish" instead."

Robin chuckled, "Ironic, isn't it? Gerry was one of the few here I was cool with at first while you and Tommy picked on me."

She looked down, feeling a small amount of guilt at her decisions early on, picking on him at Sonyai's request and participating in the prank Alex did, which got the page and Robin suspended.

"Now Gerry's the dick and you, Tommy...we're on better terms." He smiled and looked at her.

There was a small chink in the hardened armor that was Ethel's disposition, but she kept her face stoic as usual.

"Hmm, good talk." He stood. "I'm going upstairs before I start my shift. See ya!"

"Yeah," she replied and went back to reading her paper.

Ethel worked the next two hours on returns while Robin worked the three o'clock hour and came back to relieve Gerry at five, to work the final hour with Tommy.

"You're relieved," he told Gerry nonchalantly.

He stood in front of the young clerk, arms folded. "I'm waiting for an apology."

"You'd have a better chance waiting for Rickey Henderson coming back to New York, cause that sure as shit ain't happening."

Tommy looked at each of them nervously, thanking his lucky stars Sonyai was out and Augustus had left for the evening.

"Hey, I didn't invite you to be a smart ass to my friends," Gerry began.

"And I didn't go to be treated like some 10-year-old hanging around a bunch of old-timers playing spades and drinking Old English! If I went with you to that bar, your friend Blue would have told me to run around the corner for some cigarettes and gave me a 100-dollar-bill!"

Gerry blinked hard at the assumption.

"I would have taken that money and went home. That shit got old REAL quick when my grandfather and *his* friends did it!"

Gerry looked around and leaned in. "You know what he would have done?" he whispered. "He's *killed* people for less than that."

"I don't care. I did you a favor taking you to Hair-o-Matics, and I paid for our shoe rental, so how am I wrong? You know, what if I invited *you* to hang with all my college buddies, huh? If you'd have shown up with your afro and jeans, my friends would have clowned you so bad it would have been humiliating!"

"Okay, alright, you have a point. Maybe you were too young for the crowd. They had a little fun at your expense. That's what we did back in the day. That's your heritage, okay? Respect where you come from is all I'm saying!"

"Hey, fuck all that! *My* heritage is Bubble Goose and Timbs, Carhartt Hoodies, Smoking L's and hitting the lunchroom tables for a beat. It's watching the *Cosby Show* instead of *Good Times*, watching *Martin* instead of *What's Happenin?*, listening to mixtapes instead of an 8-track!"

Gerry stood quietly as Robin pointed.

"You can stay in your time warp if you want, but don't diss the next generation just because you can't understand it!" He turned his back to Gerry and stood at the terminal, finishing the conversation. Gerry nodded and left the desk. Whatever had to be said by them was said.

CHAPTER FIVE

New York was in a solemn mood Friday morning as the world mourned the death of former first lady Jacqueline Kennedy Onassis. The branch was quiet all day, even through the lunch hour rush. Heywood sat thinking to himself at the information desk when Eugene walked by.

"Hey," he called out to the guard.

Eugene stopped and turned around. He walked back over. "Yeah?"

"Angie's coming with me to a concert that Jackie's doing. Um, you doing anything tonight? I could use a buffer."

"I gotta pay for the ticket?"

"No, it's on us."

"You got yourself a third wheel!" he said with a wink.

Heywood laughed. "Thanks."

After his morning classes, Robin took a trip up to the computer lab where he found a group of students surrounding a desktop personal computer. Curiosity got the best of him as he approached and asked, "What's going on?"

"We're registering for a CompuServe account," one of them answered.

Robin was fairly familiar with the growing popularity of the internet but had no clue what to use it for. "Any particular reason?"

There were exchanged glances throughout the group as they quietly debated on letting him know. "Um, we heard that Aerosmith is doing a promotion," another from the group began.

"They're allowing subscribers to CompuServe a chance to listen to an exclusive song from their upcoming album."

"And save it on your computer for free!"

"It's not for free. It costs 10 bucks an hour to be on the internet!" Robin exclaimed. "And besides, they'll just play the song on the radio eventually, so you're willing to waste money on something you can get for free."

"I told you we shouldn't tell anybody!" someone whispered.

"Nevermind, have fun. I'm off to use the computer to make a spreadsheet with Lotus 1-2-3, something *productive* instead of listening to music."

Janelle was at home in her room watching the *Ricki Lake* show. There was a knock on the door.

"Come in!" she yelled.

"Hey baby, how you feelin'?" Janelle's mother Luanne asked, opening the door.

"I'm fine, Mom."

Janelle sat up from her bed as she sat down next to her. "Janelle, I was wondering if..." she sighed and gathered her words. "I was wondering if you would consider...staying with your grandmother after you graduate."

"Huh? She lives all the way down in Jacksonville...sh..she's basically living in a loony bin!"

"It's a senior-citizen facility. They also take in unwed teen mothers until they're 25."

"There's nobody I know down there. All my friends, my job, I..."

"Just think about it, please. The paperwork would need to be filed now, and I don't think they would put you on the waiting list due to you being related to a resident." She reached out and grabbed both of her daughter's hands. "Listen to me. Your father will NOT let you stay here after you have that baby. This is your only chance to start over with help. You can go to college down there and find a job..."

"I'm not going Mom, and that's final. If Daddy kicks me out, you will never see your grandchild and I will make do *in this city* on my own!"

Luanne dropped her head and hissed, "You are definitely your father's daughter. Both of you are as stubborn as a pair of mules, damn you!" She stood up and left the room.

"Thanks for coming guys. Jackie's been down in the dumps after bombing a few auditions lately." Heywood, Angie, and Eugene were all heading to the Roseland Ballroom. It was seven in the evening. Jackie was the first act scheduled to start at eight.

"Who are the other acts after her?" Eugene asked.

"Don't know, but there's at least six acts, groups and solos, ranging from metal, grudge, speed, and punk. Should be a helluva show."

Heywood noticed that Angie was strangely quiet as they walked. He turned back to Eugene. "This is the second time I've seen you in street clothes. It feels so weird."

"Why the hell does everyone keep saying that?" Eugene asked.

They arrived and entered through a side entrance. There was a huge audience standing in front of the stage while assigned seats were stacked in rows three levels high. Music personalities were warming up the crowd, then at eight-thirty the house lights turned off and an announcer introduced Jackie.

The singer walked on stage and began singing one of her original songs, "Waves of Rage". The band was loud, and the crowd was louder. Eugene was fist-pumping and head-banging while Heywood and Angie stood quietly. "It's an acquired taste," he told her and shrugged. She nodded. "It's alright," she replied.

Several songs into the set, she took a moment to talk to the audience. "Thank you! You guys are great! I'm feeling your energy tonight, are you feeling me?!"

They responded with an affirmative cheer.

"Yeah! Alright it's time, folks...Time to bring the rain!" That was her song cue to start her most popular song, "Dogs Don't See Colors in the Rain". As she sang, she broke out into a dance routine that captured Angie's attention.

"What the," she whispered.

"You feeling it now, huh?" Heywood called out over the music.

But it wasn't the music that made her stand up. The routine was very familiar to her. "I gotta go!" she yelled.

"What?! What happened? What's wrong?" Heywood asked.

Eugene turned his head as Angie started side-stepping to the end of the row. Heywood followed her.

"Guys!?" he yelled. After a moment of thinking, he shrugged. "Fuck it." He turned back to the stage.

Angie was storming off to the exit when Heywood caught up with her and tried to grab her arm. "Get the fuck off of me!" she screamed, pulling away.

"What is up with you?"

"Look, I was okay with her sporting a mohawk and wearing tribal make-up, but she's gone too far!"

"What?"

"She is incorporating a sacred Native American ceremonial dance, blatantly misappropriating our culture!"

"Oh, c'mon, you're overreacting!"

"Fuck you! We don't stand for that shit!" She stomped away through the exit as the song ended. Heywood sighed and went back to his seat. On the stage, Jackie took a bow, then looked up toward his seat and winked at him. He gave a half-smile and waved back to her.

"Great show man, we staying for the rest of it?" Eugene asked, then looked beside him at the empty seat. "Hey, what happened to Angie?"

"She, um...she had to go."

Robin woke up Saturday morning and checked in on Jon. He was surprised to see him sitting up dressing himself.

"Good morning, what are you doing?" Robin signed.

"I want to go for a walk. You up to pushing me around for a few hours?"

"It's the perfect day for it," he signed and smiled.

They left the building, Robin pushing Jon in the wheelchair. Since he was behind Jon, the elder had to direct where they were going by pointing and using hand signals. They went to the George Washington Bus Terminal as Jon socialized with his friends at the OTB and introduced Robin to everyone.

After leaving the terminal they went around to several parks and playgrounds reminiscing. Jon recalled to Robin his first day in the first grade at P.S. 132 and then graduation day from the eighth grade at I.S. 143. They went to 181st Street, and he pointed out where the Woolworth's and Wertheimer's department stores once were, sharing a story about taking a picture with Santa Claus. As they passed Fort Washington Collegiate Church, Robin remembered being a cub scout of troop 729.

At Fort Washington Avenue, they took the M4 bus up to Fort Tryon Park. There were some hard stares from the passengers as the driver had to accommodate Jon using the wheelchair lift. In the park, they followed the path to Linden Terrace Plaza, where there stood a majestic art deco flagpole with a great overview of the neighborhood. Jon surveyed the vast landscape. To his west was The Hudson and The Palisades. The George Washington Bridge was in the distance. To the east was Inwood, The Bronx, and of course, Washington Heights. He was so moved by the sight he began to tear up.

"Granddaddy?" Robin asked.

Jon sighed. "I love this town," he whispered. Suddenly he covered his mouth and went into a violent coughing fit that lasted nearly two minutes. Robin tried to hand him a napkin or tissue while looking for someone that possibly had some water.

"You okay?" he asked, kneeling down in front of him.

Jon pulled his hand out in front of him. It was covered with blood.

"I think we better go," he said hoarsely.

Robin nodded, "Okay, let's go home."

Jon shook his head, "No, not home." He looked up at Robin. "Not home."

Robin was once again in the waiting area after Jon was admitted to Columbia Presbyterian. He wasn't in ICU like the last time. They were reviewing the eligibility criteria for Hospice Care. The health care aide arrived with his Medicare paperwork and gave testimony on his condition. This was the beginning of the end. It was a few minutes after four in the afternoon. Doctor Kelsloan approached Robin as he was staring out a window.

"Mister Walker?"

"Yes?"

"What are you looking at out there, son?"

"Across the street, the infamous Audubon Ballroom...where the assassination of Malcolm X took place."

"Yes."

The structure, a decaying empty shell of a building in the midst of being demolished, stood in the middle of the two parting streets of Broadway and Saint Nicholas between 165th and 166th. After years of being abandoned, the city finally made plans to tear it down and build a medical facility for Columbia University, but there had been resistance to preserve and award it landmark status.

"There's an urban legend," Robin began. "On that fateful afternoon Brother Malcolm was pronounced dead by physicians at Harlem Hospital down 135th Street." He turned away from the window to the doctor. "Now considering Columbia Presbyterian was right across the street, why is it that he was taken over 30 blocks south only to be pronounced dead on arrival when there was a chance to sustain him a mere 100 feet away?"

Kelsloan just stared back at him upon hearing the question.

"Could it be that there were no patients of color allowed here at the time?" Robin asked.

"What are you insinuating Mister Walker?"

"You know damn well what I'm trying to say. My grandfather is somewhere in here dying and you are doing NOTHING to prevent that from happening!"

"I see. You have finally arrived at stage two...anger. Lashing out at everyone around you as the frustration builds. You can draw your own conclusions and place blame, you're entitled. But when you reach the final stage, I'll be expecting an apology from you, sir."

"Don't hold your breath," Robin snarled.

Robin went upstairs to Jon's room. The elder had a catheter put in and a breathing tube in his nose. His frame was thinner than before. It was hard to tell when he was wearing his clothes. This was the worst he had ever seen his maternal guardian, even after the health scare seven years earlier.

"Don't fucking cry on me, boy!" Jon barked. "You hear me?! Not one tear!"

Robin shook his head and shut his eyes, holding back the tears. "No sir... not one tear," he repeated.

"I still got some time, so listen carefully. I know you're scared, but I took care of all the precautions for...after. You're going to be taken care of," he wheezed and took a moment to collect his breath. "You're going to be fine," he signed.

Robin nodded. "Try not to talk," he signed back to him.

"Too weak to keep moving hands," he whispered. "Just bear with me."

"Okay."

"We need to discuss life, things I should have told you sooner, but we'll have to push through it now. First, don't marry the first girl you have sex with."

"Granddaddy..." he sighed while blushing. Jon believed he was still a virgin. Little did he know, Robin lost his virginity right before starting high school at George Washington.

"Travel..." he gasped. "See the world. Do it while you're young. Don't grow old and die in the same damn city you were born and raised in."

"I promise," Robin smiled. His eyes were watering. He blinked hard to hold back the tears.

"In the event of another war, you tell the government you're a conscientious objector if they dare to bring back the draft!" He coughed violently and took a moment. "What I've seen and done...for pride and country..." He left the thought unfinished and just shook his head.

Robin pulled up his blanket. "Okay, that's enough talk for today. Warm up, get some rest. I'll be back tomorrow."

A nurse entered the room. "He'll be with us for a little while longer. He still has some strength in him."

"I know," Robin replied, and walked past her out of the room.

"Alright, no more playing around. I'm serious, Jon is in the hospital again, and he is in Hospice. He doesn't have that much time left. This is it. You NEED to come home, now. Don't call me and ask how is he? Don't ask for his number in his room so you can say your piece over the phone. I don't care what happened between you two but now is the time to be the bigger person. He's your father, Mom! I've tried calling Regina, Sydney and Marcus. No one's picking up. Look, you need to be a grown-up about this. He's on his deathbed and you need to come home and say goodbye!"

Robin put the receiver on his forehead as he looked down and took a breath.

"Mom? Mom I'm scared, my hands are shaking as I hold this phone saying all this. C...can you please just come home? Please? I can't do this by myself, I...I'm not that strong. I can't keep it together. I need you, I need you, here."

He felt the lump in his throat. "Just come home, okay?"

He pressed pound and the answering service confirmed the message recorded in its entirety. After pressing the button to end the call on the wireless phone, it slipped out of his hand and fell on the floor. Leaning his back against the wall, Robin slid down to the floor and curled into a fetal position. With no other options, he did the only thing that he could think of at a time of crisis. He prayed.

Tanya was sitting in her homeroom class as first period began Monday morning. She was confident she passed Friday's quiz and looked forward to playing baseball outside at DeWitt Clinton Park for gym class.

Suddenly a squeal of microphone feedback came from the loud-speaker, causing a hush among the students conversing. "Attention! Your attention please!" a woman's voice boomed throughout the school halls. "Will Tanya Brown please report to the principal's office? I repeat, Tanya Brown please report to the principal's office."

Tanya's eyes went wide as she felt the stares of the entire class. *What the fuck?!* she thought. She looked ahead to her homeroom teacher who gave her the nod to get up and leave. Within seconds she was up from her seat and out the door. She was greeted by Mister Notice, the school administrator (he was offended by the term "Secretary").

"Miss Brown?" he asked with a heavy African accent.

"Yes?"

"Principal Frohlich will see you now," he said, gesturing toward the door to her office.

She walked past him and approached the open doorway. She went through the hundreds of possibilities she was being summoned. Vickie Florence had left her alone since she finally started dating Johnny Jones. There was nothing else she could think of.

"Miss Frochlich?" Tanya asked from the entrance.

Natalie Frochlich was sixty-years-old and stood at 5'11 over a rusted metal desk. For twenty seven years she served as the principal of Park West High School. She was wearing a green and white plaid skirt with a white blouse and black loafers. The pale white skin on her face was colored heavily with make-up in a feeble attempt to retain her youth.

Her office had no windows, but the principal was facing the wall away from the entrance as she stood with her arms behind her back. "Step forward, Tanya, step forward. I'm afraid I have some news."

There were three chairs in front of the gunmetal gray desk. She walked in and took a seat in the middle chair.

"I did NOT ask you to sit down, now did I?"

She sprang back up. "N-n-no you didn't...sorry," she stammered.

The elder turned around to face the student, her face completely emotionless. "Follow me, please," she ordered. She walked around her desk and Tanya followed behind. They walked out to the hallway toward the school entrance.

"I received an interesting phone call this morning," Frochlich began. "It seems that there has been a death in your family...apparently."

"What!?" she gasped.

"Yes, and the memorial is this afternoon, which is quite sudden, I might add."

"Who...who was it?"

"Your grandmother."

That's impossible! she thought. She struggled to keep up, but then another thought crept in the back of her mind. "No wayyyy..." she whispered.

"What was that?" the principal asked.

"Um, nothing! This is all so sudden. I...I'm speechless. Um I take it someone is picking me up?" She was trying really hard not to smile.

They arrived at the door to the school and looked at each other.

"Young lady, I wasn't born yesterday. I saw *Ferris Bueller's Day Off* too, and for someone to be THIS stupid to pull a stunt like this..."

Tanya looked down sheepishly, expecting the worst.

She sighed. "However, I've reviewed your school record, your current grades and even remember speaking to your mother in the past so I know she is VERY strict with you."

"Yes she is, ma'am."

The principal sighed again. "You know, I am two years from retirement. I'll get my full pension and I can stay as long as I want. But I've been overlooked for several advancement opportunities and I...I just don't give a fuck anymore." She nodded. "I believe your ride is here to take you to "the memorial"."

She looked ahead to see a stretch limousine waiting outside in front of the school.

"Wow."

"Go, before I change my mind."

Without another word, or even a second glance, Tanya sprinted out the door.

The limousine driver opened the door when she approached. She looked in to find Franklin sitting in the backseat.

"Don't draw any suspicion. Get in."

She smiled and climbed inside. The driver closed the door and Tanya wrapped her arms around Franklin's neck in a tight embrace. "You're fucking crazy! Is this your car?"

"Of course not! This is just a rental," he grinned. "Where to, Beautiful? South Street Seaport or City Island?"

"City Island!" she squealed.

"Great choice." He lowered the divider and called out, "City Island and step on it!"

"Yes sir," the driver replied.

Franklin pressed a switch, and the divider went up, giving the two some privacy to make out.

"58th Street Branch Library, Sonyai Yi speaking," the senior clerk answered her phone.

"Good morning, Miss Yi, it's Robin. I'm afraid my grandfather is in his final stages...of his life. He's been admitted into hospice care and I need to be by his side."

"I...I understand Walker. I can remove you from the schedule for the week."

"No."

"Excuse me?"

"No, once this happens I'm going to need someplace...someplace to go to get out of the house."

"Very well, call me tomorrow if you need more time."

She hung up the phone, waited a few minutes, then picked it up again and dialed.

From her desk, Ethel lowered her newspaper. "The kid's grandfather?" she asked.

The senior clerk nodded.

Ethel sighed and stepped outside to give Sonyai some privacy. Tommy was processing book reserves received from other branches, placing them on the shelves above the VHS file cabinets. Gerry was at the reference corner, writing in his notebook, when Ethel approached him.

"I know the two of you aren't talking, but Walker's grandfather is on his deathbed."

"That's unfortunate," Gerry replied nonchalantly.

"Coltraine, show some damn compassion."

Gerry stopped writing and looked up. "What do *you* care about some compassion, Jenkins?"

She narrowed her gaze and waved him off with a scoff. "You know what? Fine, be as cold as you want...if the positions were reversed, I'm sure Walker would offer his condolences. That just proves he's the bigger man between the two of you!"

Gerry thought about a response, but noticed Ethel was walking away. He picked up his pencil and resumed his writings.

Doctor Kelsloan was making his rounds when he walked into Jon's room. Robin was holding a silent vigil while Jon was taking a nap. Kelsloan checked Jon's vitals and made a notation in his chart.

"I've noticed you've made several calls to other hospitals and physicians," he began. "Trying to find some advanced treatments and experimental drug trials that are looking for test subjects. I must admire your resources."

Robin said nothing, refusing to acknowledge his presence in the room.

"This would be stage three, bargaining."

His eyes darted up to him for a moment, but he kept his composure and remained quiet. After a moment of lingering, Kelsloan walked out back to the hallway.

Robin let out a sigh of relief, then jumped when he heard Jon whisper, "Is he gone?" He opened his eyes and looked at Robin, who nodded and gave him a thumbs-up.

Jon sat up and signed, "Good. For a doctor, he has terrible bedside manner."

"You okay?"

"Yeah, just dying, that's all."

Robin grinned as Jon looked over to him.

"I'm tired of signing. My hands feel like bags of sugar," he whispered.

"Okay."

"I know you want more people to come, but I'm letting you know now, no one is. Not Esmeralda, Pepsi, Regina, Sydney, Marcus, or your mother. Nobody's coming."

"That's bullshit!"

"Watch that mouth, boy!" he exclaimed. "I can beat the tar off ya, even in this condition!"

"They should be here."

"But they're not! And I've accepted their decision. Now I want you to promise me you will hold no ill will against them, and that you'll forgive your mother and let go of all your hatred for her."

"Never!" he spat in anger.

"Promise me!"

"NO! I'll forgive everyone else, but *she* doesn't get a pass!"

Jon shook his head and sighed. "Robin, please. I'm not asking for much, Son. Your mother loves you."

"I don't believe that."

He closed his eyes and took a breath. The heated argument was taking its toll. He wiped a tear from his eye and looked back at him. "She's your mother. No matter how much hatred in your heart, you only have one mother in your life. You can forgive her, or just cut her out of your life forever, but please, think hard about the major decisions you will face in your journey ahead."

"How...how will I know?" Robin cringed. "You've been there for me, all the way. What will I do now?"

"There will be a time...when you believe that you are alone. When you don't know what to do, and when you don't have the answers. You'll be searching inside yourself for guidance and the will to go on."

Robin looked on and listened.

"You'll be at a crossroads...with two paths before you. When that happens, think of me and remember, Son. Your eyes...they will not see anything, and your ears will not hear a sound. But it will be as if I'm standing right beside you, and the path will present itself."

The youngster was moved as the words stayed with him, still fighting back the tears.

"Remember that, Son."

"I will, I'll remember, and...I promise to...try to forgive Mom," Robin relented.

Jon nodded. "Good, good. Okay, listen, just a few more important things." He took a breath. "First, go to England before you're 25. It's a wonderful place. And when you get there, I need you to do something for me."

Robin listened to a set of instructions given to him by his grandfather, who also shared more personal information to know after his passing. Jon said that he would be contacted by a stranger, who would identify himself with a unique phrase...something about Speedy Gonzales. His speech became slurred as he started to get tired. Robin wondered if everything they discussed was nonsensical. Jon once again went back to sleep as Robin continued watching over him.

Tanya and Franklin were walking around the southernmost tip of City Island, surrounded by the Pelham and Eastchester Bays along with the Long Island Sound. The neighborhood was quiet and serene, with barely a soul in sight.

"I can't believe you actually did this, and it worked," she said.

He chuckled. "I live dangerously. It makes life more fun."

"True, so...tell me about yourself. Is this how you get all the girls? Taking them out in limousines and playing hooky?"

"Nah, this is for those special types, you know? As for me, hmm, where would you like me to start?"

She shrugged. "I dunno, what's your family like?"

"Well, my mom's a stewardess. She flies for Carnival Air. They're a small airline working the east coast. I barely see her. I live with my dad who works maintenance for the apartment complex we live in."

"That's cool? Any brothers or sisters?"

"Yep, one of each. I'm the middle kid. Think that gives me a complex. You?"

"Nope, only child...think that also qualifies for some issues. My father died when I was around six. Mom's been doing what she can since."

"Wow."

"Yeah."

They approached a rail in front of the shore at Belden Point, over-looking the beach.

"There's something else going on with you. I sensed it at the library," Franklin said.

"Wha...what do you mean?"

He tightened his gaze at her. "You've been hurt recently...an ex maybe?"

She looked down at her feet, making an attempt not to blush. "Maybe."

"I knew it," he said with a nod. "So, am I just someone to make him jealous, eh?"

"It's not..."

"No, no, I'm cool, I just wanna know...so I can up the ante," he said, a huge smile growing across his face.

She smiled back. Then he put his arm around her waist. "We're going to have *so much* fun." They leaned in for a long kiss.

At three, the limo pulled up in front of the branch. Franklin came out first and nearly got hit by a car driving down the street. He then walked around and opened the door for Tanya, who was carrying a huge stuffed teddy bear he had won her.

Inside, Lakeshia, Alex, and Janelle looked out through the wall of glass and noticed Tanya's arrival. Behind the circulation desk, Sonyai and Andrew Friedman stood and turned to see what caught the pages' attention.

Tanya looked in and caught a glimpse of Andrew behind the desk. Franklin saw her reaction and looked in as well. "That's him, isn't it?" he asked.

She nodded.

"Well, let's give him a taste of his own medicine, shall we?"

Without hesitation, she pulled him close, and they proceeded to tongue each other down in an exaggerated and sloppy series of wet kisses. She went even further by reaching down and lightly grabbing his crotch, which he was unprepared for. Tanya looked back over her shoulder and the faces of the pages, along with Andrew, were frozen with shock. She reached into the car for her book bag as Franklin stood in place, blinking rapidly.

"See you around."

"Uh, yeah..." he sighed.

She giggled and turned around, strutting to the entrance. Once inside she greeted everyone as she skipped through the floor to the door upstairs, "Hi y'all," then greeted Andrew with a snort, "Andrew."

Andrew Friedman looked back at Sonyai, who rolled her eyes and turned back to her terminal.

The afternoon went by with little tension. Sonyai saw Andrew walk toward her as he prepared to leave at five o'clock.

"Thank you for coming in. Walker believed his grandfather wouldn't last the night."

"No problem, um...next time I think I'll send one of my other clerks if you need any help," he replied.

She wanted to ask why, but held her tongue. "I see. Very well then."

They shook hands, and he turned to leave. Andrew gave one last look at Tanya as he walked by the shelves and then quickly stepped through the exit turnstile. A smile came across her face. *Bye, bye!* she thought.

Sonyai was working the last hour with Tommy when she noticed Lakeshia collecting several returned books behind her. A concerned look was on the teen's face.

"Is there something bothering you, Miss Seabrooke?" Sonyai asked.

"Um, I was just wondering why Robin called out today. Is he sick?"

"He should be back tomorrow. You seem very upset by his absence."

She blushed at being confronted about her feelings by the supervisor. "I...I..uh, it's nothing, jus..."

"Miss Seabrooke, I can read you like a book, as corny as that sounds. You have affectionate feelings for Walker and despite my warnings, they are starting to affect your work."

"No! Please, I...I, we're just friends, and we'll stay that way. I'm sorry I brought it up." She hurried away back to the shelves.

Sonyai took a deep breath. "These girls," she whispered. "They're going to be my death!"

It was nine-thirty at night and the hospice ward was eerily quiet. In the past few hours, Jon only had two visitors whom Robin had never seen before. Later, a priest stopped by working on behalf of the hospital, offering to perform Jon's Last Rites, but he politely declined.

Every ten minutes, Robin would check Jon's wrist for a pulse. He was cold as ice. His eyes were closed as his head leaned over to the side. Robin checked the heart monitor which registered a steady pulse. Leaning forward, he strained to hear if he was still breathing.

"Granddaddy?" he whispered. "Granddaddy!" he called out in panic. *He can't hear you, dumbass.* He looked out to the hallway and was about to wave for a nurse when...

"Still here," Jon whispered.

"Oh! Jesus!" Robin exclaimed, he clapped his hands and signed, "Don't do that!"

"I'm just resting, damnit. When I'm dead, you'll know!"

He sat back down and held in a giggle. "I...I love you, Granddaddy," he whispered and smiled.

Jon played the "I'm still here" game several more times, but the lapses between breaths were getting longer as his heart monitor registered his pulse slowly fading.

Robin was bouncing his foot to take his mind off the rising urge to urinate. The nurse noticed his foot as well.

"Honey, why don't you go to the bathroom? He has a few more hours, we don't need you making a mess on the floor."

Robin gave Jon a longing look. His face was sunken in, his eyes were half-closed, and the heart monitor was beeping slowly but steadily. He nodded and mouthed the words as he signed, "I'll be right back."

He waited for a reaction from Jon's mouth or hands, some sort of reply. He lowered his hand back to his side and took two steps from the bed, looked back, then walked out to the hallway. The nurse walked around the bed to Jon's right side. His hand suddenly shot up and grabbed her arm with the last of his strength.

She gasped in shock as he pulled the oxygen mask off and turned to her. "Thhhhh...aank you," he hissed quietly. With his last breath, Jon David Walker whispered, "Diddddn't. Wanttt. Toooooseeeeehh." His final words came out in a guttural death rattle as he flatlined.

His arm went limp. The nurse laid it back on the bed and looked up at the clock on the wall. Doctor Kelsloan stepped in to acknowledge the code blue. "Time of death..."

The doctor heard running footsteps from the hallway and quickly turned back to the doorway. Robin ran full speed into the physician's arms as he held the youngster at bay.

"No!" he screamed.

"Let him go, Son! He didn't want you to see..."

"NOOOOO! LET ME GO! GET OFF ME!" Robin cried.

"Time of death, 9:59 pm," the nurse announced.

"He's gone Son, he's gon..."

Robin socked the doctor in the jaw with a thunderous right cross. He fell to the floor like a ton of bricks as Robin ran past him to the bed and dropped to his knees.

"No, no, no...You ROBBED me of saying goodbye to him!" he screamed at the nurse.

"He didn't want you to see him pass. It was his final wish..." she said, shaking her head.

"I DON'T CARE! It wasn't your decision to make for him!" he screamed in anguish, shaking the bed. "GRANDDADDY!!! GRAND-DADDY!!! NOOOO, OH GOD PLEASE NOOOOO! PLEASE GOD PLEASE!"

His sobs resonated in the halls as the staff left him alone in the room for privacy.

CHAPTER SIX

Robin sat alone in the chapel. After walking the halls randomly, he followed the signs, took a seat and waited for thoughts to come to him. Everything felt surreal. It was as if he was living in a nightmare, begging to wake up. A shadow appeared at the doorway and Doctor Kelsloan walked in.

He was still holding his jaw when he sat down next to Robin. "You have a solid right hand there," he began. "Felt like a cinder block."

"What kind of doctor holds a family member at bay while a patient dies on his deathbed?" Robin asked, staring out into space.

Kelsloan looked down and sighed.

"I...I imagine what it would be like," Robin said. "Slowly slipping away, completely unaware of my cries of protest, screaming at the top of my lungs and it's just white noise to him." He turned to the physician. "It's not right."

"He didn't want you to see. It was his dying wish," he replied flatly. "We respect that above all things."

They sat in silence. Kelsloan attempted to say something, but Robin spoke first.

"I never understood the logic behind having one of these in a facility dedicated to science and medicine. They make strange bedfellows. They don't belong together. If a patient survives, it's because of the skills of the doctors...faith has nothing to do with it."

He turned and looked at the doctor.

"I mean, you think that one patient whose relatives came here to pray deserves to make it over the next patient who just trusted the doctor's competence? Huh?"

Kelsloan had no answer.

"I refuse to believe it works that way. Would my grandfather still be alive if I came here and prayed?"

"Stage four is depression, Mister Walker. You're almost through."

Robin shut his eyes. He didn't want to give him the satisfaction of getting him angry with him counting off those damn stages. He cleared his head and sighed. "This reminds me of a conversation I once had. A teacher once asked me, 'What are you going to do to help the world when you get older?' and it made me think."

"A valid question if I ever heard one."

"So one day, when I was 12-years-old, I told my grandfather, I was going to kill the devil."

The doctor raised his eyebrows and gave the youth a questionable look.

"He asked me why. I told him that the devil was responsible for all the bad things that happened in the world. I wanted to stop bad things from happening so the world would be a happier place."

"Okay."

"So then he says, 'Well, the devil lives in Hell. How you gonna get down there and kill him?' and I answered, 'The only way I know how.' So, he laughs, actually laughs, and I'm looking at him all weird-like."

"Not the reaction I'd expect, Son."

"I know!" He shook his head with a smile from the memory and continued, "So, after laughing he tells me, 'So you know the only way to go to Hell and face the devil is to commit a sin.' He told me this to scare me, but I thought about it for a minute and asked him, 'If I sin to go to Hell and then kill the devil, God would forgive me, right?' "

"Wow, you missed your calling. You should have been an attorney," the doctor said. "Such a clever boy at 12."

"Heh, yeah, I guess...Granddaddy tells me, 'It doesn't work like that. Once you're in Hell, there's no getting out.' I was quiet after him telling me that and then he said, 'So if you go to Hell, kill the devil, you'll spend the rest of your time down there alone. You will become that which you have set out to kill,' and that was the end of the philosophical debate."

"Remarkable. He left his mark on you. Whatever you do in life, I'm sure you will honor him."

Robin nodded. "That made me think and eventually do some serious research as I got older. Everyone says the devil was once an angel who challenged God and was cast out down to Hell for him to reign, never to return. But who exactly said that? Who wrote the bible? All the stories? Adam and Eve, David and Goliath, Noah and the Ark, all the testaments, new and old, King James, and the rest..."

The doctor looked at him blankly.

"Man. *We* came up with it. When bad things happen in the world, we blame it on the devil because we are taught to believe that God doesn't let bad things happen. It's not him, it's the OTHER guy! But what if it was wrong? We know the devil exists because he IS the source of evil for all the bad things that happen, going back to the Ice Age!"

Robin stood up and began to pace back and forth.

"The dinosaurs being wiped out, all him! When man comes along, and the devil is still making his presence known...The rise and fall of the Roman Empire, the Ming Dynasty, the Mongolian Empire, the Crusades, Camelot, the Victorian Age, all dealing with the darkest moments of history, under the devil's influence. Napoleon, Jack the Ripper, Adolf Hitler, so then what does man do? Huh?"

Doctor Kelsloan just shrugged.

"He comes up with that mythical tale, of a wonderful place, a place you can only go if you are GOOD. And running that nice place is the Creator himself, big guy, white flowing beard, sound familiar? Santa Claus, that's right, a creation of man. We came up with Santa

Claus to scare the children into being good or they won't be rewarded, and now we have Santa Claus for the adults, too."

Robin looked crazed. He raised his hand and pointed to his temple.

"God...is a creation of Man. It's the chicken and the egg. Man wrote the bible, so Man created God. And the devil, the source of all the evil in the world, the one that is convincing everyone that he does *not* exist was the one fucking up the world from the moment it all began!"

The doctor just looked at him after listening to the story. Robin was out of breath, on the verge of tears. He sighed. "And from that day forward...he understood my behavior. He knew that there were good intentions behind the bad things."

After the tirade, Robin stood as if struck with an epiphany. His mind was clear now. He had finally come to terms with what just transpired.

"I suppose you don't believe in God, then," Kelsloan challenged.

Robin grinned. "Are you kiddin'? I'm a God-fearing Christian. Of course I believe in God."

"What?" he gasped.

"It was *just a theory*."

The doctor blinked while scratching his head. He began to question the young man's sanity.

"Ahem, with that said, I um, believe I have some sort of paperwork to fill out, sir?"

"Yes, that is what I was looking to tell you." He stood up. "I believe you have just reached stage five...acceptance. Follow me, please."

"Lead the way, Doctor."

In the event of a patient's death, the next of kin has to officially identify the body, confirm the mortuary it should be sent to, then fill out forms for the death certificate and social security death index. Doctor Kelsloan walked Robin to the lobby once everything was completed.

"Mister Walker?"

"Yes?"

"I did some research and discovered something interesting."

Robin turned to look at the physician.

"It seems that around 3:30 in the afternoon on February 21st, 1965 a patient was brought into the emergency room on the third floor in this hospital and pronounced dead after 15 minutes of life resuscitation methods."

Robin cocked an eyebrow.

"He was believed to have over 20 gunshot wounds, including a close-range shotgun buckshot impact to his chest. The patient was described as slim, over six feet tall with reddish hair and officially listed as 'John Doe' on file due to lack of any identification on his person."

He lifted a file confirming the details.

"He was later identified by next of kin as Malcolm Little, also known as Malcolm X."

It was late and Robin was tired, but he looked down apologetically, caught off guard by this new information.

"So you see Son," Kelsloan took a step toward him. "We doctors don't see skin color when it comes to treating patients, because underneath that one-millimeter layer of skin," he pointed to Robin's arm making him flinch. "Your ligaments, joints, muscles, cartilage, veins, blood vessels, nerve endings, and bones..."

He reached over for the youth's left hand and suddenly ripped off his glove, making him grunt in surprise.

"...all look the same! You think about that before you call me a racist!"

With his point made, Kelsloan handed back the glove. Robin took it back and slipped it back on.

"Sorry for your loss," the doctor said in parting, then turned and headed back to the elevators.

"Yeah," he whispered back.

"Alright you bitch, the inevitable has happened! You fucking hear me?! Any chance for closure has gone out the window! I really thought you were better than this. I thought you could be the bigger person. You're a role model for fuck's sake. How could you be so petty? You know what? I'm not surprised. You've been nothing but a vindictive bitch as long as I've known you! You have NO SOUL whatsoever! Leeching off that bimbo, your little paycheck with an IQ of a pumpkin! Fuck you! I hate you so goddamn much right now that if I see you, I'm gonna rip your spine out of your throat and use it for dental floss! You're a disgrace, and no matter WHAT Granddaddy did, you don't have to worry about him anymore...your father is dead. I hope you're fucking happy now."

He slammed the phone down and threw it against the wall. Taking out his rage on his mother wasn't making the pain go away. The apartment was completely quiet. Sixteen stories up, he couldn't hear a single car horn from the streets below, nor a screeching airplane among the clouds above. Robin looked around the living room, unsure of what to do.

"If you can hear me," he began, his voice hoarse and full of desperation. "If there truly is another form of existence out there...spirit, soul, or ghost, give me a sign that you're still with me."

All that remained was the silence.

"Please! Move something, knock a book over, make a noise, compel someone else to, anything, a whisper, a faint cough, a bell, anything to break...to break this quiet feeling of emptiness!"

He fell to his knees. Like a twisted reversal of paralysis by sound, Robin was unable to function. Using his voice as a grounding point in the middle of an invisible hurricane. The quietness endured, breaking Robin, shattering his mind at the mercy of the deafening silence.

It was four in the morning when Robin staggered down 2nd Avenue, nearly passing Walter's brownstone. A six-pack of Budweiser was hanging off his gloved left hand while he held a bottle of Coors Light in his right. He knocked on the door, calling out, "Waaaaaaaaaaallllll-llltttttt....Walt!!! Open the door, it's Robin!"

There was no answer. The windows were completely dark.

"My...my, granddaddy's gone, Walt...I need...I need to talk to someone. Open the door!!!"

The door flew open. From the darkness inside, Robin heard a tirade of French obscenities, "Sacré bleu! What is it with you Americans?!" yelled Jacques Sarte.

"Hey! Inspector Clouseau! Mister Pink Panther, lemme in. Need to talk to Walt!" Robin said to Walter's roommate.

"He is not here, now go away before I call the police!"

Jacques moved to close the door, but Robin pushed his way inside, screaming at the top of his lungs. "Waaaaalt!! My granddaddy! He's dead, man...he's fucking dead! Where are you!?!?"

The dark hallway made him trip, and the bottle fell on the floor. "Shit!" he hissed. "What the fuck, man!?"

Robin had no memory of what happened next. He felt a thump at the back of his head and then woke up back outside. The six-pack was on his lap as he sat in front of the door in a collapsed heap.

"Walt, man...where you at?" he whispered to no one.

Tuesday morning in the staff room, Augustus was conducting a meeting with Zelda, Heywood, and Angie. There was a box of donuts in the middle of the kitchen table. Only Zelda helped herself to one.

"...and that's our schedule of events for the remainder of the year. Are there any questions?" Augustus asked, concluding the discussion. Everyone was quiet. Heywood and Angie were avoiding eye contact.

"Very well, see everyone downstairs."

The head librarian got up to leave. Zelda followed behind him. The remaining two information assistants sat for several minutes, then finally looked at each other.

"Tell me," Angie started. "You ever hear of The Boston Tea Party?"

Heywood nodded. "December 1773, 300 boxes of tea from the East India Company were destroyed and the remains were thrown overboard in the Boston Harbor. It was a protest against the imposed taxation of imported goods, including said tea. The actions were done by one of the earliest groups of political radicals in the country's history, the Sons of Liberty."

"Yeah, what the history books leave out is that the Sons of Liberty disguised themselves as natives of the Mohawk people so *they* could be blamed and retaliated against." Her gaze turned cold. "People have been impersonating and stealing every single aspect of who we are."

"Look, I'm sorry you were offended. Jackie told me stories of her living on reservations back in Washington. She made friends, learned from them, I would like to think that what she's doing is...is homage."

"Well I don't see it that way."

She stood up and walked out of the room.

Sonyai walked inside the 96th Street Branch Library at eleven in the morning and made her way to the circulation desk. A stout African-American man with a noticeably large head was standing behind the counter with a face of no expression.

"Sonyai Yi, senior clerk at 58th Street," she identified herself. "I believe Ms. Coons is expecting me."

The clerk nodded. "The clerical office is to the left, down the hallway."

The senior clerk walked past the desk, down the hallway, and knocked on the door at the end.

A sultry voice called out, "Come in."

Behind the door, in a small office, a middle-aged white woman wearing a red blouse and gray business slacks sat at her desk. Sonyai walked in and took a seat as Jessica Coons looked up and greeted her with a slight grin.

Sonyai matched the grin with one of her own. "How are things going for the regional senior clerk these days? You and Yosemite Sam working well together?"

Jessica let out a throaty chuckle. "He leaves me alone, I leave him alone," she replied, referring to Cleopheous Baker. Unlike the rival librarians Augustus and Cleopheous, the senior clerks were actually good close friends.

"I need to ask a favor," Sonyai began.

"Let me guess, you need a vacancy for Janelle Simms."

Sonyai didn't surprise easily, and you would have never guessed she was taken off guard if it wasn't for a small twitch at the side of her mouth. "Wow, you *are* well informed."

"To say I heard it through the grapevine, old friend, would be putting it lightly...it's like a secret that all the women are aware of but none of the men. Which is life, them being all oblivious and thinking with the *wrong* head." A smile finally came across her face.

"Indeed," Sonyai remarked. "Can you help me?"

"Well, we're fully staffed here, of course, with a waiting list for clerks and pages. Webster and Yorkville are also without any openings. Which leaves 67th Street and Cooke-Cathedral."

Sonyai winced at the mention of the two unfavorable branches in their midtown cluster. "Those two would be a punishment worse than hell. A remote tourist trap and an underground newsstand!"

"Beggars can't be choosy, Sonyai. You know how this is. Have you gone through the official channels yet?"

"A formal request has been submitted. She's out of school already, her graduation ceremony is a month away, and she can't stay a page for too long."

"I sympathize, but options *are* limited, and you know I would help you out in a heartbeat. We go back, you and me. The three of us back then. You, me...The Man in White, we look out for each other."

Sonyai let out a sigh at the mention of her mentor. "Yes, I know...well, if you hear anything..." She stood up to leave.

Jessica got up and walked around to meet her with a parting embrace. "Stay strong...Freckles," she whispered.

Sonyai smiled, actually smiled at their private nickname. "You too, Red, you too."

At two o'clock, Robin slowly walked in the branch past the circulation desk to the clerical office. Despite a fresh set of clothes, he was physically distraught as evidenced by his gait and was not wearing his book bag.

Sonyai saw him walk in. They looked at each other. "Walker?"

"I..I'm going to need...to go on bereavement leave," he muttered.

She nodded. "I'm sorry." She opened a drawer in her desk and pulled out a form. "Which days? This week, next week?"

"Thursday and Friday, that's it. We're off Monday for Memorial Day, right?"

"That's correct." She handed him the paper. "Please fill this out. You okay to work today?"

He nodded. "Yes." He took a seat and proceeded to fill out the form. He handed it back to her and went back to the door. "I'll be upstairs."

Sonyai almost called back to him, but by the time she opened her mouth, he was quickly out the door.

As Robin passed through the floor to head upstairs, Ethel and Gerry exchanged glances behind the circulation desk, while Angie noticed him from the information desk. When he entered the staff room, Tanya was lying on the couch reading an issue of *Vibe* magazine. She looked up and flinched when she saw the look on his face.

"Hey," she greeted.

"How's it goin'?"

She wanted to say he looked like shit, but decided not to. "Um, I uh, never got to say thanks for um, taking care of that thing I was going through with Vickie Florence at school..."

Robin chuckled. "Heh, figured out it was me, eh?" He thought back to a few weeks after he started at 58th Street. Tanya had inadvertently attracted the affections of a boy at school, which made another girl jealous to the point of following Tanya around with the intent to do her harm.

"Yeah, not to sound ungrateful but, I can take care of myself, Cuz. Next time, I won't be needing anyone to fight my battles, okay?"

"I'll keep that in mind," Robin replied, remembering when he tied Vickie up and held her on the roof of the high school. "I didn't do it for *you*, Lakeshia asked me for help on your behalf."

"Yeah, I kinda figured, but like I said, no offense, thanks, but um..."

"Gotcha," Robin nodded.

He moved to the other couch as Tanya started reading again. A moment went by when Robin said, "Hey Tanya."

"Huh?"

"Can I ask you something?"

She shrugged. "Sure."

"Yeah, umm...what's with...um, the way you talk?"

Tanya frowned. "What'chu *mean* how I talk?"

"Like you grew up watching nothing but *The Dukes of Hazzard*, *The Beverly Hillbillies* and *Hee Haw*..." he held up his hands. "Sorry if I offended you, just asking."

Since she was being frank with him, he'd decided to return the favor.

She snorted. "I grew up in Yonkers, was there 'til I was 10." She stood up. "But trust me, you won't catch me rocking no Daisy Dukes!"

Robin watched her walk out of the room, thinking about her last remark, then shrugged and laid down for a quick nap.

"I received a call last night," Zelda began, "A few minutes after David Letterman from Babs."

She had just finished filing away some reports on her desk while Augustus was sitting quietly at his desk in deep thought. "Hmmmm," was all he let out, completely disinterested.

"Walker's grandfather passed away last night."

That brought his attention to the assistant librarian. "That's...unfortunate. I take it he was Walker's guardian?"

She nodded.

"He's still young," Augustus said. *And susceptible...* he thought. "This will be very hard on him."

"I agree," Zelda nodded. "I hope the rest of the branch goes easy on him. He needs their comfort and acceptance even more now." She stood and walked out of the office.

Augustus agreed with his assistant's statement but his personal experience taught him not to expect any kindness from those who see you as adversarial. Perhaps he could reach out to the outsider and use his offered condolences as a way to manipulate...

A knock came from the door which interrupted his thoughts. "Yes?" he called out.

Heywood opened the door and walked in. "Sir, I've been meaning to ask you about returning the box. I feel uneasy keeping it at home."

"I understand your anxiety, but I need you to hold on to it for a few more days."

"Sir, I—"

"When I asked you to remove it from the branch, I was trusting you more than anyone else here, including Zelda." Augustus stood up. "I know you won't let me down."

Heywood swallowed hard. "A few more days."

The head librarian nodded.

"Uh, yeah...I can do that."

"Good. When you bring it back, place it in the auditorium closet upstairs." After stepping around his desk, he rested his hand on Heywood's shoulder. "I won't forget this, Learner."

The two men left the office together, with Augustus closing the door behind him.

At the end of his first hour, Sonyai walked up behind Robin holding an inter-office manilla envelope. He turned and looked at her.

"This came for you this afternoon from a courier. You can open it inside."

"Thanks," he said with a nod, then walked inside. Ethel stepped out to the desk to join Gerry in a corner after Tommy relieved him from the returns side. All four clerks were looking at each other as Robin sat alone inside.

Unlooping the red twine holding the flap close, Robin opened the envelope and pulled out a card that read *Our deepest condolences...* on the outside. He opened it and there were numerous personal messages expressing sympathy. *From the staff of the Fort Washington Branch Library,* was at the top of the card's inside page.

Sonyai and Gerry stole side-glances inside as Robin sighed, reading each message. He was very moved by the gesture. Gerry then looked back at Sonyai who looked back and mouthed the word, *"What?"* Robin emerged from the office. He stopped halfway past the circulation desk and turned to face all the clerks, who were secretly following him with their eyes.

"I know I haven't been here that long for you to get to know me personally," he began. "Coming here to work keeps me away from my empty apartment, thinking about how my grandfather is now gone. I know you feel obligated to do or say something for my loss, but I'd rather mourn quietly without anyone bringing it up or being the center of attention. Is that cool?"

Everyone nodded in agreement. Robin turned to the pages out among the shelves, hoping they heard him, then toward the information desk. The staff seemed to have gotten the message, while the patrons were confused at what was happening.

Robin nodded and then whispered, "I'm going down the block for a slice, anyone want anything?"

The group declined awkwardly all at the same time, which didn't make him flinch as he turned and left.

"His branch sent him a card. That's something *we* should have done here!" Gerry hissed at Sonyai.

"Why are you mad at me? You could have easily gotten a card and we could have signed it!"

"She's right, man," Tommy whispered anxiously. "If you really felt that way, *you* could have gotten the card."

"What? She's the supervisor, she should have done it. What do you care anyway, man?" Gerry asked Tommy.

"You should talk, you're the one that's on his shit list after that argument y'all had!" Tommy said.

The trio bickered among themselves as Ethel looked on, shaking her head.

Since there wasn't any request from the staff, Robin walked up to McDonald's on 3rd Avenue instead of getting pizza. He ordered a number nine (which was a filet of fish and fries) then took a seat in the dining area upstairs. Looking over the card again, he remembered each staff member from his previous branch fondly. Even Trevor Guzman wrote something poignant: *Robin, sorry for your loss...fatboy. - Trevor.* He shook his head and snickered, "Fucking Trevor."

He ate and read some more and then noticed something odd. There was someone he remembered that was unaccounted for. He thought he was mistaken and scanned the card front and back to confirm his suspicions. *She would have written something...*

"Rose?" he whispered to himself.

The last twelve hours had been a blur. After washing out at Walt's place, he had returned home to take a shower, barely getting any sleep. There was so much he had to do for the wake and funeral. No one from the extended family had contacted him after he reached out, making phone calls all morning. Fortunately, Jon planned ahead and made most of the arrangements.

His grandfather only took Robin to Wadsworth Baptist Church on holidays but the pastor was the closest person to a spiritual advisor for conducting the ceremonies. After talking to Pastor Amaro this morning, all he had to do was wait until Thursday evening for the wake and then the funeral Friday morning.

Sonyai changed the clerical schedule so Robin could leave at five. It was ten minutes before the hour when Gerry finally walked up to him.

"Hey man, about before...I just want to say..."

Robin waved his hand dismissively. "It's cool, man."

"And um, sorry for your loss."

"Thanks," Robin replied. He extended his hand out for a handshake of friendship.

Gerry grabbed his hand and pulled Robin toward his chest, embracing him with a hearty hug. "You need anything, man...you let me know!" Gerry gasped.

Robin's eyes grew wide with shock by the emotional gesture. "I *need* you to let me go!" he mumbled.

Gerry released Robin as the youngster took several steps back. "Sorry, I just..."

"I get it, I get it...thanks, um, I gotta go. My ride's waiting for me."

"Yeah," Gerry waved dismissively at him.

Robin double-timed it around the circulation desk, through the threshold, and out the exit where Cervantes was waiting outside. He was quiet most of the ride home, but once the cab passed the 145th Street exit on the West Side Highway, Robin asked his driver and friend to take the regular streets up to 179th Street.

"Something on your mind?" Cervantes asked.

The cab driver had always been someone Robin could talk to since helping the immigrant avoid getting robbed over a year ago.

"Yeah, I gotta question, man...what do they do in Ghana when someone dies?"

"Believe it or not, it is a time for celebration when someone passes on."

"For real?!"

"Yes, the family of the departed have a huge party, with food, drink, and dancing. They remember the person's life, focus on their successes, happy moments and achievements. The Americans here are always so serious and sad with their crying and carrying on."

"I haven't shed a tear. I refuse to!" *"Not. One. Tear!"* he remembered.

"The body is buried in style! The coffins are made as a representation of who they were, what they did, like a carpenter would have a coffin in the shape of a hammer. A cobbler? His coffin would be made to look like a shoe!"

"What!? That's crazy!"

"And there would be billboards and skywriting all over the city. We don't mourn death, young man...we celebrate life!"

"Celebrate life..." Robin said with a nod.

Lakeshia sat quietly in the car as her brother Derrick drove home. She was worried about Robin. Something about his demeanor was off as he left for the day.

"You alright, Sis? You look like Daddy's gonna beat our asses for some reason when we get home. Something I don't know about?" Derrick joked.

She shook her head. "No, I...I'm just feeling sad for Robin. His grandfather passed away. With his mother away, his grandfather was all Robin had to raise him." She looked down. "He's all alone, now." A tear slid down her cheek.

I wonder if it would be too much to attend the funeral... she thought.

Derrick took a quick glance at his sister then focused back on the road. "Lakeshia, I know you have feelings for this boy but you need to let him grieve and get through this. Remember Romans 8:28."

"And we know that in all things God works for the good of those who love him," she recited, *"who have been called according to his purpose."*

He nodded in agreement.

"I just want to be there for him, to comfort him."

"Comfort him as a Christian? Or *comfort* him, comfort him?" he asked with some emphasis and a grin on his face.

"That's not funny!" she snapped while blushing a bright red on her fair skin. "Don't tell Mom and Dad about any of this, either!"

"Oh they already know, Sis...they already know."

The wake for Jon David Walker took place on the evening of May 26th, 1994, from five o'clock to seven. Robin greeted each person as they arrived and signed the visitor's book at the hall of Benta's Funeral Home.

Aside from the direct family, there were very few visitors that he was unfamiliar with. Several MTA employees, who were also retired, came and shared fond memories they had of Jon. Franklin and Supa arrived to pay their respects. It was the first time Robin had seen the man wearing something other than his uniform as he shook his hand wearing a black business suit.

Franklin hugged Robin, patting him on the back. "Sorry, Bro. He lived a good, long life."

"Thanks, man."

Over his shoulder, he saw a group of five young men his age walking up to the entrance.

"I brought the crew," Franklin said. "I think it's time."

He stepped back from Robin as Clay, Greg, Al, Keith, and Hector all walked up and stared at the two. They were all once friends from the age of ten to fifteen. Running through the neighborhood, riding bikes, playing sports and video games at each other's apartments throughout the high-rise. After a disagreement, Robin distanced himself from the others with Franklin as the common link between them, his allegiance divided.

They all looked at each other in silence until Clay nudged Al to step forward and say something. "Uh, hey Robin."

"Alec," he replied coldly. His resentment was still strong against the would-be "leader" of the group of friends he once associated with.

Franklin put his hand on Robin's shoulder. "C'mon man, it's been three years. They're here out of respect."

Robin cleared his throat. "Thank you for coming," he said and extended his hand in friendship.

Al nodded and shook his hand and stepped past him inside. The others did the same, then Franklin smiled and looked at him with an approving nod.

Robin checked his watch for a moment, which read six-thirty. He looked up and gasped at a figure crossing the street. He ran to meet his cousin, Sidney Jordan halfway at the corner and greeted him with a hearty embrace. For the first time since Jon's death, he felt some relief at seeing a close member of the family.

Sidney was a pilot in the Air Force stationed in Greensboro, North Carolina. Like Robin, he was fairly light-skinned. With a lean frame and clean-shaven standing an even six feet, his hair was cropped with a military issued Caesar and he had green eyes that Robin had always been jealous of.

"Thank God, Sid. I've been a mess. Where's Marcus and Auntie Gina?" he asked, looking around.

"It's only me, Robin. I'm sorry."

"Huh? Damnit, they need to be here! It's about respect!"

"Robin, I know he raised you and everything. You owe what you are to him, but...when it comes to our mothers he..."

"Look, I know things weren't easy for them. He was raising two girls by himself. He might have been strict, but..."

Sidney waved his hand. "I don't wish to speak ill of the dead, but there's a damn good reason why momma, auntie and my brother aren't here. Maybe someday one of us will tell you, but it's not going to be me."

He stepped past and continued to the entrance. "I'm paying my respects and then I'm back on the 8 o'clock Trailways Bus back to North Carolina."

Robin ran to catch him. "Wait, wait, wait! What about the actual funeral service?" he asked, putting his hand on his cousin's shoulder.

Sidney pushed his hand off and turned to him. "Robin, they don't even know I'm here. If they find out, Momma may actually disown me."

A scowl came across his face. "Alright, fine!" Robin spat. "Marcus always *was* a basket case! The shit you and him pulled at sleepovers when I was five...I still remember. I'd almost believe he'd be in jail by now..."

"Hey! That's my brother..."

"I don't care! You go in and leave for all I care. I'm sick of this disrespect! Thanks for nothing, you tight ass stick in the mud!" He pushed past Sidney and went inside, pretending their conversation never happened.

Robin was in no mood to sleep in an empty apartment the night before the funeral, but to his surprise, the apartment wasn't as quiet as it had been the last several days. It was eight o'clock when he stepped off the elevator on the sixteenth floor, walking down the hallway past several strangers...who were coming from his apartment!

"What the...?" he whispered.

He couldn't believe his eyes as he stepped inside to find distant family members and close friends scrounging around, claiming items in his apartment for themselves. They were at the wake several hours ago and were barely familiar to him.

"Make sure you check under the bed!" someone yelled in the apartment's hallway to their bedrooms. No one stopped to acknowledge his appearance at the doorway, so Robin slammed the door behind him and locked the door. He then reached behind the writing desk next to the closet and pulled out a genuine Louisville Slugger baseball bat.

"Who the fuck let you in here!?" he yelled.

A tall, bald African-American man Robin recognized as "Cousin Avery", the oldest of Jon's nephews stepped forward. He was holding a sterling silver picture frame with Jon and his two other siblings from twenty-years-ago. "Mom gave us the key so we could get a few things...HEY!"

Robin swung and missed his Grandaunt Esme's oldest son by inches, leaving a mark on the wall behind him.

"Hey, good reflexes!" he complimented. "Let's see how good you are at running the bases..."

Avery side-stepped and moved around the living room, being chased by Robin swinging wildly after him. He then turned his attention to another man trying to unhook the cable box from the living room television.

"And what the hell are *you* doing!?"

The man was an elderly gentleman, wearing overalls and a tee-shirt, with sandals and no socks, exposing his toes. "My name's Artie Finkleberg. Jon promised me his tee-vee set!" he answered with a southern drawl.

"You're not taking the TV," Robin said flatly. "Let go of the wires or—"

"Jon know me from OTB for over 30 years! We go back now, Son...before you were even born. He owe me this..."

Robin brought his bat down hard on the old man's left foot. He howled and fell to his side, screaming in agony. Several other people came into the living room, drawn by the commotion.

"Let me make this clear. Nobody is taking *anything* from this house. I don't care who you are or if my grandfather promised you the Brooklyn Bridge!" He turned to Avery and held his hand up.

"I'll take those keys now...you can put down that picture as well."

"My mother said..."

"Your mother didn't even go to the hospital to see him in his final hours, NOT EVEN ONCE! Give me those damn keys or I break bones!"

"You've got a lot of nerve..." Avery mumbled as he fished out a pair of keys from his pocket.

Robin snatched the keys and went back to unlock the door. "You come back here after the funeral, and I will personally send each and every one of you to the afterlife so you can meet Jon again! Now get the fuck out of here, you vultures!"

They all started to move toward the door, but Robin closed it. "Drop everything first!"

One by one, they took out items they had hidden on their person and dropped them to the floor. Robin shook his head and opened the door, staring with disapproval as they walked out.

CHAPTER SEVEN

THERE WERE NO MORE THAN THIRTY ATTENDEES AT THE FUNERAL. Esmeralda and Pepsi were joined by Pepsi's brother and two sisters who all came from out of town. Obituaries were handed out while solemn music was played on an organ. Opting against a business suit, Robin was wearing black slacks and a matching turtleneck instead. His book bag was laying at his feet, fully packed while his jacket was draped over the back of his chair. He was sitting in the office wondering if he could get through the service when Pastor Anthony Amaro walked in.

"Are you ready for this, Son?"

"I really wish more people were speaking on his behalf," he replied.

While planning the funeral, there were very few family members that offered to speak during the services. The program had only a few presenters. What was originally planned for at least two hours would only take forty-five minutes.

"We will make do with what we can. It's time to start."

"Okay."

Pastor Anthony started the service while Robin sat alone in the front pew. The open casket with Jon's body stood behind a podium where he addressed everyone. He explained how death should not be mourned, for Jon's spirit was on a new journey and his body was at peace. After his speech, he waved his arm and called Robin up to deliver Jon's eulogy.

Robin stepped up to the podium. He felt all the eyes on him and fought to remain calm. He cleared his throat and began. "Um, thank you all for coming. I'm not very good with speeches, so please forgive me if I'm a bit crass." He turned back to the pastor standing behind him and then looked back to the attendees.

"My mother...is a whore who cheated on her husband," Robin began.

There were gasps from the crowd. Pastor Amaro's jaw dropped. He then did the sign of the cross on his chest and whispered, "Mother of God, Father forgive him."

Sensing the outrage, Robin put his hand up for the attendees, and looked over his shoulder to reassure the pastor. "I'm... I'm going somewhere with this, bear with me here, Padre."

He cleared his throat again. "As I was saying... my mother, after five years of marriage, cheated on her husband and had an affair. The result, she got pregnant with me. After she divorced, she had no qualms about reminding me that I was the reason her marriage failed, even at a young age. She, uh... never loved me, favored her daughter more than me and repeatedly treated me like garbage. But I digress. This is not about me. It's about Jon David Walker.

A man who raised two daughters by himself after losing his wife in a bus accident, doing the best that he could as they grew up and moved on to live their separate lives. And my mother, after coming to the conclusion that she could not raise her son while managing the budding career of her daughter and turning her into a cash cow, guilted her father into taking me in when I was six while she circumnavigated the globe 48 weeks out of the year.

Out of sight, out of mind, to the point where she barely acknowledges her own son to this day. Jon Walker did the best he could to raise me, the same way he did the best he could to raise them. His resources were limited, his patience was thin, but he got the job done.

And now that he's being laid to rest, I would like to share my best memory of him.

I... I was not an easy child to take care of. I suffered from separation anxiety, I developed very late, I was non-communicative. I grunted when I had to use the bathroom. I'd moan or grunt when I wanted something. Doctors thought I was either deaf or retarded.

But then one day, when I was three years old, my mother took me to Jon's house so he could babysit me. She laid my blanket down in the living room and...he came out of the bathroom and walked across the living room toward the kitchen. He turned and waved at me nonchalantly and at three-years-old I noticed him, waved back and said...'Hi.'

Just out of nowhere, 'Hi.'...No 'Mama', 'Dada', 'Baba'...'Hi.' At three years old after being silent for so long, they couldn't believe it. From that day on, I knew that there was a bond between me and him that would last an eternity."

He turned to the coffin, held in his tears and whispered, "Goodbye, Granddaddy." After turning back to the crowd, he cleared his throat, stepped down from the podium and took his seat in the front pew.

For the last presentation of the service, a woman stepped forward that Robin had never met. As elderly as she appeared, she had a sense of style and grace to her presence. Without any introduction, she pulled the microphone from the pulpit and dedicated her performance to Jon. With no backup music, she proceeded to sing a soulful, sultry ballad that chilled whoever heard it to the bone. There was not a dry eye in the room.

Once she was finished, she took a seat and Pastor Amaro concluded the service. Robin received more condolences from those who attended. Amaro walked up to his side. "That... that was a nice speech. I just had issues with the beginning. Need I remind you of the fifth commandment young man? Honor thy mother and father?"

"I was raised to follow by example, Padre," Robin replied, "If my mother didn't honor her father, I refuse to honor her."

Robin eased through the crowd and found the performer. He put his arm on her shoulder and she turned around.

"That was a beautiful song, ma'am."

"Why thank you, thank you," she replied with a toothy smile.

"You're welcome. What was the name of it?"

"It's called, "Gloomy Sunday". It's originally by Ella Fitzgerald."

"Wow... may I ask, who are you? How did you know Jon?"

"My name is Gloria Evelyn Robinson, but everyone knows me as Miss Glory. Jon used to see me perform every Friday night at the Cotton Club from 1947 til '52. I promised him I'd sing at his funeral. I just wished he had a few more years left in him."

Robin nodded, "Yeah, I did too."

"I knew he had two daughters, but he never told me he had a son."

"Oh, actually I'm his grandson," he chuckled. "But he raised me like the son he never had."

Gloria adjusted her glasses. "Oh, my apologies, young man."

Someone behind them called for her. She nodded to him. "Sorry for your loss, please excuse me." She picked up a cane and slowly walked away from him.

Jon didn't have any pall bearers, so six Benta's employees carried the coffin and placed it in a hearse behind the building in the parking lot. Pastor Amaro and Robin climbed into a Lincoln Town Car and followed the hearse to Saint Raymond's Cemetery. They arrived at eleven fifteen. The plot where Jon was laid to rest had a tombstone already placed for his wife, Agnes, who was killed back in 1957.

Robin stood with Pastor Amaro as he said a final prayer. No one else was with them. The casket was slowly lowered. A representative from the funeral home asked him to sign some forms, completing their service, and the pastor joined the other employees back at the two cars so they could return to Manhattan.

Cemetery gravediggers were filling the grave as Robin watched over them. It was past noon as he stood with his book bag on his shoulders. Another twenty minutes went by and one of the diggers turned to him. "You mind? We really don't like to be watched while we work."

"Just pretend I'm not here," he said. "Or there'll be someone *else* in that grave with him."

The man looked back at him. He stared back blankly, completely emotionless. *Nothing. To. Lose,* he thought. The rest of the workers were done and waved their friend away to join them. After staring at Robin he said, "It's your lucky day."

He shook his head. "Not by a long shot," he answered and watched as they walked from the freshly filled grave. Once he was alone, standing in front of the grave, Robin took a deep breath and performed the Lord's Prayer in sign language. He faltered halfway, but finished, then did the sign of the cross and kneeled.

Another hour went by and then another as Robin was approached by another person who informed him that grounds close at four-thirty. At three, he finally walked toward the exit. He left from the gate leading to East Tremont and took the Bx40 bus up to Westchester Avenue. From there, he got on the 6-train.

Over the next forty-eight hours, Robin Walker rode the subways aimlessly, stepping off and on stations, transferring to lines, and exploring the abandoned tunnels all throughout the four boroughs. Over four-hundred destinations among twenty-two subway lines. He even took the tram to Roosevelt Island. Surviving on food and drink in his book bag and whatever he could buy from platform news-stands, sleeping and relieving himself in the tunnels, it was his final tribute to the tracks his grandfather worked on for nearly thirty years.

It was Sunday night, fifteen minutes to midnight, when he stepped off the 7-train at 42nd Street and Times Square. He took the escalator upstairs and walked to the four-track platform for the shuttle to Grand Central. He specifically picked this location because the train would be empty on the platform waiting for the conductor to arrive and start on the single destination across town.

He was tired, and it was time. He was ready. Entering the car on track two, he took a seat in the corner. *Don't want to draw attention to myself. Have to make sure the blood is barely visible against the wall,* he thought. With a sigh, he psyched himself up for what he was about to do, inhaling and exhaling through his nose and out his mouth. He lowered the book bag and opened it, slipping out the gun he took from Vickie Florence back at Park West and putting it into his jacket pocket.

Looking up and then around to the rest of the car, then out on the platform, Robin braced himself for the end. He saw no other outcome beyond the next several minutes. He didn't want to live anymore. College, the library, his mother, his sister, Franklin, the crew... he was done with them. This decision was made the moment Jon passed. *Nothing. To. Lose,* echoed in his head.

It was almost midnight. At a minute after the hour, the conductor would find him on the train. He needed to act quickly. After taking one last breath, Robin whispered, "Here we go."

Before reaching inside his pocket, he heard a sound, faint, and approaching footsteps. Heels... a woman? She walked around track one and approached his car. His eyes followed her as the rest of his body froze. As she stepped in and took a seat across from him, a smile grew on her face. She was as beautiful as she was the first time he saw her on the 6-train that fateful morning.

"My name is Shinju Hasegawa. It's nice to finally meet you."

"I must apologize for my appearance," Robin said.

The two were alone in a nearby coffee shop. It was twelve forty-five in the morning. Robin was drinking orange juice while Shinju quietly sipped a cup of tea. She looked tired. As if she just finished working an estimated eight to ten-hour shift followed by several hours of socializing with her co-workers after work. Despite that random assessment, she was still breathtaking to him.

"I won't pry, but you appear to be in a state of distress," she replied.

Her voice was soft with her Asian accent very pronounced.

"I recently had a loss in my family. I needed to do a bit of soul searching to determine what I was going to do next."

"I see. In Japan, there is a forest at the bottom of our tallest mountain. After a traumatic event like a divorce, or death of a child, people travel outside of the city to this forest as a pilgrimage. They enter and walk among the trees until an answer comes to them. Sometimes they are never seen or heard from again."

Robin nodded. "Wow, that's some pilgrimage. I wouldn't use that word for what I was doing. My intention was to wander aimlessly for as long as I could." He chuckled. "I just find it very amusing that we would cross paths after so many near misses."

She smiled. "Yes, I must admit, ever since I saw you on the train I wondered if we were destined to meet."

"What happened all those times? It felt like you would just disappear into thin air."

She chuckled, a light, enchanting sound. Robin felt butterflies in his stomach when he heard it. "I'm currently doing a 12-month internship at the Museum of Modern Art. The very first time I saw you on the train I got off at 51st Street so I could walk there."

Robin nodded. "Ah..."

"Then, at the study hall I noticed you hiding and talking to another student for a moment, but then I dropped my pencil and bent down to pick it up."

"Ha! Really? You were still there, just underneath the table?"

"Yes, but what happened to *you* that time at the nightclub?" Shinju asked. "One moment I saw you approaching me, the next minute..."

"It's a long story," Robin interrupted. "What about Grand Central? Where are you coming from or going to at this time of night?"

"Some of the other interns and I were attending a film festival near 42nd Street and 8th Avenue. I live in a small studio out in Queens. I normally take the E-train to Long Island City, but it runs terrible after midnight, so I took the shuttle from Times Square in order to catch the 7-train, and that's where I saw you."

"Wow. Just... wow," Robin whispered. He noticed he was staring when she looked down sheepishly, breaking eye contact. Just like on the train. He snapped out of it. "Well, ahem, I'd like to um, walk you back to Grand Central and wait for the 7-train to make sure you get home alright. If you don't mind the company."

"Oh, I don't mind... actually, I would like that very much."

The two exchanged glances, smiling at each other for several minutes.

"We're closing in 30 minutes!" the cashier behind the counter announced.

She blushed and stammered, "W... we should go."

"Yeah," Robin agreed, and they stood up to leave.

It was six o'clock in the morning when Robin made it back to Washington Heights. He stepped off the A-train at the 175th Street GWB Bus Terminal station and entered the connecting pathway leading inside to the busy promenade. He was exhausted but in high spirits. After escorting Shinju all the way to Queens, she gave him her phone number in order to set up a date on Saturday night.

In the hallway leading to his apartment, he sat sideways on the window sill, looking out northeast toward The Bronx. From the sixteenth floor he could see Highbridge Pool and Yankee Stadium in the distance. He just stared out across the cityscape, thinking. He was so close to ending it all. He felt the gun weighing heavy in his jacket pocket. He had no idea what he'd do with it now — keep it, throw it away — his thoughts were a scattered mess swirling around in his mind.

He would need to decide what to do next, but for now, all he was thinking about was a hot shower. Walking down the hallway, he fished out his keys and stood in front of the door knowing that Jon was not inside. His hand shook as he turned the key and entered. His heart stopped at the sight of a figure standing by the window. For one frantic second, he believed Jon's spirit was in the living room, greeting him with his warm smile one last time.

"Granddaddy?!" he gasped.

The silhouette moved. As Robin's eyes adjusted to the sunlight spilled out in the room, the stranger's features revealed themselves. He was shorter than Jon, yet old like him. At first, he had believed the stranger's pale skin matched his grandfather's but he could see now the elder was white. The facial hair almost made him look comical, but his most haunting feature were his green eyes that danced in his sockets. They looked familiar to him in some mysterious way.

"It's about time..." the visitor began. "...I've been waiting here for days..."

Robin drew the gun from his jacket pocket, took a step to square himself, and aimed and squeezed the trigger. The shot was loud, but the sound would unlikely be heard within the concrete walls. The stranger had little time to react as his right arm exploded. He was mid-sentence when the pain took hold of him and he flinched, expecting the worst.

"Holooooooohley SHIT! You shot me!" he yelled.

Robin didn't wait to see what he said next. He reached over and grabbed the baseball bat from behind the desk again. He advanced on him and delivered a swift blow across his face. Jon taught him when attacking an intruder..."*Break the jaw so they don't scream, then break the knees so they don't run.*"

Waving his arms frantically and incoherently mumbling, the man fell back against the window and slid down to the floor as his legs gave out. He looked up, eyes wide open and pleading as Robin prepared to bring the bat down on his crown.

"Speedy Gonzales! ...Speedy Gonzales needs to stop drinking coffee! ...Speedy Gonzales needs to stop drinking coffee!" he yelled.

Robin stopped in mid-swing and remembered Jon's final instructions to him. "What!? What did you say?!" he asked, out of breath.

"You fuckin' shot me. I don't believe it..." the old man panted.

"Speak up! What are you doing here and how do you know that saying?" Robin ordered.

"M..mm...my name is Synclair. I'm a friend of your grandfather. I was at his funeral, didn't you see me, damnit!?"

"No, I fucking didn't! If you came up to me and shook my hand back then, instead of breaking into my apartment, perhaps I wouldn't have shot you! What are you doing here? How did you get in?"

"Esme gave me the *second* copy of the key after you took the first copy from her son. I came right after the service waiting for you... can I have a towel or something? I'm fucking bleeding here!"

"Don't fucking move. Don't even get up, just lie there." Robin took a few cautious steps backward, then went to the bathroom for a towel.

"Trust me, I'm not going anywhere. Fuck!"

Robin returned with a towel, a bottle of hydrogen peroxide, and gauze. He handed them to the mysterious stranger and took a step back. He was still holding the bat with his left hand. "My aim was off. I think I just grazed you."

Synclair glared at him due to the cold treatment received. He moved his hand, looking at the wound. The skin was broken with a deep gash dripping blood, but there was no sign of penetration. Robin stared quietly as the old man began tending to his wound. Ripping the sleeve of his shirt, he poured the peroxide on the towel to clean it.

"You can put that bat away now," he whispered hoarsely.

Robin simply shook his head in reply.

Twenty minutes later, the two were sitting at the kitchen table. Robin didn't know what to make of this weirdo, but Jon's instructions were explicit. Whoever said the phrase was to explain everything to him. "For someone as old as you look, you're pretty tough," Robin said.

"It's not the first time I've been shot," the elder replied. "But I figured Jon raised you to have better manners."

"So, Mister Sinclair..." Robin began, ignoring the quip.

"It's *SYNclair*, with a Y. You're pronouncing it wrong."

"Okaaaay, what's your last name so we don't have to keep with the correcting?"

"We're done with formalities. You can just call me "Synclair with a Y" and we'll keep it at that. Jon entrusted me with the task to bring you to the executor of his estate. Do you know what that person does?"

"Something about his will and the belongings he left to his family," Robin answered.

"Very good, young man. As you may or may not know, Jon's relationship with his daughters was estranged."

"That would be an understatement."

"Yes. Your colorful eulogy reflected how you felt about your mother. Well, originally I had planned to take you to the executor after the service Friday, but since you fell off the face of the earth for the holiday weekend, we can go this Friday."

"Okay. We have to go early. I'll be working around 2 pm to 6 pm."

Synclair stood up. "Understood. I'll be here on the 4th at 9 am sharp."

"Works for me," Robin said, still sitting down.

The elder seemed annoyed by his lack of manners. "Ahem, I'll see my way out." He grabbed his jacket and bowler hat and walked to the door. Robin stood up and called after him from the living room. "Mister Synclair with a Y?"

The man stopped at the door and turned to him. "Yes?"

"Why did Jon ask you to do this? Where do you know him from?"

His eyes danced in his sockets again with a weird glazed look as he prepared his answer. "Jon ever tell you about his service in the military?"

"Briefly. He said he did things he wasn't proud of."

"He wasn't the only one. We served together. He was lucky enough to get out when he did. He asked me because no one else would have done this for him. Have a nice day, Son." He turned back to the door, but stopped and looked back at Robin. "By the way, if you were going to off yourself, a .22 caliber wouldn't do the job. The bullet would have gotten stuck in your brain, and left you alive but a vegetable."

Robin narrowed his eyes and stood quietly as the mysterious visitor left the apartment. He didn't think about the possibility of Jon leaving him anything in his will while planning his suicide on the train. Until meeting Shinju last night, he didn't care. School, the library, the apartment...Mister Synclair with a Y would have been waiting forever if it weren't for the chance encounter. Now, with his restored faith in life, he planned on living it one day at a time.

Lakeshia arrived at the branch at three o'clock. She went upstairs and placed her things in her locker, then checked the staff room. Robin had taken time off, going on bereavement leave. She was hoping he would come back today. There was no sign of him. *Only one other place he could be,* she thought. She walked into the auditorium and found him playing "Mad World" by Tears for Fears on the piano. His voice was so full of melancholy.

"Wow, I've never heard that song before," she said to get his attention.

Robin still hadn't turned around. He just looked straight ahead at the wall. "Yeah, everyone knows "Shout", "Everybody wants to Rule the World", and "Head over Heels"...but they always forget "Mad World". It's pretty easy to play too, practically a scale in E minor." He swung his legs around to look at Lakeshia and smiled. "It's great to see you, Leelee. I kind of figured you've been worrying about me."

"I'd be lying if I said I wasn't." She took a few steps inside and stopped in the middle of the room. "Robin, I'd like to share something with you I've never shared with anyone before."

"I'm listening."

"My father has two other brothers. Originally there were six siblings. Three boys and three girls. My grandmother passed away when I was six years old. They all took it kind of hard. But no one took it harder than my Aunt Priscilla. She was the youngest of the bunch at 19. She felt that she knew her the least amount of time and it really hurt."

Robin was now staring attentively at Lakeshia.

"Two weeks after Granny's funeral, Priscilla took me to the movies to see *Rainbow Brite and the Star Stealer*. It was just around Thanksgiving break. We spent the whole day together," she said with a smile at the memory. "When she dropped me off, the apartment was empty, so she was waiting with me until mom and dad came home. She turned on the tv for me and went into the bathroom. I sat there watching cartoons for a while, then noticed she hadn't come out."

Lakeshia's voice and demeanor had changed now. She was very somber.

"I remember knocking because I had to use the bathroom, and when I couldn't hold it anymore, I just pushed the door open. For a moment the room looked empty, like she just disappeared. Then I stepped in and saw her feet. They were just dangling, no more than 20 inches off the floor. We had one of those high clawfoot bathtubs so it was just a matter of tying the knot on the towel rack and looping the rope securely on the light fixture, then stepping off the side of the tub."

Robin was stunned, but remained quiet as she finished the story.

"I...I wasn't scared or shocked. I just stood there, not knowing what I was seeing, but kind of understanding what happened and why. I'll never forget that look she had on her face as she walked in the bathroom. It looked like she knew what she was about to do and there would be no more pain. There wasn't any look of doubt or fear in her eyes." She moved to the piano and took a seat next to him. "I saw that same look on your face last week right before you left...and I'm just glad you're still here."

"Wow...Leelee, I'm so sorry."

"It's okay. Like I said, just glad you're alright."

Robin couldn't believe how close to home her story was. He didn't even think how his suicide would have affected her. It was really eye-opening. They both stood up from the piano and turned to leave the auditorium.

"Lakeshia," he called out, stopping for a second.

She turned after taking a step ahead of him, shocked he called her formally by her first name.

"This may be bad timing, but with everything that's been going on, I'd like to lighten things up with a joke."

The page frowned at the odd request, but nodded. "Okay."

"Batman and Robin were patrolling the rooftops of Gotham city one night," he began, "swinging from building to building, rooftop to rooftop. Suddenly, Robin misses a landing and slips off the edge of a 10-story-drop. Batman does nothing and Robin at the last minute fires his grappling hook and swings back up to safety. When he catches up to Batman, Robin asked, "Why didn't you try to save me back there?" To which Batman replies, "I knew you'd fly back up and eventually come back to me." The boy wonder was astonished. "What makes you believe that?" he asked. Batman turns to him and just says, "Because I named you 'Robin'."

There was a collective moment of silence between the two after the joke. Lakeshia then burst out in a stifled giggle that turned into an odd laugh. Robin smiled and started to join her in laughing. The two looked at each other as if they were pretending to laugh with a studio audience watching a sitcom for canned laughter.

Tears started coming out of Robin's eyes and suddenly his knees started to buckle. His laughing became loud and before he realized it, he was hysterically crying on the floor.

Lakeshia reached out and pulled him close to her, wrapping her arms around his shoulders, trying to comfort him. "It's okay, okay! Let it out!" Before she knew it, she was sobbing along with him.

"He's gone! I'm alone! I'm so alone!" he cried.

"NO! You're never alone, you'll never be alone! Not while I'm here, Robin, you'll never be alone. I'll be here!" she answered him.

After days of holding strong, remembering his grandfather's words, Robin finally broke down in his emotions. He never would have imagined Lakeshia, of all people, being there with him. He crumbled into a fetal position as she drew him in... unaware of what was transpiring.

His face is in my bosom... she thought. *His face is in my bosom!*

My face is in her bosom! he screamed in his head.

"Whoa!" Robin recoiled with a gasp. She crossed her empty arms against her chest as he backed up a few inches from her and wiped his face. "I...I...I don't know what came over me just now." He thanked his lucky stars the room was soundproof so no one would have heard their emotional outburst.

"It's okay, it's okay..." Lakeshia tried to assure him. "You've been through—"

Robin sprang up. "I need to go, um...yeah, I'm sorry, I...I...I'm due downstairs." He hurried around her and rushed to the exit. Still on the floor, she looked back to him, thinking of something else to say, but he was gone without another word.

"You'll never be alone..." she whispered, wiping her face.

Ethel and Sonyai noticed Robin rushing from the staircase door past them to the clerical office inside.

"The kid's been through the wringer lately."

"It will take time, but Walker can recover from this personal loss, Jenkins."

"I really hope so. I think we were too hard on him when he got here, due to Simms' situation."

Sonyai furrowed her brow but didn't reply.

Ethel noticed the cold reaction and felt apprehensive. "I apologize, Yi... I'm just thinking... about the future."

"Meaning?" she asked sharply.

Ethel was hesitant about tipping her hand, but the senior clerk was owed early notice if she decided to follow her plans. "I'm thinking of retiring at the end of the year," the elder clerk revealed flatly.

Sonyai slowly turned to her. "Jenkins?"

"I've been approached by my sisters. They're buying a house down south. It needs some work, but—"

"You still have a few years before reaching 55 for early retirement," Sonyai interrupted. "Let alone 62... where is this coming from?"

Ethel sighed. "My health's been taking a turn lately. I'm a Type-2 diabetic now. I need to slow down."

"I...I don't know what to say."

"Don't get all soft on me. It's not like I'm leaving tomorrow! All I'm saying is we really need to keep everyone we have here. We can't have a bunch of rookies who don't trust or support each other bringing this branch into more chaos. We need to be a unit again."

"And we *will* be, but believe it or not, I still need you," Sonyai emphasized. "Your wisdom, your experience... without you I'm just a den mother barking at the boys."

"We're all replaceable, Yi... they can find some other dusty grump to plop their butt here after moving all around. People come and go, but this situation we're currently in has to get better...or I won't be the only one leaving, you hear?"

"I...I hear you, Jenkins... A leader is nothing without their followers. Once Miss Simms has been given a full-time position, I will make efforts to strengthen the bond between the clerks here. I really hope you reconsider leaving."

Sonyai turned to accept a patron's returns as Ethel stood quietly...hoping she got her point across.

Franklin stepped out of the back door from the stockroom Wednesday morning at ten to find Robin waiting for him, leaning against a brick wall.

"Holy shit! You've been waiting long out here? A visit while school is in session? I'm honored."

"Yeah, now that I'm on my own, I'm taking the risk of socializing with who I want when I want in hopes it doesn't affect my grades."

"So you mean to tell me it was your grandfather who told you not to hang around with me while going to work and college? You really expect me to believe that pile of horseshit? Don't disrespect his memory like that. Using him as a scapegoat for your antisocial tendencies!"

"Hey man, I'm not getting into it with you over this because I need a favor. You're not gonna like it, but I'm calling in a marker, here."

"What?" Franklin asked hesitantly.

"I've... met someone," Robin said with a grin on his face.

"Oh really? Ha!" Franklin laughed.

"You remember at The Tunnel before your *incident*?"

"How could I forget!?" Franklin gasped, thinking back to when a would-be thief nearly sliced his manhood off.

"There was a girl. One that I saw on a train, then on campus. We kept missing each other until she found me after the funeral." He didn't wish to share details of what he almost did at the time. "We finally sat and talked and she gave me her number."

"So, you wanna do a double date? For a first date? I can call one of my standby's..."

He shook his head. "No, I wanna... I wanna head out to Ozone Park."

Franklin nodded and smiled. "Ahhhh—make out near the airport! Robin Walker Corny Date #27 in the cub scout guidebook of macking!" Franklin laughed out loud at the thought.

"Uh-huh, laugh it up, Cadbury. You're driving us out there!"

Franklin stopped when he heard that. "Wait, you don't mean!?"

"Yep, we need the *Prizm*."

Franklin got his driver's license the minute he turned sixteen. Months after, his father purchased a 1991 Geo Prizm. He was only allowed to drive it when Supa let him. Until he turned twenty-one, then the car was his. Franklin and Robin had gone on joyrides when the opportunity presented itself, but it was not an easy task.

"No, no way...not happening. My father would kill me!"

"You owe me," Robin said flatly.

"I'll pay you back doing something else. The last time my father caught me taking the 'Priz out, he took it to Yonkers and left it at my grandmother's house for three months. The summer's coming. I can't afford to lose it."

Robin took a few steps to face Franklin eye-to-eye. They were the same height, and neither wavered. "I checked your balls, man. Make it happen." He turned and started walking. "I'll swing by Friday after work and we'll come up with a plan," he called back, then disappeared into the shadows.

CHAPTER EIGHT

Friday morning, after a shower and getting dressed, Robin answered the door to see the mysterious Synclair with a Y standing in the hallway. He was wearing a different suit than the last time, but still wearing his signature bowler hat.

"Ready to go?" he asked.

"Yeah," Robin answered.

They took the elevator down and headed outside. They walked north toward 181st Street. "We taking the 1-train downtown?" he asked the elder as he followed. He didn't answer, and they went the rest of the way in silence. When they got to the corner of Wadsworth and 181st Street, Synclair turned and crossed the street, heading toward Broadway. The pair arrived at 656 West 181st Street, a huge office building that took up the entire block on top of a series of several boutiques and a beauty supply store.

"Hey, I know this place," Robin said as he heard the intercom door buzz open.

Inside, they climbed the staircase to the second floor and took a right down a long hallway, then stopped at an unmarked door with only a number seven on the glass. Synclair took off his hat and knocked on the door. Without waiting for an answer, he turned the knob and pushed the door open.

The office suite was huge and had very little furniture. There was a desk in front of the glass window revealing the busy sidewalk below. A skinny redhead wearing a miniskirt and matching blazer sat in her chair, expecting the visitors. Despite her figure, her face was full and her chin was elongated, reminiscent of comedian Jay Leno. It had been over ten years, but Robin still recognized Carmen Hernandez in all her glory.

"Robin! You little cachetón, look at you! You've gotten so tall, lost some of that weight!"

"Hello Carmen," Robin greeted nonchalantly.

Carmen was a close friend of the family. She went to school with Robin's mother and encouraged his sister, Raven, to pursue a career in modeling. Carmen eventually became Raven's first manager, but was betrayed by her friend when Raven chose her mother to take over as manager when she turned eighteen.

"It's been what? Over 10 years since I saw you last? You were starting the first grade at P.S. 132. How's Ronnie? When's the last time you saw her?"

Robin winced at the sound of his mother's nickname. Everyone called her 'Ronnie' and never by her actual name. "She's fine, I guess. It's been almost a year. Both she and Rave came to my graduation from dubs."

"You graduated from George Washington? Nice! Are you in college?"

"I'm going to Baruch, down near 23rd Street on the East side."

"Hmmm, not bad, a business school, lots of pencil pushers get their calculators from there. Jon mentioned you were working over at Fort Washington with the books at the library. You still there, too?"

"I transferred to be closer to school...um, I had no idea you would be handling his will. Can we get on with it?" he asked sharply. He was tired of catching up and answering questions.

Carmen stared blankly back at him. "You're right. Sorry for my unprofessional manner."

He didn't mean to be so cold, but Carmen was just as responsible for Raven's success as his mother was, which didn't place well in his book. Carmen was a woman of all trades. Lawyer, manager, accountant. There was nothing she couldn't do once she put her mind to it. Seven years ago in the office they were sitting in, she ran a private ambulette company with her husband at the time. After a messy divorce, the company went out of business and she started working on her own, providing services she had any expertise in.

She nodded to Synclair. "Thank you, Synclair. You can wait outside for a moment."

"Yes, ma'am," he replied and started for the door. Robin called out to him. "Hey! How come she doesn't call you '*Synclair with a Y*?'"

Without turning around to look at Robin, he said, "Because she says it correctly," and left the office.

He rolled his eyes and turned back to face Carmen. She pulled out a file from her desk and opened it. In the center was a manila envelope with the name *Jon David Walker* written in the middle.

"Jon prepared his will back in 1988," she began.

Robin nodded. "After his heart scare. He knew back then his time was running out." His voice faltered at the end of the sentence.

"Before I open this, I have to ask for the verbal phrase he gave you to make sure you were there in his final hours."

Robin sighed. "Speedy Gonzales needs to stop drinking coffee." An image of Jon in his hospital bed flashed in his mind for a moment. Carmen nodded, acknowledging the phrase, and explained. "It's common practice to use a nonsensical sentence that no one could guess. That way his last wishes are honored correctly."

"Okay," he said with a shrug.

She opened the envelope. "Jon's finances were set aside for several purposes. You haven't paid the rent for June, have you?"

"No. There's a few thousand in the savings now. I'm trying to figure out how I'm going to pay all these bills by myself."

"Don't worry. Your grandfather set aside funds that will pay the rent on the apartment for the next six months."

Robin's eyes bulged and his jaw dropped. "You're shitting me!"

"You'll still be responsible for the cable and phone bills so don't get excited."

"No problem."

Carmen continued to read and a concerned look came over her face. "Okay, there are some other aspects that will take months to finalize, which is why he took care of the rent for you. Because there are no other beneficiaries, all of his material possessions are yours."

"He... he didn't leave anything to Mom or Aunt Regina?" Robin asked, shocked.

"They weren't on good terms. I take it neither of them were at the funeral?"

Robin simply shook his head.

"There might be a chance one of them, or both will contest the will, but if that happens, you call me. You're the only person mentioned in all his papers so by the end of the year if no problems arise you'll get the rest of his funds set aside, minus my fee and a small payment for Synclair."

"Look...Sinclair, see? I'm saying it correctly, right?"

She sighed. "Robin, you have a lisp. You always had it. Some words just don't come out right for you."

"That's bullshit!"

"Say 'Far Rockaway'."

"Far Rahockaway."

She looked at him quietly, proving her point.

"So... six months you say?" he said, changing the subject.

"Yes, now, I know you're only 18 and this would be presumptuous to ask of you, but you have to be a responsible adult now. Eating right, no fast food every day, household chores. Do you even know how to do laundry? Wash dishes?"

"Okay, Jon raised me right! I'm not sliding across the living room in my underwear, stealing the car or having sex with Rebecca De Mornay. I *know* how to take care of myself!"

"Good, because Jon didn't pay me to check up on you, and if I find out the bills aren't being paid or you're blowing through the money in the account, I have instructions to start a trust at my discretion. I can hold up whatever's left until you're 21."

"That won't be necessary."

She smiled. "I didn't think it would be. I'll be available at this office on the first Friday of every month. Here's my card in case of an emergency." She stood up and handed Robin a business card with her name and number. He took the card and put it in his pocket, then started walking to the door.

"Robin," she called out to him.

He stood in the middle of the office, waiting.

"No one will tell you this, but Jon raised you well. You're a constant reminder of the good he tried to accomplish, despite what most people thought of him."

Robin looked back, remembering the outburst at the wake. He wondered about the legacy Jon left and the secrets he took to his grave. So many people believed Jon was a monster. "Whatever he did, his past shouldn't be a stain on his memory." He opened the door and closed it behind him.

After walking the hallway back to the steps, Robin saw Synclair waiting for him at the exit.

"So, we done here?" he asked when he met him at the bottom of the staircase.

"For now. When Carmen has everything ready in five or six months I'll come for you."

"Do me a favor and either call or knock on the damn door. If I catch you in my living room again, I'll beat you senseless no matter what you say."

The old man chuckled. "I'm going to let you in on a little secret, Son... your grandfather and I were snipers during World War II. And we were *really* good. I could pierce your earlobe from Saint Nicholas Avenue while you're standing on Broadway. Don't try me."

Robin stood there imagining Jon with a Winchester 70 model on Japanese infantry, leveling it on his arm, looking into the scope. "Woah," he whispered. He was so caught up by the revelation he didn't notice the mysterious stranger had left without a trace.

"I see congratulations are in order," a voice said as Augustus looked up from the chair at the information desk. He was surprised to see Cleopheous Baker in the flesh standing before him on the library floor. The senior clerk was wearing a blue suit with black alligator shoes and sunglasses.

"Cleo, what do I owe for a personal visit in the middle of the day? What congratulations are you talking about?"

"Don't play dumb with me. I know you've seen the numbers from your little experiment and it's no surprise 58th Street won the media bonus by a landslide."

"Really? Wow. That's news to me," he said with feigned enthusiasm. He was indeed aware of the results since this morning, but Cleopheous wasn't the type to praise in person when a simple phone call would do. Something was amiss.

"Why don't we step inside my office..." Augustus began as he stood up.

"No, what I have to say won't take long, but *needed* to be conveyed face-to-face," Cleopheous interjected while removing his sunglasses.

"Okay, what's on your mind?"

"We have a saying back at Goose Creek, *"If the rooster didn't wake you up this morning, the weasel got him."*..."

Augustus stared back at him blankly, waiting for him to continue.

"Back on the farm, the weasel was one of the sneakiest bastards around."

"Really, and all this time I thought he only goes 'POP'," the librarian joked.

The visitor chuckled back for a moment before making his point. "Now the only way to handle a weasel when they're sneaking around the chicken coop is to set a trap. So Augustus, if somehow the scales were tipped in your favor, well... that just wouldn't be right, now would it?"

Augustus's face darkened, flushed with anger. "You accusing me of something, Cleo? I'm sure you can take your grievances to upper management and see what comes of it."

"Now, now, let's not get testy here. I'm just letting you know that things better be on the up and up, because sooner or later...that weasel's gonna get caught, ya hear?"

"Well, to use your colorful dialect, *I reckon so.*"

That got another chuckle. "So glad we had this chat. Congratulations again...spend that bonus well." He turned to leave and never gave a glance back.

"Y'all come back now, ya hear?" Augustus hissed in a taunt that no one else heard.

Gerry pretended to be writing in his notebook as Cleopheous Baker walked by the circulation desk through the security threshold, leaving the branch. The exchange between the regional head librarian and Augustus appeared intense from his vantage point. Since it was still early morning, he was alone handling checkouts and returns when a patron walked up to him.

"Uh, excuse me?"

"Yes, how may I help you, sir?" the clerk politely asked.

The white man was short, with a thinly shaved head of graying hair. He was wearing a striped, purple short-sleeve polo shirt and white shorts. "Um, there's a man back there who is kind of menacing to anyone who gets near him..." he pointed over his shoulder without turning around to the opposite wall where the homeless patron, John Paul Jones was sitting at his usual table.

"I really think he should be removed from the premises."

Gerry was already familiar with the antics of the frequent vagrant, but looked to where the patron was pointing at to show concern. He then looked back to the timid patron. "Well, this is a public sanctuary for undesirables, sir... legally we can't do anything provided he keeps to himself and doesn't make a disturbance."

"Okay, I get that, but there's a book I'm looking for near him and I can't seem to grab it from the shelf without him growling at me."

"I would suggest waiting for him to move along then. Just be patient," Gerry suggested. He could tell the patron had never been in a situation like this. He probably drove instead of taking the subway, never walked through a park, just lived a sheltered life, oblivious of the forgotten man. The two usual options when dealing with the homeless were to stay away from them or pretend they weren't there.

"He's been there since you opened. I have places to go. Can't you—"

"Sir, if he's sitting there and reading, then there's nothing we can do," Gerry interrupted. "If it means that much to you to have this man ejected from the branch, you can stand up for yourself and get the book off the shelf near him. If he attacks you, we will throw him out!"

Embarrassed by the sharp response, the man's face reddened. He tilted his chin up with a snort of contempt. "You know, I bet if he was a *white* guy you'd have no problem throwing him out!"

The clerk refused to take the bait. He learned to check his anger when confronted by patrons after being warned by Augustus, due to heated exchanges in the past. "You would be mistaken, sir." He extended his hand toward the information desk. "Perhaps the head librarian can explain our policies better to you. He's right over there."

The patron turned and looked across the room, then rolled his eyes. "Forget it," he said, returning to the shelves to look for other items.

The phone next to Gerry at the desk rang with an interoffice call and he picked it up. "Yes?"

"You handled that well," Augustus complimented from his desk.

Gerry turned to see the librarian on the phone looking back at him with an affirmative nod.

The clerk grinned. "Thank you, sir." He hung up the phone.

Robin and Franklin entered the parking garage through the side entrance in the lobby. Both of them were dressed for a night on the town. It was six o'clock in the evening and his date with Shinju was at eight.

"Alright, run this plan with me again, Ferris?" Franklin asked.

Robin smiled. "Funny. It's really simple. The Prizm is parked in an obscure corner spot far in the back behind a pillar. We slip out of that parking spot and place a similar-looking car in its place. From a distance, your dad will think the car is still there and nobody's the wiser...huh? It's the perfect plan."

"Okay, but where are you going to get this other car from?"

They were standing in the middle of the lot, with entrances from opposite ends. One of the doors started to open, and a car pulled in. While the car was blue, it hardly looked like a Prizm.

"What the...?" Franklin gasped.

"Hi Robin! You looking sharp, hon!" a female voice yelled.

The car door opened and twenty-year-old Gabrielle Smothers leaped out the driver side to greet them.

"Heeeeey, Gabby! Thank you for doing this," he said with a wave.

"Isn't that Diedre's cousin? Isn't this kinda taking advantage..." Franklin whispered.

Gabrielle always had a crush on Robin, despite being a couple of years older than him. She backed off out of respect for her cousin when Diedre and Robin met in high school. Like Diedre, Gabrielle had a mental disability with the childlike capacity of a sixteen-year-old.

"I brought the car over like you asked, did I do alright?" she asked.

"You did great, Gabby, thank you SO much! Now, we're going to park it over there..." he said, pointing to where the Prizm was parked. "...then you come back after you and your friends go to the movies."

"And drive the car back home!" she finished. "This is so much better than parking it on the street where I could get a ticket."

"Right! Now, don't forget to swing by McDonald's after the movie and meet us back here around 11:30 pm, okay?"

"You got it!" she cheerfully affirmed.

"Okay, we're going to move our car, and then you park it there." He smiled and walked over to Franklin with a nod. They both headed toward the Prizm.

"I don't like this…" Franklin started. "You know she's…she's…slow. This feels wrong."

"We're not taking advantage. She's not getting in any trouble. She's going to see *The Flintstones* with her friends. She needs to be home by midnight. We'll be back by eleven and switch the cars back, no problem."

"Okay, but she's driving a Nissan Sentra. Dad's going to know the difference," Franklin said.

"Only if he walks up and takes a good look, which he won't," Robin reassured him.

They got inside and Franklin started the engine. He pulled the car out of the spot and stopped a few feet from the garage door leading to the 178th Street side. Gabrielle moved her car to park it the same way as the Prizm, and the deception was complete.

Franklin drove down Saint Nicholas toward downtown, then got on the FDR. He was feeling more relaxed as they drove. They arrived in Long Island City and used the directions Shinju gave to her place. They made it by seven-thirty.

"She said she'll come out at eight," Robin said.

"So, what do we do till then?" Franklin asked.

Robin shrugged. "We wait."

They sat in silence for a couple of minutes.

Franklin suddenly asked, "What do you think happened to Cameron at the end of *Ferris Bueller's Day Off*?"

"What?!"

"When his father came home, and the car got wrecked, what do you think the father did to him? They never let you know… that really bugged me."

"His father probably went nuts and shipped his ass to the army," Robin said after thinking about it.

"Think so?" Franklin asked. "Would have been a fucked up way to end it."

"Which is why they left it... ambiguous."

"I hate weird endings like that. It's like telling the audience, '*You figure it out*'. Same thing with *The Graduate*, *The Shining*, or *The Thing*... fucking bullshit, man."

Robin chuckled.

"What?"

The Shining and *The Thing* I can understand, but what's so ambiguous about the ending of *The Graduate*? They get on the bus out of town and live happily ever after."

"What do they do? Where do they go? The looks on their faces, they're scared shitless. Reality sets it."

"That's what makes it a great ending," Robin explained.

"Yeah, right, just like in *Ferris Bueller*? I don't think so."

The conversation ended, and they waited in silence for ten minutes. When the door to the building opened, Robin stood up. "This might be her, head's up!" He opened the passenger door and climbed out.

Shinju stepped out just as Robin came around the car and stepped on the curb to meet her. Holding an arrangement of flowers in his hand, he smiled when he saw her face. She was radiant. Her face brightened as she saw the bouquet.

"Oh! No one has ever brought me flowers before!" she gasped and blushed while accepting them.

"Now *that* I find hard to believe," he said, leaning in for a peck on the cheek. He took her hand, and they walked to the car where Franklin was leaning on the hood.

"Shinju Hasegawa, this is Franklin, my best friend. He'll be driving us tonight."

Franklin did a friendly bow. "Nice to meet you." He opened the back door and gestured. "Step inside and enjoy the ride."

The couple slid inside and Franklin closed the door behind them, then went around to the driver's side and got in.

"Where are we going?" she asked.

"It's a surpriiiiise," Robin and Franklin said in unison.

It was dark now as they traveled down the Long Island Expressway. They passed the Queens Zoo, then took the Van Wyck south.

"I've never been this deep into Queens before," Shinju said. "Does your friend always drive you around on dates?"

"Uhh, no...Franklin owes me for the numerous times I've helped him out in a jam. We wash each other's hands, you know?"

"Yeah, I'm afraid you'll have to take the train on your next date!" Franklin joked.

They got off at Atlantic Avenue and took it down to Woodhaven.

"Ah, here's our first stop!" Robin exclaimed as they pulled up to a Japanese Bistro. He opened the door and helped Shinju get out while Franklin stayed in the car. The two got a table and looked at the menus.

"Will he be alright waiting out there?" she asked.

"Yeah, I can't tell you how many times I've been on dates with Franklin being the lookout or chaperone. He'll be alright."

Robin scanned the menu. He was way out of his comfort zone when it came to the cuisine. He had no idea what to order. "Uh, what would you recommend?" he asked with an uneasy smile.

She lowered the menu. "You've never eaten Japanese food before, have you?"

"Uhhh..."

"And you only picked this place to accommodate me. Why?"

"Because...you're important and the date should be all about you?" he asked frankly.

She scowled. "C'mon! Let's go!" She stood up and pulled him from the table.

They came outside and walked across the parking lot. Franklin stepped out of the car confused but Robin waved him down to wait. "In all those conversations over the phone, you didn't once ask what I liked to eat," she said. Across the street was Romeo's Pizzeria. Ten minutes later they were back in the car with a medium-size pie. She handed Franklin a brown paper bag with two slices.

"When I came here, the first thing I ate was a slice of pizza. It was like nothing I'd ever experienced."

"A woman after my own heart," Robin said with a smile. "I think it's time we move on to our second stop." He nodded to Franklin who nodded back.

It was nine-thirty when they pulled up to a vacant lot in the shadow behind the Aqueduct Racetrack. Robin and Shinju stepped out of the car. They walked to the rear in front of the trunk.

"What is going on? What are we doing here?" she asked.

He stepped on the bumper, made his way on top of the car and held out his hand.

"Don't worry, Franklin won't mind. It's a sturdy vehicle, let me help you up."

She took his hand, and they were sitting on the roof looking at each other.

"I'd thought it would be nice to just look up at the stars, take a look," Robin said while pointing to the dark sky.

She looked up. "Ohhh, wow..." she smiled. "It's beautiful."

"Yes, yes it is," Robin agreed, staring at her. "Absolutely beautiful."

She looked back at him and blushed. He then knocked on the roof twice.

Inside the car, Franklin turned on the stereo and the speakers began to play, "I only have eyes for you" by The Flamingos. The song echoed in the night air. She looked around, appreciating the music as it set the mood and nodded.

"Nice," she whispered. "This is real... nice."

They moved a little closer to each other, then laid on their sides face to face. After a few moments of whispering in each other's ears, Robin caressed her face.

"Got any more surprises?" she asked.

"My last one should be happening... right about..."

There was a loud roar when suddenly a Boeing 747 commercial airplane flew over them. The craft was approximately 800 feet above them, but it appeared so close you could almost reach out and touch it.

Shinju was terrified. She screamed and grabbed onto Robin in fright, which made him laugh out loud in excitement at the thought of her in his arms. It was like watching a horror film and the girl buries her face in your chest right when the killer strikes.

"It's okay...it's okay, it's just a plane, it's just a plane leaving JFK nearby."

She was trembling. "That's not funny! What if they crash?"

"They won't. You get used to it after a while. They take off and leave every 10 to 20 minutes."

He noticed she was still holding on to him. She felt safe in his arms. They looked at each other. He nodded, "Look, here comes another..."

Shinju looked up as another plane swooped in real low and went by. She laughed and reached out in a feigned attempt to feel it as it passed. "Wow!" she exclaimed. She looked back at him and leaned in, giving him a long, passionate kiss. Robin kissed back and pulled her close to him.

Franklin was whistling along as "Cruisin" by Smokey Robinson was playing. There was a loud bump from the roof as the car suddenly started to rock and shake. "What th...?" he yelled. Then smiled. "Damn!" he said as he chuckled to himself. "Go 'head, man!"

They made it back to Long Island City by eleven o'clock. Shinju was sleeping on Robin's chest as he grinned from ear to ear.

Franklin put the car in park and looked at his rear-view window. "Is she alive?" he asked. "Y'all were really going at it..." he smiled, "...at least from the bouncing point of view down here!"

Robin grinned then looked down and stroked her hair, waiting for her to stir. "Ba...baby? We home, Baby..."

"Hmmmm?" she slowly opened her eyes. "Baby?!" she exclaimed.

"Whoops, sorry," he apologized with a smile.

She squinted. "I don't like 'Baby'... but you can call me 'Shindy'. It sounds like 'Cindy'... like from *The Brady Bunch*! I watched that as a child and always liked the youngest one...with the curls."

"Okay, Shindy it is..." he said with a smile.

They kissed again. Robin saw stars in his eyelids as he felt her soft lips on his.

"Call me as soon as you get home. I won't go to sleep tonight until I hear from you."

"You got it!" he answered.

"It was nice to meet you, Franklin," she said, turning to him.

"It was nice to meet you, too."

She stepped out of the car carrying her bouquet and went inside the building. Robin waved at her as the car pulled off, then sighed heavily while slumping in the backseat. "Damn," he whispered. He noticed Franklin looking at him and smirked while raising his eyebrows.

"Okay, okay you... got your eyebrows jumping up and down like Magnum P.I. We gonna talk about the dents in my roof later!"

She was positive Mr. Kani would stop by the branch again if she didn't show, and she wanted to avoid another embarrassing visit by him.

She was walking toward the lunchroom for sixth period when she saw a student reading the *Village Voice*. She reached out and grabbed the paper out of his hand. "May I borrow this for a sec, thank you!" she called out. After sitting on the corner alone at a vacant lunch table, she opened the paper to the back of the newspaper with the club listings and classifieds.

There were parties from club nights listed on Friday, Saturday and Sunday, but she knew she couldn't do a club those nights without her parents finding out.

But a Thursday...

After minutes of searching, she found a listing for an after-work party on Thursday, the ninth.

She ripped the page out and walked through the cafeteria, finding the student eating lunch that she borrowed it from. "Thanks," she said as she slapped it back on his lap.

Sonyai was working the desk with Tommy at two o'clock. There was a calm after the lunch rush with things winding down. Occasionally someone would walk by giving a long, lingering stare at the senior clerk who stared back defiantly.

"Ma'am, I'm not going to pretend to ignore the tension in the building, but..."

"I'm alright, Thomas," she interrupted. "We're almost done with the day without incident."

She spoke too soon.

A patron came up to the returns side and asked Tommy, "Excuse me? I'd like to check out this book, please."

Tommy looked to Sonyai and back to the elder gentleman. "Uh, sir, this is the returns side. You'll have to step over to the other side in order to check it out." He extended his arm showing the way.

The patron looked at Sonyai and stood in place. "Can't *you* do it?" he asked.

Sonyai narrowed her eyes.

"Sir, I see nothing wrong with you stepping over..."

"Well I do, son. So I'd like YOU to check out this book...please," he insisted.

She stepped across to Tommy's right side. "Is there a problem here, sir?"

"Nothing personal. I would prefer not to speak to you, *miss*."

"Oh, I'm sorry, have I offended you in some way, sir? Do you have a problem with me personally, *sir*!?" she snapped.

"I have no qualms with you personally, ma'am, I just wish not to have anything to do with you people considering the significance of today."

Sonyai said nothing and Tommy did his best not to reveal his disdain. "Well, I'm sorry sir, but if you want that book you have to go to her. End of story."

A moment passed, and the patron chewed his lip. "Fine." He dropped the book on the desk in front of Tommy. "I'll go someplace else, where I don't have to see any *gooks*!"

He turned around to leave. Sonyai shut her eyes, resisting the urge to say something...she failed.

"You got a problem with Japanese people, you racist!?" she spat at his back.

He froze and turned around to face her. "I have a problem with 2400 dead military and civilians in Hawaii because of some rice-eating, slanty-eyed cowards!"

She nodded. "Pearl Harbor. It always comes down to Pearl Harbor, doesn't it? I am 36 years old! I was born 16 years AFTER it happened. I have nothing to do with what happened that day!"

"If not you, your parents, uncles, cousins, you people were responsible for the USS Arizona!"

"Not everyone in Japan was in favor of the war! My parents brought me and my brother here to the United States in 1969, after hearing the words of John F. Kennedy seven years earlier. He was a visionary, representing the land of the free! Words that inspired every person that heard his voice...and what do you do? Shoot him dead! Martin Luther King, Jr. Dead!"

Sonyai's voice began to attract glances from the rest of the floor. She started to pound her chest. "My father was a scholar! He reached thousands of people with his writings, and what did he do for a living when he came here? He worked in a hospital as a janitor!"

The patron's face turned red with rage. "I lost *my father* when he was stationed there as a missionary...he was a peacekeeper! He wanted to *help* people! He didn't deserve to die cowering in the corner of a hospital room when the bombings began!"

"So you want me to personally apologize on behalf of all the Japanese!? You, who killed MILLIONS of innocent people?" She gritted her teeth. "You talk about losing 2000? Tell that to the people of Hiroshima and Nagasaki."

Tears were running down her face as her voice began to break. "All we want is a chance...at the American Dream, and we are treated unfairly, discriminated against! You held an entire generation accountable for something they had nothing to do with! Even after 50 years, nothing's changed. Nothing WILL change."

The man looked back at her, stunned. He shook his head and whispered, "It was WAR. They were casualties..." he raised his voice again. "We needed to send a message!"

"It wasn't a message...it was *genocide*."

Zelda stepped up to the circulation desk. "I know this is a touchy subject, but I must ask you to refrain from continuing this conversation please."

Sonyai and the patron stared at each other, then without another word the man left through the exit. It was almost the top of the hour. Robin walked in and noticed Sonyai walking in the clerical office wiping at her face. He looked at Tommy.

"Uh, did I miss..."

"Just drop it, Walker...before you even ask," he dismissed.

It was five o'clock and Augustus was leaving for the day. He stopped at the information desk to see Heywood and Angie sitting in the two seats while a huge cardboard sign explaining the history and the meaning of D-Day was propped up on top of a table next to the phone.

"Seriously you two, is the sign really necessa—"

"Yes," they answered deadpanned in unison.

He nodded. "Alright, but I don't care how many times they ask next year, we won't be doing this again."

"Deal," they agreed in unison again.

The head librarian turned and walked toward the exit.

As Augustus passed the circulation desk and exited through the security threshold, Robin and Gerry stood at their stations preparing for the final hour.

"You follow basketball, man?" Robin asked.

"I've been a Lakers fan forever," Gerry admitted. "They haven't been the same since Magic got HIV."

"Yeah, they always tussled with the bad boys from Detroit. Me? I'm all about the Knicks, baby..." Robin did a sidestep jig that got a grin from Gerry.

"Think they can pull it off and beat the Rockets?"

"I have faith. All those times losing to the Bulls has prepared them for this. It's their time, now."

"Well...we'll see," Gerry replied with a shrug.

Janelle was pushing a shelving cart in the fiction section when she stopped suddenly and winced in pain. "Oooooh..." she exhaled. Nearby, Lakeshia heard the gasp and approached her with a concerned look.

"You okay?" she asked.

"I'm... fine... it's just..."

The young page looked at her with doe eyes, waiting to continue.

Janelle smiled and giggled, "...oh my God... the baby's kicking! For the very first time..."

She grabbed Lakeshia's hand and pressed it on her stomach. "Here, feel that?"

A moment passed as she felt and waited. "I don't feel any..." she stopped as her hand felt movement.

"There! Did you feel that?"

"I did!" Lakeshia giggled. "Wow... I really felt that!"

They both noticed their voices were high from excitement and both covered their mouths with another series of giggles. Lakeshia feeling the kick made her mind wander for a second.

She imagined herself in a kitchen, the oven cooking at four-hundred-and-fifty degrees, and a pitcher of Kool-aid being stirred in the sink. She catches her reflection in the window, then glances down to find her stomach protruding as if she swallowed a beach ball. Her hand caresses the unborn child as suddenly a pair of arms surprise her with an endearing embrace.

"I'm huge," she jokes, pretending to be sad.

"You're beautiful," Robin replied.

He placed his hand on top of hers.

"Thought about names?" he asked.

She nodded. "I think if it's a boy we name him Jon... and if it's a girl, we name her..."

"Priscilla?" he finished. "Works for me."

He turned her around, and they stared into each other's eyes, then slowly leaned forward, their lips inches apart...

"Uh, earth to Lakeshia Seabrooke!" Janelle said snapping her fingers.

She snapped back to reality and shook her head. "Oh my God, I'm sorry! I don't know what came over me."

Janelle looked in several directions, wondering about the page's mental state for a second.

"Um, I know this is a weird request, but on your next appointment, could I tag along with you and Miss Yi?" Lakeshia asked.

"Since my parents haven't been very supportive, Miss Yi has been keeping my appointments a private affair. She was even hesitant about me inviting Avery."

Lakeshia looked down with disappointment.

Janelle let out a breath. "Uh, if she's okay with it...I guess you can come."

She perked up and smiled again. "Thanks." She backed away, disappearing among the shelves.

Sonyai rarely went to the Pig 'N' Whistle. She was not what you would call a casual drinker. Times when the staff celebrated holidays or someone needed moral support, she'd indulge in a drink or two, but she never got sloppy drunk.

The heated exchange left a hole in her soul that she was attempting to fill, sitting alone at the corner of the bar.

"That wouldn't happen to be sake, wouldn't it?" a female asked from behind.

Ethel approached and took a seat on her left as Sonyai gave a light chuckle.

"Bacardi and Coke, please," she ordered from the bartender.

"It would be stereotypical to actually be drinking that swill, so no...my brother and I were always fans of Brass Monkey. Could be the Orange Juice..."

"There's always a Screwdriver," Ethel suggested.

"Not strong enough."

She nodded as the bartender placed a napkin in front of her along with her drink on top. She took a sip as they both drank in silence.

"Wanna talk about it?" Ethel asked.

"How do you do it? How do you deal with the bullshit?"

"Shit, we've been dealing with it longer than y'all, that's all...for 375 years now going on...what you went through today was cake and ice cream compared to anyone black and over 40 from the south."

"It's not right. It's just not right. Back in Florida, I never experienced any prejudice. I was invisible."

"That in itself can be considered prejudicial."

"I suppose, but I didn't care. No one messed with me so I didn't mess with them. That's the way it should be."

"Amen to that," Ethel saluted and downed the rest of her drink.

A moment went by, then Sonyai sighed. "Times like this I wonder what *he* would say."

"The Man in White?"

Sonyai nodded. "He once told me, "The world will never let go the atrocities of the past, to do so..."

"...would make one cease to be human," Ethel finished. "I remember."

"It would be so different if he were still here."

Ethel ordered another, and the bartender placed it in front of her. She lifted it up for a toast. "Well, here's to wishful thinking..."

Sonyai lifted her glass. "...here, here!" They clinked their glasses.

"We're going to Coogan's to watch game I, wanna come?" Robin asked Franklin.

The two were in Robin's living room while he was finishing a drink of water. It was seven-thirty Wednesday night, and the game was scheduled to start at nine.

"Who's 'we'? What's wrong with watching it here?" Franklin asked.

"Shinju and the gang from school...I don't want all those guys messing up..."

"Pass," he interrupted. "You know I'm not hanging with them..."

Robin didn't pry. Since starting college Franklin refused to mingle with his friends from Baruch and he accepted that decision. He himself felt the same way about his former circle of friends that lived in the high-rise apartment complex.

"Alright, speaking of Shindy, she's staying over the weekend for the first time."

"Yeah? You getting ready to...*Enter the Dragon*?" Franklin asked with a smirk.

Robin smirked back at the crude joke. "We're getting there... taking our time, fooling around and exploring each other's bodies..."

"Uh, huh."

"There's no need to rush things, and that's the end of that discussion."

Franklin shrugged. "Okay...BUT, just in case...I hope you're *prepared*." He tossed an item to Robin, who caught it with both hands. Robin held up a cassette case with a tape inside.

"Is this what I think it is?"

"Yep, made a copy just for this special occasion..."

He thumbed it around in his hand. There was no tracklist written, only two words in magic marker: *THE TAPE* on a 90-minute TDK cassette blank. A collection of Slow Jams, R&B and Soul tracks with the power to remove the panties of the most stuck up of girls.

"Remember, when you hear "Love T.K.O." by Teddy Pendergrass, that's the cue for the photo finish cause the tape's about to end."

"Hey, who MADE the tape between the two of us here?" Robin asked.

"Who's *performed* to the tape... multiple times I might add...between the two of us?"

With a chuckle, he opened the case and also found a three-pack of condoms with the tape.

"Nice touch."

Franklin nodded. "Hey... we gotta look out for each other. Can't be getting her pregnant and ruining your life." He pointed at him. "Let no bitch tear asunder..."

"...the two brothers from different mothers!" Robin finished, and they slapped hands.

"Don't be calling her no bitch, though," Robin pointed.

"My bad, my bad!" Franklin raised his hands apologetically.

At eight-fifteen Robin stepped off the M100 bus at 168th Street and Broadway where the Irish Bar and Restaurant Coogan's was located on the same block as Columbia Presbyterian Hospital. He spotted Shinju buying a pack of gum at a newsstand near the A-train station stairway and greeted her with a kiss.

"Hey," he greeted.

"Hey," she said back. They shared wide grins.

"Um, everybody's inside waiting. I came out here hoping to catch you so I could give you this."

She held up a gift-wrapped box.

"Huh, what's this?" he asked with a shock.

"Just a little something... I saw it and I immediately thought of you."

Robin looked down sheepishly, trying not to blush.

"What's wrong?"

"It's just... I can count on one hand the number of people who've bought me something... except my grandfather." He looked up at her. "I didn't get you..."

She interrupted him, "It's okay. Open it!"

"Okay, but first..." he reached over and gave her a long kiss which caught a few glances from onlookers walking by.

"Wow," she whispered with a giggle.

He smiled and opened the present. Inside the box was a very long silk scarf. It had fringes and multiple colors. He didn't know how to respond to the garment, but he acted as if he was given the golden fleece.

"I love it!" he exclaimed. *A scarf? Who gives a man a scarf? What kind of gift is this? Oh my God, I hope she doesn't expect me to wear it!* he thought.

"Here, let me show you how to wear it..." She took it out of his hand before he could react and she looped it around his head three times before letting the ends rest on his shoulders. She stood back to take a long look.

"It's perfect!"

Robin felt like a preppy. The fabric felt smooth around his neck but he wasn't used to something this extravagant.

"It even goes with your cap! C'mon, let's head inside and show the others..." She pulled him to the entrance as a worried look came across his face.

Coogan's Restaurant and Pub was a lively establishment where anyone could drink like a sailor or feast like a king. Patrons vary from a rare mixture of hard-hat construction workers side-by-side with local politicians, actors, poets, musicians, and a large number of doctors and nurses from the hospital next door. The dining tables were in the middle of the floor boxed in, with the bar and kitchen located in the back. There was a stage for live entertainment and karaoke and a huge 32' television in a corner above the bar.

Shinju and Robin joined Walt, Kim, Gillian, Jarvis, and Mouse at a pair of tables pushed together at the corner of the dining area facing the bar. The three ladies took seats with their backs to the tv since they had no real interest in the game. Robin squeezed in at the far end, crushing Mouse, who was next to Jarvis.

"Nice scarf, Robin," Kim complimented.

Walt leaned forward from the opposite end to get a glance, then everyone but Robin and Shinju burst out in laughter. She rolled her eyes and mouthed the words "Ignore them," while he blushed bright red from embarrassment.

"Man, we just playing. She showed us the scarf before you came...it's all good," Jarvis said.

It was a few minutes before the tip-off. Marv Albert was doing pregame commentary as the guys were hyped up to see the Knicks start their final series for the NBA Championship. A waitress approached the table wearing a white apron with *Coogan's* written in green letters on it.

"Alright, I see y'all are here to watch the game so let me give some house rules. There's a two drink minimum for each of you, club soda and Shirley temples unless you got ID's and water doesn't count. Nuts are $3.00 a bowl with one refill. The kitchen's closed so no meals, but we got plenty of pizza to warm up. Keep the chatter down to a minimum or we WILL toss your sorry asses out of here. Got me?"

"Damn," Mouse whispered.

"We'll be cool," Robin reassured. "Can I have a watered-down screwdriver at least?"

"We don't have orange juice," she replied with a nasal tone.

"Alright, two bowls of peanuts..."

"Mixed nuts," she interrupted.

He rolled his eyes. "...and a round of club sodas to start us off."

She nodded and walked off.

"What a bitch!" Jarvis said once she was out of earshot.

"Yeah, we are definitely watching game 2 someplace else!" Walt chimed in.

At halftime the Knicks were down 46 to 54. Hope was fading among the people at the bar that New York was going to take the first win. Robin and the guys were still expecting a better second half.

"C'mon guys...we can still win this!" Robin cheered.

There were groans all around the tables.

"Nah, man... this one's going to Houston," Mouse said.

"We should bounce," Jarvis added.

"It ain't over, till it's over..." Robin said.

Everyone was still watching the game until the bartender stepped up and turned off the tv.

"Ayyo! Turn the game back on, man!" Robin stood up and yelled.

"The set goes off at 10:30, no exceptions! We like the night to end *quietly*," the man barked back.

Shinju pulled his arm, but Robin stepped away from the table. "I paid my money for your shitty-ass nuts and pissy drinks. Turn that the damn tv back on, NOW!"

At the table, the group exchanged worried glances. Kim chucked her thumb towards the door, the rest of them nodded.

"Alright kid, you're done...get the fuck outta here before we throw you out!"

Robin pointed to the tv. "Turn the goddamn tv on, man!"

Mouse, Jarvis and the others all stood up to leave. Shinju pulled on Robin's arm again. "Let's not get into trouble," she protested.

The bartender pulled an aluminum baseball bat from behind the counter and came around approaching the dining area.

Robin just looked back with a grin on his face. "Oh, what'cha gonna do with that, huh?" The group was through with Robin's bravado. Four pairs of hands grabbed him from behind and pulled.

"Hey!" he yelled.

"We appreciate your loyalty to the Knicks..." Kim started.

"...But we are not going to jail tonight!" Shinju finished as she walked ahead of Walt, Kim, Mouse, and Jarvis pulling Robin to the exit.

Robin struggled in protest, but was no match for his friends as they pulled him to the exit.

"And don't come back!" the bartender yelled, waving his bat.

Right before he was pulled through the door, Robin yelled, "Only pussies use aluminum, dickface! Get yourself a wooden bat!"

Tommy was working Saturday, so with his day off this Thursday morning, he took the Long Island Railroad out to Ronkonkoma. His parents lived in a luxury apartment complex on Peconic Street. After signing in at the gate, he proceeded to Unit 2 in Building 12. After a quick knock, the door opened and Maureen Carmichael greeted her son with a hearty embrace.

"Thomas! How are you? How are Sarah and the baby?"

He stepped inside and looked around. "They're fine, everybody's fine...where's dad?"

"He went out for a swim. Been at that pool every day since it opened after Memorial Day weekend. He's getting his laps in now before the end of the school year and the kids take over."

Maureen was just as tall as her son, but very thin. She had worked for NYNEX as a switchboard operator back when it was known as AT&T. Now retired, she spent most of her days painting landscapes and scrapbooking. Tommy poked his head into the apartment's second bedroom, which was made into a studio with various paintings on walls and easels.

"Looking good, ma... thinking about putting these in a gallery and selling them?"

"Oh please," she scoffed. "These are just for keeping my mind sharp. I gave a few to the senior center up the street to put up in their lobby."

"They're really nice..."

The door opened and Jarlath Carmichael walked in wearing a black-and-white-striped 50's style swimsuit. He was 5'8 but built like a circus strongman with huge long arms and a chest the size of Texas.

"Maureen! Call the building manager. They're putting too much goddamn chlorine in the pool! My eyes are burning and I'm already wearing goggles!"

"Hey dad!" Tommy yelled.

"Wha..th...? Tommy! When did you get in? C'mere and give me a hug!"

"Jarlath! You're still wet!" Maureen cried out, but it was too late as Tommy bent down and embraced his father, damp swimsuit and all.

"You're looking well, boy...how's the wife, how's the baby? She should be due in a few weeks. You ready?"

"Everybody's fine and we're ready as we'll ever be."

Maureen approached both men, giving each a towel.

"Be right back. I'll change into something more presentable..." Jarlath disappeared into the hallway leading to the main bedroom.

"He's coming back wearing a robe, isn't he?" Tommy asked.

"Oh yes," Maureen quickly replied. "I got some corned beef and cabbage in the kitchen. Take a load off."

Twenty minutes later the three were talking and laughing, their plates empty after a hearty meal.

"Son, you need to learn to drive so you don't have to take the train out here! I'm scared more of those damn niggers are going to shoot it up again..."

"Jarlath! Don't use that word," Maureen scolded as Tommy cringed.

"What? It's true... they're trying to work their way over now... shooting and slashing each other in Brooklyn, Bronx, and Queens... this Colin Ferguson takes the train in December during rush hour and just starts shooting... what the hell is this world coming to?"

"They're not all like that, dad... I work with two black guys and five ladies over at the library... that was just an isolated incident..."

"It always starts with one, Tommy..." Jarlath said, raising his finger. "When our grandchild is born, I want you back here living nearby within the next five years..."

"Oh please!" Maureen snapped.

"No way will you be raising a child in that hellhole!"

"Oh yeah, Sarah will really like that, dad... we'll be fine. And if you won't come to the city, you're never going to see our child face to face..."

"Alright! There'll be no more of that! The two of you always get into a shouting match when your father talks about the city. Knock it off right now!"

The men went silent. Apparently, Maureen's word was absolute in the Carmichael household.

After a moment, Jarlath simply grunted at Maureen and then pointed at Tommy, which reminded Maureen of something she wanted to tell him.

"Oh, by the way, your father heard that a school is looking for a football coach a couple of towns over. Someone can put in a good word..."

"I don't want to coach football, I want to *play*," Tommy dismissed.

"You're wasting your time stamping books in and out for people. You can do so much more!" Jarlath exclaimed.

Maureen put her hand on her husband's arm to calm him down. "Jus..just think about, okay Tommy? No rush, if you don't wanna coach, maybe you can be a... what you call it? A coordinator or something?"

"Just... think about it... like your mother said, that's all we ask... talk it over with the wife, you know? Best decisions are always made together. Don't keep her in the dark about anything! That's how you keep a marriage strong! No secrets. Remember that, Tommy!"

"I will, dad... I will... now, let's talk about something else, huh?"

His parents both nodded.

"Okay... are you having a boy or a girl?" Maureen asked as Tommy rolled his eyes.

Alex was pushing the shelving cart through her section after putting away all her books. It was the last hour, and she was hyping herself up to head out to the nightclub in a few minutes. She parked the cart at the corner of the circulation desk where Robin was working the checkout side with Gerry on returns.

"So how 'bout them Knicks?" Gerry asked.

Robin turned to give him a scowl while saying nothing, then looked back out to the floor.

Alex let out a fake chuckle at Robin's expense, which he ignored, then headed upstairs to her locker. After applying makeup with a mirror on the inside of her door, she noticed she had an audience. Tanya and Janelle were at the doorway to the staff room.

"What you getting gussied up for?" Tanya asked.

"None of your business..." she dismissed.

"You've been acting weird, lately, Alex... what's going on? We're just looking out for you." Janelle said.

"I'm fine, butt out!" she said with a slam of her locker. She stormed away from the pair and went downstairs.

Lakeshia was putting some books back in the fiction section when Janelle and Tanya approached her from opposite directions.

"Hey, what the hell?" she gasped.

"Miss Yi and Chavez left for the day..." Tanya began. "Along with

Alex, looking like she's getting into trouble," Janelle explained. "We need you to cover for us. We're going to follow her."

"What? I can't close by myself!"

"Just do what you can and leave the rest of the books at the circulation desk. Don't worry about it," Tanya assured the young page.

The two headed toward the branch exit. Lakeshia stomped her feet. "Y'all suck!" she hissed.

"Don't you think she'll take a cab?" Tanya asked as they stepped outside.

Janelle looked around and saw Alex walking toward Lexington a half-block away. "Nope. She's taking the train. She doesn't want her uncle picking her up like usual... c'mon!"

Janelle was right. They followed Alex as she took the 4-train to Union Station. Alex walked upstairs and started heading further east while staying on 14th Street. Tanya and Janelle were still close behind.

"Where is she going?" Janelle asked.

"I think I know," Tanya answered.

This time it was Tanya who was right. Alex walked along the line and waited at the end of what led to the entrance of Webster Hall. A nightclub that was for the 18-and-older crowd only. The two girls circled around the block and stood from the corner of 3rd Avenue and 11th Street, looking down to the club in the middle of the street.

"This doesn't make sense. There's no way she can get in there..." Tanya said.

"Somehow, I think she can," Janelle whispered.

Alex stood in line. She spied her two shadows standing at the corner behind her up the street and smiled. She'd spotted both of them previously as they followed her from the train. *They couldn't resist, could they?* She almost changed her mind to try again later, but there was a chance another party like tonight wouldn't happen before the freshman orientation at Hunter College.

The line started moving, and she calmed herself of any jitters. She remembered what the ID guy said and got her purse ready to show it. *It's all about confidence...* she thought. She stepped forward to the bouncer and handed her ID with a smile. The bouncer looked closely at the picture and looked up to her. He squinted in hopes she would crack. Alex kept a straight face, daring him to say something questionable.

After thirty seconds he shrugged and waved her in, then gave her back her ID. Alex took it back with a smug grab and stepped inside. A huge smile slowly crept across her face.

"I don't believe it!" Tanya yelled. "She got in! What the hell?"

"There's only one way they let her inside without a second glance..." Janelle said.

"A fake ID!" they said in unison.

CHAPTER TEN

IN 1962 SYLVIA WOODS, A FORMER BEAUTICIAN, HAT FACTORY WORKER, and waitress, opened her very own restaurant at 328 Malcolm X Boulevard, several blocks down from the Apollo Theater. Every Sunday morning, gospel breakfast was served between ten in the morning and two in the afternoon from their legendary soul food menu. When Zelda stepped inside a few minutes after one o'clock, she received a few glances and turned some heads.

She walked to the back of the establishment where she took a seat in front of an African-American woman who was just finishing a plate of catfish and eggs. Despite the hearty meal, the woman had an athletic figure any other 36-year-old would kill for. Her dark hair was relaxed at the shoulders, natural brown skin complemented by the gray sleeveless sheath dress she was wearing.

"What brings you to Harlem, Zelda Clein?" the woman asked.

"Hello, English. We need to talk about Cleopheous."

Kathy 'Kat' English took a sip of Grandma Julia's fruit punch and looked directly across to Zelda. 96th Street's assistant librarian was Cleopheous Baker's right-hand woman. Their unorthodox relationship baffled the entire midtown cluster, but despite being polar opposites, the pair agreed on everything when it came to office politics.

"It's Sunday. Why don't you help yourself to some greens and grilled shrimp. It's the best in town, I swear to it."

Zelda raised her hand. "He made a personal visit to our branch, Kat. He's under some strange presumption that the results of the experiment..."

"...and with good reason, Zelda. We can't prove anything, but we know...not everything's on the up and up."

Zelda leaned forward. "Kat, we go back, you and me, we both know *you* should be in charge of the region. Hell, you wouldn't even be there if it weren't for me. He's barking up the wrong tree here."

She sighed. "Zelda, I'm patient. I'll probably be old and gray like you when I finally get my own region..."

Zelda blinked hard at the thought.

"...but I will get there, and the fastest way to do so is not to betray my head librarian."

Kathy rose to leave. "He's coming for Augustus, Zelda. Your guy got sloppy, and he's going down. If not by us, it'll be from the inside."

"He won't go without a fight, Kat...and your hands aren't clean," Zelda warned.

"Neither are yours, Zelda," Kathy replied. "Neither are yours."

Deacon Patterson and his brother Macallister (Mac for short) were coming home from playing basketball all afternoon. Deacon was the older of the two at 21, but 17-year-old Mac was the better player. As they approached their building, they spotted Ethel in front of the courtyard entrance holding two bags from McDonald's.

"Auntie Ethel!" Mac ran up and greeted her.

"Hello boys, got a minute for some burgers and fries?" Ethel asked.

The three were eating while leaning against the hood of a car parked in front of the building.

"Alright boys," Ethel started. "Your mother, Elisse, got this crazy ass scheme about buying a home down south... how serious is she?"

The boys looked at each other. "She's doing it, aunt, it's real serious," Deacon said.

"Yeah, she's just waiting till I turn 18 in September," Mac added.

"You two comfortable living on your own? You're still young... how will you pay your bills?"

"Mac's going to NYU after he graduates. I'm doing alright working at the garage, but I'm bringing in a roommate to help later. I'm also going to night school."

Ethel looked closely. "This roommate... it wouldn't happen to be a *girl*, would it?"

Deacon blushed and looked down with a smirk. "Nah..."

He's got it all figured out... she thought. His own little bachelor pad, and in two, three years, he'll be bringing down a baby for Thanksgiving. *Not if I have anything to say about it!* she shook her head.

"Mac?"

"Yes, Auntie?" the youngster answered.

"Why don't you take our garbage to the can up the street on the corner?" She flashed him a five-dollar bill for his troubles.

"Sure!" A second went by and Mac was halfway up the block.

Now that Ethel was alone with her eldest nephew she took a step closer. "Deacon, I don't want you having no babies the minute your mother leaves you alone to live..."

The boy sucked his teeth.

"Your mother won't get a dime from me unless you assure me you'll be a responsible young man, understand?"

"Yeah, I get it...but if you won't help...she's going to find a way to make it happen... with or without you, aunt..."

She looked at the young man and saw the determination in his face. The deal was more serious than her sister let on.

Robin met Shinju in front of her building at two in the afternoon, then escorted her to Cervantes's cab.

"This is Cervantes," he introduced to her.

"Pleased to meet you," she greeted. "You have a lot of friends with cars," she said to Robin.

"Heh, heh... it's just these two, I assure you..."

"Yes, but you will NOT be making out in or on top of my cab!" Cervantes added.

Robin cleared his throat and glared at the cabbie. "Funny guy..."

They drove back to Manhattan and made their way north. When they passed the GWB and bus terminal, she looked at Robin. "I thought you said you lived..."

"We're going somewhere else before we go to my place. You're going to love this."

Fort Tryon Park was located on Fort Washington Avenue between Washington Heights and Inwood. It was a vast park overlooking the West Side Highway and the Hudson River. Cervantes pulled up to the entrance. A huge green sign greeted them with the name of the park. Robin came out and ran around to open the door for Shinju. She stepped out with a smile due to his chivalry and closed the door with a double pat to signal the driver to take off.

She read the sign and noticed that underneath it said, *The Cloisters, Weather Garden, and Cafe.*

"What are...The Cloisters?" she asked.

Robin grinned. "You'll see." They started walking the path to the entrance leading inside.

The walking path was smoothly paved with benches on both sides. There were plaques on the benches dedicated to the many benefactors who donated generously to the park. The paths lead in several directions. There were encircled ledges with stone walls up to the waist to lean over for a view leading down. The path also wound down and sideways, almost in a stairway pattern to a section where there were arches and tunnels to explore.

But Robin led Shinju straight, passing through the park approaching a majestic structure.

"Oh...oh my!" she gasped.

"Miss Hasegawa, I present to you, The Cloisters..."

The medieval architectural gem stood before them, a towering sight. It served as a museum, library, and cafe. Opened in 1938, transported and rebuilt piece by piece from France, the four separate quadrants come together in a Frankenstein style of synergy.

"It's like something out of the ancient past! We can actually go in?" she asked in awe of the castle.

"Sure!" he said and led her inside.

It was six o'clock when they finally arrived back at Robin's apartment. Shinju was floating on air, amazed by all the sights she saw today.

"I have never seen such beautiful art in my life! The tapestries, the gardens, statues, the stained glass windows... oh Robin, it was remarkable! Thank you for taking me there."

"I knew you would enjoy it..."

She came up to him and they shared a long kiss. His eyelids lit up with a display of fireworks.

"I will never... forget this day, for the rest of my life," she whispered.

"There's something we can do...to make it VERY unforgettable," he whispered back.

They kissed again. Robin slowly reached down to unbuckle her pants.

"Robin," her voice was so soft he almost didn't hear her. "Can we just... wait a little longer?"

He blinked hard and held his breath, trying not to sigh. "Yeah... it's okay," he said, moving his hands away.

"You're not upset or anything?" she asked, her eyes looking into his.

"Of course not," he said with a smile. He rubbed her hand with a warm caress. "Let me show you around and you can unpack, get settled, then we can watch some tv." He led her around the apartment, from the kitchen, to the living room, then to his bedroom, where he gave her some privacy to change.

"So... tell me about Japan," Robin said as they sat on the couch. The tv wasn't on and the sun was beginning to set behind them.

"My father took care of me from birth. His occupation had us moving a lot. Japan has 47 Prefectures...what you would call 'states'. I was born in Suzu, Ishikawa. When I was six, we moved to the wards of Tokyo."

"Wards?" Robin asked.

"By your standards, Wards would be considered Boroughs... like here in New York City. You have five, Tokyo has 23."

"Wow, fascinating. How do they live? Are there stores, malls, supermarkets? Do they play sports, have concerts? Is everything they do like here, just different?"

She laughed. "Of course, silly! We're just as civilized as here! What, you think we all live in poor villages, praying in temples and challenging each other in Kung-Fu?"

Robin blushed. "No, not really, but... I'm sorry. I feel so stupid for asking."

"It's okay. My misconceptions of Americans were just as bad when I came here five years ago."

"Five years? Wow, I figured you'd been here much longer."

There was a brief silence as they looked at each other.

"Robin?"

"Yes?"

"What happened to your hand?"

He blinked hard, looking down and then back at her. "Burn accident," he explained coldly.

"May I see it, please?"

"Can we just... wait a little longer before you see it?" he asked, echoing her words.

She looked down and nodded. "I'm sorry... of course."

He reached over and took her hand. "You're not afraid of heights, are you?" he asked.

She shook her head no.

"Good," he said.

They went back to his bedroom, and he moved the curtain, revealing the balcony door.

"Robin! We're 16-stories up!" she yelped.

"It's perfectly safe. Trust me."

He unlocked the door and pulled it open. After stepping out, he turned and saw her standing at the doorway. The neighborhood shined below them.

"I... I might have been mistaken about what I said earlier," she stammered. Her knees started to buckle.

"Don't they have skyscrapers in Tokyo?" Robin asked.

She swallowed hard and nodded yes.

He extended his hand. "C'mon... one little step. I've lived here for 12 years, and you only need to worry if you're crazy enough to walk on the railing."

She took his hand and slowly stepped forward. The balcony floor was a foot lower than the bedroom tile floor. As her foot landed on the concrete, she brought her other foot down and balanced herself.

"You can even jump!" He took a small hop to demonstrate, and she gasped in fright and grabbed him.

"Okay, you're going to stop scaring me to get me to hold you... once bitten, twice shy."

He smiled, wondering where she learned the idiom from. "You have my word, no more frights... unless we see a scary movie, of course."

He noticed she wasn't holding his hand anymore and standing comfortably. "Take a look around," he said with a flourish. "It's a great view..."

She took a few steps to the steel mesh railing and made the mistake of looking straight down. "Oh my G..." she retreated closer to the doorway.

"It helps if you look *out* across the horizon rather than down," he said with a grin.

Shinju bent her knees and sat on the step, halfway in the bedroom and halfway outside. "I think I'll look at everything from here," she said.

Robin grabbed the folding chair and took a seat next to her. "Fair enough."

She let a moment go by before she asked, "You lived here with your grandfather? Where are your parents?"

"My mother left me with him to manage my older sister. She's a model. I never knew my father, only that mom ended her marriage by having an affair with him."

"So sad, my goodness..."

"Shindy, I'd be the first to admit life hasn't been kind to me. Don't get me wrong, I'm grateful for everything my grandfather did for me... he saved me from being a thoughtless sadistic thug. But now that he's gone, I'm so lost..." he looked down, then looked up at her. "You're the only thing now that's keeping me going."

She looked at him, astonished by how devoted he presented himself.

"Robin."

"Yes?"

She took his hand and looked into his eyes. "I want us to sleep in each other's arms tonight. I want you to wrap yourself around me... like a cocoon. Do you understand?"

He nodded.

She leaned over and kissed him on his cheek. They both stood up and she held his hand, leading him inside. They left the balcony door open. She walked back to his bed. He slid on top of the comforter first, with his back to the wall, and she joined him, her face nuzzled into his chest. His arms enveloped her as they lay together, limbs intertwined like a braid of hair. Nothing happened intimately, but if you would ask either of them, both Robin Walker and Shinju Hasegawa would say that two souls became one that night.

Heywood woke up Monday morning to find Jackie awake and gone already. Their relationship had been strained in the last few weeks with the failed auditions. There was a note on the refrigerator when he made breakfast. He chased his cup of coffee with a shot of bourbon then walked to his closet and produced Augustus' box.

Since bringing it home, it had been a mystery he was dying to solve. He was instructed to take it home, not to open it and to hold it for two weeks without any questions. The first night he shook it for over thirty minutes in hopes of hearing a clue of what could be inside. When he got tired of playing detective, he put it up in his closet and forgot about it.

Now it was time to take it back and ask some questions.

Zelda sat behind the information desk, looking up to Augustus as he leaned on the desk with his back to her. He rubbed the left side of his temples as he listened to her recap of the conversation with Miss English.

"Kat says Cleo has it on good authority you fixed the results. Her words were '...*your guy got sloppy.*' And that if they don't do it... it'll be from within. They know something. So does someone else here."

"He's got nothing...thank you for talking to her. Consider this matter concluded." He stood up straight in front of the desk, preparing to step away.

"I wouldn't take this lightly, Gus," Zelda warned. "Advantage is a better soldier than rashness, *Henry V*, Act 3, Scene 6."

"Trust me, Zee...I'm not."

The conversation ended as Heywood entered the branch. He nodded to Augustus and walked past him to his office. The head librarian turned around and walked past his colleague toward his office.

Shinju woke up in Robin's arms to the sounds of the neighborhood coming in from the open balcony door. She sighed contentedly and noticed the glove on Robin's injured hand. She wondered if she could slip it off gently. He appeared to still be asleep as she pinched the end of the garment with her thumb and forefinger.

She slowly started to lift it back when she heard, "Did you know you talk in your sleep?"

Her hand immediately released the glove as she gasped. "Huh?"

Robin grinned while his eyes were still closed. "In Japanese AND English, I might add. It's very impressive...but kind of hard when you're trying to get some sleep."

"Yeah, right... you're kidding..." she said.

He started repeating the Japanese he heard throughout the night. "I'm sorry father, I do not wish to disappoint you... Obasan, talk some sense to your brother... Obasan, Obasan... you said that word a lot, what does it mean?"

She turned to face him, her mouth open wide in embarrassment..."Ah!" she gasped, her face turning bright red.

She gathered her composure and looked at him seriously. "You... you have a problem yourself as you sleep... you stop breathing... for minutes at a time...that is very dangerous."

He looked at her skeptically, wondering if that was true or if she said that to change the subject.

"Let me wash up first. That way I can make breakfast... no classes today, so... wanna take a jog after?"

She turned around and lowered her legs off the side of the bed. "Sure."

"Great!" He stole a kiss at the back of her neck and leaped out of bed to the bathroom. She laid back down and brought his pillow up to her face to take in his scent. After a deep breath, she sighed.

Finding her bathrobe, she entered the bathroom and took a shower. Robin was waiting for her with a well-prepared breakfast, consisting of English muffins, scrambled eggs, toast, dry cereal, and pancakes.

"Robin! This is way too much to eat as the first meal of the day..."

"Well, it's a rare occasion that I'm entertaining company. I guess I'm being a little over-the-top."

She sat down and just stared at the table of lavish food. "I don't even know where to start..." She picked up an unfamiliar item and asked, "What is this?"

"Thomas English muffin," he replied.

She took a small bite and chewed slowly. Robin sensed her apprehension. "What's wrong? Try the cereal. It's Rice Krispies."

She looked at the bowl. "Rice...Car-risp-ees?"

He picked up a cup of milk and held up the bowl to her face. She looked at him questionably as he poured some milk on top of the cereal, causing the reaction that startled her.

"Fireworks!? How can you eat such food that makes noise!?"

He laughed, "Snap, Crackle, Pop!...It's puffed rice, the milk makes it come alive!"

"I'll just have the eggs and pancakes," she said sheepishly.

He pulled the bowl back. "Okay."

It was almost nine when they were standing near the door, preparing for a morning run. Robin had his sweats on with a Nike T-shirt while Shinju was wearing a jogging suit.

"Try to keep up. I'm big, but I climb hills and go far," Robin warned.

"I'm your shadow, just stay the course and no surprise deviations."

They exited the apartment and took the elevator to the lobby. The pair sprinted out of the building as Robin led Shinju through his usual path down Wadsworth Avenue to 181st Street, then uphill past Broadway toward Fort Washington. He thought about stopping at Bennett Park but remembered Diedre and changed his mind. Instead, he made a left turn heading south at Fort Washington, passing the bus terminal.

"For a second," she huffed, "I thought you were going to run back up to The Cloisters..."

He laughed. "No way!"

They arrived at J. Hood Wright Park on 173rd Street. The path went past a children's playground and led deeper into the park, which was further uphill. They climbed some steps to an elevated enclosure with park benches. The George Washington Bridge stood behind them as they took a break.

"This is a lovely park," she said.

"One of many here in the heights...I love it here." He nodded at a bench. "Let's sit for a bit..."

"I have to admit, you can run. It took a lot to keep up with you."

"That's why you treat yourself to a hearty breakfast," he said, patting his chest.

She noticed he was staring at her. "What?" she asked with a giggle.

"You look beautiful in a jogging suit."

She blushed and wiped the hair out of her face. "We should head back," she nodded.

They jogged down 173rd Street from Fort Washington to Wadsworth, then walked the rest of the way to 178th. As they approached the building, two girls stepped out of the lobby and stopped when looking in their direction. Robin's eyes narrowed as he recognized Mercadees and her twin sister Porshia glaring at Shinju while walking next to him.

He grabbed her arm lightly and quickened his pace to pass them by.

"Hey Robin!" Porshia called out, "What's with you and that ching-chong chick!"

She almost turned around, but Robin whispered, "Ignore them. Just some skanks from around the building..."

"What, you think you're too good for the sisters, now?" Mercadees taunted. "Messing with that chop suey bitch like a sellout?"

He took the bait. "Watch that shit, you two! I'll knock your fucking heads together like Tweedle-Dee and Tweedle-Dum!" he yelled while turning around.

They didn't back down. "You ain't knocking shit!" Mercadees barked. "You walking around with that chink on your arm is disrespectful!"

"Hey, I don't remember you giving me the time of day back at I.S. 143 when I asked you out to the dance..."

"That don't give you the right to just drop us all together, just because my sister shot you down!" Porshia yelled. "You an embarrassment to our race!"

Robin took a step toward them, clenching his fist. "Fuck you stupid-ass bitches, so damn dumb y'all be chewing Juicy Fruit instead of Doublemint gum!"

"Who you calling a bitch?!" they both yelled. Robin tensed up and got into a defensive stance when Shinju pulled him back.

"Don't," she pleaded as he looked at her.

He turned back toward them and did a fake flinch that made the twins jump back a few inches. Robin smiled at the scare and turned around, walking inside.

"Don't let me catch you in the laundromat next time, Robin! Throw some bleach in your and that slanted eyed bitch's face!" Mercadees yelled at them.

They rode the elevator up in silence. Robin noticed Shinju's hands were shaking. When they were back in the apartment, Robin told her, "Ignore them. I don't know what I saw in..."

"You can't go around hurting people all the time! You have to control your temper!" she suddenly yelled.

Robin opened his mouth, registering her genuine mortification. "They were disrespectful! I was defending your honor!"

"You...you're like that big green guy that's always angry! The Thing!"

"Hulk, Shindy... The Thing is the orange guy made of rocks."

"Whatever!" She waved her hands in the air.

"Look, those two have always messed with me, and I don't mind... but the minute they say anything about you, well yeah, it's on!" he said, punching his open palm.

"You need to be Zen."

"What's 'Zen'?"

"Buddhists from Japan developed a way of life, a religion you might say... teachings that value the importance of non-confrontation, to achieve inner peace."

Robin took a breath. "Look... I'm sorry, you're right... losing Granddaddy has me going back to my primal state... I'll try to be better."

She caressed his cheek. "It *was* nice... defending me, defending us... I never thought about it, but people on both sides may object to us going out."

He brought his hand to hers, which was still on his face. "Is that why... you haven't introduced me to your... Obasan?"

She tensed up. "In good time..." she said with a nod. "I'm going to take a shower." She gave him a peck and headed to the bathroom.

CHAPTER ELEVEN

AUGUSTUS WALKED INTO HIS OFFICE. HEYWOOD WAS STANDING IN FRONT of his desk and there was a gym bag on the chair in front of him.

"I believe the coast is clear for you to take this back." Heywood gestured toward the bag.

The head librarian walked to the chair and removed the box from the bag. "Yes, I suppose it is. I know I asked you to put it upstairs, but I'll do that myself later." He put the box back in the supply closet on the top shelf... way in the back.

Heywood turned to leave, but Augustus cleared his throat, which made him stop in his tracks and turned around.

"Zelda spoke to Kat English from 96th Street. Cleo's going to make a move. We need to make sure this doesn't get out..."

"You have nothing to worry about with me," Heywood replied.

"Very good. I assume you didn't open it, correct?" Augustus asked, handing Heywood his gym bag.

"Curiosity *was* getting the best of me, sir."

Augustus tilted his head.

He let out a chuckle. "But no, I didn't open it."

"Excellent, dismissed."

Heywood nodded, then turned and left.

Tanya was so excited Monday evening. She came home after work and showed her mother the latest quiz that she passed. The ladies sat at the kitchen table later eating dinner as Tanya continued to convey her enthusiasm about her schoolwork.

"Very good, Tanya..." her mother began. "With two weeks of school left, you've been more focused and it's paying off. There haven't been any more incidents between you and those co-workers, like that sex book nonsense!"

Tanya blushed while looking down sheepishly.

"Which brings me to something I've been meaning to discuss with you. You listening young lady?"

"Yes Mama," Tanya answered.

"Hear me out before saying anything..." she folded her hands before her. "If you pass this semester, in September you'll be a junior...even though you *should* be starting as a senior."

Tanya rolled her eyes and continued to listen.

"I want you to work this last summer at the library and then quit in September."

"But Mom..." Tanya began in protest.

She held up her hand. "I'm not finished, just listen." She took a breath. "I know you appreciate earning your own money. It makes you feel independent, which is good, and you're learning important skills that you will need in life...but you need to work harder at school with no distractions."

Tanya stared back, waiting to speak.

"In exchange, I'll give you a $50 allowance every week."

The child's eyes went wide as her jaw dropped.

"And an extra $25 for some simple chores around the house like taking out the trash, washing the dishes, and sweeping and mopping the floor."

Tanya was earning four dollars and twenty-five cents an hour and working twenty-four hours every two weeks. She was lucky to get eighty dollars every paycheck after taxes.

"Mama," she began. "How can you…"

"Don't worry about where the money comes from, Baby, just think about my offer. I know this job means a lot, but school is more important. I hope to see a good report card at the end of the month. If not, you're going to summer school and you WILL quit this job."

Tanya swallowed hard. The pressure was definitely on her now. What would she do without Alex and her friends?

"Okay, you got this…it's all about confidence. Knock 'em dead!" Heywood said, rubbing Jackie's shoulders.

"Thanks, Stringbean. It's great that you came with me. Just sit quietly in the audience, okay?" she asked.

"Sure."

It was six in the evening as the couple walked to the back entrance of The Pyramid Club between 6th and 7th Street on Avenue A in the East Village.

There were ten performers lined up for the open auditions. One by one they performed and failed to impress the club owner. When it was her turn, Jackie came out from backstage and introduced herself.

"My name is Stormin' Jackie Daze, and I bring the rain!"

She then gave the band behind her the cue and started her performance.

After thirty seconds, the club manager raised his hand, and the band stopped. Jackie froze in mid-stride, confused by the interruption.

"Thank you, we'll call you," the manager dismissed.

"But I only sang for…"

"Heard all I needed to hear, we'll call…"

"I was promised a five-minute audition!" she yelled.

"Well then read the paper aloud for four-minutes because you can't fucking sing! You're all spectacle and gimmicks. I'm surprised you don't burn a guitar thinking you're Jimi Hendrix!"

"You're just judging me on my looks!"

"No, I'm judging you on your talent, which you have none of."

Heywood stood up and ran backstage, sensing trouble.

"You asshole!" Jackie screamed. "I've been singing for over 20 fucking years! Who are *you* to tell me?"

The manager chucked his thumb. "Get this bitch outta my sight!"

Two bouncers in the audience stood up and approached the stage. Heywood ran on stage behind Jackie. "We better go. Those guys look like they mean business."

"I'm not going anywhere. I want my five minutes! And I'm not leaving 'til I get..."

The bouncers approached from both sides, towering over them. One took off his sunglasses, while the other cracked his knuckles. Heywood grabbed her hand and stammered, "W... we'll be going now."

The back door flew open. Jackie struggled against Heywood's grip as he pushed her out to the alley.

"Lemme go, lemme GO!" she protested.

Once the door was closed, he obliged her. "Sorry, but those guys were going to pound us."

She started to stomp back and forth. "Fucking sonofabitch! This is bullshit. I should sue!"

"Yeah, okay, we'll sue... c'mon, let's go," he said with a wave.

The back door opened again as the couple flinched. The bouncer with the sunglasses stepped out to the alley. Heywood stepped in front of Jackie protecting her. "Hey man, we're leaving... no need..."

"Hold on," the bouncer said. He was at least seven feet tall with dark skin, his head shaved smooth like Augustus. "I just got a call. The manager may not be interested, but I represent someone you need to talk to. He's really busy in and out of town right now, but if you give him a call, you may get a fair chance at working with... 'The Man'."

"The who?" Heywood asked.

The giant pulled a business card from his pocket and gave it to Jackie. "Leave a number with him and wait for the call... don't blow it."

She took the card and the bouncer knocked on the back door twice, then stood back as the other bouncer opened the door for him. The door slammed shut again. She looked down at the card. It simply said 'THE MAN' and there was a phone number underneath. Heywood looked at her and asked, "Who the hell is 'THE MAN'?"

It was a day New York City would remember forever. Wednesday, June 15th, 1994, the sun shined brighter, the Hudson River appeared bluer, and the sidewalks were bright with smiles of the residents of the five boroughs. Because last night, the New York Rangers won the NHL championship trophy, the Stanley Cup, for the first time since 1940.

Eugene Iscaro entered the branch at eleven, with Zelda walking behind after letting him in. The security guard was still wearing a New York Rangers jersey and screaming from the top of his lungs.

"YEEEEEEEAAAAAAAAAAAAAHHHHHHHHHHH!!"

From the circulation desk, Gerry and Ethel looked at the security guard as if he was insane, as Augustus and Sonyai both emerged from their separate offices. Only Tommy and Heywood understood the outburst as they stood out on the library floor.

"How 'bout them Rangers!? 54 years! The curse is broken!" He walked to Tommy, who high-fived him, then Heywood shook the guard's hand as they fist-pumped together.

Ethel shook her head and walked back inside the clerical office. "White people..." she said under her breath.

"I got like three hours of sleep last night, I was celebrating so much!" Eugene said.

"Me and Jackie caught the end of the game at a bar off 14th Street. People were dancing out on the sidewalk!" Heywood added.

Tommy nodded. "Sarah was asleep, but I went across the street and celebrated with my neighbors. What a heart-stopper!"

"Gentlemen," Augustus approached the trio. "Let's try to contain ourselves, shall we? While it's wonderful news for the city, we still have an image to maintain in the eyes of the public."

"Yes, sir," all three said in unison.

The head librarian nodded, but couldn't help to break into a smile himself before walking back inside his office.

"Well, here I am," Robin announced, walking in the clerical office. "It feels funny coming in at 4 pm. My day is just beginning, but around this time, I'd normally be halfway through my shift." Sonyai and Tommy were out working the circulation desk, while Gerry and Ethel were at their desks.

"About time you joined the late-night rotation," Ethel said.

"Hey, from what I hear, this place is a ghost town after 6 pm. Only a few dedicated regulars. What's to complain about?"

"Well, leaving here at 8 pm can be dangerous at times, especially in the winter when it's dark at night," Gerry explained.

"Which is why the clerk who works the late-night makes sure the page working with him is escorted to the train station. We look out for each other," Sonyai said from the door.

Robin turned to Sonyai. "All these precautions wouldn't be due to the pages being all girls...would it?"

Sonyai gave Robin an icy look and then turned to attend to a patron returning books.

Gerry wheeled his chair to Robin and leaned forward. "Hey man, if you want to stay on her good side you're gonna have to get off her about the female pages thing. You've been here long enough."

"It still bothers me, man...doesn't it bother you?" Robin asked.

"I learned to let it go. You should too, just a word of advice." He went back to his desk.

At five, Gerry and Ethel took the desk while Sonyai briefed Robin in the office.

"You're entitled to a 15-minute break where the information assistant can cover for you. Just don't stay away too long."

"Okay," Robin said.

"After closing the cash register and locking the funds in the safe, you wait until the page you're with is ready and you leave together. Got it?"

"I got it," Robin whispered closely. "I shouldn't have to worry about being paired up with a *certain* page during a late Wednesday... right?" he asked, cocking an eyebrow.

"For the sake of peace, you and Alex will *never* do a Wednesday late night together," Sonyai declared with a nod.

"Ever?"

"Ever."

"Glad we see eye-to-eye," Robin said and relaxed a bit.

"Well, I must get ready to leave."

Sonyai turned when Robin tapped her on the shoulder. "Hey! That reminds me of a joke."

She sighed. "Walker..."

"C'mon, this'll be quick. Stop me if you've heard this before... James Patterson, John Grisham, and Stephen King are at the gates of heaven..."

"Stop," she flatly dismissed and walked outside the clerical office.

The staff said their goodbyes and minutes later there was a lull throughout the floor defined by an eerie silence. It was only six twenty and Robin felt like he had been behind the desk for two hours. *Boy, they weren't kidding. Time is standing STILL here!* he thought. Lakeshia walked in and collected a few returned books from the carts and went back to the shelves.

"Leelee?" he asked, catching her attention. "Is it always like this?"

She nodded. "Yep," and resumed walking.

Even Eugene appeared to be nodding off as he sat in his chair. Tired from celebrating until the wee hours of the morning.

Ten minutes later, he took a seat on one of the shelving carts. By six forty, he started pacing in a circle. A few minutes after seven, the door opened and Shinju walked in. She was wearing a black leather skirt with a red tube-top. There was no way she left the museum dressed like that. She was out to entice.

Along with the outfit, she wore a pair of white low top sneakers that silenced her footsteps as she walked to a table furthest from his view at the circulation desk. He couldn't help noticing that the table she chose to sit at was usually reserved for the homeless vagrant, John Paul Jones. Luckily he wasn't known to stay during late nights, probably seeking shelter for the evening elsewhere.

Robin pretended not to stare, but was watching her every move from the corner of his eye as he checked out a few books for a patron. Once he was alone again, Shinju found a paperback to read and sat back at the reading table, this time with her legs facing him. She opened the book and held it up to her face, her eyes peeking at him from the top of the cover. She gave him a playful wink.

Lakeshia noticed Robin staring at the new patron, and curiosity got the better of her. She pushed her shelving cart to the New Books section. She saw the two of them pretending not to be looking at each other, and her blood boiled. Robin looked mesmerized, like in the cartoons when cupid shoots someone in the ass with his arrow. *What does he see in her? She doesn't look all that!* she thought. She caught some off-hand gesture by him as he walked around from the circulation desk toward Angie Trueblood.

"Can you cover me for my 15-minute break?" he asked.

The information assistant stood up and stretched her legs. "Sure. Nothing's going on here."

"Thanks." He walked toward the door leading upstairs.

A minute later, Lakeshia saw the girl in the black skirt slink her way to the door and follow him.

Robin looked down from the second floor as he saw Shinju climb the steps up to him.

"We got 15 minutes," he said, greeting her with a kiss. "Wanna see the staff room? They have a comfortable couch." The two started making out while approaching the entrance. Two minutes later, the door from downstairs opened and Lakeshia tiptoed up the stairs and put her ear to the staff room door.

Robin and Shinju were on the couch. His hands were all over her and she was kissing his neck. "Chill, don't give me a..." but it was too late. Shinju bit down and inhaled a deep breath with a loud sucking sound. He gritted his teeth and growled in pain as he received the hickey, then used the opportunity to slip his hand in her skirt and finger her. She had a wet spot on her panties that he rubbed while his other hand caressed her nipple. "Ohhhh..." she moaned.

Lakeshia slowly opened the door and peeked inside. She held in her gasp as she watched them on the couch. All the illustrations and pictures from the books were no comparison to watching the real thing. It was very jarring. She closed the door and walked halfway back to the stairs. Tears streaked down her face as she sobbed uncontrollably.

Robin returned to the floor and walked back to the circulation desk. A moment later, Shinju emerged from the door, attempting to look nonchalant among the few patrons in the branch. She returned to the table, gathered her belongings and walked through the security threshold to leave. Lakeshia grabbed the book she left and re-shelved it in its correct place.

The branch closed without incident. Robin and Lakeshia waited while Angie set the alarm and locked the entrance. She waved at the pair, wishing them a safe trip home, and walked toward Lexington.

"So, you want me to walk you home?" Robin asked.

"My brother is picking me up," she replied coldly.

"Okay, I'll wait 'til he shows up."

"That's okay, I'd rather you just leave!"

"Hey, what's wrong?" Robin asked, hurt by the cold shoulder.

"Nothing, I'll see you tomorrow! My brother's here..." she walked off quickly to the curb.

Derrick pulled up and Lakeshia walked around the car and got in the passenger seat. Robin scratched his head and shrugged, then walked East. Derrick drove past Robin and then looked over to Lakeshia before heading past Lexington to get on the FDR Drive.

"Um, something you wanna tell me, Sis?"

"Just drive," she said, fighting back her tears.

CHAPTER TWELVE

GEORGE WASHINGTON HIGH SCHOOL WAS LOCATED ON AUDUBON Avenue between 192nd and 193rd street. It was the middle of second period Friday morning as Robin climbed the steps to the main entrance. He greeted the receptionist at the main desk and she directed him to the office down the hall to the left. The name on the door read *Arturo Ramirez*. He knocked on the door.

"Come in," a male voice answered.

Robin walked and closed the door behind him. "I've come to confess. I cheated on my Regents Exam in Biology," he said, a huge grin growing across his face.

Mr. Ramirez looked up from his desk. "Is that why you barely passed with a 67%?" he asked, smiling back.

The two looked at each other deadpanned, then both broke down in laughing hysterics.

"It's great to see you, Robin."

"It's great to see you too, sir. How are the kids treating you here?"

"Ah, can't complain. How have you been?" George Washington's guidance counselor asked.

Robin took a seat in front of his desk. "I've been fine... considering."

"Yes, I understand today is a somber anniversary for you. A year to the day, yes?"

"Yeah."

One year ago...

George Washington High School Senior Breakfast, class of '93.

"Robin, it's not working out. I've been accepted to Rutgers. I'm moving to New Jersey."

"Diedre please, don't do this to us," Robin pleaded. "I love you. I don't know what I'd do without you."

"I don't want to hear it! I know you have feelings for that bitch at your job! I saw you KISS her!"

"She kissed ME. I was caught off guard!"

"Everyone's seen you two together outside the library. I'm not a fool, Robin!"

"Who? Who's telling you these lies!? Your so-called friends? Don't you see? This is what they want! They want to see us broken up and fighting. They're fucking jealous! Please! Can't we just talk about this?"

"There's no more to talk about, Robin. We're through!"

Robin sighed and dropped his head, then snapped it back up. "You know what? Fine! For four fucking years, this entire school has made fun of you, calling you 'retard'... and I defended you!"

She gasped.

"I've kicked so much ass in your name, it's a miracle I'm graduating! Without me, you would have been running home every day crying your eyes out and this is how you do me?"

Robin started pointing to himself. "I was the only one who ever treated you like a normal person because you are! But you know what? You can be a normal BITCH, too!"

He stormed off. "Have a nice time going to Rutgers," he called back to her. "Someone like you will fit right in over there in New Jersey!"

"You realize it wasn't your fault, right?" Ramirez asked Robin.

"I tell myself that every day, sir."

"And?"

"I don't fucking believe it," Robin said bitterly. "Now, it's worse."

"Why?"

He sighed. "Because my grandfather's dead, too."

"I'm... I'm sorry," the guidance counselor said.

"I've never felt so alone. The only reason why I keep going is..." Robin trailed off.

"Is?" Ramirez inquired.

"Nevermind. I'm looking for answers and solace... I won't find them here. I'm just living in the past." He rose to leave. "Thank you for listening, I gotta go."

"If you need help, I know people you can talk to. Think about it!" Ramirez called back to him.

Lakeshia stepped out of school five minutes after two o'clock excited about acing her latest quiz. She was certain she would pass all her classes with straight-A's with only two weeks of school left. Her parents promised her a trip to Six Flags Great Adventures over the summer if she did. She was looking up and down the street for Derrick in the car when a voice from behind got her attention.

"Happy birthday..." Robin said.

Without turning around, she smiled and said, "That's my line!"

"Beat you to it..."

"...to save some time," they said in unison. She turned to see him behind her and smiled. "What are you doing here?" she asked.

"I wanted to talk about the other night. I got the feeling you discovered my little secret."

She looked down sheepishly. "Oh. That."

"Yeah, that... I know you want things to be more...*personal* between us, but with all that's been going on, losing my grandfather and all that, I've been lucky enough to have met someone. We just bumped into each other finally after missing a few opportunities at school."

"So... she's your... girlfriend?" Lakeshia asked.

Robin nodded.

"I see..."

"Leelee, remember what I said when we talked after the basketball game? I meant it. You've been there for me at my lowest point. You're like a sister to me... the sister I always wanted instead of the *conceited bitch* of a prima-donna I have now."

She giggled.

"I want us to be friends, okay?"

"Okay!" she agreed.

A car horn got their attention as Derrick pulled up next to them and stepped out of the car. He approached the pair with a grin on his face. "Hey, hey, what's going on here? You mackin' on my baby sister at school now?"

Lakeshia rolled her eyes while Robin blushed. "Uh, nah, just so happened to be in the neighborhood... heh, heh..."

Derrick patted his shoulder with some enthusiasm, "Man, just pulling your leg! Matter of fact, I wanted to say sorry for being hard on you at our place. It was all in fun... we cool?"

Robin rubbed his shoulder. "Yeah... we're cool."

He looked at Lakeshia. "Ready to go? I'll drop you off at the library." He looked at Robin and nodded. "You can ride with us, too, if you want... but um, you sit in the front seat with me!" he said with a laugh.

Lakeshia sucked her teeth. "Derrick!" she hissed.

"Nah, it's okay, um, I'm actually off today..."

Lakeshia rolled her eyes. "...I'll be in the car." She walked to the car.

Derrick looked back as Lakeshia headed to the vehicle. "Sisters..." he said. Shaking his head, he shook hands with Robin and jogged behind her. Robin waved at both of them as the car pulled off.

Sonyai noticed Lakeshia walking in the branch more chipper than usual, which made no sense considering Robin was out today.

"Good afternoon, Miss Yi," the young page greeted.

"Good afternoon, Seabrooke. I couldn't help noticing your demeanor today. You *are* aware Mister Walker is off today?"

She waved her hand. "I know you were afraid we were getting too close, but things have changed and I'm cool that he's with someone else now. We are and will always be... just friends."

"Oh, he has a girlfriend now? How interesting."

Lakeshia thought about mentioning Robin's little make out session in the staff room, but she knew that would get him in trouble and he would resent her for it, so she said nothing else and pushed a shelving cart full of books out to the floor.

As the senior clerk observed the page moving out to attend to her shelves, she noticed a hand signal from Angie sitting at the information desk. Sonyai walked over to the branch phone near the checkout side and dialed an extension.

The phone rang at the information desk and Angie answered in a low whisper, "We need to start looking for the box again."

"How do you know he still doesn't have it hidden somewhere outside the branch?" Sonyai asked.

"We've waited long enough, and if I know Augustus, he's likely to use it again."

"I agree. Where do we start?" she asked.

"I'm checking the supply closet again, but when you get a chance, try looking upstairs in the staff room and the auditorium."

Sonyai turned to look directly across the room at her, narrowing her glance. "I'm not accustomed to taking orders, especially from an IA who is still earning her associates in night school."

Angie saw the glare, cleared her throat and looked down. "Sorry. I'm beginning to believe you now about his deceptions and I admit, I'm becoming... overzealous."

"There's nothing wrong with a little enthusiasm. Just watch that *tone*." She quickly hung up the phone and went back to her station behind the checkout terminal.

Alex walked into the staff room at four-thirty to find Janelle, Tanya, and Lakeshia sitting at various locations between the couch and the kitchen table.

"What the hell's this? Why are y'all staring at me?" Alex asked.

Janelle stood up from the couch and folded her arms. To the untrained eye, her loose clothing disguised her pregnancy well, but she was starting to show as she approached six months. "We know about your fake ID, Alex."

"And we believe you're about to do something... stupid," Tanya added.

"Like what?"

"I remembered when you showed me that guy's business card. I asked around the school and some of the seniors told me all about him. Calls himself a promoter slash talent scout, but he's just a scumbag looking for girls on behalf of a college fraternity... The Dragonslayers."

"You don't know shit, Tanya! This guy's legit. He can get me in music videos and TV..."

"He's just gassing your head up, Alex!" Lakeshia said. "He probably says that to hundreds of girls every day..."

The two other girls agreed.

"We're just looking out for you," Janelle insisted.

"I'm a big girl. I can handle this," Alex replied.

"Alright, look, this is serious." Tanya stepped forward. "I don't wanna turn snitch, but I WILL tell Miss Yi if you don't run that ID right now!"

"Really Tanya? It's like that?"

"Yeah, it's like that Alex. It's like that," she replied nodding assertively.

"And what if I said you gonna have to come MAKE ME give you that ID?" Alex taunted taking a defensive step forward.

Lakeshia started to tremble as her eyes darted back and forth between the two. Janelle stood in place worrying where this was escalating to.

"I kept your secret about fooling around with Andy in the beginning, Tee...you owe me," Alex hissed through her teeth.

"And I'll pay you back another way, but I'm not about to let this guy trick you out."

Tanya clenched her fist for emphasis as Alex squinted in a death stare. All four girls were looking around the room, none of them saying anything. Alex weighed her options and after another tense minute she sighed. "Fine." She took the ID out of her pocket.

Lakeshia exhaled while the rest of the girls relaxed. Alex snapped the card in half and let both pieces fall to the floor.

"Thank goodness," Janelle stepped to Alex. "Now, I want you to promise me you won't get another ID and try to go to the college party we heard about, please."

Alex raised her left hand. "I promise..." she rolled her eyes. "Y'all suck, you know that?"

Lakeshia sprang up and gave her a hug, Janelle and Tanya joined in. "Yeah, but we care," Lakeshia said smiling.

Tommy was pacing back and forth near the returns side at the circulation desk. Gerry looked up from his notebook and said, "I can cover both sides if you need to go to the bathroom, man."

"Funny... I'm going out of my mind..."

"Again? More childbirth classes?" Gerry asked.

Tommy shook his head. "Worse... Sarah's baby shower is this Saturday."

Gerry winced. "Ouch."

"20 to 30 Puerto Rican women in a church hall, pampers everywhere, onesies, booties, and stuffed animals."

"Don't forget balloons," Gerry added.

"Please tell me there's a way I can avoid all this..."

"Nope, you're screwed."

He turned to look at him. "Thanks."

"Why don't you just invite some of your friends to balance it out?" Gerry suggested.

"Do YOU wanna go?"

"Hell no! What am I? Your only friend or something!?" Gerry yelled.

"Shhh!" Angie held her finger to her lips as she sat at the information desk. Sonyai stepped near the doorway to the clerical office. She scowled at both clerks, then disappeared inside.

Eugene walked up to the desk. "What's up?"

"Wha'cha doing Saturday?" Tommy asked.

"Going to the range with some friends, why?"

"His wife's having her baby shower," Gerry said, jerking his thumb toward Tommy.

"No shit? Congrats. Babies are fun, man."

"You got kids, Gene?" Gerry asked.

"Nope, and that's why they're fun," he replied with a chuckle.

Gerry rolled his eyes and went back to writing in his notebook.

"What's the big deal anyway? All you have to do is hand her presents, smile for pictures and fade into the background, get loaded then duck out early, ha!"

Tommy looked at the guard. "Not with my wife, geez,"

"I got two sisters, two nieces and three nephews. They love 'crazy ol' Uncle Gene'. Was the kid planned?"

"We conceived on Halloween, of all days."

"Nice," Eugene said with a big grin.

"We went to a costume party dressed up as Little Red Riding Hood and The Big Bad Wolf."

Eugene raised an eyebrow. "Not going to dignify that with a response," he whispered.

"She took a pregnancy test right before Thanksgiving and when we told everyone Christmas. It was the best news in the world." He sighed. "All that seems like it was just yesterday, and now... we're a month away. I just can't believe this." He laughed and shook his head.

Eugene slapped his shoulder. "Hey man, it's gonna be alright. If I wasn't firing off some rounds this weekend, I'd definitely crash those festivities. Speaking of," he nodded to Gerry. "You wanna come hang with us this weekend, Gerry?"

"Bunch of white guys with guns... I'll pass," Gerry replied, not looking up.

Eugene looked back at Tommy and shrugged, then went back to his chair at the turnstile.

"I don't get it, man...we went to The Cloisters, took her on the balcony, we got close, but she put on the brakes."

Robin was at Franklin's apartment watching him play *Super Castlevania IV*. Franklin was sitting on the floor in front of the tv while Robin was lying down on the bed reading a copy of *Electronic Gaming Monthly*.

"Then she comes to the branch on my late-night, wearing this killer outfit to tease me, and we go up to the staff room and I tell you, we were seconds away from ripping our clothes apart..."

"Dude, chicks be crazy. I always told you that," Franklin said. "You remember Claudia from I.S. 143? I called her *Cloud*ia because her head was always in the clouds."

"This is different. We'll see how things go at her place this weekend. Maybe she wants the home-court advantage."

"Yeah, maybe she's got some special outfits for that first time, huh? Damn! Stupid skeletons!"

"Heh, good one."

Franklin paused his game and looked at Robin. "Look, I like her for you. Y'all look good together... so here's my advice, stop overthinking shit."

He looked up from the magazine. "Isn't it usually *me* giving you dating advice?"

"And I've heard enough to spit some back at you, okay?"

He resumed his game and sighed in frustration when a skeleton killed Simon Belmont. "Shit! I'm skipping this level. Look in my notebook and get me the password for level seven, will ya?"

"Which level is that?" Robin asked, looking around the room.

Franklin turned to him, grinning. "The long library."

Robin made it to the branch at eleven in the morning and rang the doorbell. This was his first Saturday at 58th Street since the "Paper-Bag Prank" and he was hoping there wouldn't be any incidents involving Alex this time. Sonyai arrived at the glass door and unlocked it. Stepping outside, she pulled out a pack of cigarettes.

"You were due at noon, this is kinda early, Walker." Before lighting up she asked, "Do you mind if I smoke?"

He grinned. "I don't care if you burn."

She lowered the cigarette and gave him an annoyed glance.

"Didn't you ever watch *The Honeymooners*? They do a marathon every New Year's Day on Channel 11!"

She continued to look back at him deadpanned.

"I'm going to make you laugh one day if it's the last thing I do," he promised, waving his finger. He then arched his eyebrow and asked, "Is it safe to go in?"

The senior clerk pouted at his attempt of humor. "Yes, Walker, I made sure there would be no problems this morning."

He stepped inside to find the branch in its normal state. Heywood was sitting at the information desk while Ethel stood at the clerical desk. Janelle and Tanya were pushing shelving carts nearby.

"Satisfied?" Sonyai asked, stepping in after finishing her cigarette.

He nodded. "Looks cool. Thank you."

Robin walked around to the circulation desk and started setting up the terminals. Sonyai started to pace behind him. "So, I hear you are seeing someone. Thank you for letting Miss Seabrooke down gently and remaining friends."

He turned to look at her. "I didn't know my personal life was such a hot topic of conversation, but I, too, am glad things between us didn't require signing a *silly* fraternizing contract."

She ignored the taunt. "Yes, well I tend to be overprotective of my girls. I didn't want young Lakeshia to get hurt. She is the most innocent of the four and I'd like to keep it that way."

"Of course," he nodded.

She turned and walked back into the clerical office.

This is going to be a long four-hour day, Robin thought. No Tommy, Gerry, or Lakeshia. Just him, Sonyai, Ethel, Tanya, and Janelle as well as Angie and Heywood.

"A long day, indeed," he whispered.

He walked over to check the desk schedule on the wall next to the clerical office entrance. He was doing checkouts with Ethel when the branch opened at noon, then taking a break at one. Then he was doing returns from two-thirty to three with...

"Woah, what the hell?" Robin cocked his head when he noticed that Janelle was scheduled to work the desk for an hour. From two o'clock with Sonyai, then with him at two-thirty.

"Is there a problem?" Sonyai approached the wall when she noticed him studying the schedule.

"All that freaking out you did when Leelee practiced checking out a book, and you're letting Simms work the desk... with me?"

"Miss Simms is the eldest of my pages. She has already finished high school and is on the waiting list for a clerical position. Unlike Miss Seabrooke, she is experienced enough to work the desk during off-peak hours, including the weekend."

"Well, I'd rather not work the last half-hour with her..."

"You have no choice," she interrupted. "I will not rewrite the schedule to accommodate you, Walker. *That* is final!"

He rolled his eyes and walked away from the schedule. He turned to look out to the shelves and noticed that Janelle was nearby staring, likely to have heard their conversation.

Great, he thought.

She went back to pushing her shelving cart while he kept to himself the rest of the morning.

When the branch opened, the first hour was mostly quiet, to Robin's surprise. His Saturday at Yorkville had him busy, but like his evening shift after six o'clock this past Wednesday, the branch had very few patrons today. Ethel seemed preoccupied which kept the idle conversation to a minimum. Before he knew it, one o'clock came around and he was relieved by Sonyai.

At the same time, Heywood relieved Angie, who made her way toward the door to the second floor. Robin quickened his pace to catch up with her.

"Hey, want some company for lunch? I brought some sandwiches from home," he asked.

"I'll have to take a raincheck on that. Just going upstairs for something from my locker," Angie replied.

He shrugged. "Suit yourself."

They made their way upstairs. Angie stopped at her locker while Robin went inside the staff room. Once the door was closed, the information assistant looked around and walked over to the auditorium door. She searched the room quickly, checking both closets, looking behind the television cart. The film projector was packed in a small suitcase, which she searched under. Angie even opened the grand piano and looked underneath the lid.

While checking the second closet, which was reserved for storing the piano, Angie found several broken folding chairs and an overhead shelf that wasn't in the first closet.

"That's interesting," she whispered, looking up.

She found a broken chair that was sturdy enough to stand on. Her eyes nearly jumped out of their sockets as she gazed upon the elusive cardboard box she discovered in the supply closet weeks ago.

"Gotcha!" she gasped in excitement.

Robin came back from his break in the staff room upstairs and saw Sonyai and Janelle talking privately at the circulation desk. He approached slowly, so not to overhear anything they were talking about. Janelle appeared to receive most of Sonyai's attention among the pages, which he found puzzling. He cleared his throat, and the pair turned to look.

"Oh my, it's 2:30 already... this day is just flying by," Sonyai said.

He nodded and stepped aside while the senior clerk left the desk to step outside for a cigarette. Robin took his place in front of the returns terminal while Janelle turned her back to him.

Good. If we don't say anything to each other, this half-hour will be over in no time, he thought.

He accepted a few returns and watched as the page performed several checkout transactions effortlessly.

"You impressed yet?" she asked, still not looking at him.

"You could be faster," Robin quipped nonchalantly. "You're lucky it's so dead here today."

Janelle turned at the dismissal. "I'll have you know that Miss Yi has taught me everything I need to become a clerk, you..."

A male patron came forward, placing several books in front of her. She snapped to attention and grabbed the lightpen. After checking his wallet, the man looked up sheepishly. "I've seemed to have forgotten my library card," he whispered with a depressed sigh.

Janelle panicked and stammered, "I... I suppose we can hold these books for you while you go home and come back with your card another time...we can set them aside for three days..." she looked around nervously for Sonyai as Robin observed while folding his arms.

"I live out in Queens. I was just in the neighborhood. Isn't there a way to check these out? Please?" he pleaded.

"Um, just a moment, sir... I, I apologize. Give me a moment..." She walked over to Robin and whispered, "I... I don't know what to do."

Robin smiled and looked at the fear in the child's eyes... *I guess I waited long enough.*

He stepped across to address the patron. "Sir, we need your library card to check these books out to you," he explained.

"But..." the man began.

"However, for a $1 fee and some identification, we can look up your record this one time and process the transaction that way."

The man's face brightened. "I have my driver's license if that helps."

Robin accepted the payment and the ID. He passed the ID to Janelle. "You know how to do a patron search?" he asked.

She nodded and Robin took the dollar to the cash register. She was able to find the patron's record and proceeded to check out the books. The patron thanked her and passed through the security threshold to pick up the items and leave. When they were alone, she sighed. "Tha-thanks."

"No problem. Looks like you still have a few more things to learn before you move on to a clerical position someplace else."

She looked up at him. "Yeah... I guess I do." A moment went by, then she asked, "Hey, can I ask you something?"

"Sure."

"Why didn't you take a clerical position at Fort Washington, where you were a page?"

"They encourage you to venture out, see other locations and explore. Each branch has its characteristics, the people they serve, their personalities. Why would you stay in the same place doing the same thing over and over? You work as a page in one branch, get a clerical position at another, then maybe become a senior clerk and take charge of a branch of your own... that's what they try to teach the pages at Fort Washington."

"Does that mean *you* want to be a senior clerk one day?"

Robin looked at her and began to laugh, which caught the attention of everyone on the floor, including Ethel in the clerical office. He caught himself and coughed quietly, shaking his head. "Um, no...I'm only doing this while I go to school. Once I graduate, I'll be on the first plane to Seattle working for Microsoft... you going to college in September?"

She blushed at the question. "I..." she started.

Ethel walked out of the office again. It was three o'clock. Janelle stepped forward. "Guess my time's up..." She looked at Robin. "Um, thanks again for your help." She took a few returned books and headed out to the shelves.

"You're at checkout," Ethel said to Robin.

"Okay," he said, switching positions.

The rest of the afternoon would play out with no other incidents. As far as Saturday's go at 58th Street, Robin felt it might be better to cluster abroad occasionally.

"So who do you think this 'The Man' person is?" Jackie asked Heywood.

The couple was spending Saturday evening at Union Square, walking near the drinking fountain monument.

"Don't have a clue. Do you believe he actually exists?" he asked.

"There are rumors in the industry of several individuals calling themselves 'The Man': James Brown, Miles Davis, B.B. King…"

"Well, you left a number. We'll be hearing from him sooner or later."

"He's my last hope. I'm running out of clubs looking for singers."

"Have you thought about…doing something else?"

She stopped and looked at him. "Like what?"

"I dunno," Heywood shrugged, "something temporary. A waitress, a bartender, a…"

"All I know is singing. If I'm not doing that I might as well be dead."

"Hey, there's more to you than that, okay? All I'm saying, is to brace yourself for the possibility of doing something else. You're still young. You have your whole life ahead of you…"

"Do you know how many times someone has told me that?" she asked. "When I first started in music, I went by the name of *Jack Daze*. I wanted to be the female version of Method Man from the Wu-Tang Clan… he calls himself 'Johnny Blaze' after the comic book character, Ghost Rider."

Heywood noticed her intensity as she continued her story.

"Promoters kept thinking I was a guy named Jack, so I changed it to Jackie Daze. I scored some gigs singing Soul and R&B, but when it comes to women, R&B singers are a dime-a-dozen. So I spent time with friends in Washington, developing an aggressive persona. I got interested in wearing a mohawk after reading *X-Men* comics with Storm, then one day I was hearing the news about the Gulf War. There was this general, Norman Schwarzkopf. The news nicknamed him 'Stormin' Norman' and that's when Storming Jackie Daze was born."

"Wow, what a story."

"I've been bringing the rain ever since, Stringbean... it's what I'm good at... I can't see myself doing anything else."

"Okay... okay, sorry I even brought it up. We're going to get you back on the stage... where you belong." He smiled and the two held hands as they exited the park.

Tommy pushed the huge wicker chair slowly into the hall. It was seven-thirty and Sarah's baby shower was due to start in a half-hour. Father Carmine was nice enough to rent the hall out at Saint Mary's for a steal, and Tommy had been working since five o'clock with the decorations and food. There were balloons and streamer backdrops in all the corners, tables placed for gifts, food, and a stereo system with over fifty folding chairs divided in two sets of twenty-five. The wicker 'throne' was the final touch, where the guest of honor would be seated and be the center of attention.

Tommy centered Sarah's throne perfectly in the front of the hall before the chairs when he heard a voice echo out of nowhere.

"She needs a cushion to sit on."

He gasped in shock and turned around to see Acindina standing in the middle of the room.

How on earth did she sneak in here wearing heels? he thought.

"That wood is going to be murder on her back and behind. She'll need some pillows," she barked.

"I'll get some before everything starts at eight," he assured Sarah's mother.

She nodded. "Don't you have to get dressed? You're not wearing sweats and a T-shirt for my niña's baby shower, are you?"

"No, not at all. Now that I'm done, I'll go change. Excuse me." He hurried past her then jogged toward the exit.

By nine, the celebration was in full swing. Children were running around playing while the adults were dancing and having a good time. Guests were wearing capias on their lapels and having drinking contests with baby bottles. Sarah was wearing a peach maternity dress with a matching paper crown on her head as she sat on her throne fanning herself.

"Baby, can you do something about the air conditioning? I'm dying here."

"I checked three times, hon. This is as cold as it gets. We do have a lotta people in here generating some heat," he said with a chuckle. They had planned for at least forty guests, but the hall's capacity was nearly at maximum.

"OKAY! It's time to open presents!" Lorenzo yelled, getting everyone's attention. "Grab your plates and sit down!"

Tommy stepped up as Acindina walked over to the table where there were at least thirty gift boxes. "Let's speed this up. We got until 11 pm and I'm not cleaning all this up by myself!" she ordered. She took the first gift and handed it to Tommy, who presented it to Sarah. She opened it, tearing the wrapping paper apart.

"Don't forget to put the ribbon on the hat!" Acindina reminded.

"Pampers!" she said with a smile.

"Can never have too many of those!" Tommy added.

Ten minutes later, Sarah unwrapped the fifteenth set of pampers out of twenty gifts. "More pampers," Tommy laughed. "Keep 'em coming!" he cheered.

"Drop the enthusiasm," Sarah hissed.

"Yes, dear," he quickly replied.

"Ay dios mio! Whatever happened to originality? Here, open mine!" Acindina handed Tommy a small wrapped box. Sarah opened it and pulled out a bracelet with a tiny black fist charm. Sarah sighed, moved by emotion. "Mama!" she gasped.

Tommy was confused. "Wha, what is that?" he asked.

"El Azabache," Acindina explained. "It protects the baby against the dark forces, mal de ojo!"

He leaned in and asked Sarah, "Mal the what?"

"Mal de ojo...The evil eye," she said.

Tommy shrugged. "Okay! Moving right along, next present!"

By ten thirty, most of the guests were gone with Tommy, Lorenzo and a few others cleaning the hall up. Sarah received thirty-seven packages of diapers, several articles of baby clothes, and a copy of *"Que puedes esparar cuando estas esperando,"* a Spanish translated version of *"What to Expect When You're Expecting"*.

"You did a good job, Tomas," Lorenzo said to Tommy.

"Uh, thank you, sir."

"I remember, we had our baby shower in my father's basement. It was barely big enough to hold 12 people. Good thing only five showed up." He threw some streamers in the trash. When the hall was clean, Tommy and Lorenzo took the garbage bags out to a bin in the back of the church.

"You're a good provider, Tomas," Lorenzo said. "And you'll be a great father to my grandchild."

"Yes, sir."

Robin exited the train station around seven forty and walked to Shinju's building. He rang the intercom and she buzzed him in. The door was cracked open once he climbed the steps to the fourth floor. He walked inside and worked the lock behind him. Shinju was wearing an oversized white tee-shirt and nothing else. Her hair was up in a bun as she prepared a bowl of lentil soup.

He made himself at home by hanging up his jacket and his bag with an extra pair of clothes. Ten minutes later they were sitting comfortably on the couch. He changed into a New York Giants

Rodney Hampton football jersey. A rerun of *Empty Nest* was playing on the tv. She finished her soup and snuggled up to his chest.

"Robin?"

"Yes?"

"I think that little girl at your job likes you."

He blinked hard being put on the spot. "We're just friends," he dismissed.

"She was spying on us while we were upstairs the other night. I saw her."

"Oh," he replied dryly.

Shinju looked up at him.

"Shindy, she's 14 and I'm 18. I look at her like a kid sister. We're just friends... that's all."

She turned the tv off with the remote, sat up and stepped away from the couch. Robin reached out to her, but she turned around and pushed him back.

"Shin..."

She pressed her finger on his lips. "Shhhh... Stay right there, don't move," she ordered.

She quickly walked to her bedroom. Robin sat on the couch puzzled as he heard her moving things around, opening and closing drawers and closet doors. She came back out to the living room with a wool jump rope.

"Uh, we're..."

"Stand up and turn around," she interrupted.

After raising an eyebrow over her giving him orders, he obliged. She tied his wrists together, turned him around and sat him back on the couch. Robin was smiling now, anticipating some kinky action. "Shouldn't I have a blindfold?" he asked.

She walked to her stereo and selected a record from her collection, then cued it up on her record player. "Oh no, I think you'll *want* to see this..." She dimmed the lights, turned on the stereo and ducked inside the bedroom.

Robin tested the bonds for a moment as the music started to play on the speakers. It was a familiar tune, a Japanese strings assortment.

His eyes became transfixed as Shinju slowly came out and performed a tantalizing striptease in front of him. Singing along with the song, she extended her legs and gyrated her hips, along with various other body parts with ease.

It was a side of her he had never seen before. He was completely flabbergasted. After the song ended, she removed the needle from the record and stood before him in her revealing attire.

"Was... was that the Siamese Cat Song from *Lady and the Tramp*?" he asked.

"If you please," she purred, reciting the lyrics.

He laughed. "Oooooh, you better untie me, my Siamese pussy cat!"

"This was to teach you a lesson. Your little co-worker better accept that she can't have you... or I'll scratch her little eyes out!"

"Ooooooh, feisty... last chance, untie me," he teased.

"I think I'll tease you a little while long... aaaaahhhhh!"

Robin slipped out of his bonds and she screamed as he leapt off the couch. He hooked his arms around her knees and lifted her over his shoulder.

"Down! Put me down!" she giggled.

"Ah, ah, ah... if I please!" Robin carried her playfully into her bedroom.

CHAPTER THIRTEEN

Robin woke up Sunday morning with the sun shining in his face. Being four stories up, Shinju didn't have any curtains or even a window shade to pull down. He had a bad taste of morning breath, so he headed to the bathroom to wash up and brush his teeth.

Shunju was in the kitchen wearing nothing but his Giants jersey. He had to admit, it looked good on her.

"You're staring at my ass," she said without turning around.

"Yes. Yes, I am..." he admitted.

"Have a seat. It's time I make *you* a traditional Japanese breakfast."

"Well, alright," he said, taking a seat at her kitchen table.

Ten minutes later they were both preparing to eat. There were several bowls, but nothing was on a plate. She poured him a cup from her tea kettle.

"Be careful, it's hot," she warned. "Let it sit, then blow."

He looked around the table and asked, "Uh, no chopsticks?"

"Do you know how to use chopsticks?" she asked.

"No."

"Then you don't need them," she said with a smile.

"Where do I start?"

"There's no particular order. Just pick a bowl and... dig in!" she laughed at his awkwardness.

He shrugged and started with a bowl that looked familiar to him... picked up a fork and started eating. His guess was correct. It was brown rice.

"What are these green things?" he asked.

"Genmai... Brown rice mixed with green tea leaves," she explained. "Try this one next..." she said, pointing to another bowl.

The second bowl was also rice, with something orange in the middle, which turned out to be an egg yolk. After a taste, he nodded. "Well alright, pretty good," he said, taking a sip of tea. Without knowing, he moved on to another bowl which had some soup. Switching from fork to spoon, he held the bowl up and took a spoonful. Once it went down his throat, he immediately froze. His eyes got wide and began to water.

"Uhhhh, what is this?" he whispered.

She looked at his hand. "Miso Soup."

He lowered the bowl slowly, and started to shake, his voice became raspy. "What's. In. It?"

"Robin, it's just fried tofu and seaweed..."

"S..S... SEAWEED?!?" he gasped. He sat up, ran to the bathroom and closed the door.

Shinju was dumbfounded as she heard him violently retching. She continued eating her breakfast, shaking her head. "Americans..."

Across Queens from Robin and Shinju at Flushing Meadows Park, a team of teenagers was warming up and practicing for an upcoming game of lacrosse. A whistle sounded and Angie stepped forward to address the team. She held a clipboard in her left hand and a lacrosse stick in her right. A black plastic whistle was on a lanyard around her neck.

"Okay, let's pair up and start some quick stick drills!" She blew the whistle again. "Hustle, hustle!"

The local league had eight teams, which she coached on Sundays since 1990. As the players started their drills, Angie saw a shadow approach from her left side. Zelda walked to the edge of the field, catching her attention.

"How did you know I'd be here!?" Angie asked. There was shock and fear in her voice.

"I have my ways," Zelda answered flatly while adjusting her glasses.

"My private life outside the library is mine to—"

"What were you and Sonyai looking for that evening?" the elder interrupted.

"Nothing!"

"You've been secretly searching the branch, everywhere from Augustus' office, the staff room and even recently the auditorium."

How does she know these things!? Angie thought. Could Heywood be revealing her actions? No, she'd been careful not to share anything, not even to him. "I don't know what you're talking about!" she said, shaking her head.

"Look," Zelda hissed. "Everyone's been talking! Baker is sniffing around and questioning this damn media experiment Augustus created and it has something to do with a cardboard box that's been going around like a hot potato!"

This was a side of the assistant librarian Angie had never seen before. However, despite the outburst she refused to give in. "I'm saying this for the last time!" Her eyes stared back with such defiance. Angie was done being the timid, neutral outsider. If this was what Augustus and Zelda were about, she wanted no part of it. "I don't know what wild conspiracy is taking over the library, but I would appreciate it if you keep our conversations there and nowhere else!"

She turned away from Zelda, focusing on the team she was coaching. "Now if you don't mind, our game starts in 15 minutes."

When there was no reply for more than a minute, Angie turned back around to find the assistant librarian nowhere in sight.

After walking around her neighborhood and picking up some snacks from a corner deli, Robin and Shinju came back to her place at three forty-five. He dropped the bags on her counter.

"Nice area out here. Queens is looking better and better."

"I can't believe you've never been out here before," she said.

"It has a reputation. Can't help it."

He noticed there was something tucked away under her couch. He cocked his head. "Hey, what's this?" he asked.

Shinju started to panic as he walked over and reached underneath. "Robin, wait!"

He pulled out a dusty guitar case and stood it up. "Wow, you're full of surprises!" A grin growing across his face, he flipped the locks and opened the case to reveal an acoustic guitar.

"You play?" he asked, looking up at her.

She sighed. "Let me put this stuff away. You really should ask before touching someone's things."

Robin sat down on the couch, pulled the instrument out of the case and rested it on his lap. After checking the chords, he began to play a simple scale with his fingers. She looked at him, impressed by the performance.

"Where are your picks? I don't see any in your case."

"Check the cushions. Is there anything you CAN'T do, Robin?" she asked sharply.

He ignored the snide remark and fished around between the couch cushions. He found a plastic pick and began to strum a few notes.

"Don't play too loud. I have neighbors downstairs," she warned.

"Is that why you play with plastic? Wooden picks are the way to go." He started playing the intro to "What's Up" by 4 Non Blondes.

She started to smile. "I like that song. Know any others?"

"There was one we always had to sing in music class. Even performed it for graduation." He strummed an intro and sang the first verse and the chorus to "Cielito Lindo".

She clapped and giggled after the performance.

"What's so funny?" he asked.

"You sound like Ricky Ricardo when you sing that."

He scowled. "Lucyyyyy!"

She giggled again when suddenly her phone rang. She gasped and froze, looking at Robin, then the phone.

"Aren't you going to get that?" he asked.

"Umm, I'll let the machine answer," she dismissed nervously.

He frowned as she walked over and lowered the volume of her answering machine.

"What's wrong?" he asked.

"Nothing! I just prefer to..."

"Is it your family? Obasan? Do they know about us? Are you ashamed of me?" he asked, concerned.

She ran across the room to him on the couch and put her hand on his shoulder. "I would *never* be embarrassed by you, but I value my privacy and screen all my calls except for yours. Just trust me, please."

He looked at her as she matched his gaze. *What is she hiding?* he thought.

"Umm, we forgot orange juice. I'm going around the corner to get some." Without any hesitation, despite her protests, he got up and left the apartment. Once alone, she walked over to the answering machine and replayed the message left for her.

The rest of the evening was tense between the two. Very little was said as they ate dinner. Robin even contemplated heading home early but decided to stay. They were sitting on opposite ends of the couch, staring at each other. The tv was off, and the clock on the wall read 6:17 pm.

"Are you mad at me?" she asked.

Robin shook his head. "No."

They continued to stare at each other in silence.

He outstretched his arms. "Why don't you put up your feet and lay over here while we watch some tv?"

She smiled. "Okay."

He turned on the television as she snuggled into his chest. He traced his forefinger across her crown and kissed the top of her head.

"Are you mad at me?" she asked again.

He rolled his eyes. "Stop it, no..."

She smiled and sighed, whispering something in Japanese.

The news was on television. A sports segment was discussing the NBA finals and Houston's attempt to even the series at three games apiece while staying alive against the Knicks, who were one win away from the title.

"Oh my God!" Robin exclaimed sitting up. Shinju slipped off the couch to the floor landing on her behind.

"That's tonight!? Game 6? What time is it?" He looked around and noticed it was a few minutes before seven. He grabbed the remote and frantically searched all the channels. He found the pregame show, then leaped over the couch and ran to the kitchen.

"Robin!" Shinju called out.

He ignored her as he searched the refrigerator, grabbing a loaf of bread, then opened the pantry for the peanut butter. She couldn't believe her eyes as he proceeded to make several sandwiches as well as spreading the peanut butter on a plate full of crackers. Shinju stood up to find the nearest object she could throw at him. When she failed to find anything worth breaking, she stormed into her bedroom and slammed the door behind her.

Robin watched the entire basketball game alone in Shinju's living room, oblivious to her hurt feelings. He completely snapped into *fanatic mode* and cheered at the possibility of the Knicks beating the Rockets in Houston for their first title in over twenty years. First, the Rangers and now history was being made again.

Alas, Houston stole victory from New York's grasps edging them out, winning by two. With Game 7 scheduled for Wednesday. With the game over, Robin's fanaticism evaporated from his body, and reality set in. Shinju had not come out of the bedroom the entire time, not even to go to the bathroom.

Did she go to sleep? he thought. He walked to the door and leaned his ear on it while trying the doorknob.

"Uh, Shindy? You awake? Um, the door is locked... you think you can, um... unlock it for me, please?"

There was no sound coming from inside. Robin wiped his brow as he tried not to stammer.

"I uh, get why you're kinda mad and I... I just wanna say I'm sorry... it was wrong to just zone out and focus on the game... I'm such a tool." He took a breath and waited. *I really fucked up.* He leaned his back against the door and started to slide to the floor. "I feel, really, really, really, bad, Shindy. If you could just open the door and we can talk... I'll do anything. I'm on my knees, here."

There was a sound of movement in the bedroom. He heard the whine of the mattress and footsteps approaching the door. He turned around and stood on his knees in time to see the door open. Robin looked up to see Shinju glaring down at him. He immediately started to bow profusely and kissing her feet.

"You're pretty good at begging," she complimented.

"I can roll over and play dead as well," he said and started panting like a dog.

She stifled a giggle, trying to stay angry at him. "You better not *ever* ignore me again in favor of some sporting thing on television. You hear me?"

"Yes," he nodded and kissed her feet again. "Let me suck your toes to make it up to you..." he pleaded.

She smiled finally. "Actually," she pulled up her shirt over her head and dropped it on the floor. "There's something *else* I need you to suck on."

His gaze went wide upon her exposed breasts as if he was staring at the gates of heaven. She turned around and went back inside the bedroom. "Stay on your knees... and crawl," she called back to him. Robin bowed several more times and did what he was told.

Tommy walked in the branch Monday morning a complete wreck. His eyes were bloodshot, his usually groomed hair a tattered mess. Gerry and Ethel looked at him from the circulation desk.

"Damn, you look like you got hit by a truck," Gerry said.

"I feel like it, too," he replied. "I worked my ass off this weekend with this baby shower. The house looks like a pamper factory exploded. Sarah started craving guava pastelillos last night at 10:30. I searched all around Queens looking for guava paste. Do you have any idea how many stores are open after 10 pm? Not many! Let alone a store that has guava paste!"

"Calm down, boy, you're gonna give yourself a stroke. Trust me, I know!" Ethel said.

Tommy sulked his way to the office and collapsed into his chair. Sonyai turned from her desk and looked at his pupils. "I take it the shower was..."

"Respectfully, ma'am, I really would not like to discuss anything from this weekend," he interrupted. "In fact, you can put me on the desk for the first two hours... it'll wake me up."

She nodded. "Very well. For what it's worth, Thomas, what doesn't kill you, only makes you stronger. Remember that." She turned around back to her desk.

Tanya was working the 000's in the afternoon, her mother's ultimatum still on her mind when she saw Lakeshia and Janelle whispering in the Foreign Books corner. Janelle nodded and walked away, heading toward Tanya.

"Hey, what was that all about?" Tanya asked.

Lakeshia's smile beamed. "Nellie has another appointment the night before she graduates Thursday. I'm going with her and Miss Yi."

"Why the sudden interest? You're just learning the *'Birds and the Bees'* as it is."

She pouted. "Very funny." She moved past her, but Tanya called her back. "Leelee, wait."

The page turned around and came back, noticing something was bothering her. "What's wrong Tee?"

"I'm worried...about passing this year. My grades are okay, but something's come up," Tanya explained.

"I'm sure you'll make it through. Why all the pressure?" Lakeshia asked.

"My mother warned me that if I fail the 10th grade, she's going to make me quit the library."

"What?" she gasped.

"She thinks the job is a distraction. It didn't help with you borrowing that sex book and not returning it."

"So this is MY fault?"

"I didn't say that, dang..." She sighed. "My grades are my grades. I'm sure I'll pass, but I'm scared that she might make me quit anyway."

"It's bad enough that Nellie's going to leave one day. It would suck if you left too..."

"Yeah."

"Alex would drive me crazy!"

They two shared a laugh as Tanya playfully shoved her. "Leelee!"

"Don't worry about it, Tee... your mom's just trying to motivate you. My parents are promising me a trip to Great Adventures with friends from school, so I'm definitely hitting the books to pass!"

"Cool, thanks Leelee. I was so worried, I didn't even wanna tell Miss Yi. I needed that pick-me-up... don't tell anybody about this, okay?"

"Your secret is safe with me."

She nodded. "Uh-huh, seriously... DON'T tell anyone!" she warned with a smile.

It was several minutes after the branch opened Wednesday. Tommy and Sonyai were working the desk while Gerry and Ethel were in the clerical office.

"Hey Gerry?"

"Yeah?"

"You ever think... about the future?"

"Sure, when I'm rich, retired and married to Janet Jackson? Think about it all the time," he said with a smile. "What are you worrying about now, Jenkins?"

She chuckled, a rarity for her. "This stays between us, you hear me, Gerry?"

"My lips are sealed." He thought about sliding across to her but knew Sonyai would notice. Ethel checked outside for a moment, then whispered, "My sisters are buying a home down south. They want me to retire and run off with them."

Gerry nodded. "Hmmmm... you thinking about it?" he asked.

"I don't know... I've been out of it lately. I'm just worried about my health. It's too early to talk about retiring, but I'm getting to a point where I just don't wanna work anymore."

"Wow, well... there's only one piece of advice I can give you, Ethel."

"And what's that, Gerry Coltraine?"

"Win the lottery," he said and laughed to himself.

Robin was finishing his last hour with Gerry. The two were talking about the Knicks' chances tonight winning Game 7 and if Gerry wanted to check the game out with him somewhere. Jarvis, Mouse and the others were in no mood to watch the game in another bar and Shinju wasn't about to let him watch at her place. Eugene walked up to him at the desk.

"I hear you're looking for a place to watch the game."

"Yeah."

"I'm going to a bar a friend of mine runs nearby. Got a VIP booth with a huge screen tv."

"Uhhh, I'm sick of the bar scene," Robin said.

"Free beer and nachos, trust me... win-or-lose tonight, you'll thank me tomorrow."

He thought about it. "Alright, you're on."

Eugene nodded. "Okay, we'll head out at 6 pm."

"Hold up, don't you have to stay here until 8 with Tommy?" Robin asked.

"I got someone to cover for me," he said and walked back to his chair.

Six o'clock finally came and Tommy emerged from the door leading upstairs. An African-American gentleman in a security uniform entered the branch and talked to Eugene. Tommy took the circulation desk, then Gerry, Robin, and Eugene left for the day. Augustus was at the information desk while Alex worked the shelves.

An hour into the late shift, Alex sat on a cart at the circulation desk taking a break.

"I hear Nellie graduates tomorrow," Tommy said to the page.

"Yeah, have you heard anything about where she's going for a full-time position?"

"They're still looking for openings. It may take a while."

She looked down and shook her head in frustration.

"Alex, you need to lay off hating on Robin. It's not his fault she has to transfer someplace else."

"Bullshit. That fat asshole's dog meat to me," she hissed. "And nothing's going to change that!"

There was a sound of a throat clearing as the two turned to see Augustus standing at the returns side. "Control your voices, you two... there may not be many patrons here, but the few that are deserve their silence."

"Sorry, sir," Alex whispered.

"Sorry," Tommy repeated.

"Be that as it may, Miss Stevens, Tommy's right. Your animosity toward Walker will only make things more difficult if you wish to continue working here."

The librarian returned to his desk and Alex whispered to Tommy, "He's going to find out soon. Miss Yi better find a position soon."

"I trust her, Alex. Don't worry."

She went back out to the floor and disappeared among the shelves.

"Where the hell is this place and why did we have to walk?" Robin asked Eugene.

They were on 1st Avenue approaching 60th Street after walking east past Lexington and 3rd Avenues.

"It's right around the corner. We're almost there. Now I need to warn you, this is a high-class bar we're going to. Keep your cool. We might see a celebrity or two. Don't be embarrassing me."

"What high class? What the hell are you talking..." they turned the corner and Robin trailed off, "...about? Oh, holy shit!"

Once he saw the black awning, he knew he had arrived.

Scores wasn't just a sports bar... it was a gentleman's club. Rumored to have mob ties, everyone from John Gotti to Howard Stern was known to frequent the establishment. There was already a line forming to the entrance, but Eugene walked alongside as Robin followed, and with a nod from the security guard they both walked past the bouncer to enter the club.

Sonyai led Janelle and Lakeshia inside the clinic. Lakeshia wondered why Janelle would have an appointment in a place that was closed, but she didn't say anything.

"I know you may have some questions, Miss Seabrooke," Sonyai began, "...but the less you know, the better it will be, young lady."

"Yes, ma'am," she replied.

The nurse was waiting for them. She greeted Sonyai and Janelle, then gave a puzzled look at Lakeshia.

"It's okay. The child is a friend. She won't say anything," Sonyai assured.

"Thought father of baby was coming," the nurse said.

Sonyai looked to Janelle. "He... he said he was coming, maybe he got the wrong address."

The nurse shook her head. "Very well, let's get started."

"Will you calm down? You're creeping out the waitresses."

Robin and Eugene were sitting in a booth within the isolated VIP section on the second floor. There was a huge television across the room. It was even bigger than the one at Coogan's. The tv wasn't what was drawing his attention though. It was the topless dancers performing on a stage below on the main floor.

The waitresses that Eugene had mentioned wore silver and black, revealing string bikinis, leaving little to the imagination. There were women of all races working. It almost made him forget about Shinju... almost.

"You act like you've never seen tits before."

"I've seen tits, but what these women got I've only seen on channel 35 after midnight! It's the Robin Byrd Show up in here!"

It was nine o'clock and the tip-off was minutes away. Eugene was already on his second beer while Robin was nursing a screwdriver that Eugene ordered for him. Robin had already seen several politicians, actors, and musicians in the last couple of hours. Once the game began, he tried to focus, but the live entertainment was more alluring. Houston was leading by two at halftime. After the third quarter, Houston was still leading 63-60.

"Starks is blowing it!" Robin said. "He's bricking everything in sight. Oh my God!"

Eugene just shook his head. "It's over man, they're running on empty. Fucking Rockets man, they got this." He sat up. "I'm going downstairs for some food to go, then I'm calling a cab." He took out a twenty from his wallet and dropped it on the table.

"Fine, I'll stay here until the end of the game," Robin said.

"You can't stay here without me. It costs $100 an hour to sit in VIP."

Robin flinched. "What!? You're kidding!"

Eugene jerked his thumb to a pair of bouncers in the back. "Two minutes after I leave, those guys are gonna step up and toss you through the back exit. You're too young and there's a dress code, kid."

Robin looked at them, then back at Eugene. "Man, fuck this shit! Thanks for nothing, man!" He stood up and stormed downstairs to the nearest exit.

Eugene shrugged and looked back at the game. Houston's lead was getting bigger in the fourth quarter. The fans were already celebrating. It was over. "Ahh fuck!" he spat and slowly descended the steps to the main floor.

"Baby is looking well. Have you had any weird food cravings lately?" the nurse asked Janelle.

"Well, a month ago I started eating... weird stuff like..."

She held up her hand. "Don't need the details, just want to know if you have them," she dismissed. "We need to talk food allergies, certain foods you need to stay away from that can hurt the baby."

"Like what?" Janelle asked, concerned.

"Raw meat, deli meat, fish, shellfish, all possible for contamination unless cooked correctly. Also soft cheese like Limburger, Feta, Cream Cheese and Brie."

The teenager nodded. "Okay, I'll make sure not to eat any of that."

The ladies were leaving the facility as the nurse locked the door behind them. A pair of footsteps approached the trio. Avery Boone hurried to the entrance and stopped when he saw the hard stares upon him.

"You're late, young man," Sonyai scolded.

"I'm sorry, I got here as fast as I could..." he said apologetically.

"You have to take this seriously, Avery," Janelle said.

"I am, I am. It's just hard with school and everything."

"You are nowhere near *hard* yet... you think it's easy raising a child?" Sonyai asked.

"I... I know it's not, ma'am... I watched my mother struggle raising me and my brother and I wouldn't wish that on any woman."

He walked in front of Janelle and caressed her hand. "I know I'm doing a terrible job so far, but I promise, I'll be better."

She looked up at him as Lakeshia rolled her eyes and Sonyai pursed her lips.

"It's okay. It was just a routine appointment anyway. Everything is fine, the baby's fine. Let's go." She nodded and smiled. "Got a big day tomorrow."

"Ugh," Lakeshia grunted. "I have to take the subway home. I did NOT think this through."

Everyone laughed as the group made their way up the street to the nearest train station.

New Yorkers everywhere were in a slump Thursday morning, the high of the Rangers winning diminished by the Knicks losing the NBA finals in game 7. Shinju walked in the study hall to find Robin face down on the desk in the back. He wasn't sleeping, just distraught. Occasionally a moan of despair would be heard.

"Robin?"

He moaned louder.

"I know you're sad, but we have English class in 15 minutes."

"What is that thing that Samurais do where they slice open their abdomen as a form of suicide?"

"It's called *Seppuku*," she answered.

"Yeah, that... does it have to be self-inflicted? Could someone else do it for them?"

She shook her head and pulled on his arm. "C'mon, let's go!" He reluctantly got up and she led him out of the hall to class. Once the rest of the students filed in, a white man with curly blond locks wearing a tweed suit walked in and stood in front of the blackboard.

"Now I know most are disappointed by the local basketball team losing the championship last night," Professor Fries began. "I was planning on having a quiz this morning but considering the circumstances, I'm willing to postpone the exam to a later time."

There were sighs of relief heard from the entire class.

"Jussssst kidding! Close your books and pass this sheet around." He presented a student up front with a stack of stapled quizzes for the entire class.

The students groaned in agony.

After the class Shinju was walking down the hall with Robin. She reached out and held his hand. "Is there anything I can do to cheer you up? It hurts to see you like this."

He tried to smile at her effort. At this point, even sex would bring him to the verge of tears right now. They exited the building to see several students outside waiting for them. Asian students.

Xian Zhe Hong and his friends surrounded Robin and Shinju from all directions. He pointed at Shinju and said something in Japanese.

Robin hadn't seen Xian since their scuffle at a college party that resulted in him getting tossed out a window, then Robin breaking Xian's arms in return. "Whoa, what's going on here? What is this?" he exclaimed, looking around.

Shinju was upset by the remarks and yelled back at the group in Japanese. Judging by the exchange and body language, this was becoming more than an intense conversation. He felt lost, not sure what to say or do as more voices yelled out against them.

"Speak. English!" he yelled.

Xian obliged him. "Whasamatta black boy, you got yellow fever?

That's why you were sniffing around where you shouldn't be at? You don't belong with our kind!"

"What the? Are you? What the fuck?" Robin began to clench his fist, but this time it was Shinju who acted first. She yelled something in Japanese, took two steps forward and socked Xian in the jaw. Robin was stunned as she proceeded to take on all of Xian's allies, who attempted to avenge their fallen friend.

Robin laughed at the spectacle. He was definitely in high spirits now. "Okay, so all that talk about Zen, being non-confrontational and walking away from a fight, tha-that was all bullshit, right?"

Someone grabbed her from behind and she elbowed him in the face. "Number one rule when it comes to being my boyfriend," she chopped another attacker on his shoulder, "...do as I say, not do as I do!" She dispatched the last person as he charged at her with a jumping roundhouse kick.

"Let this be known to all who hear me..." she yelled. "My dating preferences are my own and *none* of anyone else's business!" She cocked her head. "Let's go." She started walking up the street. Robin surveyed the group of students sprawled out, groaning in pain.

"Yeah, look at y'all... That's MY girl who just kicked all your asses... my girl, mine!"

"ROBIN!"

He took off behind her. "Coming!"

Senior clerk Annabelle Doyle sat in her office at the Yorkville Branch. She heard a sound outside and stepped out to investigate. The entrance was being closed again by one of the IA's as a figure slowly walked to the middle of the floor.

"Who the bloody hell..." she whispered under her breath.

"God save the Queen, Miss Doyle!" Cleopheous Baker greeted. "If I may have a moment of your time."

CHAPTER FOURTEEN

The Julia Richmond high school auditorium was packed with proud parents and school faculty. Lined up in the hallway outside, the graduating class of 1994 waited for their cue to march in. Dressed in their gowns and mortarboards, the teens were talking and playing with their tassels.

"Keep them on the right side, ladies and gentlemen!" the principal shouted while walking up and down the line. "When you walk across the stage and receive your diploma, you then switch your tassel to the left side and walk off the stage to the back of the auditorium."

"Yes, sir," the students said in monotone unison.

"Do NOT throw your cap in the air, and do not attempt any extracurricular celebration stunts...like *mooning!*"

"Who told!?" a male anonymous voice yelled.

"Just wave to your parents for them to take a picture and keep walking! We have over 150 graduates and only three hours. We have no time for delays!"

Janelle was in the back of the line due to her last name starting with 's' but she didn't care. It was graduation day. She had made it. Four years of hard work. She was trying to hide her stomach, but in the past six weeks since her gown had become a little tight. In front of her, some students were talking amongst themselves.

"Are you excited?"

"Yes! I can't wait to start college. I just got accepted to NYU. Where are you going?"

"I'm going to Lehman. My mother went there, so it was important that I go there as well. I have no clue what I'm going to declare as my major... hey Janelle, what are you doing after graduation?"

Janelle blushed by being asked. "Uhh, I'm taking a break...traveling abroad, seeing the motherland, checking out Europe for a bit... finding myself, you know?"

"Cool!"

"Alright, show time. We'll be calling names signaling you to come in. Get ready!"

Everyone straightened up as the band inside started playing "Pomp and Circumstance".

Inside, among the audience, Luanne and Chester Simms sat and waited patiently. Luanne had a Kodak disc camera ready to snap pictures of Janelle while Chester was folding his arms in annoyance.

"You sure that ol' camera even works?" he asked. "It's got to be at least 10 years old."

"I'm sure, tested it yesterday," she replied and looked at him. "You *could* be more pleasant about this. Our only child is graduating high school!"

"She ain't my child," Chester mumbled. "My child wouldn't be six months pre..."

"Hush!" she interrupted. "I'll hear none of that today! If you can't say anything positive, just sit there quietly and pout!"

She gasped as Janelle marched inside. "There she is!" She pointed her camera and pressed the shutter as the students walked against the wall to the back where they gathered. The principal addressed the crowd of faculty, students, and parents. There was a performance by the senior music class, a poetry reading, then the school valedictorian delivered her commencement speech.

"And now without further ado, I present the class of 1994!" The principal announced and proceeded to read off the students' names in alphabetical order.

Once the ceremonies were over, all the students exited the school without incident. The parents were then dismissed to meet their children out in the courtyard. Janelle was saying her goodbyes to her friends, exchanging hugs and posing for pictures when Luanne approached her in tears.

"My baby! You did it! I'm so proud of you!"

Chester was stoic as he stood and waited, watching them. Janelle sensed her father's anger, and she looked down sheepishly.

Luanne noticed the tension and resolved to do something about it. "Baby, why don't you take a picture with your father real quick? I'm sure he's just as proud of you as I am."

Chester began to protest. "I am not taking no picture..."

"CHESTER!" Luanne yelled, startling everybody around them. She took a step toward her husband. "You will NOT ruin this day for her. Now stand over there and smile or I will make *such* a scene, you hear what I'm saying!?" she ordered him through her teeth. He looked at the scowl on her face and matched it with a scowl of his own, then slowly walked over to Janelle's side.

She held up her camera. "Okay, smile..." She waited a moment as he refused to grin.

"CHESTER!" she yelled again.

He relented and put on a fake, toothy smile while Janelle smiled nervously.

The camera flashed, and she cooed, "There, that wasn't so bad, was it?"

Chester grunted, "Alright, I gotta get back to the office."

Janelle was once again disappointed. "Daddy?"

Luanne waved her hand. "Oh, let him go. We're meeting Auntie Jessie and her daughter at the Central Park Zoo."

She perked up. "Cousin Missy!? Oh, I haven't seen her in years!"

Luanne sighed as she saw Chester a half-block up the street, walking away. She shook her head in frustration at her husband's stubbornness and led Janelle away from the school.

Alex walked through the library floor, heading toward the exit after finishing her shift at four o'clock. She planned to only stay at Hunter College for an hour, then meet Janelle at Central Park. She made sure Tanya and Lakeshia were upstairs, so they didn't see her leave. The page left the branch unbeknownst to anyone.

When she arrived at the campus, it took her a while to find Lowe Plaza, where the party was being held. The guy guarding the door to the gallery asked for ID and she handed him her second fake ID she swiped from Steven the forger with a smile on her face. Once inside, she scanned the area carefully. The space was usually for art exhibits or theater events related to the Kaye Playhouse next door.

Music was playing from a sound system as college students danced, drank and ate while partying the night away. Drinks and snacks were offered by caterers in business suits. There was a solid number of guys, but more than double the number of girls, some dressed reserved, while others were scantily clad. After searching for ten minutes for Mr. Karl Kani from the nightclub, she had seen enough and was about to leave.

Then a familiar face approached her. "Heeeeeyyyy! Glad you made it, Spunky Brewster!"

Instead of Karl Kani clothes, the so-called party promoter was wearing the school's colors with a Hunter College sweater.

"My name is Alex, okay? Enough with the nicknames."

"It's cool, my name's James... as in "Ladies Love Cool James." He flashed a smile.

She rolled her eyes. He was hardly in the same comparison with the popular rap star he referenced. "Look, I'm not staying long, so hurry along with the introductions, connections, and formalities..."

"All in due time. Make yourself comfortable. Walk around on your own for a bit, have a snack and take a drink."

Alex shrugged and reached for a glass on a tray that was held by one of the caterers when James caught her by the wrist. "Ah, ah, ah... you're pretending to be 18, not 21. The light stuff is at the table over there." He pointed to her left.

She noticed he was still holding her wrist and pulled away.

"Sorry, just looking out for you. Guys be slipping stuff in drinks trying to take advantage. Stick with me and the sodas, okay?"

She nodded. "Okay, just don't be grabbing me."

"Hey, it's all about respect... Alex," he said with a slight bow.

The gesture made her more relaxed. She even let a smile creep across her normally serious face.

"So, yeah, help yourself to some treats, walk around and show them dance moves. Anyone asks, you're with me. I'm going to talk to a couple of scouts and see if we can get an introduction going. Maybe even an audition, cool?"

"You better be real with me, or I'm bouncing," she got serious again.

"Hey, my actions speak for themselves. I'm not like all those 'fake line' brothers... you'll see."

More like 'weak line' brothers, instead, she thought, then just nodded as he stepped away.

Once alone, Alex started making her way through the crowd, enjoying the music.

James walked through the crowd, greeting other students, male and female. He stopped at a male student who was drinking a glass of vodka. The student's dark eyes surveyed the room like a leopard stalking a herd of antelope on an African landscape.

"I got the perfect girl lined up for you, Chapter Leader Longstroke, sir," James said as he pointed at Alex, who was dancing by herself.

"Well, well, well, you did good, Poser-in-training James. You did real good... I'm actually familiar with this particular dragon," the fraternity leader admitted.

"Really?"

"Do you know who she is and who's her father?"

"No."

He chuckled. "You should really do your homework..." He leaned in and whispered the secret in James' ear.

"Really?" James looked out to her again.

The fraternity leader nodded and handed him a green pill. "Here, take this... and when she's ready to be slayed, you find me."

"Yes, sir!"

It was five-thirty when Janelle walked into the branch. She had changed out of her gown into regular clothes. Lakeshia and Tanya emerged from the shelves and met her at the entrance.

"Hey there, college girl, thought you were out celebrating today!" Tanya said.

"I was, have you seen Alex?" Janelle asked.

"We thought she was with you. She left early at four, I think. I didn't see her leave," Lakeshia said.

Janelle shook her head. "No, I waited for her and she didn't show up."

"Wait, you don't think she went to that college party, do you?" Lakeshia asked.

Across the floor at the circulation desk, Robin tilted his head, eavesdropping on the conversation.

"She promised us she wouldn't, Leelee..." Janelle said. "...I'm starting to think she did."

"You don't think anything's going to happen to her, do you?"

"They're going to drug her."

The three girls turned to see Robin walking toward them. Gerry was temporarily watching both sides of the desk behind him.

"They're going to slip something in her drink, even if it's water..." he continued, "...she'll become lightheaded and someone will suggest she sit down somewhere isolated until she feels better. They'll take her upstairs and put her in a bedroom. She'll be giggling and totally out of it. She won't even notice them slipping off her clothes. They'll run a train on her."

"A train..? What's a train?" Lakeshia asked.

"It's when three or more guys have sex with a girl one after another," Tanya whispered.

"Over, and over, and over again..." Robin let out a sinister chuckle.

Janelle gave him a look of disgust.

Tanya stepped forward and pleaded, "You have to help us find her and prevent that!"

"The hell I do!" he snarled. "The only thing I *have* to do in life is eat, drink, breathe and die!"

Lakeshia said, "Look, I know the two of you can't stand each other but you seriously can't stand idly by and let this happen!"

"Oh no? Watch me!" *If they only knew...* he thought, remembering the racially insensitive practical joke Alex played when he worked his first Saturday at 58th Street. He was sworn to secrecy by Augustus under penalty of repaying a lump sum of money he accepted to sweep the incident under the rug.

"You're disgusting!" Janelle stormed off and exited the branch.

Lakeshia grabbed his arm and pleaded, "Robin, please, look at it this way... you do this, you prove that you're better than her!"

He turned his back to the pair. "That's the problem, Leelee... I'm not." He walked back to the circulation desk.

Lakeshia dropped her head as Tanya gritted her teeth. "What are we gonna do now?" Lakeshia asked Tanya.

"We're going to do this... ourselves."

The branch closed at six with no headaches or problems. Robin saw Tanya and Lakeshia rush out, on their way to Hunter College. Guilt was eating him up inside. *Just let it be and go home.*

He let out a sigh, picked up the phone and dialed a number. "Hey Jarvis, it's me Robin... your cousin went to Hunter, right? Does he still have his college sweater?"

Alex was talking to a Hunter sophomore who was working on his undergraduate degree in economics, when James walked over and tapped the guy's shoulder, then chucked his thumb.

As he left, Alex yelled, "Hey! He was nice!"

"He's a nobody. Besides, you've caught the eye of someone better," James explained as he pointed across the room.

Alex strained her neck to see a dark-haired white man wearing a red blazer and black slacks. He looked like a movie theater usher to her.

"Who's he?"

"You ever hear of "Changing Faces"?"

"No."

"They're an R&B duo. Got a song coming out called 'Stroke you Up'. It's going to be big," James explained. "And *he's* directing their music video." He waved to acknowledge their presence. The man waved back.

Alex was less than impressed. "Okay."

James turned and looked at her after waving. "He *also* wants YOU to be the lead in the video. The video has a storyline about a girl hooking up with a guy... you would be that girl!"

Alex raised her eyebrows. "Word? You serious?"

"Yeah, he just needs to talk to you. Make sure you can take direction... so check that attitude of yours, okay?"

She nodded then he said, "Great, follow me. We're going to one of the rooms upstairs."

He moved through the crowd toward a staircase at the corner and she closely followed behind.

Tanya and Lakeshia emerged from the 6-train at the Hunter College station. Once upstairs and outside on the street, they looked around the campus. The trio of buildings was connected by a pair of overhead glass hallways. Students were walking around, mixed in with regular pedestrians.

"Geez, where do we even start?" Lakeshia whined.

"Excuse me?" someone said behind them.

The girls turned to see a homeless man sitting in a corner. There was a shopping cart full of aluminum cans next to him, along with several sacks and garbage bags of his belongings.

"Can either of you spare some change so I can get something to eat?"

Tanya cringed. "Sorry, can't help you." She then grabbed Lakeshia by her arm and pulled her toward the east building. "C'mon, let's check here first."

After asking around and checking flyers on several bulletin boards, the pair learned there was a fraternity event at a gallery near the Kaye Playhouse. When they arrived at the entrance and saw that IDs were being checked, Lakeshia turned to Tanya. "Great, how are we going to get in?"

Tanya looked over Lakeshia's shoulder to see a group of well-dressed caterers smoking in front of a door around the corner from the entrance.

"Think I found our way, let's go!"

The door to an empty room opened as James led Alex inside. He flipped a light switch on, and the space lit up from fixtures in the ceiling. There were no chairs, only a table a few feet away.

"Okay, see that X on the floor with tape? That's a mark. You stand right there and when the director walks in, you put on your biggest smile, got it? Really pour it on. 80% of this business is charm."

Alex was getting excited now, feeling the moment. She had forgotten all about Janelle and celebrating her graduation, focusing instead on the task at hand.

"Speak clearly, try not to stutter, and keep your answers short. This ain't Miss America. He's not going to ask you how to save the whales or anything..."

"Okay, okay, quit fussing all over me!"

"Hey, he puts you in that video, you'll get $1000.00. 10% goes to me, so excuse me for—"

"Hold up!" Alex interrupted. "10%?! We ain't sign no contract or anything. What makes you think you're owed 10%?"

"Hey, agents get 15% in this biz. 10 is charity! You don't wanna be down, there's the door," he pointed. "I can find someone else who wants to be famous."

Alex quietly thought it over. She got this far, and he'd been on the level up to this point. "5%," she said, "Then we got a deal."

James blinked hard in astonishment. "You're crazy...nine!" he countered.

"Six," she said back.

"Eight!"

"Seven! Final offer." Alex held her chin up, preparing to walk out the door.

"Fine, 7%" James agreed. *Not that it mattered,* he thought and then pulled out the green capsule that was given to him. "Here, take this mint. There's a bottle of Evian on the table."

As he started walking toward the door, he called back, "I'll leave the door unlocked for him. He should be here in five minutes."

Alex popped the capsule in her mouth and took a swig of the water. "Fine."

"Remember, stand on that mark. Big smile!" He closed the door behind him.

"Jerk," she whispered.

Alex walked back to the X from the table and stood there waiting. Her eyes started to suddenly lose focus as a wave of dizziness overcame her. With her knees buckling, she started to breathe heavily and the room started to spin. Before she could cry out for help, everything went black.

Despite sneaking in through the back door, Tanya had no clue where to start looking for Alex. There were at least a hundred people in the room. The ratio was seventy-thirty girls to guys.

"How'd they get all these girls in here?" Lakeshia asked in awe.

"I have no clue but we..."

"HEY!" a voice called out, freezing the pair in their tracks. A nerdy student approached them with an accusing finger. He had on a varsity sweater with a sticker labeled "POSER" on the upper left side.

"You two are kinda young, ain't you? You sure you're in the right place? Because if you're not, you got to go, now!"

Tanya stammered, "We belong here, uhhh, ummm, we're... we're..."

"These fine ladies are with *me*," a voice came from behind them, accompanied by a pair of arms around each of their shoulders.

"And you are?" the poser challenged.

"Clemente, Roberto Clemente," Robin answered. He was wearing a varsity sweater as well, but with no label. In a sorry attempt at a disguise, he had a thin mustache that was penciled in with eyeliner. He also gelled his hair straight and to the side. "Foreign exchange student... from the Dominican Republic."

The girls looked behind at the sound of the familiar voice. Tanya nearly laughed as Lakeshia's eyes went wide.

"Clemente?" the nerd asked. "From the Dominican Republic?"

"It's a common name... for obvious reasons. Ladies, I've been looking all over for you. I turn to get you something to drink and you wander off? Tsk, tsk, tsk..."

Tanya and Lakeshia looked at each other and then both started rubbing their hands up and down his chest while smiling. "Sorry, Bobby, dear..." Tanya cooed.

"Okay, *Bobby*... just making sure we don't have any teenagers in the party, you understand?" the nerd asked.

"I understand completely," Robin said with a dismissive wave.

Robin led the girls to mingle among the crowd. When they were out of earshot Tanya asked, "Is that eyeliner on your lip?" and began to laugh.

"Keep it down and look for Alex. We don't have much time!"

He lowered his arms and stepped in front of them. "You two nearly got caught because you look like nuns in here. You need to show more skin!" He reached out to grab Tanya's shoulders and ripped the sleeves to her sweatshirt off. "What the fu…" she gasped as he then produced the switchblade he took from Vickie Florence and slashed the bottom-half of the shirt revealing her belly button.

"Shit! You could have warned me, man… my gear ain't cheap!" Tanya barked.

"It sure tore apart like it was," he replied, then turned to Lakeshia.

He pulled out the bottom of her blouse and tied a knot that rested just below her bosom. With a quick slice, he made a slit on the right side of her skirt that stopped five inches from her waist. Her thigh was barely visible due to her thin legs.

"You got a set of chopsticks kiddo and nothing to show, but it'll do."

She huffed at the insult and winced when he reached up at the top of her head. "One last thing…" he said and wrapped a rubber band around a handful of hair to make a ponytail.

"Alright, back at my side, and keep your hands on me at all times. I'll try to get us upstairs to see if there are any bedrooms." The girls resumed their positions as they returned to the crowd. "Watch those hands, Leelee…" he whispered.

"I got that dragon lined up to be *slayed*, sir," James whispered with some excitement.

He was in the hallway talking to the fraternity's chapter leader, the white man from the crowd. "That's *Chapter Leader Longstroke*, sir, Poser-in-training James," he corrected sharply. "Learn those formalities. They're crucial to the elevation of your status."

"Yes, Chapter Leader Longstroke, sir! My apologies, Chapter Leader Longstroke, sir!"

"Ah, that's better. You gave her that pill I handed you? What bull-shit story did you tell?"

"Told her you were a music video director," James chuckled. "She negotiated my cut like a real business deal. What a sucker. She should be unconscious on the floor by now, Chapter Leader Longstroke, sir!"

"Alright, good job, Poser-in-training James... help me pick her up and get her in my room," he instructed as they walked back to the door. "I'll make sure she gets a *'special'* audition," he added with a smirk.

After moving through the crowd downstairs, Robin and the girls found the staircase leading to the second floor. There was a long hallway in front of them with doors on either side.

"Geez, it's like a 'Needle in a Haystack' up in here!" Tanya said.

Robin scanned the doors, then sniffed the air. "I smell weed, and there's a red light coming from the bottom of that door on the right." Robin darted ahead and leaned his ear on the door. He waved them over.

"I'll knock to get him to the door, then you ask if you can join the fun, got it?"

They both nodded and Robin knocked on the door, then stepped aside.

"Find another room, we're busy!" someone yelled from inside.

"Hey, is it just one-on-one in there or can we join in on all the fun?" Tanya called out, Lakeshia giggled for an added effect.

They heard footsteps approach the door. Robin counted three seconds and then rushed the door shoulder first. It slammed inside and the thud of a body hitting the floor echoed in the hallway. Robin stepped over the fraternity leader as the girls stepped inside. Lakeshia closed the door behind her. They found Alex passed out on a King-size bed surrounded by an assortment of drug paraphernalia. A red light bulb was attached to a ceiling fan.

Robin found an entire bookshelf of vintage liquors and spirits, everything from Thunderbird to Absinthe. "Sweet Mary Christmas! These guys are hardcore!" He ran to check on Alex on the bed.

"What kind of kinky shit...?" Tanya grunted with a look of disgust.

"Alex! Alex, wake up! Hey!" Robin shook and slapped her on her face, but got little or no reaction. "She's out, help me stand her up!"

Lakeshia was standing over the leader as he lay unconscious on the floor. "You sonofabitch!" she swung her leg back to deliver a swift kick, but Tanya stopped her. "Don't! He'll wake up!" She turned to Robin. "We gotta get out of here!"

There were no windows, but there was another door that led to the bathroom. Lakeshia ran in and found a window next to the toilet. "Over here!" she yelled.

Robin carried Alex in his arms and sat her on the toilet seat. He then checked the window. It was big enough to step out of and only a one-story drop to the ground. He came back to the bedroom, pulled out the switchblade and ripped the sheets off the bed.

"Okay, you two climb down, take this comforter with you. I'll drop her from the window and you catch her stretching it out like a fireman's life net."

"Are you crazy!? That's not gonna work!" Lakeshia screamed. "Let's just sneak her out!"

They heard a groan and turned to see the fraternity leader slowly coming to. Robin had his makeshift rope of bedsheets out the window already. "C'mon!" he yelled. Tanya slid down and caught herself to a stop. Lakeshia slowly shimmied, nervous and not looking down. They stretched the comforter, grabbing each corner.

Robin closed the bathroom door, buying more time and lifted Alex to the window. He stuck her out feet first, holding her wrists. "Ready down there?" he called.

"Ready!" the girls replied.

Robin let go and Alex's limp body fell backward, landing square in the middle. The girls held their ground, making sure she wouldn't drop through and hit the ground.

"We did it!" Lakeshia cheered.

"I can't believe that worked," Tanya exclaimed.

A huge garbage bag landed next to Alex.

"What the...Robin! What are you doing?"

"Saving the booze!"

"Really?!!?" they yelled, then lowered the comforter slowly and picked up Alex.

"There's a Liverty Cab waiting. Run around back to 69th street! I'll catch up with you! Don't forget the booze!"

"How are you getting out!?" Lakeshia asked. But Robin was gone from the window.

The leader was on one knee, shaking his head. He looked around, wondering what was going on. Inside the bathroom, Robin looked around for a weapon or something to cause a distraction. He pulled open the shower curtain and found a hanger with an interesting choice of costume.

"Who's in there? Come on out, now!"

Two kicks and the door gave way. The fraternity leader gasped as he saw a strange man wearing a black cape with matching mask and sombrero.

"What the hell?" he yelled.

"QUE HORA ES?!" Robin screamed as he rambled incoherently in Spanish. The outfit disoriented the student enough to freeze him in place.

"Who you calling gay?"

Robin rushed him and the two wrestled throughout the bedroom, crashing through everything. They were both screaming as he continued ranting in Spanish.

"HOY ES MIERCOLES!" Robin caught the fraternity leader's wrist and applied a judo flip that sent him crashing on the bed. Robin turned around in time to see the door open and two other members wearing red jackets standing in the hallway.

"Hey, you!" one called out.

He dove between the two and darted down the hallway.

A voice behind him yelled, "Stop him! Somebody grab that maniac!"

There were gasps of surprise from students on the floor as Robin weaved his way around everyone, his cape flapping in the air. The exit was in sight until he slammed face-first into the stomach of a 7'2 400-pound Linebacker and bounced several feet back. "Damn!" he yelled. It felt like running into a wall.

Arms came from all directions as Robin was held and stood up by four members while the leader came down the stairs. A smirk was on his face. "I forgot I had that costume for a bit of role-playing later." He shook his head. "Shame it doesn't look good on you... search him for ID!" he ordered.

Outside, Lakeshia and Tanya were still waiting for a sign that Robin was okay.

"I don't like this... we need to do something," Lakeshia said.

"I got an idea. Hold Alex and give me that bag for a second." Tanya reached in and pulled out the green bottle of Absinthe, then tore a piece of cloth from the rope of bedsheets.

"I'll be right back!" she said and took off running.

Lakeshia was barely able to hold Alex up by herself. "Hey!" she cried out, then started grunting. "Damn Alex, what do you be eating!?"

"No ID on him, Chapter Leader Longstroke, sir!" one of the guys answered after a thorough search.

Robin laughed out loud when hearing the leader's name for the first time. "What? Longstroke? What kind of dumb name is that?"

"I'd think twice before disrespecting the Dragonslayers Fraternity... Zorro The Gay Blade."

That got a laugh from everyone in the room.

"Uh, this is *your* costume, remember? Why the hell didn't you just say 'Zorro'? What are you, a Film Major or something?"

Longstroke slapped him across the face with the back of his hand. "SILENCE!" he barked. He then removed the hat, mask and pulled the string that tied the cape around his neck. The cape fell to the floor as Robin looked back at him, his cheek red from the slap.

"You are SO going to pay for that!" he hissed.

The leader studied his face. "I don't recognize you from campus. How did you get in here and where's the girl?"

"Who? The 16-year-old you just tried to rape!?" Robin yelled out loud. Another slap came, along with a punch and a kick to the ribs.

Tanya ran back to the window from around the corner with the bottle and the sheet sticking out on fire.

"How the hell did you do that?" Lakeshia yelled.

"The bum from the corner had a lighter. I hope this works, I've only seen it in the movies!" She hurled the bottle toward the window. It landed inside and exploded with a crash. The bathroom ignited and smoke blew out into the open sky.

"Put him on his knees. I'm making an example of those who crash the parties of the Dragonslayers..."

The four applied pressure and made Robin kneel.

"I don't know who you are, fat boy, but you're in a heap of trouble!" Longstroke turned to address the room. "What say we do to him, brothers?" The room of men roared cheers of suggestions. One of the men holding Robin said, "I think we oughta strip him naked, grease him up and toss him into the ladies' sorority house!"

There were more cheers at the idea.

"That... sounds like a good time, actually," Robin replied with a grin.

There was muttering around the room as they agreed. The leader shook his head and rolled his eyes.

"You're not too good at this whole 'hazing' thing, are you?" Robin taunted.

"SHUT UP!" Longstroke yelled.

Everyone froze as smoke started to billow down from upstairs, followed by a smoke alarm going off. Sounds of concern began to fill the room. "What the hell is that? Someone check it out!" Longstroke ordered. A girl screamed, "Fire!" and everyone started running for the exits. Robin took this time to run for it himself in all the chaos.

The fraternity leader was followed by three other guys as he ran upstairs. People were running everywhere. They made it back to the room and saw the bathroom fire burning ablaze.

"Get a fire extinguisher. Campus PD will shut us down if we don't contain this!" he ordered.

"Oh my God, Tanya! You burned the place down!" Lakeshia squealed.

"C'mon, Robin should be able to make it out now..." she nodded.

The pair carried Alex and went around back, heading north toward 69th Street. Cervantes had been circling the block for the last ten minutes, looking for Robin. He spotted two girls carrying another and honked the horn. They walked up to the curb and he got out.

"Are you girls with Robin?" he asked.

"Yeah. You the cabbie he talked about?"

"Yes, where is he? We have to get out of here!"

A voice called out to them, "CERVANTES!"

They all turned to see Robin running toward them. "Start the car, GO!" he yelled.

Tanya opened the door. Lakeshia went in first and helped as they eased Alex in the middle, then Tanya climbed in. Cervantes was back in the driver's seat as Robin grabbed the handle to the front passenger door.

He pulled the handle a few times to find it locked. "Let me in up front!" he pleaded.

"After him!" someone yelled, and five or six fraternity brothers started rushing toward them.

"No one rides up front. Those are the rules!" the cabbie explained.

Robin pounded on the glass. "C'mon man! There's no time! There's no room! We gotta go, now!"

Cervantes just looked back at him with a blank stare, shrugging his shoulders. The group was getting closer. Robin went to the backseat. After a few moments, the door pulled closed, and the cab took off.

The fire was put out in minutes. Fortunately, the shower curtain was the only item that caught on fire.

"Sonofabitch!" muttered Longstroke. "This guy's gonna pay!"

"Campus Police are here. We're probably gonna get probation for this..." a fraternity brother said.

"Clean up the bedrooms and stall them downstairs. NO ONE comes up here, got it? I'll handle all this. I got some pull with the board."

They all dispersed, leaving Longstroke alone in the bathroom. He looked ahead to the open window, then down at the floor. Something caught his eye. There was a white card covering part of the tile floor. He bent down and slipped the card out from under the toilet. Lifting it from the floor, he turned it around and smiled.

It was an identification card from Baruch College, with a picture of their party crasher. A Mister Robin S. Walker.

CHAPTER FIFTEEN

"Where does Alex live? Either of you two know?" Robin asked.

"No, but Nellie does. We should go to her house. She lives in Kingsbridge."

"Heading toward the FDR," Cervantes announced.

"I hope you saved that bag of booze," Robin said.

"It's in the trunk," Tanya replied.

Alex was slumped over at the far end of the backseat while Tanya was on the opposite end. Seated in the middle, Lakeshia was sitting on Robin's lap, her eyes wide open and very nervous.

"For the last time, Leelee... that's my *belt buckle*..." Robin said, steadying her in their awkward position.

The Liverty Cab pulled up to the building at ten. Tanya got out first, followed by Lakeshia, who couldn't resist rubbing her behind. Robin stepped out, glaring at Lakeshia with Alex in his arms. She was finally coming to, but still groggy and moaning.

"What are you going to do?" he asked.

Tanya was already on the intercom explaining everything.

Lakeshia wrapped her arm under Alex to hold her up. "We're putting together a story. We're gonna call her parents and say we were all celebrating Janelle's graduation and we're doing a sleepover. We've done it a few times before during school recess... they should buy it."

"Sneaking around and spreading lies, what would Miss Garrett say?... Tootie."

"Huh?"

"Nevermind." He went to the trunk and got his garbage bag, then closed it again. With two taps on the trunk, Cervantes pulled off and disappeared into the night.

Janelle opened the door to her building. "My parents said she can spend the night. I told my mother she got food poisoning and she'll sleep it off." Lakeshia nodded and turned around to find Robin gone. She looked at opposite ends of the sidewalk, wondering what happened to him. Tanya waved her over, and she carried Alex inside.

Robin climbed the steps to the downtown side of the elevated 1-train tracks at the 231st Street Station. He didn't want another stare down with Janelle so the moment she stepped out of her building he quickly ran across the street and hid behind a parked car. The train arrived, and he took it back to Manhattan.

An hour later he arrived at Walter's place, knocking on the door. Walter answered, and he walked in.

"Robin, what the..."

"Shhhhhhhh..." he said with his finger to his lips. "Yo, call all the boys over, get some glasses, and put on the '36 Chambers' tape...have I got a fairy tale to tell you." He pulled out a bottle of Wild Turkey and took a swig. "You motherfuckers ain't gonna believe this shit!"

Forty-five minutes later, Jarvis and Mouse came over with a few others. Each was given a glass of Jack Daniels as the guys drank well into the night. Robin had told his story over and over again in the last hour. There were at least twelve of them spread out on three different couches.

"So I rushed him yelling, 'QUE HORA ES?' and he yells, 'I ain't gay!' and I'm knocking the shit out of him!" he laughed. "It was hilarious. I thought that stupid bitch was done for! What a night!"

Everyone else was laughing around the room when suddenly the music stopped.

"Huh?! What the fuck? Put that Wu-Tang back on. Method Man is next, you know? The M-E-T-H-O-D Man! Put that shit back on!"

"Hey man, we've been listening to that same tape forever. I got something new here you should hear. There's more to rap than Wu-Tang Clan and A Tribe called Quest."

Robin looked at the one speaking and didn't recognize the visitor. "Blasphemy! Who tha? Who the fuck are you, anyways?" He nodded to Jarvis. "Yo, Jarvis, pass me your gat, nigga I'm about to bust a cap in this kid's ass..."

Everyone laughed as Robin attempted to stand up and address the newcomer. "Listen to me, muthafuckah...there is NOTHING more to rap and hip hop than...Wu-Tang, Tribe called Quest and Leaders of the New School...THAT'S IT! No Fu-Schnickens, no Das-Efx, no EPMD..."

"Fuck you, I like EPMD," another visitor said across the room.

Robin grabbed an empty bottle and tossed it, missing the person my inches. "Shaddap!... now, where was I? No Big Daddy Kane, no Kool Moe Dee, no Eric B and Rakim, none of those corny ass 80's rappers! RUN-DMC, Biz Markie, Fat Boys, Doug E. Fresh, Slick Rick...all that beat boxing shit! That music was cool when I was 10-years-old, but this is the 90's. Their time is done!"

There were cheers and dismissive sounds that divided the room.

"All nine members of Wu-Tang are gonna release solo joints, you'll see... Busta Rhymes is gonna go solo, too... and Tribe will keep dropping album after album till they're in their fifties and still be rocking. Tribe will live on forever!"

Jarvis finally stood up, trying to get Robin to sit. "Alright, alright Robin, calm down, man."

"Put that damn tape back on!" Robin ordered.

"Okay, I'll put it back, but give a listen to these guys first okay? Just check them out..." The new guy pulled out the tape and tossed the case in the air. Robin caught it and looked at the cover.

"Who the fuck are they? Let me see this cover... hmmm, Lost Boyz? What kinda Peter Pan shit is this? They can't even spell, and they all rocking braids. Fuck are they, a spinoff group of Das-Efx? Or some rasta niggas?" He waved his hand. "Fine, put it on! If I don't like the first three songs, we going back to Wu-Tang."

Twenty minutes later everyone was singing choruses from several songs, including "Lifestyles of the Rich and Shameless" and "Jeeps, Lex Coupes, Bimaz & Benz".

"Alright, alright!!" Robin yelled. "I'm man enough to admit I'm wrong... sometimes! These cats are okay!"

The rest of the group agreed.

"I'm buying that album first thing tomorrow!" Jarvis yelled.

"Word, great call there, kid... whoever the fuck you are!" Robin said with a boisterous laugh and took a swig of tequila.

Soon, the group was laughing and drinking again until someone started a snapping contest.

"Your mother is so stupid, she thought Garfield the cat was a former president of the United States!"

"Yo, YOUR mother is so dumb, she took a spoon to the super bowl!"

"Your mama so dumb it took her three hours to watch *60 Minutes!*"

Everyone was laughing along and then turned to Robin.

"C'mon Robin, give it a try!" Mouse said.

"Ummm, okay..."

The group looked at him and waited.

"Your mother is so stupid she put Hot Wheels in her hair and hot curlers on those orange plastic tracks."

Silence filled the room as they all looked at each other, then an explosion of laughter erupted while Robin passed out.

Friday morning, the Dragonslayers fraternity was the joke of the Hunter College campus. There were repercussions that would have to be dealt with, but the punishment they received was light. The members were having a briefing placing blame for what went wrong last night.

"First off, bring me that idiot Poser-in-training who invited the girl. Joe, was it? No, James! He's accountable for this. Her friends were the girls that came to find her, and to find out she's 16 on top of who her parents are...he's in for a world of hurt."

There were nods from everyone around the table.

"We're adjourned, for now. I'm going on a personal outing. Don't wait up."

"I don't think you should go by yourself," a subordinate remarked.

"I'll be fine. He won't know I'm coming for him."

Walter filled a cup of cold water and tiptoed into the living room where Robin was asleep on a couch in the living room. He poured the cup over the sleeping teen who started screaming and sat up with a start.

"Now, we're even," Walter said with a smile, remembering when Robin got him in the shower.

Robin had a choking fit and looked at his friend. "You're lucky I have stuff to do this morning, or you'd be limping to a hospital."

"I couldn't resist. I made breakfast to make up for it."

"No time. I'll grab something on the way. I gotta go!"

"Wait, class ain't for another hour. What's the rush?"

"Tell the professor I'm not coming to class today. Something came up, she'll understand. It's my first absence."

Robin was already heading to the door. Walter was close behind asking, "If you're not going to class where are..." The door slammed before he finished the question.

Chapter Leader Longstroke arrived at 23rd Street and Lexington and surveyed the Baruch College campus carefully. He was willing to wait all day for a chance to catch this Robin Walker and have his way with him.

Robin arrived at the study hall looking for Shinju, but there was nobody there. He checked a couple of floors looking around, but it was still early. A growl from his stomach echoed in the hallway. He needed to eat something. There were a few possibilities for something to eat across the street, so he headed toward the building's exit.

A Dunkin Donuts was down the street nearby. Robin stayed on 23rd but left Lexington heading east. He was still buzzed from all the drinking last night and would have been an embarrassment in class. There were questionable glances from people as he passed. He *was* still wearing his clothes from yesterday, and his hair was still straight from the mousse, but he didn't have a care in the world.

It was a stroke of luck, or maybe even genius, Longstroke thought as he caught the back of Robin Walker walking down 23rd Street heading toward 2nd Avenue. He followed him from a distance, stalking his prey like any other would-be conquest from his past. Blending in the crowd, knowing he wasn't discovered yet, he continued to stay out of sight.

Longstroke saw him enter a donut shop and waited at the corner to see where he would come out and go to next. After waiting for five minutes, he wondered if he missed the interloper coming out somehow, but his doubts were eliminated when he saw him emerge from the store and double back to 2nd Avenue.

Robin was eating a jelly donut and looking for a park bench to sit and eat the bagel. He also brought a cup of orange juice to collect his thoughts. He was approaching 1st Avenue, still walking. He turned south to 20th Street entering Peter Cooper Village. Longstroke was still close behind, wondering where Robin could be going.

The fraternity leader turned a corner and felt something land on his right side. He instinctively turned his head to see a glob of jelly on his shoulder. A shadow suddenly appeared, indicating that someone was behind him. In that split second, he had no time to react.

"Peek-a-Boo!" Robin yelled, followed by a blow to his head.

Longstroke woke up in a large, dimly-lit room. He looked around to see a table, a tripod in front of him, and a video camera. A few feet away was a door where Robin was talking to someone. Looking down, he found himself tied to a chair. His hands were behind him, but his fingers felt wet. Robin finished the conversation and closed the door, then approached while holding a manila folder in one hand, and a jelly donut in the other.

"The old 'shoulder trick'," he started, waving his donut. "Drop something on the shoulder, then knock them out when they look that way. Works with pickpockets, muggers, and other criminals." Robin took a bite for effect and smiled.

Longstroke just stared back at him.

"Feel free to scream your head off. We're in an underground parking lot at an isolated far end of Alphabet City," Robin said.

"I don't feel like—"

Robin socked him across his jaw, interrupting the comment, as the fraternity leader's head dropped into his chest.

Robin then propped his head up by his chin and looked at him eye-to-eye. "I told you, you were gonna pay for hitting me, didn't I?" He let his head drop down again and stepped away from him.

"Thank you, by the way, for returning my college ID. It costs $15 to get a new one."

"I'm not alone. Others will be looking for me..." he started, a trickle of blood running down his chin.

"Hmmm... nahhh, I don't think so...your ego wouldn't let you do this with help. You thought you could handle me all by yourself. So let's get started. We have PLENTY of time to get to know each other."

"What the hell are you talking about?"

"Oh, let me explain... a few years ago, I beat the shit out of this guy who insulted my girlfriend. Now the two of us are friends, imagine that! Well, that guy's father turned out to be a police lieutenant. As a reward for teaching his son a lesson, this cop gave me access to their resources from time to time."

"How fascinating. What does that have to do with me?" Longstroke asked.

"Glad you asked! I took the liberty of having you fingerprinted, which is why your hands feel funny. Imagine my surprise when I found out you have a bit of a criminal history! I have a copy of your file right here," he said, waving the folder. Robin opened the file and started reading.

"Chapter Leader Longstroke of the Dragonslayers Fraternity at Hunter College...better known as Roy J. Urich. Suspected for sexual assault of over 12 women from March 1992 to April 27th of this year."

A sick sadistic smile grew across his face. "12? Pretty sure that number should be over 15 by now. Must have missed a few."

"Oh there's more. I was just reading the top page, let me continue. Graduated from John F. Kennedy High School, valedictorian. Dean's List, Debate Team, Yearbook editor. Mother was the president of the PTA, father was Kennedy alumni. Did I miss anything?"

"Voted most likely to succeed, but I digress."

"Pledged for the Dragonslayers freshman year, made Chapter Leader by sophomore, now a junior going for a bachelor's degree in Integrated Media Arts... Film, I knew it!" he exclaimed.

Roy rolled his eyes.

"But here's the kicker!... Full name..." he chuckled. "Fauntleroy Julian Urich!" Robin laughed so loud it echoed throughout the empty room. "That is the WHITEST name I've ever heard! Were you named after "Little Lord Fauntleroy"? The book by Frances Hodgson Burnett..."

"Okay, enough fucking fun! I don't think you got it while you were reading my record, but I've never been charged with anything, why? Because I'm rich! I'm powerful! My family RUNS this god-forsaken city, okay? So you better let me go or I'll make YOU disappear, understand?"

"More than you'll ever know, Roy, my boy... which is why I brought all this equipment here..." he gestured to the video camera and tripod. He stepped away and plugged the video camera into an electrical outlet, then put in a VHS tape. The machine clicked on and there was a small preview screen focusing on Roy's face from the chest up. Robin placed the camera on the tripod and pressed a few buttons.

"What do you think? 'SP' records for two hours, but that probably won't be enough, 'SLP' records longer, but then the quality suffers. We want to keep a nice clear picture, right?"

"What is this?" Roy yelled.

"We'll go with the middle, 'LP'...that records for four hours. That should be enough. Okay! We're recording!" Robin propped the camera directly at Roy. The little red light on the machine flashed in the darkness.

"Now, let's talk about..." he checked the file. "Karen Vanderslice. March 17th, 1992."

Roy chuckled. "Okay, I'll play along... Karen... we met at a bar. It was raining and she was a bundle of nerves. Three drinks later and she was flying to the moon..."

In the hours that followed, Robin and Roy discussed over thirty sexual encounters, down to the smallest detail. It made Robin's skin crawl that the deviant before him was walking around with impunity. The fact that he was in such a position to prey upon women with ease, not even Alex deserved what possible heinous acts he had in store for her. Something had to be done.

"Okay, I think we're done here." He clicked the camera off and ejected the tape, which was almost full. "You'll have to excuse me if I look like I'm about to throw-up. I'm extremely nauseated. I have to say... everything about you, even that stupid frat name completely repulses me. I mean, do you even know the purpose of a fraternity? It's not about drinking, doing drugs, and having sex with hundreds of girls... it's about *brotherhood*. It's about having each other's back. Solidarity. Assholes like you are just corrupting an idea created for good intentions."

"Spare me the sanctimonious bullshit!" Roy spat. "We are the future. We are better than anyone else and we will become champions of industry, destined for greatness! The world is ours for the taking, and there's nothing you can do to stop it! You probably don't know it, but there's a great chance me and that black bitch would cross paths down the line anyway!" He nodded to the camera. "You give that tape to the cops, I'll just tell them those confessions were given while I was under duress and they'll be thrown out."

Robin held up the tape and smiled, "Oooh, look at you! You're in the wrong field of study. You should become an attorney, Mister Law Degree! You're a regular Benjamin L. Matlock..." he taunted. "No, no, no, the tape will stay with me...for insurance purposes only."

"Insurance!? Insurance from what?" Roy asked.

"In case you get any ideas... for retaliation. If anything happens to me, copies of this tape will be sent to the police, the media, and the Hunter College faculty. Everybody in the world will know what you did. You'll never get a job or transfer to another school anywhere in the United States."

Roy finally registered something he had never felt before... fear. "W..w... why would I need to retaliate? Wha... what are you doing?" he stammered.

Robin walked to a nearby light switch on the wall. There was a glazed look in his eyes as he stared out to nowhere in particular. "What am I doing?" he asked. He clicked the lights off. "I'm going to make sure you never even THINK about raping a woman... ever again."

"He's been gone since yesterday. I think we need to go to the police," said Chapter Lieutenant Flowereater, the second-in-command at the fraternity. The brothers all convened for their morning briefing Saturday morning. It was ten minutes to eight.

"I think someone has to be missing for 48 hours before you can file..."

One of the pledges ran in the hall. "Brothers! Come quick!" he yelled and then ran back out. Everyone looked at each other, then ran out to follow.

The pledge pushed open the door leading outside and held it. Moments later over fifteen Dragonslayer Brothers filed out and froze in their tracks, stunned. Hanging from a tree branch by his arms with his legs anchored to the trunk, Roy Urich was found suspended and unconscious. He was wearing a woman's dress, a wig, and his face was smeared with blush and eye-shadow.

"Get him the fuck down!" Flowereater ordered as six men ran to the tree a few feet from the building. As they approached, they saw the leader's mouth was covered by a scarf tied to the back of his head and there was writing on his arms. He was cut down and someone checked his pulse.

"We need to get him to a hospital!" a frat brother called out.

"No! Take him inside. We can't let this get out to any newspapers or tv! Nobody says a word about this! You understand? NOBODY!"

The six of them picked up their fallen leader like pallbearers and carried him inside the campus building.

Shinju woke up Sunday morning very concerned. Robin wasn't answering any of her calls and she didn't see him in class Friday. It was as if he fell off the face of the earth. After a shower and breakfast, she called his apartment again and got no answer. She thought about calling Walter, Jarvis or Mouse, but if Robin was doing anything with another woman, they would cover for him. She wouldn't admit it, but she could have a mean jealous streak at times.

There was one friend that wouldn't lie on Robin's behalf. She picked up the phone and dialed Franklin's number. It rang twice before he quickly picked it up.

"Hello?" he answered.

"Good morning, Franklin. It's Shinju. Have you seen Robin? I haven't heard from him since Wednesday and he wasn't in class Friday morning."

"Hey Shinju, my father and I are getting ready for church so I can't stay on the phone long... I haven't seen or heard from him either... but considering the date, I have a good idea where he might be. Got a pen? Take down this address..."

Saint Raymond's Cemetery opened every morning at eight. Shinju stepped out of the cab at the entrance after paying the fare. Inside, the facility was vast with markers beyond what the eye could see. There were signs for the various sections, which were named after saints. She opened a piece of paper with the handwritten directions. "Saint Mark, Range 13..." she read aloud.

After walking for several minutes, she heard a voice in the distance. Moments later, she found Robin on his knees at his grandfather's gravesite.

"...I miss you so much. It's only been a month and I'm barely holding it together..."

He was sobbing while pouring his heart out. He never even saw her walk up behind him.

"...I don't know what to do. I'm regressing to my wildest impulses, like when I was a kid. The kid mom couldn't handle. I need your discipline, I need your guidance. I'm scared of what I might do next."

There were several beer bottles at his side and he was currently nursing a bottle of Miller Lite.

What has he done? she thought. She was afraid to ask him, so she continued to listen.

"I... I met someone. She's so special, Granddaddy...you would have loved her. She's the only thing keeping me sane. We've only known each other for a short time, but I feel we're meant for each other. I... I almost think... you sent her to take care of me, you know? It's just so not fair!" he crumbled to the ground bawling like a newborn.

"Robin," she called out to him.

He gasped and turned around, jumping to his feet, he wiped the tears from his face. "Shinju! How long have you...!? How did you find me?"

She took two steps forward and kissed him, pulling him close and held him for a long, passionate, earth-shattering kiss.

Back at Robin's apartment, there were candles lit everywhere possible in the bedroom. After coming back and taking a shower, he put the infamous 'Mixtape de Romance' in the cassette player and hit 'play'. "Flex" by Mad Cobra started playing in the room. Shinju's naked body sat on the bed before him. Her eyes were mesmerizing as the candlelight danced in her pupils.

He undid the belt to his robe and climbed on the bed to join her. They looked at each other for what felt like hours. They studied each other's facial features, every pore, hair, and especially their lips. There was only one thing that bothered her. She traced her finger down his arm and attempted to remove his glove, the only article of clothing he still was wearing.

Robin recoiled and pulled the hand back. "No," he whispered.

She looked at him. "It's okay."

He shook his head, refusing to budge.

"It's. *Okay*," she insisted.

Robin's eyes went soft and he nodded once. She carefully held the hand and slowly pulled the glove off by the middle finger. Staring at the charred hand, she studied it like a painting from the museum.

"Fascinating. The texture... it's... it's really beautiful."

Robin was moved to tears. He had never felt so vulnerable, not even with Diedre. A tear dropped down his cheek. "Thank you."

They embraced each other. She moaned as he kissed her neck, then laid back and he mounted her. The music and the passion went on, as they did, with breaks in between. "Always" by Atlantic Starr was playing as they were resting between bouts. Once the song ended there was silence, then the tape clicked off.

"Is there music on the other side?" she asked.

"O..o..other side?" he asked.

She stared at him with a hungry look.

"Umm, yeah there's music on side two."

"Same songs?"

"No, a whole different arrangement of songs..."

She got up from the bed, flipped the tape over and pressed Play.

"Good," she said and stepped back to the bed with a smile.

The candles were extinguished, and the room was dark. Even the sun was beginning to set as the lovers spent all day in each other's arms on the bed. Shinju was lying on Robin's chest again, the rhythm of his heartbeat lulling her to sleep like a lullaby.

"No one has ever made me feel this way..." she whispered.

He started to stroke her hair. "I'll take that as a compliment," he said with a chuckle.

She smiled at the dirty joke, then let out a sigh. "Robin?"

"Yeah, baby?"

She decided to let the pet name slide this one time and asked, "Are you going to stay here in this big apartment by yourself?"

He pondered the reasoning behind the question for a moment. "You looking to move in here with me?"

She giggled, "No..."

Robin gave a look of disappointment, but she didn't see it.

"What I mean to say is... would you leave all this behind and start over someplace else?"

"Someplace else, like where?" he asked.

"Nevermind, I was just..." she quickly shook her head, dismissing the subject.

"No, no, no... let's talk about this," he pressed.

"Well, my internship is only for a year, and I'm halfway through so I was thinking in January when it's over..." she turned her head up to look at him, "...of going overseas."

He remained silent.

She looked into his eyes. "Would you go with me?"

He chose his words carefully. "I...would need to prepare. There are some loose ends I'd need to take care of."

She sprang up and moved to sit at the edge of the bed. "I should have never had asked..." she said in a panic. He sat up and put his hand on her shoulder.

"Woah, woah, woah... I didn't say 'no'. I just said I would have to get my things in order first."

She turned to look at him and he put his hand on her face. "I have an inheritance from my grandfather. It won't be ready until November or December."

She smiled, feeling his touch. The hand was soft and soothing as a cloud.

"Once that's resolved, I'll follow you to the ends of the earth. I promise."

He drew himself close to her face. They were cheek-to-cheek, and he whispered in her ear, "I love you Shinju Hasegawa."

She gasped at the declaration, then he took her hand and placed it on his heart.

She whispered something in Japanese that he didn't hear clearly.

"Huh?" he grunted and blushed.

"In Japan, there is technically no official phrase that means 'I love you.'. We express ourselves quite differently when it comes to affection."

"I see."

"But we have three common phrases which define the...degree of love you feel..."

"Like saying it to a family member or about a place or thing like, 'I love pizza' or 'I love school'!"

She nodded and exclaimed, "Yes!" then whispered, "But when you really mean you love someone, we say...*Koishiteru*."

He smiled. "One simple word meaning three of our words...I like it."

They kissed again and then he sighed. "I don't know about you, but I'm *very* hungry!"

"You shouldn't be... you've been *eating Japanese* for hours," she said with a dirty grin.

He playfully slapped her on the ass and she giggled again.

"I'm sure you still have an appetite for *Black Cock* as well..." he laughed, after putting on his robe he walked to the living room. "I'll grab some menus."

Alex arrived at the branch and went upstairs. In the staff room, Lakeshia and Tanya were reading the newspaper. When she saw Alex come in, Tanya waved her over.

"Alex! C'mere! Check this out, you're not gonna believe this!"

"What?" she asked, approaching the table.

Remember those assholes from the party Friday? Read this!" Tanya handed her the Daily News. She read the headline and gasped. There was a picture of the guy with the red jacket at the party. He was tied to a tree and dressed as a woman, complete with makeup.

"Hunter College student falls victim to hazing. 21-Year-old Roy Urich, a Junior at Hunter College was found wearing a dress, wig and makeup while tied to a tree." She read the rest of the article quietly, then gasped and read aloud again, "...a gag was removed and shoved in his mouth were six pairs of women's panties...a proctologist was called in to remove another six..." she trailed off for a moment and then lowered the paper.

"What's a...proctologist?" Lakeshia asked.

"A butt doctor. There were 12 panties shoved in his mouth AND ASS!"

"EWWWWWW!!!! Gross! Who could have done all that to him?"

"Take a wild guess..."

The pages went downstairs and spread out among the floor. Alex pushed her shelving cart to the front of the branch working on the New Books. She tilted her head near the circulation desk and noticed Robin finishing a checkout with a patron. He noticed her looking in his direction and they locked eyes. They didn't say anything but

Alex's glance faltered as several tears streaked down her cheeks followed by a lip quiver.

For a split second, they both acknowledged how close things were for her. Had it not been for his actions, things would have been a lot worse. He nodded slightly. She nodded back and for that brief moment, there was mutual respect between the two bitter enemies.

CHAPTER SIXTEEN

ROBIN CAME HOME AT SIX, DROPPED HIS BOOKS OFF, THEN PICKED UP the phone and dialed Franklin's number. After a few rings, he answered.

"Sup?"

"Meet me at Blimpie's on Broadway in 10 minutes. Sandwiches on me."

"Bet!" he hung up the phone.

Ten minutes later Robin was at a table near the back of the sandwich shop when Franklin walked in and saw him.

"Man, I haven't been here since graduating from P.S. 132. Damn they still got *Robocop*, *Ajax* and *Street Fighter II* arcade games..." He froze as he looked at Robin.

"What?"

Franklin smiled and pointed. "You fucking did it! You climbed Mount Fuji!"

"Will you shut up? The whole damn world doesn't need to know. Sit your ass down!" he hissed.

Franklin laughed. "Cut another notch on the motherfucking belt! How the hell was it?"

Robin looked at him seriously for a moment, then broke into a huge smile. The two laughed, then slapped each other five. Franklin then picked up his sandwich.

"Man, it was amazing. I am *still* on Cloud Nine. I basically zoned out through school and work today."

"Awww."

"Shut up!" Robin shoved him and laughed.

"She called me looking for you, too... what did you do all weekend, besides her?"

He gave an abridged version of the events involving the girls, including his conversation with Roy Urich.

"Wow, I'm surprised you helped her. So you took the information to the press anonymously, then got fucked up and went back to see your grandfather. That's where she found you?"

Robin held up the newspaper with the article about the Hunter student. "Yep. Thanks for sending her there. I appreciate it, man."

"No problem, so did you go back to her place or..."

"Nah, I had the home-field advantage," Robin answered.

"Did she, uh... um, you know... your hand?" Franklin asked while pointing.

He nodded. "She said it was beautiful. I never took it off that one time with Diedre. She's the first... to ever see that vulnerable side of me."

"Wow, well I hope you had a DIFFERENT type of glove on while invading Tokyo."

"Heh, oh yeah... Granddaddy didn't raise no fool... and I ain't raising no babies!... Hahaaa!"

"That's right! Did the tape help or was it one of those quiet moans and deep sighs moments?"

"Tape worked fine...she even liked the songs by Shai, Portrait and Boyz II Men..."

"Wait a minute... those are all songs on *Side Two*. You got to Side Two?!"

"Un-huh, even went back to Side One... then Side Two again, and so on and so on..."

"WHAT!? That's... over... three hours..." Franklin said, astonished.

Robin raised his eyebrows.

"GET THE FUCK OUTTA HERE!" Franklin yelled.

Robin looked at the counter where several customers and employees were looking back at them. "Shhhhh!" he hushed.

"Sorry," he whispered. "Damn man, you got stamina..."

"Think next time we use a 120-minute tape, with a whole updated arrangement of songs..."

"Well..." he shrugged. "I can go that long, too! Who am I kidding, no I can't. Damn!"

Robin snickered at his friend's admission and took a bite from his sandwich.

"Have y'all talked since?" Franklin asked.

"We didn't see each other at school today, but I'm off from the library tomorrow. After school we'll probably hang out at her place."

"Awww yeah, round two!" he laughed.

"We'll see. I'm not assuming anything," Robin said and grinned. "She may need time to recover." They both started laughing and slapped fives again.

"I was starting to doubt you, man. Didn't think you could figure out her *Chinese Arithmetic*..."

He caught the reference to the Eric B. & Rakim instrumental track and rolled his eyes. "You and your euphemisms. You got a million of them!"

Franklin backhanded his shoulder playfully, then asked, "Hey, you got a quarter?" he nodded behind Robin. "I wanna see if I'm still good at *Street Fighter*."

Robin fished out a quarter from his jeans and flipped it to him. "I hope E. Honda 100-hand-slaps your ass," he joked.

It was one o'clock when Robin and Shinju emerged from the 6-train Canal Street subway station. The sidewalk was so full of people coming and going, the couple had a hard time walking side by side.

"Wow, I've never seen a street with wall-to-wall people like this,"

Robin said. "How 'bout you lead and I follow since I don't know where we're going." He slowly let her step ahead of him.

"It's not too far from here. Just a few blocks ahead," she said.

They were walking east and had passed Centre Street, then Mulberry.

"Wow, there really IS a Mulberry Street, just like the Dr. Seuss book!"

Shinju rolled her eyes. "Everything to you is about books, isn't it?" she asked.

"Well, I do work in a library..."

When they arrived at Elizabeth Street they turned the corner, finally leaving the congested main street.

"Where exactly are we going?" he asked.

"It's a supriiiiiiise." she looked over to him and winked, repeating his phrase back to him.

They walked up to a building at 15 Elizabeth Street. The words *Elizabeth Center* were over a window on the side of the entrance while the rest of the building had Japanese symbols embossed on the walls. Shinju pushed the glass doors in and stepped inside, followed by Robin. The interior was a three-level shopping mall full of small stores where vendors sold a wide variety of Asian products.

"Woah," Robin said in awe. "This place is awesome!"

She smiled. "I always come here when I yearn for a taste of home."

He surveyed the floor. "Video games, Japanimation, Gundam models," he gasped. "Kung-Fu movies! Let's check 'em out!" He pulled her toward a store as she laughed.

Robin spent a little over two-hundred dollars at the Elizabeth Center. Rather than carry all their bags on the train, Shinju suggested taking a cab that she paid for after his over-the-top shopping spree.

"I can't believe you bought all this stuff, Robin... it's just too much, you went crazy!" she said as she unlocked the door to her apartment and walked in.

Robin followed, carrying a handful of bags in each hand, with a few under his arms. "What can I say? I've been taken over by Japanese Culture."

Twenty minutes later they were eating lunch and wearing kimonos that he had bought for both of them.

"I love the Japanese sense of style. These robes are fly," he said.

"They're *kimonos*, not robes," she corrected.

"What's the difference?"

They watched several VHS movies, which led to a debate between them.

"*The Big Boss* is definitely Bruce Lee's best film. Everything after that, pales in comparison..." Robin said.

Shinju shook her head. "*Fist of Fury* is way better. It's a better story, has a cult following and went on to have three sequels."

They laughed. "Well, can we at least agree his worst film was *Way of the Dragon*. It's so overrated," Robin offered.

"Agreed. I never understood why everyone loves it so much. It's like "The Godfather" of Martial Arts movies," she replied.

He gave her a skeptical look. "What do you know about *The Godfather*?"

"I like all those gangster movies! *Scarface, Goodfellas, A Bronx Tale, Carlito's Way*...Robert DeNiro and Al Pacino are my favorite movie stars."

"Really?"

"Yes! They dress up in nice clothes, drive nice cars, being all rich and powerful..."

"And killing people," he added.

"It's the American Way! You glamorize violence to the point that gangsters are worshiped like superheroes here in the United States."

"I... I guess I never saw it that way."

"I take it you're the opposite. I saw all those posters of Bolo at your place," she grinned. "You do favor him a little."

"Oh, yeah?" Robin slipped off his kimono, exposing his bare chest and flexed for a minute.

She stood up from the couch and went into a playful defensive stance. "Let's see what you got, eh?" she taunted.

Robin flexed again and got up to answer her challenge. They paced around the living room, sizing each other up. She attacked first with a telegraphed light kick that he blocked, then he wrapped his arms around Shinju's waist and spun her around. She giggled uncontrollably.

"No fair! That's cheating!" she protested.

He stopped. "It's not cheating! American Karate!" he yelled. "Unorthodox... but effective! Hyah!" he grabbed her wrist, then flipped her on his shoulder and spun her around. Her legs were kicking air.

"I just ate! You're gonna make me sick!"

"Okay..." he said as he lowered her back on the couch.

She took a breath, then quickly swept her leg out across Robin's left calf, knocking him back and causing him to crash on the floor. Before he could react, she was on top of him. "Gotcha!"

The wind was knocked out of him, but he managed to let out a soft chuckle. "Your neighbor downstairs is going to be upset," he said in a hoarse voice.

She took off her kimono and leaned forward inches away from his face. "I lied. The apartment underneath me is empty." She kissed him.

The sun was in and out of the clouds with an occasional ray of light coming through the window as Shinju and Robin laid naked on the hardwood floor. Her head rested on his chest and he stared up at the ceiling.

"You're awfully quiet," she said.

He sighed. "It's unreal... I keep thinking... that maybe this is all a dream. That I never met you in that subway car and I'm dead, and

this is all just a wonderful fantasy. Where you and I can exist forever."
He started to stroke her hair.

She smiled. "Robin I..." she gasped as the intercom bell rang out, echoing in the apartment.

Robin lifted his head. "You expecting someone?" he asked.

Shinju sprang to her feet and ran to the intercom. She pressed the TALK button and said something in Japanese, then held down the LISTEN button. A female voice replied in Japanese and her eyes grew wide with fear. She pressed the DOOR button, giving the visitor access in the building.

"You have to go, now!" she yelled. "Get dressed quickly!"

"What!? What is it? What's going on?" he asked.

She was picking up their clothes and frantically running around the apartment. "I'll explain later, just please..."

There was a knock on the door. She turned and cursed in Japanese. She tossed Robin his kimono and threw the rest of their clothes in her hamper, closing it shut. "In the bedroom closet and don't say a word!" she ordered.

Robin began to protest but saw her eyes pleading with him and quickly ran into the bedroom.

She gathered herself and calmly opened the door.

Robin stood in the closet holding his breath. His mind was racing with scenarios that could be happening and what he would do if he was discovered. He heard a new voice from the living room. A female who was speaking Japanese.

"What took you so long to open the door?" the visitor asked Shinju.

"I was using the bathroom. I needed to freshen up," she answered.

The visitor started walking around. Robin heard the footsteps echo in the next room and a bead of sweat trickled down the side of his face.

Then he heard the visitor speak again... and she sounded familiar. Robin opened the closet and slowly stepped out of the bedroom. He couldn't believe his eyes as he saw Shinju... and Sonyai Yi both looking back at him.

Sonyai turned to her niece and yelled at her in Japanese, then turned back to him.

"You're...Obasan?" he asked.

"It's Japanese for 'Aunt'," Sonyai explained. "Of all the boys in this city!" she yelled, looking up at the ceiling.

Shinju looked back and forth between the two. "You know each other?"

"She's my supervisor at the library...." he started.

She turned to her aunt. "You told me you worked in a flower shop!"

"Flower shop!?" he exclaimed.

The two women started arguing in Japanese again as he stood there, in his kimono, completely stunned.

Sonyai said one last thing that made Shinju run past him crying into her bedroom.

"I think you need to leave, Walker... right now."

He nodded. "Right, I'll be leaving... but if you could just open that hamper and pass me my pants..."

"Walker, I'm going to count to three..."

Robin was out the door in the blink of an eye.

After an awkward train ride home, Robin returned to Washington Heights at seven-thirty in the evening. He was barefoot and only wearing his kimono as he carefully walked down Saint Nicholas Avenue from 181st Street, past the confused glances he received from people on the street.

He made it to Franklin's apartment and knocked on the door. Franklin answered, and before he could react Robin quickly walked in.

"Wha... dude, what are you doing in that bathrobe? What happened?"

"It's not a robe, it's a kimono!" Robin yelled. "I need my emergency keys..."

Franklin went to his room as he waited next to the door. Supa came from his room and stopped when he saw Robin.

"What the hell is going on? Why the hell are you wearing a robe, boy?" he bellowed.

His knees buckled as he stammered, "It's... it's a kimono, sir... long story."

"Let me get this straight," Franklin began.

He and Robin were upstairs, and after a shower and fresh change of clothes, Robin was pacing around the living room while Franklin sat on the couch. They were sharing a plate of french fries by passing it back and forth between them.

"You see this girl on the train, then had a few missed chances to talk to her, until she finally finds you alone on another train..."

Robin took a fry. "Yes," he nodded.

"After roughly a month of dating and hooking up, you're telling me that she ends up being your boss's daughter?"

"*Niece*, you idiot. Quit saying daughter!" Robin corrected him.

"Wow, that's amazing!" he said eating a couple of fries. "What are the odds? You need to buy a lottery ticket!"

"YOU need to shut the hell up before I send you flying over the bridge to Fort Lee!" Robin scowled.

"Alright, alright, no need to get heated, man. Chill."

Robin sighed. "Man, I really thought she was the one..."

"Aww c'mon man, you say that all the time! You said you loved Diedre, and *she* was the one..."

"I DID love Diedre you goddamn dick!"

"Did you!? Because you had a fucked up way of showing it if I remember!" Franklin yelled back.

He was right, but Robin didn't feel like looking back on the tumultuous relationship. "I dunno what I'm gonna do tomorrow..." He shook his head.

"Hey, just walk up in there and say, 'Hiya boss, did your niece tell you how long my dick is?' "

Franklin passed him the plate, and Robin just stared at him. "You are SUCH an asshole...you've never been in a situation like this."

"Well, there was that one time I got caught having sex with a mother and then her daughter...on two separate occasions. Is that close to what this is?"

Robin stared at him again.

Franklin laughed. "Dude, I'm just trying to lighten things up..."

"I know." He couldn't help but laugh as well.

Franklin took another fry. "Cause you see," he waved the fry as he talked. "The crazy thing about life is, tomorrow's always a brand new day where even MORE shit can go wrong." He popped the fry in his mouth. "Things are bad now, yeah, but just imagine what's waiting to kick you in the balls tomorrow!"

Robin took a moment to acknowledge what Franklin was saying. "That's pretty fucking deep."

He waved dismissively. "Yeah, I got a million of 'em. I should write a book. What do you think the call number for that would be?"

"American humor and wit?" he asked.

"817!" they said in unison.

Monday afternoon, Robin slowly walked in the clerical office and closed the door behind him. Sonyai was sitting at her desk with her back to him.

"Um, hi, I..." he began.

"Your clothes and belongings are on the shelf in front of you. We will not have any further discussions about the events that occurred yesterday evening," the senior clerk said sharply.

"Understood, but it's just one thing bothering me, ma'am. Your last name is Yi. Her's is..."

"My brother and her mother are not married. She took her mother's last name because my brother has enemies in his line of work. It was for her safety," Sonyai explained.

"Okay... also, why did *you* lie about where you worked?"

She refused to answer.

He shrugged. "Fine, I can understand the safety concerns. She mentioned her father's occupation but, um, I didn't see..."

She snapped her head from the desk to give him a deadly look.

"Umm, a certain student was missing from their classes this morning..." he stammered.

"The person you speak of is none of your concern... not anymore."

"Meaning?" Robin challenged.

She sighed. "She is... *gone.*"

Robin gasped in horror. "You... KILLED her?"

"Ay! My own niece? You actually believe I'm capable...?"

"When you say it like *that*, what else am I to think? Where is she?"

"It doesn't matter, Walker. She is gone. You will never see her again, that is all."

"Okay, I know you're mad," he put his palms up and out in front of him, "and you don't approve, fine, but can you at least give me a number to call, or an address to send a letter? Just to say goodbye?"

She shook her head. "No. It's better this way."

Robin gasped and collapsed to his knees. "PLEASE! Don't do this! I beg you!" he pleaded.

"Get up and keep your voice down." She looked at the closed door, worried his voice would carry. "What is wrong with you?"

"PLEASE!" he yelled again. "I... I'll do whatever you say!" Tears began to stream down his face as he pleaded hysterically. "After I lost my grandfather, she was the only thing keeping me alive! Just let me say goodbye at least!"

"Out of the question. Get a hold of yourself, young man!"

"Look, ever since I got here, you've wanted me to leave, and I've tried! Chavez won't let me, but just let me say goodbye. Give me some closure, and I'll walk out of here, right now...you'll never see me again. I'm on my knees. Please, tell me where she is!"

"No!" she yelled. "It's over. Wipe your face and get some air outside before you start your shift!" She turned away from him.

<*"You will regret this..."*>

Sonyai turned, her face frozen in shock as the words chilled her to the bone. It wasn't WHAT Robin said, it was the fact that he was speaking... in her native Japanese tongue... perfectly.

He slowly lifted his head, his eyes red with rage, his voice cold and calculating.

<*I'm saying this in Japanese so you understand me clearly... I loved her. She guided me out of a dark place at the lowest point of my life."*>

He went back to English. "So you have two options... you either tell me where she is so I can say goodbye, or you see a side of me very few do and it will NOT end well."

"You don't scare me, Walker..." she replied defiantly, yet her hands began to tremble.

He was standing now, staring back at her. "Fear is something you have to make someone acquainted with over time. And when you have nothing to lose, you practice a *lot* of patience."

He signed three letters with his hand. "W...A...R."

Robin waited in silence for her answer. She whispered to him in Japanese.

He nodded. "So be it," he hissed.

They locked eyes for what felt like an eternity, then Robin opened the door and left.

CHAPTER SEVENTEEN

Franklin entered his apartment and turned on the lights.

Robin was sitting on the couch calmly and startled his friend so much he jumped in place and screamed, "Jesus!"

"Lord's name in vain," Robin whispered coldly.

"What the fuck is with the Batman shit?! How did you get in?"

"Your father let me in, actually. He told me you should have been home sooner. He even asked me to tell him if you came in after 7 pm."

It was seven-fifteen, but Robin was no snitch. After Franklin gathered himself, he noticed his friend's cold demeanor and icy stare. "Oh, shit. I've seen you like this before."

Robin nodded. "Nelson Suarez hit Diedre with a snowball... January '92."

"Yeah, we did a number on him. I take it things didn't go too well at work, huh?"

Robin shook his head. "She's gone, man."

Franklin's eyes went wide. "She killed her?"

"That's what I thought too, but no. She's just gone. I went to her place after work and it was empty. Wiped clean, like she was never there." He let out a sigh. "It's straight out of Jimmy Hoffa. Who the hell can do this within 24 hours?"

"I... I dunno. Maybe you dodged a bullet here, man...these people may not be the types to be fucked with."

Franklin looked at Robin. His mind was already made up. "Yeah... the look. This means what I think it means?"

Robin nodded as the two friends said it together. "We're going to war."

"So... where do we start?" Franklin asked.

"First rule... know the enemy and know yourself," Robin said. "And how do we get to know the enemy?"

"Reconnaissance, observe and report. Got it."

"She's never seen you, so rent a car or follow her on foot and find out where she lives."

"Okay, I can take a few days off... what exactly are we looking for?"

"I don't know, but we watch her like a hawk and see if she has any secrets worth exposing. Sooner or later, I'm gonna make her pay!"

After a string of days over ninety degrees, there was finally some relief Thursday morning on the last day of June. The rain was coming down steadily as Sonyai approached the entrance to 58th Street. She closed her umbrella and sneezed loudly then looked in her purse for a napkin. A hand extended behind her as she gasped to see Annabelle Doyle offering her a tissue.

"Doyle?" she asked.

"Those summer colds, Sonny... they're the worst," she greeted.

She accepted the napkin, turned her head and blew her nose privately. "What are you doing here?" she asked.

"I gave you a heads up about Gussy's little project and then next thing I know I get a visit by Big Bad Baker himself, walking in my branch like he owns the place. I thought we were mates, Sonny. Tell me I'm dreaming and you're not turning rat on me, yeah?"

"What the hell are you talking about?" Sonyai asked.

"Baker is going on about some mad conspiracy that your boy fixed the numbers of the experiment..."

"And what exactly does that have to do with me?"

"Is it true?"

Sonyai said nothing.

"Bloody hell!" Annabelle yelled.

"Doyle, listen to me."

"Sonny, do you have any clue what could happen? How did he do it? I'm in this mess with you

already, so you better be straight with me!"

"I'll tell you everything when we have the evidence, Doyle. I'm working with the IA Trueblood, who discovered how he did it by accident and we're working together to find the..."

"You working her, or is she working you? For all you know she could be in on it, too."

"I trust her. She's neutral in all this."

"She's not one of us, Sonny... you're playing with fire collaborating with an IA. They're just as well librarians themselves. They think the same way, serving the people and not thinking of the branch!"

"Like I said, I trust her... she is not the threat. Baker is."

"Well, you nip this in the bud, Sonny... as quick as the changing of the guard, eh? I don't need no Yanker shitting on the lawn, get me?"

The senior clerk registered a look of confusion at the parting statement as Annabelle turned and walked back into the downpour, unaffected by the rain.

"And stop calling me 'Sonny'!" Sonyai called out to her.

Sonyai entered the branch, left her umbrella open in the middle of the floor to dry and walked in the clerical office. The door closed behind her and she jumped in fright from Angie, who was leaning against the wall next to the doorway with a huge smirk on her face.

"Damnit! Why is everyone sneaking up on me this morning?" she barked.

"I'm sorry... will *this* brighten your mood?" Angie asked as she pulled her hand from behind her back to reveal the box with the paper, signature stamp, and stickers.

"You found it!" Sonyai gasped.

Angie nodded. "Last week!"

She looked inside at the contents for herself. It felt surreal. *I got him, I finally got him!* she thought. She had an idea, inspired by the fact that outside factors were now in play. She had Annabelle and Yorkville branch to consider before making her next move. "Where did you find it?" she asked.

"Upstairs, in the auditorium. What are we gooooooooing..."

Sonyai interrupted and pulled her arm as they exited the office.

Upstairs the two quickly entered the reception room. "Are you sure about this?" Angie asked.

"Yes," Sonyai nodded. "We can't tip our hand just yet, so you're going to return the box where you found it, but we'll take a few pages of the memorandum stationery sheets to examine."

"We should just go to S.I.U. They'll bust Chavez for sure."

Sonyai turned to her. "Why are you so anxious to get him removed? What's in this for you?"

"I've seen how he's been treating Heywood lately."

"I see. Well, Baker has approached Annabelle Doyle from Yorkville branch and accused her of having inside information about Chavez's deception, so we have to make sure this evidence implicates him and him alone. Knowing that bastard, he may claim he received these materials from her and get off scot-free."

"Wow, good thinking," Angie complimented.

"We'll check out these pages and figure out how he's done all this and how far it goes. Great work, Angie." She handed the box back to her. "Put the box back exactly how you found it."

"You got it."

Sonyai returned to her office. She held up the memo pages in her hand. "After all these years, Nat... I'll get him... for you," she whispered. She heard noise outside from Gerry and Ethel arriving and quickly slipped the papers in her desk.

The Baruch College photography laboratory was temporarily located in the school's newest addition, the William and Anita Newman Library on 25th Street. Robin stepped inside the darkroom which was lit only with a red 25-Watt light bulb.

"Mar?! You in here?" he called out, adjusting his eyes.

"Ain't nobody here but us chickens," a female voice answered.

He grinned and walked toward his best guess of where the reply came from. He hit his leg on a chair. "Ow!"

"Careful," she called out. "Walk with your hands in front of you."

"Thanks for the advice," he growled. His eyes finally made out objects in the room. He approached Jeannimar Martinez as she hung developed photos on a clothesline. The student was wearing a leather biker skirt and a jean vest with a green t-shirt underneath that read *House of Pain* on top of a gold cross. She was also wearing a pair of green Doc Martens and matching green leather gloves.

Her brown skinned face had patches of acne and her hazel eyes were surrounded by eyeliner. She was wearing a baseball cap turned backward on top of her short brown hair.

"Robin Walker," she greeted. "I haven't seen you since we had Accounting 1001 freshman year. What brings you to my neck of the woods, Chico?"

"I'm going, uh, bird watching during the break and I need to borrow your camera."

She stopped in the middle of swishing a picture in its stop bath. "Camera? You wanna borrow my camera? I don't have a *camera*, Robin. I have an $1800 piece of equipment! And if you want to use it, you better make it worth my while."

"Okay, I apologize. Um, how do you propose I do that?"

"I dunno... surprise me," she said in a sultry voice.

Robin's head leaned back in shock as he raised an eyebrow. "Last I checked, you weren't hitting for our team... so once again I ask, how do you suppose I do that?"

She reached down and pulled the zipper to her skirt up and

opened her legs. She was not wearing any panties. "My lawn needs a good mowing. Make like a billy goat and *chew the grass.*"

Robin started doing a few head twitches. "Wow, now there's an invitation if I ever heard one."

"Mmmhmm..." she hummed.

"But you know, I've had a death in the family recently, then my girlfriend got sent somewhere unexpectedly..."

"Robin if you don't stop with the Eeyore-sad-story bullshit and make like Winnie the Pooh, you're not getting my shit."

He shifted his glance from her face, down to the skirt, and back to her face, blinking hard.

Sonyai and Robin were working the circulation desk at four o'clock. Neither would look the other in the eye, nor were they speaking. Behind them in the clerical office, Gerry elbowed Tommy and nodded, "Hey man, what's that all about?"

Tommy looked out at the pair and shrugged his shoulders. "Got me."

"Something happened Wednesday. I heard them going at it before he started his shift. The kid's been a pillar of stone ever since." Gerry said.

"None of my business," Tommy said. "Things are cooling off here, pardon the joke. Don't stir up the hornet's nest unless you want the Queen to sting ya."

Gerry turned his head. "You come up with that one?"

"Heard my dad say it a few times."

He pulled his notebook out from his back pocket and grabbed a pen. "Stolen," he said, writing the quote down.

Lakeshia walked by the circulation desk several times and noticed Robin's emotionless stance. It puzzled her. She was pushing her shelving cart, looking over her shoulder when Alex stepped into her path.

"Hey!" she whispered.

Lakeshia turned around to see Alex stopping the cart with her hand and froze. "Oops! Sorry!" she whispered.

"Watch where you're pushing that truck, Leelee," Alex warned her.

"I'm sorry, I was wondering what was wrong with Miss Yi and Robin..." Lakeshia nodded behind her. "They look like statues..."

Alex craned her neck. "Hmmm, reminds me of when my parents have a fight. Something must have happened between them. Maybe she will finally fire his ass," she said and walked off as Lakeshia gave her a dirty look.

Tommy exited the clerical office to relieve Sonyai. The senior clerk went inside to get her purse, then waited a few minutes for Heywood to take over the information desk from Angie. The two ladies left together through the exit turnstile in front of Robin. While Tommy checked the cash register, Robin signaled Franklin, who was sitting near the revolving shelves holding the paperbacks.

Franklin walked up and met Robin at the checkout side. "Follow her and call me with your location," the clerk ordered.

His friend nodded and left the branch on the heels of the senior clerk and IA. As he left the branch to shadow the two, he breathed a sigh of relief that Tanya was off for the day so they didn't bump into each other.

Forty minutes later, the phone rang and Heywood answered. The IA nodded at Robin, indicating the call was for him.

Robin picked up the phone and asked, "Where are you?"

"Followed them to... get this, *another* library. 79th between 2nd and 3rd."

"Yorkville?" he asked.

"I guess so. This cluster is all new to me. It's closed, too."

"Stay on them. I'll be there in a half-hour." He hung up the phone.

Angie and Sonyai arrived at Yorkville and knocked twice on the door.

A teenager answered the door. "We're closed," one of the pages said after partially opening the entrance.

"We're here to see Annabelle Doyle," Sonyai said.

"And you are?" the teen asked. She was tall with dark hair, pale skin, and braces.

"It's okay, Brittney," Annabelle appeared behind her. "I'll take it from here. Come in ladies."

The page stepped back as Sonyai and Angie entered the branch. Annabelle closed and locked the door behind them.

"Are we alone?" Sonyai asked nervously.

"You can relax. Mister Ballard is long gone and young Brittney here was just leaving," the Yorkville senior clerk explained, referring to the branch head librarian, Matthew Ballard.

The three women walked to Annabelle's office, which was separate from the rest of the area designated for the clerical staff at Yorkville. There were pictures of Princess Diana and Prince Charles, as well as the rest of the royal family. The Union Jack hung on the wall behind her desk.

"They do spoil you here, Doyle," Sonyai said, looking around.

"When you manage one of the oldest substantial branches in the entire system, let alone your cluster, you acquire some perks, Sonny."

"Sonny?" Angie whispered to Sonyai, who waved her off and shook her head.

Annabelle sat behind her desk. "So, you told me over the phone that you found this box with materials that prove Gussie's making his funny-money memos, eh?"

There were three chairs in front of the desk. Sonyai and Angie each took a seat. Sonyai leaned forward and pulled out the stationary pages from her purse. "He was somehow able to purchase the same paper along with a stamp of the president's signature and the sticker of authorization."

"Interesting," Annabelle remarked. She searched her desk and pulled up an office memorandum announcing the upcoming summer festival schedule. Then she extended her hand for the pages in question. Sonyai passed the pages to her, and she held them both side by side.

"Practically identical, even in texture. Remarkable. That cunning devil."

"We have to find his source," Angie said. "He must have discovered where the officials buy their supplies and created a separate account."

"There's no proof of that, Miss... Trueblood was it?" Annabelle asked.

"Yes," she answered sharply.

She laughed. "Ain't we a couple of Sweet Valley Twins with this, eh?"

Sonyai shook her head. "Uh, there's three of us, Doyle."

Annabelle shrugged. "Well, I'm sure there's some sort of mystery-solving triplets out there as well..."

Robin arrived to meet Franklin and pulled the camera from his book bag. He then attached the zoom-lens and pointed the camera at the branch's huge glass windows. Despite being closed for the day, the facility was very well lit and he could see much of the interior inside.

"You sure they didn't leave?" he asked.

"Unless there's a back door somewhere, I'm sure."

"Cool."

"Where'd you get that camera? Very high tech!" Franklin asked.

Robin focused the lens. "You don't want to know what I had to do to get it. Trust me."

"Okay Doyle you've been studying those pages for five minutes. What are you..."

Annabelle held both pages up and turned toward her desk lamp. She gasped, "Wait!" She went inside her desk again and pulled up the memo approving Augustus' proposal, then looked at the blank papers and to the festival schedule memorandum.

"Bollocks! We got him!" she exclaimed.

"What is it?" Sonyai asked.

"I heard stories of others falsifying paperwork before and there was a new security measure implemented that only a few outside of upper management knew about." She held the festival schedule correspondence close to her desk lamp and pointed.

Sonyai and Angie stood up and looked closer.

"See? In the center?"

Under the light, a faint watermark in the shape of a lion's head profile appeared. Annabelle then held up the blank pages and the proposal memo. The watermark was nowhere to be found.

"That sonofabitch!" Sonyai spat.

"We can tell the real ones from the fake and we can prove all the fake ones came from Augustus. He's as good as done!" Angie exclaimed.

Sonyai smiled. "Thank you, Doyle. Tomorrow I'll look that scum right in his eyes and demand his resignation! And if he refuses, his treachery will see the light. 58th Street will finally be free of corruption and of Augustus Chavez!"

"Did it smell?" Franklin asked after hearing Robin's story.

"Well, no..."

He scoffed. "Then I don't know what's the problem. Eating out a lesbian is like seeing Halley's Comet for a guy. That shit's like once in a lifetime."

It was almost seven and there was no sign of Sonyai leaving the branch. Robin scanned every section of the library he could, then packed up the camera.

"I'm going over to get a closer look," he said.

"Wait!" Franklin called out.

The door opened and two women walked out. It was Sonyai and Angie. They exchanged a few words and went their separate ways.

"C'mon, after Sonyai!" Robin ordered.

"Wait, we might get spotted. Let's call it for the night."

He sighed. "Fine." They watched as Sonyai disappeared in the distance.

After taking the train home, Robin and Franklin went over their notes. Franklin managed to track Sonyai to her apartment at 100 Bellamy Loop in Co-Op City, The Bronx. Outside of a few errands and several trips with Janelle Simms, she went nowhere else. The senior clerk also had a hobby in botany, going to several flower shops and plant nurseries.

"That explains why Shinju thought she worked in a flower store," Robin concluded.

"What's the connection with that page, Simms, though?"

"I don't know, but I asked Cervantes to stake out her place as well when he's off duty since he's been there before."

"Alright, let's call it a night," Franklin said, standing up. "Meet you back at the branch tomorrow evening, but I got plans Monday afternoon on the fourth."

Robin confirmed with a nod and walked his friend to the door. He then went to his bedroom and took off his clothes. On his bed, staring up at the ceiling, he began thinking of Shinju. Before he knew it, tears were falling from his face again. He sobbed uncontrollably as the pain from his broken heart released through his body. It would be hours before he finally cried himself to sleep.

After a long Friday afternoon, Augustus walked in his office a few minutes after six. Sonyai was waiting for him, sitting in his chair... holding the box.

"What the *hell* is this?!" he exclaimed.

She stood up and smiled. "*This* is the story of a young, cocky librarian who arrived five years ago. The young man worked under a wonderful woman, the legendary Natasha Santiago. A kind, caring, wise individual who was respected among her peers."

"So... S..Sonyai, let me explain..." he stammered.

"One of Natasha's closest friends was someone who was affectionately known as The Man in White, a senior clerk. The two developed more than a friendship, and despite never being physically intimate, the pair's emotional bond once disclosed proved scandalous and they both resigned in disgrace."

Augustus swallowed hard. Sweat started to trickle down his brow.

"And who was it that revealed their relationship to the public? Who shamed them for the sole opportunity of advancement and has recklessly jeopardized this branch over and over repeatedly with the morals of a snake!? You, Augustus Chavez! Well, no more!"

She dropped the box on his desk with a sharp, loud crash.

"You gave your predecessor two weeks to resign when you discovered her secret affair..." she said with a scowl. "I'm giving you two *DAYS*."

His eyes bulged at the ultimatum.

She picked up the box and walked around his desk, approaching him. "You have until after the Fourth of July holiday to turn in your resignation or I go to S.I.U. with this box and those fake memos."

Augustus stood frozen in shock as Sonyai walked past him. His body shook all over as his mind attempted to grasp what just transpired. Outside, Sonyai stepped out, put the box down and leaned against the glass door. She sighed and lit a cigarette. After a long drag, she blew out a long cloud of smoke.

"That was for you, Nat... for you," she said as a tear fell down her cheek.

CHAPTER EIGHTEEN

TANYA HAD NEVER BEEN TO WASHINGTON HEIGHTS, BUT AFTER SEVERAL dates with Franklin taking her around town, she felt obligated to meet him on the fourth of July in his neighborhood to see a movie. She got off the Bx3 bus at 181st Street and Broadway, then walked across the street to the RKO Coliseum Theater where he was waiting for her.

"Hey," he greeted her with a peck on the neck. "Got our tickets already. Want any popcorn or soda before going in?"

"Nah, can we hit McDonald's over there after?" she asked, pointing across the street.

"Sure, or we can go over *my place* for some fun." He reached behind and patted her bottom.

She couldn't help but giggle as they walked inside. Theater 6 had very few people sitting in front of the projection screen. The couple worked their way up the aisle to the back rows.

"What movie did you get?" Tanya asked, taking a seat.

"*Forrest Gump.*"

"Huh? What kind of corny shit is that?"

Franklin waved his hand. "Chill," he whispered. The last trailer played and the theater went dark. As the credits started, he tilted his head. "As you can see, there's not that many people here."

He slipped his hand to her waist and pulled down her zipper. "And *this* movie is, kinda long."

Tanya let out a gasp of surprise as he traced a circle with his fingertip. "I think I like *this* box of chocolates..."

A couple of hours later, Franklin led Tanya inside his apartment.

"This place is huge! Robin lives in a crib this big, too?" she asked.

"Yep, he's on the 16th floor," he answered.

"And, you're just on the 3rd?" she asked, scrunching up her face, unimpressed.

"My dad's the building manager," he lied. "Having an apartment on the lower floors is a status symbol."

"Ooooh, does that mean you'll get to take over when you're older?" She started to slip her blouse off.

"Yeah," he said with a grin.

They started making out. Tanya pulled his shirt over his head, and he popped the latch off her bra. Moving to his bedroom, she whispered, "Got a condom?"

"Fuck yes."

She climbed onto his bed while he reached over to his dresser. While searching, he pressed "play" on his boombox and "Flex" by Mad Cobra came on.

"No music, please!" she panted with anticipation.

He quickly turned the tape off. "Oh, you like to be loud, huh?" he said, then joined her on the bed.

She couldn't resist taking a peek of what he was working with and was impressed. For what he lacked in girth, he made it up in length. She pulled him close they started necking, teasing and biting all around.

"I'll be gentle," he whispered.

She slapped him across his face, hard. He was taken aback, mouth wide open. "You do and I'll put my clothes back on!" she hissed and wrapped her legs around his waist. "I want it *rough!*"

He reached behind her head, grabbed a handful of her hair and pulled. "Whatever you say," he growled.

They were fast, but vicious. Around three o'clock Franklin woke up with scratches and marks everywhere from his chest up. He felt across the bed and noticed he was alone. After putting on his boxers, he walked to the hallway and found Tanya in the bathroom with her clothes back on. The shower curtain was drawn and there was a towel on the toilet seat.

"My mom comes home at 5 pm so I need to get there by at least 4:30," she said.

"Give me 15 minutes and I can walk you to the..."

"No need. I know where the stop is. Starts right there around the corner on Broadway, where that Bravo Supermarket is, right?"

"Um, yeah... hey, what's with you? I'm feeling a little *"Boomeranged"* here!"

She looked at him. "Don't get caught up, Marky Mark. You knew what this was..."

He nodded. "Yeah... right, okay."

She walked out of the bathroom. They looked at each other then she turned and said, "See you."

The apartment door slammed as he walked back to his room. He took the tape out of his cassette player, then threw it against the wall. Before he went back to wash up in the bathroom, he switched on the radio to Hot97 and the song "Butter" by A Tribe called Quest came on.

"Oooh! I hate these damn fireworks!" Sonyai Yi cried out.

Janelle and the senior clerk were traveling west on 3rd Avenue in The Bronx crossing 149th Street. Despite the busy shopping hub being full of people, occasionally the popping and ear-piercing sounds of firecrackers and skyrockets could be heard in the distance.

"It's only 5 pm, not even night time! I know it's probably some rowdy teenagers in a vacant lot."

"It's for fun, Miss Yi," Janelle replied as they continued to walk. "My mother spoke to me recently. She's trying to talk me into leaving home. I don't think my father will let me stay home after." Janelle looked anxious at the thought.

"If he kicks you out, we will find a way together. There are shelters, social services that can help you." Sonyai looked at her. "You will not face this alone, child."

"I'm starting to feel like those two detectives on *Simon and Simon*," Franklin said.

"More like *Crocket and Tubbs*," Robin scoffed.

Robin had been following the two women alone until Franklin joined him a half-hour ago. They were wearing disguises while shadowing the pair from across the street. Robin was wearing a long-hair wig and aviator sunglasses. Franklin was wearing a baseball cap with an army camouflage jacket. While walking, the pair started debating which movie was better between *Speed* and *Wolf*.

"*Speed* was awesome. Best action flick in a long time!" said Franklin.

"*Wolf* was the best werewolf movie since *American Werewolf in London*. It single-handedly brought back the classic feel of the Hammerstein Studio horror movies," Robin explained. "Nicholson also proved that he's not washed up and that him playing The Joker in *Batman* wasn't a fluke."

"You're always defending Nicholson... just like how you reenact that scene from *Witches of Eastwick* all the time. Well, we'll see if he pops up in anything else. I still think he's washed up, swinging on cars with a golf club. He won't be working in Hollywood too long going crazy like that."

"We all have our moments of temper," Robin said after checking across the street.

"I wonder why she keeps meeting up with this page, though. This is their third trip I've seen on my watch... hey! Look!"

Franklin pointed as they saw Sonyai and Janelle walk into a Duane Reade.

"C'mon!" Robin yelled and they crossed the street.

Looking in the window, the pair saw Sonyai receive a bag from the pharmacist in the back. They ducked into an electronic store next door to prevent being seen when the ladies stepped out.

"You keep following them. I'm going inside for a second – I'll catch up," Robin ordered.

Franklin nodded and took off. Robin went back next door inside the convenience store and asked the pharmacist, "Hey, that Asian woman that was just here. What did she get?"

"I'm not telling you that! It's confidential!"

Robin pulled a twenty-dollar bill out of his pocket. "Is it confidential *now*?" he waved.

"Calcium and Iron mineral supplements," he answered, snatching the twenty.

"What would be the reason to be taking those?"

"What, are you dense? They're prenatal vitamins."

Robin tilted his head, very confused.

"It's NOT her, it's *her!*" Robin exclaimed triumphantly.

He and Franklin were back at his apartment, sharing a pizza pie from Tony's. Franklin was looking back at Robin, puzzled while eating a slice.

"We got her, man, we fucking *got her!*" Robin was pacing around the living room, an evil grin on his face.

"You mind cluing me in, Slylock Fox?"

"Prenatal vitamins. Sonyai was using her insurance to treat the pregnancy!" Robin declared.

"But she's not—" Franklin stopped in mid-sentence then gasped. "Oooooooooohhhhhhh!"

The two high fived each other. "Good work, man. I got it from here... the secret is coming out," Robin said with a fist pump. "And all hell's breaking loose!"

Tuesday afternoon at four o'clock. Augustus sat defeated in his office. The end was near. He exhausted all his resources and called in all his favors. If Sonyai went to Special Investigations revealing his manufactured memorandums, he'd surely be terminated. *Perhaps it's for the best,* he pondered. His efforts to make this branch reach its highest potential and influence had been an exercise in futility.

Too many times had he been brought down by his very own employees, be it Heywood, Angie, or even Zelda herself, whom he trusted the most. But Sonyai, his largest adversary, his arch-nemesis, the Moriarty to his Holmes... that was someone he refused to let be his executioner!

"How was Great Adventures, Leelee?" Alex asked.

Tanya, Alex, and Lakeshia were in the staff room on break at four forty-five. Like most days after a major holiday, the afternoon was a long drag. The branch was empty most of the day, except for those trying to beat the heat in a cool air-conditioned room.

"It was great. Derrick threw-up on the Scream Machine all over his lap! And Quinton got scared by a monkey when we drove through Wild Safari."

The girls all laughed together while she continued.

"We did everything, even the water park. I won some prizes. I wanna go back for Halloween when they have something called Fright Fest!"

"Did you go on Batman the Ride?" Tanya asked.

"Nah, the line was too long."

The door opened and all three tensed up, looking toward the entrance as Janelle walked in.

"So this is where we're hiding?" she joked.

"Yeah. Technically we're all not supposed to take our breaks at the same time," Alex said.

"Like we really do what we're told all the time," Janelle said, taking a seat on the couch.

Despite the loose clothing, the page's stomach protruded over her lap, which the other three noticed with worried glances.

"So, um, how was your weekend, Nellie?" Lakeshia asked.

"Went up to The Hub at 149th Street and 3rd Avenue window shopping with Miss Yi, then I visited Avery before he left for Basketball Camp last night," she replied. "He kissed my belly before getting on the train to Baltimore." She sighed, "He won't be back until Labor Day weekend. Then he starts his senior year."

"Anything from Miss Yi about a clerical position? It's been..."

Alex was interrupted by the door opening again. Robin walked in the room and the girls went silent. "Oh, full house in here," he said with a fake smile. He couldn't help keeping a lingering gaze at Janelle while he slowly walked to the refrigerator.

"I'm glad y'all are up here. I wanted to share something a little something I got this weekend." He opened the refrigerator door and reached inside as the girls looked at each other, puzzled.

Robin pulled out a box of Ritz crackers and a flat plastic container. He opened it to reveal a triangle slice of Brie cheese and a spoonful of jam in the corner. "I was hoping to share a delicious delicacy of cheese that my cousin gave me."

Janelle gasped, remembering what her doctor said about food reactions that could be harmful.

Robin pulled a cracker out of the box and scooped some Brie with it. "Leelee?" he offered the cracker to the page.

"Um, no thanks," she politely declined.

Robin moved around the room to Tanya, who shook her head, passed Alex for obvious reasons, and advanced slowly to Janelle. "How about *you*?" he offered with a grin.

He took a couple of more steps closer and Janelle suddenly sprang up from the couch, then shuffled to the door without a word.

"Wow, wonder what got into her?" he said, taking a bite of the cracker. "Surely there couldn't be anything wrong with eating a little cheese and jam, could there?"

Lakeshia noticed the grin across his face.

He looked at each page, one by one.

"I mean, sometimes it won't agree with you and you can get a little gas, get constipated, but what other dangers could she be concerned with... hmmm?"

They all exchanged glances and suddenly became worried that the cat was out of the bag.

"Why y'all so quiet? What's wrong?" he taunted. He was Daryl Van Horne, and they were his Witches of Eastwick. After waiting for an answer, he couldn't contain himself any further and let out a low, sinister chuckle.

"What's so fucking funny?" Alex snarled.

Yeah, she was definitely Cher... the feisty one. "Well, let's see... one other reason young miss Janelle *would* be nervous about eating cheese, especially Brie would be if she was... how do you say... *expecting?*"

Lakeshia swallowed hard with an audible gulp as Alex and Tanya kept their poker faces on.

"Don't know what you're talking about," Alex said nonchalantly.

"Oh, but I think I do, you dark and dense lump of coal!" he yelled. She flinched at the insult, but Robin continued. "It all makes sense now. Running around with Sonyai after work... SHE was promised a position here, wasn't she? That way she would have medical insurance and even go on maternity leave when she has the baby, right?"

"That's a bunch of bullshit!" Tanya stood up.

Susan Sarandon, indeed. "Shut up!" he yelled. "I'm just getting started!"

Alex started making eye-contact with Lakeshia, trying to convey a message to her.

"Then I show up and Sonyai decides to turn everyone against me to make me quit, all while using HER insurance to get treatment and care for little miss 'Brenda's got a Baby', buying time to find her another position somewhere else in the system! Am I right? AM I RIGHT?!?!?"

"Robin, please! Calm down!" Lakeshia cried out.

Damn you, Leelee! The weakest fucking link! Alex thought, she shifted her eyes to Tanya who nodded back.

Oh, Michelle Pfeiffer, the timid one, so gullible. "Everyone was in on it." He raised his finger. "Almost everyone. Chavez doesn't know... does he?" His face was contorted, almost ghoul-like, with his eyes seedy and shifting back and forth.

Alex was slowly leaning back toward the kitchen sink and let her hand reach over. Meanwhile, Tanya clenched her fist and dug her foot in.

Robin looked all around the room at the three of them in each position. "I think I'll tell him," he said smugly.

"You're not telling him shit!" Tanya hissed and lunged at him.

She telegraphed her haymaker from a mile away. Robin blocked it and delivered a backhanded slap across her face. He turned and saw Alex, bringing her arm down. He had just enough time to turn his head as the right side of his face exploded with glass and hot water.

He screamed while the coffee pot Alex grabbed from the counter shattered with shards falling between them. Robin blindly reached out, grabbing her by the throat once again. He pulled her close to his face, blinked a few times and squeezed, their eyes inches apart.

Gerry and Sonyai were working the desk downstairs when a loud crash came out from above. Eugene stood up and yelled, "What the hell was that?"

Sonyai turned to Gerry. "Stay here," she ordered, and took off for the door leading upstairs. Eugene quickly followed while Zelda attempted to calm the few concerned patrons on the floor.

Robin leaped back up after slamming Alex through the kitchen table, which collapsed under their combined weight. Lakeshia was terrified at what she had just witnessed, completely frozen in place as he advanced on her.

"I'm sorry it had to come to that. I really hate hitting girls, honest," he said calmly and quickly. Blood was trickling down the side of his face.

"R-R-Robin, please..." she trembled.

He held up his finger, shushing her. "Just relax... they're fine. I barely connected with Tanya," he coddled.

She closed her eyes, shaking like a leaf, then heard the door close. After a breath, when nothing happened, she opened one eye and noticed she was alone.

In the hallway, Robin slinked against the wall and slipped into the auditorium. The door to the first floor opened and Sonyai bolted up the steps with Eugene at her heels. Through the crack of the door, he watched as they both went inside the staff room, then came out and went downstairs. Before the door closed Eugene caught him and turned around. "Hey!" he yelled.

Back on the floor, Zelda was startled as she saw Robin suddenly burst out the door and ran to Augustus' office.

Sonyai walked in and gasped as Tanya was sitting up from the couch, shaking her head, with Alex on top of the shattered kitchen table. She rushed to check on Alex. "What happened?" she asked.

The page had a trickle of blood coming out of her mouth. She looked up, moaning. "He... he knows... about Nellie..." she whispered. Lakeshia was checking on Tanya as Sonyai sprang up and whispered, "No," she then turned and ran out of the room.

Augustus shook his head. "If I'm going down," he whispered, reaching for the phone, "I'm taking *her* with me!"

Before he could pick up the receiver, his door flew open and Robin closed it behind him. He was bleeding on the side of his face, and gasping for breath. Augustus stood up and yelled, "Walker?! What—"

"Do you have a fax machine, sir?!" he interrupted.

Eugene returned to the main floor and looked around for Robin. A second later, Sonyai came out behind him and hurried to the librarian's office. She pushed it open to find the two men smiling back at her. A piece of fax paper was in Augustus' hand.

"Well now, Yi," the librarian began with a wide smile. "You're looking very lean... for a woman *six months pregnant!*"

NO! Sonyai thought as she swallowed hard then looked at Robin slowly approaching her.

He leaned in once he was beside her and whispered, "Please know...you brought this on yourself." She closed her eyes as he walked by her and out of the office.

"Step inside... let's *talk*," he invited.

She walked in slowly and closed the door.

Robin strolled past Eugene heading back to the circulation desk. It was five o'clock and he took his post on the checkout side where Sonyai once was. From the shelves, Janelle looked on in anger as the cocky youngster stood and smiled.

A half-hour went by as Eugene stared at Robin working checkouts with a clenched fist. At the information desk, Zelda received a call and then waved to get the guard's attention. He stood and walked across the floor.

"They want to see you, inside," she whispered.

He nodded and walked to Augustus' office.

Inside, Sonyai and Augustus sat quietly as Eugene closed the door behind him.

The head librarian addressed him as Sonyai stared away, looking at a corner, "Iscaro, I need you to downplay the events that have occurred in the past hour."

"But, sir,"

"Hear me, please." Augustus pleaded. "I understand you're upset, and you'd like nothing more than to call the police on Mister Walker..."

"Two teenage girls have been assaulted, destruction of property... he's lucky he's still walking on two legs, *sir!*"

"Be that as it may, you will file a simple incident report with the Special Investigations Unit about today's events that I will go over with a fine-toothed comb before submitting and nothing else will be told to any other authorities, it that clear?"

"Bullshit! I won't let this kid get away with smacking—"

"You will if I have anything to say about it! Or do I have to remind you of exactly why you left here four years ago?"

That caught Sonyai's attention, as the senior clerk turned toward the two and Eugene's eyes went wide. Silence filled the room for over a minute as the guard's jaw tightened. He then gave a yielding nod. "Alright, I won't go to the police."

"So glad we could see eye-to-eye in this matter," Augustus dismissed.

"Yeah, if you'd excuse me!" Eugene pulled open the door and slammed it behind him.

The pages and clerks stayed past closing waiting for the aftermath. Augustus and Sonyai were heard having various screaming matches in the office earlier, disturbing a few patrons trying to read. It was a few minutes after six and everyone was waiting inside the clerical office for Sonyai to return.

The pages were on the left side of the office as Janelle sat in Sonyai's chair. On the right side, Gerry, Ethel and Tommy were standing behind Robin, who was sitting with his feet up on the corner of Ethel's desk with his hands behind his head. His face was still red from the hot water burns and there was a trickle of blood down his cheek. Shards of glass were in his hair and on the collar of his polo shirt. Eugene was guarding the doorway, blocking Robin from leaving.

"I can't believe they've been in there a whole hour," Tommy said.

Lakeshia whispered to Alex, "You okay?"

"I'm fine. Nothing's broken, just a little sore."

"You're fine because *I* absorbed most of the impact when we fell," Robin called out to her. "I learned how to do it watching WWF Superstars!"

"You're so big and tough slamming little girls," Eugene grunted.

Robin ignored the remark and rolled his eyes.

"You're looking so smug. You know she's going to kill you," Gerry said. "Like *literally* kill you."

"When I wake up in hell, I'll tell the Devil, 'Get the fuck outta my seat, nigga!'"

Gerry couldn't resist a chuckle, "Okay, but you still should go see a doctor after this."

"I'll be alright, I got…"

The door to the corner office finally opened. Sonyai stepped out, followed by Augustus. The two exchanged glances and then he closed his door and headed toward the exit. She walked to the clerical office where Eugene stepped aside to let her in.

Everyone turned to face her as Robin looked up, still resting his feet up on the desk. Her face was emotionless, even more so than usual. After looking at Robin, she turned to Janelle, who also continued to sit, waiting for the bad news.

She cleared her throat before addressing the room. "Ahem, as of next week, Miss Janelle Simms will be accepting a full-time clerical position at the Van Nest Branch in The Bronx."

The pages all gasped as Robin tilted his head.

"This Friday will be her last day," she concluded. She turned to Alex. "I'm taking you to the hospital to see if you require medical attention. The rest of you are dismissed."

Lakeshia and Tanya looked at each other, then left the office without a word.

"You too, Miss Simms. We will talk tomorrow."

Janelle sighed and stood up to leave.

Still addressing the room, Sonyai announced, "Mister Walker will have his pay docked to replace the staff room kitchen table. There will be no disciplinary actions taken and the incident that occurred this afternoon will *not* be put on record."

Robin nodded to himself and finally decided to stand up. She turned slowly to face him.

He extended his arms expecting the worst. "Alright Hirohito, make with the Pearl Harbor fireworks." He almost thought about asking for a cigarette and blindfold. *Defiant, till the end.*

Then the strangest thing happened. Sonyai... laughed. A low, long, guttural laugh.

The entire room was terrified, even Ethel. It was a sound no one had ever heard before. Robin couldn't help but smile. He finally did it, he got her to laugh.

"She's laughing like The Predator," Gerry whispered. "Is that a good sign?"

"Is it *ever* a good sign when a woman laughs like that!?!?" Tommy answered.

"I cannot begin to tell you what damage you have done... I was so close, but I'll tell you this, you were right. You did this to *hurt* me the same way I hurt you."

He nodded.

"Well, you have succeeded, young man. Bravo." She clapped her hands twice, slowly.

He was still looking at her, waiting for the guillotine to fall. A minute went by and she sighed. "We will see Miss Simms off the rest of the week until Friday and then next week..."

"If you're going to fire me..." he interrupted.

"SILENCE!" she yelled. Everyone jumped out of their skin as her voice echoed throughout the library. She pointed at him. "To terminate you now would be too lenient, and mercy is the *last* thing on my mind right now. I won't fire you, but I can damn well make your job here a living hell!"

"Short of bringing Shinju back and taking her away from me again, there is *nothing* you can do to hurt me more than you have!"

"Shinju?" Lakeshia whispered.

"We'll just see about THAT!... In due time, Mister Walker, in due time."

She lowered her arm and nodded her head. "You are all dismissed," she ordered.

Robin was the first to leave. He pulled a piece of glass off the side of his head and then flicked it to Alex as he walked out. Eugene watched him go as he left the branch without looking back. The rest of the clerks slowly filed out along with the security guard. When it was just Alex and Sonyai, the senior clerk sat down and let out a weary sigh.

"I'm calling your mother, Miss Stevens," Sonyai said as she picked up the phone. "You slipped when one of the pages spilled their soda and fell on your side... a doctor checked you out, and aside from some bruising, you're okay."

She turned to make sure the page understood the explanation. "You and Walker are not to engage each other ever again, understood?"

Alex simply nodded.

CHAPTER NINETEEN

"Nigga, are you out of your mind?!" Franklin yelled.

Robin had warned his friend about the liberties of using the word "*Nigga*", but in this instance, he let it slide. They were in his bathroom with Robin's head over the bathroom sink. Franklin was carefully picking glass fragments embedded in the right side of his face with a pair of tweezers.

"You're lucky you don't have any of this shit in your eyes," he said. "Even when this heals, the burns from the hot water are gonna have that side tender as filet mignon."

Robin groaned.

Another piece fell into the sink. Then Franklin asked, "So, what now? I take it you're ancient history. Helluva way to go out."

"I got a stay of execution. They wanna ship off that damn page before she brings the hammer down. Sending her to Van Nest."

"No shit? Ha! What a dump. You remember that guy, Shirkey? The fag who worked at Inwood, would cluster on Saturday's and flirt with Trevor?"

"Yeah?"

"Transferred over there around June '93."

"Well, the hell with both of them. If it wasn't for her getting knocked up, none of this would have happened." He grunted as Franklin pinched some skin by accident. "Are you almost done?"

"Yeah, yeah, yeah, calm down, you're lucky I know how to do this. Clay taught me how to dig slugs out after his brother Gil got clipped by those Dominicans from 185th Street, remember?"

"Crazy motherfucker trying to sell them sugar for heroin. He's lucky he walked away with just a bullet in his thigh."

"Yeah." He dropped the last piece in the sink. "Alright, that's it. Put some peroxide and a bandage on that side for the night. You should be good after that."

"Thanks." Robin sat up and checked his face in the mirror. He noticed a thin line roughly two-inches long sliding down near his right eye. "Hmmm, my very first facial scar," he mused.

"It was bound to happen sometime." Franklin said.

"Not the way I thought it would, though." He replied.

"I hope Alexandra is feeling better. She's had a rough couple of weeks," Augustus said.

Instead of a glamorous, well-known restaurant, he was dining with a guest in a local Spanish establishment located in Washington Heights. They were isolated in a reclusive corner with no one around for several tables. After ordering their meals, the pair were drinking martinis and engaging in idle conversation.

"She's a tough girl, she'll be fine," his mysterious female companion replied. "I don't believe that cock and bull story about getting food poisoning and spending the night at her friend's house, but I respect her privacy enough to leave it be."

They both took quiet sips of their cocktails, then Augustus flatly said, "We need to stop seeing each other. I'm curbing my extracurricular activities after a close call at work. I have been attracting too much attention lately."

The woman remained silent, taking the statement in with a surprising amount of calm.

"If it's because of my husband, you need not worry... he already knows."

Augustus was unsettled by the revelation to say the least. Their arrangement was to remain a secret. "I... I don't know what to say about that. I could never have a conversation with him now—"

"Gussy, my husband and I have been married for nearly three decades and were in love for only seven years. These things you'll understand when you get a little older. You were simply a distraction from a usual, mundane life, so why not continue? Unless it was about the money..."

"It was never about the money and you know that!" he spat.

His raised voice shocked her. She was not used to being addressed in such a way. "I never thought the day would come. I am truly disappointed. You Latins are so damn passionate, it's a double-edged sword."

He cocked his eyebrow as she stood up. "I think we should return to the original agreement," he said dismissively. "And keep our interactions limited to the affairs of Miss Stevens."

The woman finished her drink with one final chug and turned her back to him, storming out of the restaurant.

The waiter returned to his table as he sat alone. "Cancel her order," he told him, "and bring the biggest bottle of tequila you got."

The Landmark Tavern was in the heart of Hell's Kitchen. A classy Irish Pub which opened in the 19th century, it was known for its quiet atmosphere and exquisite cuisine. Cleopheous Baker felt out of place the moment he walked in. He would consider the establishment "artsy-fartsy" in his words. He walked to a corner table where someone was waiting for him.

"This better be important. I'm missing Jeopardy!" Cleopheous barked as he took a seat in the booth.

"I received a call from Sonyai this evening," Annabelle Doyle said as a greeting. "I'm afraid things didn't go as planned."

"No shit. Augustus did NOT turn in his resignation as planned today," he replied in frustration. "What the fuck happened, you cockney chickenhawk?"

She looked up at him from her meal with a squinty eye. "Shut your yap and listen, hayseed! All she could tell me is at the very last minute, Gussy got some dirt on her that compromised everything."

"Huh," Cleopheous grunted.

"So what we discovered will never see the light of day. They made a deal."

"What that got to do with the price of tea in China? Why don't we go to S.I.U. ourselves?"

"Because I follow a code of honor, and if we take down Gussy, Sonyai goes down with him! That won't stand with me, Gov!"

"You never would have figured out those memos were fake if I didn't tell you about the watermark! You promised *me* this stupid plan of yours would work!"

"Well, what can I say, Cleo baby? Suck it up, cheer up, forget it," she replied with a dismissive wave across her chest. "Better luck next time, yeah?"

He stared at her while she continued to eat. "Try the Shepherd's Pie, best in the whole city!" she recommended.

"I'll pass," he stood up and walked from the table.

Annabelle watched him leave. It didn't feel right working with Cleopheous, but she knew he didn't want to get his hands dirty going for Augustus's head. She was almost relieved the plan didn't work. Knowing the regional senior clerk by reputation, he would have double-crossed them somehow, the snake.

Cleopheous stepped out onto the sidewalk disgusted. He pulled out a cigar and lit it, blew the smoke out the side of his mouth, then his nose. "Hmph, never send a woman to do a man's job," He said with a grunt, then took another puff. "Okay, I guess when you want the bacon, you have to look piggy right in those beady eyes and bring the ax down yourself."

Zelda walked up to the branch Wednesday morning at eight. She was shocked when the security alarm failed to go off, then proceeded to find Augustus sitting at the information desk entering reserves into the system.

"Wow, you're here early."

"You never know how much you appreciate something until the threat of it being taken away from you arises," he replied with enthusiasm. "I nearly forgot how much fun this is, searching for the proper record, routing the copy here, filing the postcard away in anticipation." A chuckle escaped the back of his throat.

His suit jacket was draped over the back of the chair next to the desk. There were wrinkles on his shirt and the knot of his tie was pulled down.

Zelda put on a fake smile, hiding her concern. "I see, um, you realize we need to investigate how Sonyai discovered the box, right?"

Augustus finished the last postcard and his smile disappeared. "There's only *one* possibility."

She nodded. "Trueblood."

Augustus suddenly slid the shoebox of postcards off his desk with a roar, "That firewater drinking, forehead scalping bitch! I'll have her tits in a sling for this!"

Zelda didn't jump at the outburst. She merely adjusted her glasses and narrowed her eyes. "Have you been drinking?"

He didn't answer so she took a step forward. He held up his hand. "Zee."

She smelled the air and winced. "Goddamnit, Gus, go home and clean yourself up. I'll call Learner and have him switch with you for the late night." She stepped to the desk and picked up the phone. "I'm calling you a cab."

"I'm fine!" He reached for the phone, but she pulled it from the desk out of his reach after she dialed. He lost his footing and fell forward on the desk. "Zelda!" he cried.

"Get it together!" she barked back. "You've got a second chance, here. You jumped the candle and barely got your ass burned!"

He lifted his face looking up at her. His eyes were red from lack of sleep. "They're out to get me, Zee... why?"

"Pray we don't find out, c'mon." She put the phone back on the desk and grabbed his jacket. Augustus reluctantly slipped it on and they walked to the exit. She waited for the cab and helped him in. Back inside the branch, she started picking up the scattered postcards and placing them in order.

The tension had been high among the clerks and pages since yesterday. Robin kept to himself, barely saying a word to anyone when he arrived. He considered it a blessing working the late night, taking the desk for the first time at four o'clock with Sonyai. Not giving a second thought to whatever punishment awaited him, the two stood like Buckingham Palace guards behind their terminals.

She decided to break the silence. "Walker."

He nearly flinched, but turned to her smoothly, his face completely stoic.

"You may believe my actions were to save her, but on the contrary, I was more concerned for you."

"Funny way of showing it," Robin replied coldly.

A patron came and checked out several books and a CD. When they were alone again, Sonyai continued, "Shinju is my brother's only daughter. Do you have any idea what that signifies in our culture?"

Robin said nothing. He knew she was baiting him, trying to justify her blatant racism, using archaic traditions as a crutch.

She sighed. "When she was 16, Shinju met this boy in school. He was two years her senior and what westerners would call a... *rebel.* The youth was fearless, and she was drawn to charming rogues that were protective, but challenged authority."

He tilted his head, feeling that she was insinuating that *he* was the opposite.

"But there was something more to him. Turns out he was... a leader of one of the local Triads, a gangbanger." She said the last word with such disdain. "My brother discovered their relationship, and put out a contract, using rival Triads to execute it."

That got Robin's attention as he cocked an eyebrow.

She walked up and whispered to him, "The boy was found split in half, from the crotch to the top of his neck. His *head* was never found."

If Robin was intimidated by the story he didn't show it. For all he knew it was just a fairy tale she was making up and none of it ever happened... but what if it did?

"So you think he would have objected our relationship?" he asked.

She nodded. "He would have killed you. Seriously."

Shinju mentioned briefly her father's line of work, but to believe he was capable of murder... he put the idea behind him. "So, like you, he would object to Shinju being in an interracial relationship... despite the fact that your father himself did the exact same thing with your mother."

She took a step back and blinked. Being put on the spot was unexpected. "Walker, that's..."

He followed her a step and hissed, "If your mother's Scottish ancestors acted and thought the same way as you and your brother did, BOTH of you wouldn't even be here now..."

She opened her mouth to reply, but he was right, and there was nothing she could say. He turned and returned to the terminal. "*Think* about that!" he exclaimed.

They finished the rest of the hour without another word between them.

Heywood was sitting at the information desk a few minutes before six when the phone rang.

"58th Street Branch Library," he answered.

"Stringbean! It's me, Jackie! I got great news."

"Oh, hey, you found a new club for performing?" he asked.

"Even better. The Man finally called! He wants to meet next Thursday, the 14th!"

"Okay, did he give a name or any idea who he was?"

"No, but he said he wants to ask a few questions face to face and his words were, 'We'll take it from there.' This could be the big break I've been waiting for!"

"Okay, okay, let's not get too excited. I hope you set a time to meet at night so I can go with you, for... protection, you know?"

"Yes, of course. I'm trying not to get my hopes up either, but fingers crossed. I just wanted to tell you the news. I'm ordering takeout to celebrate. See you when you get home. Maybe we can celebrate... another way too." She hung up the phone as he pulled on his collar, feeling flustered.

CHAPTER TWENTY

"So what do you think Sonyai's gonna do to him?" Gerry asked Ethel.

They were walking outside after leaving for the day, heading toward Lexington Avenue. Gerry had no clue where Ethel lived, but he figured she'd be taking one of the trains at 59th Street.

"She's got a wicked imagination and you heard her, firing the boy would be too easy. My best guess, he'll be doing every possible Saturday clustering to Cathedral Branch, every late night Wednesday, and maybe even bring him in at 10 am Thursday's until he's back in school."

"I was thinking that, too. We've seen that side of her, but this... this is something else. This was personal."

"I'm staying out of it, and you should as well," she warned.

"Look, I'm not saying he doesn't deserve the book getting thrown at him, but I just want to make sure there's no bias behind it."

She stopped walking. "Everything has to be racial with you, doesn't it? We don't know the whole story. Yi and Chavez were in that office yelling for an hour, and Walker slammed Stevens through a table!"

"And she smashed a coffee pot full of hot water on his face. Why do you think *that* happened?"

"I don't know and I don't care, but the branch has been turned upside down since that boy came in and as much as I'm cool with him now, I will not miss him when he's gone!" She resumed walking at a faster pace. "You keep instigating and I won't miss *you* either!" she called out behind her.

At seven, Zelda took a seat next to Augustus at the information desk. Despite only four hours of sleep before returning at two, he managed to recover appropriately.

"You're looking much better than you did this morning."

He groaned. "Took some comp time, skipped lunch, and my head feels like someone shook the maracas too much."

"You always were a social drinker, Gus. Christmas with rum cakes, New Year's with tequila, but the man I saw this morning, I didn't recognize."

"I almost did it, Zee. My hand was inches from the phone when *he* ran in," he nodded over to Robin, standing alone at the circulation desk. "It was my last resort. Would have taken us both out. She still doesn't know, but one day I tell you, it's going to come out."

"I can't run this branch myself if you're gone, and I'm not about to start all over with some *shlemiel*. We are bleeding in the water and that shark Cleopheous is circling."

The mention of the regional senior clerk made his eye twitch. She stood and walked around to face him in front of the desk. He looked up at her.

"Bring this house back in order. Make peace with Sonyai and get past this."

He watched her turn and leave, then looked over to the circulation desk again.

Robin ignored whatever private conversation Augustus and Zelda were having as he played out the series of events from Tuesday evening in his head. He knew there would be repercussions, but Sonyai had some sort of leverage on Augustus. This was beyond Janelle and her pregnancy. Something else was amiss.

Lakeshia was keeping to herself as she worked the late hours with him. He could understand why she was upset, which made him hesitant about reaching out to her. When she came behind the circulation desk to pick up some books he called out to her, "Leelee?"

She ignored him so he tried a more formal approach. "Lakeshia, got a sec?"

Still conflicted, she quickly collected the books and left before giving in. The last ten minutes before closing were a drag. Augustus closed all the window curtains and waited for the two of them at the exit. Robin locked the day's receipts in the safe and walked up to where Lakeshia was waiting with the head librarian.

"Good night," Augustus said as he let them out.

They both replied and left. She stood outside waiting for her ride to arrive.

"I can wait with you if you want," he offered.

"It's a free country."

He pouted at the generic snide response. After several minutes he asked her, "You remember that girl that came here the last time I did a late night?"

She tried to ignore him looking out to the street, but admitted, "Yeah."

"Her name was Shinju, Shinju Hasegawa."

The name! she remembered and turned to him.

"I met her on the train my first day here back in February, but we were formally introduced later after my grandfather died."

"Okay, but I don't understand why..."

"She's also Sonyai's niece," he interrupted. "I was shocked as hell when I found out," he shook his head. "And, so was she."

"Wh... what happened to her?"

"Within 24 hours of discovering us, Sonyai sent her away. I have no clue where." His voice started breaking. "Don't you see? She hurt me because all she saw was a nigger with her precious niece and she couldn't stand it!"

"She's not a racist! You had no right to expose that she was protecting Janelle to Mister Chavez! Janelle's leaving and it's all your fault!"

"She was leaving anyway! There was no way she could stay here! What Sonyai did was wrong," he waved his arm. "But who cares, right? After all, you've known Janelle what? A little more than a year? Who the fuck was I?"

"Robin."

"No!" he yelled and pointed, "You're all alike! Again and again and again! Diedre, Rosana, Raven, even my own MOTHER!"

He felt his heart crumbling in his chest. "I thought, I thought... you were different... I thought you would understand. But I guess I should have known better." He turned his back to her just as Derrick arrived. He honked twice and Lakeshia left him standing alone in front of the branch.

Friday morning Angie was waiting for Sonyai inside the clerical office. She walked past the nervous woman and placed Janelle's farewell gift in her desk.

"We need to talk," Angie began. "Augustus hasn't said two words to me since Tuesday and I know he's figured out I..."

"You have nothing to worry about," Sonyai interrupted. "He promised no punishment or retaliation will come to you. We made a deal."

"Where's the box?" she asked, not convinced.

"It's been destroyed, burned by fire."

"I'll go to S.I.U. Even without proof they can get him."

"You do that and what I did comes to light, and we both go down. I'm sorry Angie. It's over."

"What did you do?"

She sighed. "Do you really want to know? Does it even matter? Miss Trueblood, one of my first pages I mentored since becoming a senior clerk is transferring after today, under unconventional circumstances. I made a deal with the devil and will be paying the price for the rest of my career."

"He may have promised to leave me be, but I know Augustus, one way or another." Angie took a breath, trying to relax. "I trusted you. I won't make that mistake again!" She stormed out of the office and slammed the door behind her.

Janelle walked in 58th Street for the last time as a page at two o'clock. She remembered the anxiety she felt that cold December morning back in 1990. Sonyai had greeted her and said, "You're going to do good things here, child." From that day on she faithfully served under her and played a role in shaping her successors. Now, she was leaving the nest.

After an afternoon run, Robin came home and took a shower. He stared at the bandage on his face and decided it was time. With a quick rip, he grunted, feeling the sudden sensation of pain. He chuckled to himself after checking his face, then left to get dressed. Strolling inside the branch at two thirty-five, he caught the attention of the staff on the floor.

His baseball cap was purposely tilted with the brim covering the right side of his face. He walked to the center of the floor, as the clerks, pages and librarian staff looked at him from their vantage points.

With a dramatic flourish, he removed his cap and held it in his right hand, revealing his scar to everyone. "How's *that* for symmetry!?" he yelled, frightening the patrons reading. "Glass scar on the right side," he traced his finger down his scar then reached for his glove and ripped it off, showing his burned hand to all. "And acid scarred hand on the left!"

After months of hiding behind his defect, he felt no sense of vulnerability or exposure. He was done being modest as they all looked on. If his days working at this branch were numbered, he was going to make damn sure they would remember the name Robin Walker, the boy with no fear.

You want your monster? Well here he is!

Sonyai scowed, but said nothing. Neither did Augustus. Eugene tensed up, waiting for the order to eject the clerk for the outburst. Robin threw his glove into his cap and walked to the staircase going up to the staff room.

From the shelves, Tanya saw Lakeshia swoon. "Ohhh, he's even sexier with that scar!"

Someone was missing when Robin did his lavish performance. He stopped at the top of the stairs to find Janelle emptying her locker. The two stared at each other. Five months of drama that shook up a once quiet little library, standing several feet apart.

"I thought that stupid glove was hiding something," she taunted. "The scar looks nice, too."

He entertained taking a swing at her, pregnant and all. How much *more* in trouble could he get into? He decided to stay civil. "Just so you know, it wasn't personal... collateral damage." He shrugged, "You were the means to an end. For what it's worth, I'm sorry."

She removed the last of her personal items and closed the locker. "This... this won't be the last time we see each other. I'm going to remember this day and what you did." She held her cold stare, looking up directly into his eyes. "Then one day, when you least expect it... I'm going to hurt you just like you hurt Miss Yi. It's going to be an endless circle of pain, vendetta after vendetta. There will be no one left standing. No winner, no loser. They will look back and find it all pointless. But I don't care, my only mission in life is to take care of my child and bring a massive amount of agony and suffering to your doorstep."

Robin nodded, moved by the emotional speech. "I'm looking forward to it," he replied with a wink and stepped past the page into the staff room.

"Where did I go wrong, Thomas? Where did I go wrong?"

Gerry and Ethel were outside past the closed door of the clerical office as Sonyai confided in her protégé. Tommy sat across from her next to the safe as she stared at the floor in front of her desk.

"It's not your fault. We kept it a secret as long as we could, but he would have found out, eventually."

"I should have sent her away when she told me. She was so certain I could give her the position after she finished early. Why did I listen?"

"You couldn't have predicted…"

"I should have been prepared! Planned for every contingency!" She sighed. "This never would have happened if *he* were here."

The Man in White, Tommy thought. "Ma'am, he would be proud of you. You honor him every day running things here."

"Thank you, Thomas. How's Sarah?"

"Due date's at the end of the month. I can't believe it. I'm gonna be a father, at 25," he laughed. "I don't have a clue of what to do! I'm scared as hell!"

She stood up and walked over to him. They were at eye level with him sitting down. "You're going to be a great father, Thomas. I know you can do it."

"Thanks."

She almost cracked a smile, but then a frown came across her face as she got back to business. "Uh, when Walker comes downstairs, send him in, please. Ask Ethel to stay at her post a few minutes longer before he relieves her."

He stood up. "Yes, ma'am."

"Dismissed," she instructed.

Robin walked to the circulation desk after coming downstairs. He walked to Ethel on the checkout side, but Tommy called out to him about checking in with Sonyai first. He turned in place and opened the door to the clerical office.

"I apologize for the outburst earlier, ma'am," he began solemnly.

She raised her hand and he stopped mid-sentence.

"I want Miss Simms' last day to finish smoothly without further incident, with *any* of the pages. Do I make myself clear, Mister Walker?"

"Yes, ma'am," he replied.

"I am glad you have come to terms revealing your disfigurement because you have used up all of my patience, young man. I don't want to see that glove on your hand the moment you walk in this branch from this day forward, is *that* clear?"

"Yes, ma'am," he repeated.

"Now, before you return to duty, I want to explain in full the consequences of your actions this week."

Robin held *his* hand up this time. "Save it... you have no right to lecture me on consequences! You could have prevented this."

"How dare—" Sonyai gasped.

"Do you have an idea how painful it was to have someone come in and change your life briefly and then disappear in the blink of an eye?" he asked. "I had just lost the one person who ever gave a damn about me! And then, by divine intervention, your niece..." his voice began to break, "...gave me a new outlook on life."

The senior clerk looked back at him, completely emotionless. "You talk about a new outlook. That's something Miss Simms will have difficulty with now, herself."

Robin gave her a hard look. "You know, I find it so interesting the lengths you were willing to go..." he hissed. "Defraud a medical insurance company, antagonize and discourage an innocent new hire to maintain a vacancy," he started to pace, counting off with his finger, "Engage in a massive conspiracy, all to help a teenager become a single mother, giving birth to a child she's obviously unprepared to take care of rather than terminate the pregnancy!" he spat.

Sonyai gasped in horror at his statement, personally offended while he pointed and continued, "You and all those liberal white people, thinking they're doing a service helping these mothers have their kids and then turn around and call them lazy welfare cases, living off the government when the responsibility gets to be too much for them! When all they had to do was get a goddamn abortion!"

The slap struck him right on his scar as she brought her hand up and across his face. She was so fast, all he saw was white before shaking his head, bringing his eyes back to focus. Never before had someone gotten under her skin to cause her to resort to their level. Sonyai Yi had had enough.

"Who the fuck are you to tell a woman what to do with her body?!" she yelled. The rage from Tuesday evening all came flooding back. She almost wanted to hit him again.

Being struck by his supervisor was jarring, but the clerk kept himself in check. Apparently, he got his point across and there was nothing else to say on the subject.

"Without. Further. Incident," he grunted.

He turned and opened the door. Stepping out to the circulation desk he said, "You're relieved, Jenkins," and took his post.

Against Augustus' wishes, Sonyai asked the staff (including Robin) to stay for fifteen minutes after closing for a brief farewell gathering in Janelle's honor. A variety of soft drinks and snacks were purchased and there were segregated groups conversing among themselves. Janelle was given a card for well-wishes and she spoke a few parting words.

The pages then surrounded her for one last group hug. Tears fell as they held together for more than a minute. Tanya stepped away first. Lakeshia wiped her face and walked over to Sonyai, who comforted the child. Alex was the last to let go. She looked at her.

"You need anything, ANYTHING, you call me," she stressed to her. "And I better be the second person you call when you go into labor."

Janelle giggled and nodded, then Alex turned toward Robin's direction. He was sitting on a shelving cart, leaning on the wall in the back, away from the circulation desk and everyone. She walked around, approaching him.

"Miss Stevens!" Sonyai warned.

He didn't flinch, bracing for anything. *Here we go,* he thought.

"I know you saved me, and I will always be thankful for that," she began. "But Janelle was like a sister to me. You did what you did to get back at Miss Yi, I understand that, but I don't care. One way or another, I will make you PAY for this."

Another speech. Robin wondered if everyone in the branch was just going to walk up and tell him off with a long prepared discourse. *I should have let them rape you.* He dare not say it aloud, but he knew from that moment on, it was a mistake to intervene that night.

She stepped back from him and reached for a bag that was on a reading table. She pulled out a wrapped gift. "This was originally a graduation gift," Alex said, handing it to Janelle.

"Aww, you didn't have to," she said with a smile and opened it. Inside the gift box was a cassette of Arrested Development's latest album, *Zingalamaduni.*

"Oh, wow," she gasped.

Alex stole a glance at Ethel, remembering their conversation about frugal spending.

Janelle gave her one last embrace. "Sonyai may be their surrogate mother, but *you're* their big sister," she told her. "They will look to you, now. Take care of them, Alexandra."

She swallowed hard hearing her full name and nodded, "I promise."

Janelle turned and walked toward the exit where Sonyai was waiting for her.

"Did Human Resources inform you of the details? What time you are to report at your new location on Monday?"

"Yes, Miss Yi."

"The senior clerk at Van Nest is a Mister Reginald Brantley. I wish I could have learned more, but I want you to treat him with as much respect as you have treated me. You are a reflection of me and this branch. Carry yourself with dignity and class. Remember everything you learned here."

"I will. I'll make you proud, Miss Yi."

"Say it with me, child."

They both started to recite, "The library is a public resource, where every man, woman, and child of any race, class or religion is treated fairly and equally."

The senior clerk looked at her page with loving approval. "You did great things here, child."

Janelle smiled at the memory. "Thank you for everything." She walked out of the branch to the street. She dared not look back because she knew the tears would start again. Sonyai watched the child disappear in the distance, then stepped inside and locked the door behind her.

The first person she saw when walking back in was Robin. A flash of anger flared inside her but she kept her composure.

"I stayed on my best behavior. I'll see you at the gallows on Monday."

He stepped past her and left. Zelda and the other librarians filed out moments behind him as Augustus walked back to his office. Inside, he took a seat and picked up his phone. A few rings into the call, Cleopheous Baker answered. "Hello?"

"You're going to have to try harder to get *this* weasel, you sonovabitch!"

He slammed the receiver down with a satisfying thud.

CHAPTER TWENTY ONE

Tommy was stirred awake by the sound of Sarah retching in the toilet Monday morning. He still had an hour to sleep, but her morning sickness had become routine, so he crawled out of bed instead of tuning her out. Rather than join her in the bathroom in an attempt to wash up, he rushed to the kitchen to start breakfast.

"Tommy!" Sarah yelled. "Get out of my kitchen!"

"Let me make you breakfast for once, hon!"

"I can still..." she stopped in mid-sentence as he heard her throw up again, "...still make breakfast so turn that stove off, right now!"

He threw the frying pan back on top of the range and walked back to the bedroom.

"Until my water breaks, *maldita sea*, I make the breakfast in this house!" she instructed an hour later.

"I'm just trying to help," Tommy whined.

"You wanna help? Rub my feet, fluff my pillow, and stay out of my ki..." she gasped.

He stood up as she held her side. "Ooof," she grunted.

Tommy ran to the living room to grab a gym bag that was near the door, "False alarm, false alarm!" she cried out. He dropped it and walked back to the kitchen. She was waving her arm. "Good reaction time, though. You didn't stand there all frozen with a dumb look on your face."

She took a seat to catch her breath and he knelt next to her. He held her hand in his and looked at her face. She was flushed. A curl of hair fell perfectly between her eyes. "Ay, stop looking at me like that."

"Like what? Like you're the most beautiful woman in the world?" he asked.

She looked down and he lifted her chin. Her eyes betrayed the fear she was feeling. "Are we ready?" she whispered. "Are we *really* ready for this?"

"Too late to turn back now." He leaned in. Their foreheads touched. "We'll make it work, even if I have to get a second job, hon. We'll raise this child to the best of our abilities."

She sighed. "You're incredible. I love you, *mi amado.*"

"*Te amo, mujer,*" he said back.

Gerry walked into the clerical office at eight forty in the morning. Ethel was out on the floor reading the newspaper while Sonyai sat at her desk waiting for him.

He tilted his head, looking at the surroundings. "Hey, what happened to my desk?"

"You and Thomas are sharing a desk now," Sonyai replied. "Or, you can share with Ethel. Your choice."

Gerry's desk was located in the back of the office across from Sonyai's, Tommy's was next to the doorway, and Ethel's was in the far corner. The desk was clean of his personal items.

"What's going on here? Why isn't the desk schedule up on the wall yet?"

She ignored his queries and simply said, "Thomas or Ethel, you pick."

He turned and left the office. Ethel never lowered the paper, sensing his approach.

"Uh, Jenkins, can I…"

"What do you think?" she interrupted him.

He groaned. "This is bullshit!"

"Tanya! Get out here, baby," Cynthia Brown called for her daughter.

She emerged from her room down the hall to the kitchen. "Yeah, Mama?"

"I'm doing the second shift at the hospital this evening. I want you to come straight home and call me when you get here."

"Okay."

"I've been thinking about you and this job. Just because you barely passed this year don't think I forgot about just giving you an allowance to quit it."

"We… just lost someone, Mom. She got transferred to another branch. They need me more than ever now. Please can I stay?"

Cynthia looked into her daughter's pleading eyes. "Fine!" she relented. "You can stay."

Tanya ran across and hugged her. "Thank you, thank you, Mama!"

"Hmmm. Just stay out of trouble!"

"I will, I promise!" She skipped back to her room.

"Remember, come straight home and call me!" she called back at her.

"You really think this is your last round up?" Franklin asked Robin. It was almost noon as the pair watched *The People's Court* on TV.

"Who knows? At this point I don't even care," he answered.

"Hmmm, you staying kind of late, aren't you?" Franklin asked while checking his watch.

"No train today. Cervantes is picking me up. I'm going out in style!"

"If they do fire you, what are you gonna do?"

"Find something else, I dunno... maybe I'll move, find Microsoft headquarters and start as an intern."

"Yeah, right. You couldn't get a coffee order right if you tried."

He helped himself to a can of Orange Crush in the refrigerator and took a few sips. Robin was at the kitchen table eating a peanut butter and jelly sandwich.

"Did you even try to reach out to *her* for help?"

"She didn't help before. She's not gonna save me now. I don't want her to anyway."

"Schemanske's always had a soft spot for you. Burns too. They could easily make this go away."

Robin sighed, then finished his sandwich with two big bites. Franklin walked to the table and took the seat next to him. "You're doing this because of Jon, aren't you? Because he's not here to push you, keep you at it."

He knew he struck a nerve when Robin gave him a hard stare.

"What would you think he'd say if..."

"DON'T!" he barked. "That psychological sob story bullshit ain't gonna change my mind! You walked away too, so don't you dare!"

Franklin remained calm while looking directly at him. "I left because I stopped caring," he said flatly. "But you, you still give a damn. That's why this is tearing you apart. That's why you're pretending this is the end."

He stood up. "But hey, what do I know, huh? It ain't the first time you've let me down. It won't be the last." He walked to the door. "You find yourself down in the gutter, you know where to find me." He left without another word.

Cervantes arrived at one. Robin stepped into the cab. "Take the FDR to 79th then the local streets to the branch."

The cabbie headed down to Audubon as he sat quietly. Once there were on the parkway, he took several glances over his shoulder to the backseat. "Something wrong, my friend?"

"Why do we do what we do, Cervantes?"

"A remarkable question if I ever heard one!" he replied. "I have been driving this cab for so many years and I ask myself, 'Why? I can do something else,' but I *choose* to do this because I am good at it."

He looked up to his rearview mirror. "Are you good at what you do?"

Robin looked into the mirror, his eyes looking back at him. "I don't know anymore."

"This doesn't feel right," Tommy said to Sonyai as they worked the desk. It was almost two o'clock. There was an uneasy feeling going around since the desk schedule was put up. The clerical staff were puzzled by the actions of the senior clerk, but kept their reservations to themselves.

"My decision is final, Thomas."

"But for how long? Someone will say something. This is highly irregular."

Sonyai understood the apprehension, but she was determined to see this through. *He won't last long,* she thought to herself.

At the top of the hour, Robin arrived, walking toward the clerical office. Gerry and Ethel came out and switched with Sonyai and Tommy. Robin took a second to check the desk schedule then walked in. It didn't surprise him that his name was missing. Sonyai was probably going to brief him of his termination and likely send him home early.

He stood in the middle of the office and waited for the senior clerk. She walked in and closed the door. They greeted each other with silent nods.

"I see I'm not scheduled on the desk today," he began.

She gestured toward what he knew to be Gerry's desk. "Have a seat."

He noticed it was unusually clean today. "Okay."

Once he was seated, she walked over to her desk drawer and

pulled out an inkpad and a date due stamp. Robin rolled his eyes as he saw the items in her hands and looked on as she placed them on the desk. He was all too familiar with this form of punishment. The pages at Fort Washington called it *"Peeling Potatoes"*, stamping date due cards for future dates. There were black three-week cards and red one-week cards. Once, after a fight with Trevor, he did nothing but stamp packets for a week.

"Judging by your reaction I'm sure you know what comes next. Well, I would get comfortable Mister Walker. You'll be doing this for a very long time."

She handed him a stack of cards rubber-banded and a list of dates to mark off when done. He proceeded to open the inkpad, adjust the stamp to a date, and begin the menial task. She added more stacks, followed by several more, and an additional pile to cover the entire desk.

"I want all these done *today*. Take your break and be back here promptly."

"Yes ma'am," he replied. *Hmph, no imagination,* he thought.

"This won't be a temporary thing, Walker. You are hereby EXILED. You will be doing this and nothing else for as long as you're working here. No clustering, no late nights, and crying to Miss....Schemanske? Is not going to help you."

He continued to stamp, ignoring her. He was very precise, stamping right between the lines.

She left to go outside for a cigarette. Gerry followed her with his eyes, burning a hole in the back of her head. He almost called out to her, but held his tongue.

"Let it go, Gerry," Ethel warned him.

Alex walked into the staff room ten minutes before three. There was still no kitchen table so the space was very open with the two sofas and six chairs. She rubbed her neck involuntarily, remembering Robin lifting her and stepping on top of the chair behind him, then leaping off, with both of them landing and breaking the table. The thunderous crash was still ringing in her ears.

She snapped out of the memory when Lakeshia and Tanya walked in together. They greeted each other with quiet nods, then Tanya said, "And then there were three."

"Yeah," Lakeshia added.

"Look, we've got to move on. No point moping around," Alex explained, taking on the assertiveness she promised Janelle she would. "Let's split up Janelle's shelf assignments, and when Miss Yi hires..." she didn't want to say *"a replacement"*, "...when the new page arrives, we'll do a new round of reassignments."

"Okay, but *this* time I get the ooo's!" Lakeshia exclaimed.

The three shared a laugh and headed downstairs.

Robin left at five. Sonyai set the schedule to close with each of the full-time clerks and do the late night in the part-time clerk's place. She arranged help to come from Webster and Yorkville on days when someone working a Saturday was off. This punishment may inconvenience the branch slightly, but she was determined to send a message. The senior clerk was confident the part-time clerk would resign by the end of the month.

"I'm all for teaching the boy a lesson, but you know I don't like closing," Ethel said from the checkout side.

"I've left you out of the rotation for weeks, Jenkins. Please have some patience."

"Yeah, okay," she dismissed.

Sonyai twisted her lip in a snarl of annoyance, but said nothing. *He WON'T last long,* she repeated to herself.

Tanya came home around six and turned on the TV in the living room. She took out a box of Ellio's Cheese Pizza from the freezer and broke a solid piece into three square slices, then placed them in the toaster oven. After calling her mother at the hospital to check-in, she dialed another number and waited.

"Hello?" Franklin answered.

"I'm home alone and my mom doesn't get in 'til late tonight."

"I'll be there in 25 minutes," he replied quickly and hung up.

Twenty-three minutes later, there was a knock on her door. She greeted him wearing nothing but her bra and panties. "I hope you brought a lot of rubbers."

He opened his hand and a line of five packaged and connected condoms dangled from his fingers. She stepped aside and let him in then playfully jumped on his back. Her hands proceeded to tear his clothes off until he was naked as she was.

"Fuck, I think there's smoke coming out of my dick," Franklin sighed.

They were laying together on her bed. The clock on the dresser read nine o'clock.

"I gotta hand it to you," Tanya stretched. "You've got stamina." She turned and looked at him quietly.

"What's wrong?"

"Nothing, uh, work has me fucked up. I see you, I see... him."

Franklin sat up and slid his legs over the edge of the bed, his back was to her. "He told me what went down. Believe or not, he's genuinely sorry about what happened to your friend." He sat thinking to himself, then a grin came across his face. "We can't do this anymore, can we?" a light chuckle came from him.

"You mad?" she asked.

"Fuck no, kinda saw it coming after what happened at my place. This was supposed to be fun, and it was. I hope you forgot about your boy, Romeo."

"Who?" she giggled.

He felt her hand on his shoulder and suddenly pull him back down on the bed. She moved on top of him and placed the last condom in her mouth, holding it in place with her lips. After pushing the tip out with her tongue, she winked and mumbled,

"One last time, to remember me by," then lowered her head to his crotch.

Thursday morning, Robin left the A&P Supermarket on 179th Street and Broadway, heading back home up 179th Street to Wadsworth. At the corner, he nearly dropped his bags when he saw a four-door limousine parked in front of the building.

"Are you kidding me?!" he yelled.

He crossed the street and couldn't believe his eyes as Augustus stood waiting for him to approach. "Good morning," he said cheerfully.

"If you think for a second..." Robin began.

"No tricks this time," he insisted and waved to the open door.

"Give me your wallet."

The librarian blinked. "Excuse me?"

"For assurance, I'm only going with you if you hand me your wallet to hold. That way I know you won't leave me again." He was referring to the previous time Augustus took him to The Bronx and stranded him there.

Augustus shook his head. "I'm not..."

Robin turned to enter the building.

"Okay, okay!" he yielded and pulled out a brown calfskin folding wallet.

Robin accepted the item. It felt funny in his hands, but he brought his groceries inside the car and Augustus climbed into the backseat next to him.

They rode in silence while traveling downtown. The car drove across 54th Street and stopped on the corner before 6th Avenue. The pair stepped out and Robin looked up to see that they were at the Hilton Hotel.

"Sorry sir, but I ain't sharing the honeymoon suite with you!" Robin joked.

The driver handed the keys to the hotel valet and walked down the street. Augustus glared at Robin and said, "We walk from here. Follow me, and enough of the smart remarks. I'm expressing my gratitude."

They walked down 6th Avenue a block and turned on 63rd Street. They approached a store with a red awning that read *Rochester Big and Tall.* Augustus led Robin inside. There was a vast assortment of dress clothes, as well as casual wear.

"Shouldn't you be at the branch?" Robin asked.

"I'm off today, actually, so I can work the Saturday this weekend," he replied.

"Okay."

"I brought you here because of the information you told me about Yi's deception. I'm sure she's told you all the gory details of our *arrangement*?" he asked.

"Yeah."

"Well, this is just my way of saying thank you." He stopped at a rack with polo shirts and searched among them. "What are you, a 3X?"

"Give or take." Robin looked at a price tag on one of the shirts and gasped. "Whoa! These cost over $60!" *And they're hideous!* he added.

"Well, you *do* have my wallet." Augustus replied. "Pick one and pay for it."

He looked around, there was nothing that he felt was worth wearing. The entire store was just not his style. "Um, thanks, but no thanks,"

A frown came across the librarian's face. "Walker…"

"Look, Sonyai had you against the wall and I saved you, only I wasn't trying to. I was getting back at *her!* I couldn't give a rat's ass about you… respectfully, sir." He pulled out the wallet and held it out to him. "Chalk it up to… perfect timing."

Augustus took the wallet back and pulled out a hundred-dollar-bill. "I insist on buying you something in this store, even if it's a tie, a belt," he looked down at his feet, "Or even a decent pair of shoes."

Robin was fed up with this fake act of kindness. "You justify whatever dirt Sonyai had on you, and she justifies a fake pregnancy to help a page in a messed up situation of her own doing. You're *both* wrong, and the two of you are more alike than either of you will ever admit. You don't need to buy me anything!"

"How dare you! I should leave your ungrateful ass out here again!" he hissed.

"You wanna thank me for what I did, take me back home and forget we ever came here." He turned and walked toward the exit. "I'm not for sale!"

"Integrity," Augustus whispered in disgust. "And I thought he had potential." He shook his head and followed him.

CHAPTER TWENTY TWO

THE BRANCH WAS QUIET, OPENING EARLY IN THE MORNING AS HEYWOOD and Angie were replacing the monthly periodicals with newer issues. Zelda was sitting at the information desk while Gerry was working the circulation desk.

"Isn't tonight your appointment with '*The Man*'?" Angie asked.

"Yeah, me and Jackie will be heading to the Bowery to meet at CBGB's."

"Whoa, kick-ass scene. My ex-boyfriend played there once," Angie said.

"Yeah?"

"The place was packed, and the stage was so small. It almost seemed like you were on the stage with the band."

"I never pegged you for a groupie, Trueblood," he said with a grin.

"Oh, there's a lot you don't know about me, Heywood Learner," she replied with a wink.

Eugene walked by doing his rounds. He couldn't help hearing the light conversation. "Hey, if you're meeting this mystery person you might want some backup in case something goes wrong."

"Thanks, but we can handle ourselves. Jackie's a spitfire. She can take anyone."

"Alright, keep your eyes open." He resumed his rounds while Heywood looked at Angie. "You and Jackie should really iron things out."

She scowled. "You bring her around here again, I'm giving her a piece of my mind."

At noon there was a delivery to the branch in the form of the new kitchen table for the staff room. Sonyai and Zelda helped oversee the assembly and placement upstairs in the staff room.

"I believe this is the first new piece of furniture we've had in a decade," Zelda remarked.

"That was pretty fast. I expected to be eating at my desk until the fall. How did Chavez get this table so quickly?"

"He has his ways." Zelda didn't want to reveal that Augustus used his own money to buy the table from a wholesale furniture outlet upstate.

The senior clerk said nothing further until Zelda asked, "Are the two of you okay?"

"We never were '*okay*'."

"Hopefully both of you can put everything in the past and worry about the matters at hand."

"Such as?"

"Despite his actions, there are others in the cluster who are challenging him and this branch..."

"For reasons that are his own!" Sonyai interrupted. "He manipulated statistics in favor of a lush reward. The other branches have every right to be upset!"

"Okay, he bends the rules occasionally. They are just as guilty. Will removing him really be the end that justifies the means?"

"He went too far," she pointed at Zelda. "*You* should have kept him in line, prevented him from doing this."

"And who keeps YOU in line, hmm?" she retorted. "What exactly were you thinking filing false paperwork, misusing thousands of dollars in medical expenses? There are skeletons in your closet, Sonyai, and it's time to get off that high horse of yours!"

"I will NEVER forgive him for what he did to Natasha!"

"It was five years ago, oy vey!" She looked down and pinched her forehead. After taking a breath, she looked up at her. "What's it going to take?" she asked quietly. "We Jews have a saying…"

She spoke in Yiddish as Sonyai looked at her blankly.

"It means, *"You can't move a mountain with a splinter."* I know you're angry. Your mentor was a great man. Working together with Augustus instead of against him can make you just as great as he was."

She turned and thanked the people for their assistance as Sonyai thought deeply about the advice.

CBGB was affectionately known as New York City's birthplace of Rock, Folk, and Punk music. Originally opening in 1973 as a bar that would be favored by motorcycle gangs, the letters stood for Country, Bluegrass and Blues. The irony was not lost on the owners. RFPM didn't exactly roll off the tongue.

Heywood and Jackie stepped off the M103 bus at Bleecker Street. It was ten o'clock and the club was packed with people poured out on the sidewalk drinking and smoking cigarettes. Heywood recognized the tall bald-headed bouncer who gave them the card. He was wearing a Dallas Cowboys football jersey and matching blue sweatpants.

"Emmitt Smith! Nice jersey!" Jackie said for a greeting.

"I grew up in Minnesota, I'm a Vikings fan," he said proudly. "I'm only wearing this to lay low."

"Um, okay, so what do we call you?" Heywood asked.

"*You* may call me 'sir', but I go by the name of 'Law'." He waved at Jackie, "You follow me."

Jackie wrapped around Heywood's right arm. "He comes along, we're a package deal."

"He don't sing!" Law barked.

"You heard her," he said, sticking out his chest to appear tough.

Law stared back a moment, waiting for the couple to falter. He broke into a grin and turned around. "Got two incoming, pull up," he said to a walkie-talkie.

A white limousine appeared and turned the corner from East 1st Street. It stopped in front of them and the door opened. A few onlookers began to exchange puzzled comments as Law grabbed Heywood and Jackie.

"Get in," he ordered and shoved them in.

The door slammed behind them and pulled away, running a red light.

There were sounds of protests from the rough behavior as they straightened themselves in the backseat. A smooth, calm voice came from the opposite side. "Please excuse Lawrence. He can be overzealous in protecting my privacy."

They looked up, searching for the source. The interior was dark with the windows tinted. An arm reached up and flicked a switch. The backseat light came on, revealing a figure sitting before them staring back. After focusing and adjusting to the light, they both gasped.

"Hello, Miss Daisy. It's nice to meet you."

Jackie ignored the fact that she was called, "Miss Daisy", and started stammering.

"W..w...whoaaaa, you're, you're..." Heywood said.

"Please don't mention my previous name," The Man began. "Due to my record label I'd prefer to be addressed simply as... 'The Artist'."

He was dressed all in white and wore sunglasses. A guitar in the shape of his signature symbol that also represented his current name was leaning on the corner to his right. Jackie grabbed Heywood's arm, squealing with excitement as he tried to calm her down.

"I'll get right to the point," The Artist said. "One of my backup singers has a polyp in her vocal cords and I have a tour that kicks off in the fall."

"And you want me?!" she asked.

"It will take months to bring you up to speed and we only have weeks. I don't have to tell you, this is a chance of a lifetime."

Jackie looked at Heywood. He knew her decision before she could say it. "Go for it," he whispered.

She turned and said, "I'm in."

The Artist nodded. "It's 18 months. We won't be back in the states till the end of next year. I don't mean to sound cold, but we'll need to start right away."

Heywood let out a sigh. "Right."

The high immediately got sucked out of the room. Jackie looked at Heywood again. "I..I'm... sorry. You've done so much." She reached over and hugged him. "I'll make good on this. I'll be back."

"It's okay, live the dream."

The Artist knocked on the window screen behind him twice. The car turned the corner and stopped in the middle of the block. Jackie was in tears as she kissed him one last time. "First Kurt, and now you. So many good men passing through my life."

"Take care, Jackie."

He stepped out of the limo and looked back at her. The tears streaked down her dark cheeks like icicles on a window to the night sky. She tried to smile, but failed miserably. He closed the door and the car took off like a bat out of hell.

Friday morning before going to work, Heywood walked into a pawn shop down the street from him on Clinton Street. The owner greeted with a wide smile. "Mister Learner, putting more money down on that item in question?"

He pulled out a small felt box with an engagement ring inside. He was saving up for the last two weeks after dropping a hefty deposit.

"No, change of plans. What's the policy on refunds?"

"Store credit only." The smile disappeared.

He rolled his eyes. "Great." He looked down at an assortment of chains, rings and other jewelry in the glass counter. One item caught his eye. He walked out with an eighteen-inch chain attached to a two-inch long silver cross placed squarely on his chest. Unlike Jackie Daisy, Jesus would be a mainstay in his life.

Sports had been an emotional driving point around the world during the summer of 1994, from the New York Rangers shattering their 54-year curse to the Dallas Cowboys giving the Buffalo Bills their fourth straight loss in the Super Bowl. Nothing compared to what happened last Sunday as Brazil defeated Russia in the FIFA World Cup held in the United States.

"It's insane, Learner. They take football very seriously in South America, especially in Brazil... why, it's pretty much a way of life down there!"

It was another Monday morning briefing and Heywood was preoccupied, tuning Augustus out while still thinking of Jackie. A clipboard was on his lap as he subconsciously thumbed the chain around his neck. All he heard was the end of the head librarian's rant about soccer.

"...men are literally walking up to women saying, 'Hey, Brazil just won, let's have sex!' and they start tearing their clothes off in the middle of the street! Uh, Learner? Are you listening?"

"Um, yeah, people having sex, remarkable, that's great sir! Yeah," he replied.

"Ahem, yes... forgive me. The way Mexico plays, Brazil may be the closest thing to my people winning a championship so I can't help but get excited. Back to what we were discussing, I believe your two recommendations will be fine for the final slots in August for the concert series. Great job!"

"Thank you, sir." He stood up to leave.

"If something's troubling you," Augustus said to his back, "I'm always here to talk about anything."

"I'll keep that in mind, sir." Heywood opened the door and walked out on the floor to the information desk. He jumped as the phone rang and quickly answered it. "58th Street Branch library."

"Learner, it's Gerry. Is Sonyai there? I tried to call her direct line, but she didn't pick up."

"I'll transfer you." Heywood put the call on hold and dialed the extension, then pressed the transfer button.

Inside the clerical office, Ethel picked up the phone at Sonyai's desk.

"Hello?"

"Jenkins?"

"Gerry?" she asked.

"Yeah, listen. I got a bad case of food poisoning. I can't make it today. Let Sonyai know."

"You don't have no damn food poisoning. What the hell are you doing?"

"Just tell her, damn it!" the phone clicked off.

She sighed as Sonyai walked in. "Who was that?"

"Uh, that was Gerry. He can't come in today. He's sick."

"Terrific," she sighed, but then looked at her. "What exactly did he say?" she asked, suddenly believing that this could be intentional.

"Food poisoning," she answered with a blank stare.

"Indeed."

Ethel moved aside as Sonyai picked up her phone and dialed. "Hello Andrew? Do you have anyone to spare?"

Franklin had just finished getting dressed for work when his phone rang. He thought about letting the answering machine take a message because he wasn't expecting a call, but before the third ring he picked it up.

"Hello?"

"Hi, um, is Franklin there?" a female voice asked.

He looked at the receiver. "Yeah, this is Franklin, who's this?"

"The one whose ass you were staring at while I made that 7-10 split," Denise Coltraine answered.

Franklin's eyebrows jumped to the ceiling. "Ooooooh! I could never forget that ass! Well, hello! It took you two whole months to decide whether to call?"

"Good things come to those who wait, baby. I was wondering if you'd like to help me find a bikini to wear and come with me to Atlantic City this weekend."

Holy shit! He fought to keep his cool. "Sounds like fun," he replied.

"Oh, it will be fun, Youngblood. I don't disappoint... and you better not, either," she chuckled.

After a few minutes of exchanging information, he hung up the phone and spun around in celebration.

"Time to climb that mountain!" he cheered.

Ethel was annoyed by Gerry calling out on purpose as some sort of protest of solidarity against Robin's punishment. Sonyai kept the part-time clerk stamping cards while Charlie Hooper from Webster Branch arrived to offer assistance to her and Tommy. *Sonyai and her pet footstool Andrew, offering his clerks at a moment's notice,* she thought in disgust.

She noticed something was troubling Lakeshia as she pushed her shelving cart back in place against the wall behind the circulation desk. Checking the wall clock, the clerk noticed it was ten minutes before the end of her shift. *Guess I got some time to pry.*

"Miss Seabrooke?" she called out to the page.

She turned around and stood in place. "Yes, Miss Jenkins?"

"Something on your mind, young lady?"

Lakeshia shifted her feet and looked toward the door to the clerical office, where Sonyai and Robin sat at opposite ends. Ethel noticed the gaze, then slid up the foot jam that held the door open. With it closed, she felt more comfortable to talk in private.

With Charlie working a line of checkouts, Ethel approached Lakeshia as the page whispered, "Do you think Miss Yi has a problem with..." she shifted her eyes, "...black people?"

Ethel frowned. "What would make you think that?"

She sighed. "You can't say anything, but Robin was dating this girl he met in school. She came here on one of his late nights...and I saw them necking upstairs in the staff room."

Ethel's eyes went wide.

"But it turns out...she was Miss Yi's niece and when she found out about them, Miss Yi sent her away. That's why Robin told Mister Chavez about Janelle's pregnancy."

"That's who that 'soo-hoo' person he was talking about was?" Ethel asked, remembering the confrontation.

"Shinju," Lakeshia corrected her.

"Whatever," she shook her head. "I've known her for a while. I've never seen her outright show any prejudice toward..." *Well there IS Gerry. Though she treated Friedman fairly...* "I don't know, but don't say anything to anyone else. Let's keep this to ourselves until things cool off, okay?"

"Yes, Miss Jenkins. It felt good to talk to someone about this." She was hurt by Janelle leaving, but still felt sorry for Robin and his punishment. Lakeshia walked away just as the door to the clerical desk opened.

Sonyai stepped out to relieve Ethel. They nodded to each other silently then she reached for her purse under the returns terminal. The senior clerk took her station while Ethel walked through the security threshold and left the branch.

A lot had been on Ethel's mind lately. The change of diet and medication she was taking were helping her health-wise. She was thinking clearer and feeling more energetic. After walking into her apartment at six-fifteen in the evening she poured herself a glass of water and checked the mail. A few of her credit card bills had sizable balances, and her bank statements showed limited funds available.

She was reading travel guides related to living in Savannah the last few weeks and was ready to decide on her sister's proposal. The fallout from disappointing the family would be hard, but they would understand. She planned to let her sister know face to face soon, very soon.

CHAPTER TWENTY THREE

Cleopheous Baker sat on a bench near the fountain in the center of Washington Square Park. The sun was beginning to set and he was feeding bread crumbs to the pigeons. Zelda walked up and took a seat to his left.

"I'm surprised you're not playing chess at the southwest corner," she began.

"I feed the birds for Estelle. It was her favorite thing to do Sunday mornings before she passed. We then went to the Blue Note for the brunch special. She always loved jazz." He tossed a few more pieces of bread as several minutes went by. "I heard you got a place nearby. Is the rent good?"

"I manage," she replied. "I'm here to make amends."

"Don't you ever get tired of cleaning up his messes? Doing his dirty work? I mean damn, does he even know you're here? Talking to me?" He shook his head. "I don't know if we can make this right."

"Sure we can," someone said behind him.

Barbara Schemanske sat down at Baker's right. "We can make anything right if we act like civilized individuals."

He looked back and forth and sighed. "I'm supposed to be scared because you..."

"This has nothing to do with *fear* and everything to do with the status quo," Barbara said.

"You know...our branches are like a sandbox. The six of us all have our areas, yeah. And I have my bucket with a shovel. I'm making sandcastles, and they're looking nice and neat. Then along comes Chavez, and he takes my favorite shovel! Now I can go get another shovel, but I really, really like *that* particular shovel. It's mine. I mean, who is he to just up and take it for no reason?!"

"Baker, please! Do you know how childish you sound?" Zelda exclaimed.

"Zelda," Barbara began.

"No, I'm tired, Babs."

"ZELDA!"

The pigeons flew away, startled by the outburst. Barbara sighed and in her regular voice said, "Tell him what we agreed to."

Zelda took off her glasses and cleaned them with a handkerchief. "96th Street will be awarded an anonymous charitable donation of $6,000.00. With a marker equivalent to a favor of any *reasonable* request asked upon us, no questions asked...to be used at a future time." She put her glasses back on and turned to him. "Does that satisfy your grievance?"

Cleopheous stood up. "The materials he used...does he still have them?"

"No," Zelda answered.

A minute went by then he said. "I want that check before the beginning of the fiscal year."

Without another word, he started walking toward the area of the park with the chess tables.

"What a schmuck," Zelda hissed. "If I were twenty years younger, I'd take over his branch and bury him in a reference basement surrounded by newspapers and microfiche."

"He's not worth the effort. Just a baby who's overcompensating for the small penis God dealt him." Barbara stood and looked at the park's infamous arch. "I remember hearing the beatniks spout poetry, nonsensical limericks, and rants about opposing the government. I almost believed it would be better if they were gone. Now I see they were right."

"You keep talking like we're dinosaurs, Babs, but we're survivors. Can I interest you in a glass of wine? I'm just 10 minutes away on the bus."

"We'll split a cab," she grunted. "And if I have to tell you not to call me 'Babs' again, I'm breaking the wine glass and cutting your throat with it!"

After months on a waiting list, Franklin and Robin were finally contacted by the neighborhood video rental store Kappy's about their reservation for *Super Metroid*. The Super Nintendo game was released in March and was sold out in stores within weeks. Renting it for three days had been the only other option.

The pair left Kappy's with the game and walked down 181st Street from Fort Washington.

"Why are we walking this way?" Robin asked. "We should have went through the bus terminal."

"I wanna swing by Tony's for a slice."

"We don't have time for that. At best we got an hour to play before I leave for work!"

"We got the game till Friday, and you know we're keeping it an extra day so there's time," he grinned. "Don't tell me you still shook from that time we got mugged taking home *Super Contra* from the flea market when we were 12?"

"Hey, that shit was traumatic. You weren't so tough when they put you in a yoke and pressed that barrel to your back. That'll be the last time I walk from the store down Saint Nick, flea market bunch of crooks anyway. Probably tipped off the muggers and sold the game a second time."

"Whatever. That was six years ago. Ain't nobody robbing me now. I'll kick their ass!" Franklin put his hands up in a stance while walking.

"Yeah, right."

They walked into Tony's. Behind the counter, the owner waved at his two dedicated customers.

"Three slices to go and he's paying!" Franklin called out, pointing to Robin.

"What? Since when?"

"Since a certain sexy wo-man finally called me this week."

"What are yo..." he gasped. "NO!"

"Yep!"

"Uh-uh!"

"Un-huh!"

"Bullshit!"

"Shit you not!" Franklin grinned. "I tell you, the timing was perfect, too. I just let go of this feisty piece of ass, right? Scratching, rippin' and tearing every time we..."

Robin held his hand up. "Spare me the details. What's going on with Gerry's sister? That right there is dynamite. Handle with care, man." He reached for his wallet as the slices were put in a paper bag.

"This ain't gonna be a problem for you is it?" Franklin asked as they walked back out to the street.

"Like you would pass up some action on my account."

"Heh, you right, but thought it'd be nice to ask. I'm going Martin Luther King, Jr. on this one. I'm gonna see it all from the mountain top!"

"It's 'Been to the mountaintop,' get it right, and please don't disgrace Doctor King's memory by using his words as a euphemism for getting laid."

"My bad, my bad..."

"Just be careful man, teasing these girls and breaking their hearts may be part of the game, but a woman will fuck you up if you play her. Remember that movie Fatal Attraction. Don't be having her boil a rabbit on your ass."

Franklin flinched and his eyes went wide. "Uh, I didn't see that one, but um... I'll keep it easy."

They made it to the building and he heard Franklin whisper, "...boil a rabbit?"

Tommy was scheduled to work the Wednesday late night and wasn't due until noon. Sarah's due date was a week away. It was ten-thirty in the morning and they were going over their plan with the list of people to call when she started going into labor.

"Okay, after Acindina and your cousins I got my mom. I guess I'll call the job and let them know, too."

Sarah was sitting on the couch. She was feeling queasy all morning. Tommy had his back to her, sitting at the kitchen table writing on a notepad.

"Now the clinic up the street is the closest option to go to if you get any labor pains during the day, but if it's a full-blown labor with contractions, we get in the car and head for the hospital on Main Street in Briarwood."

Sarah felt a cold sensation from her thighs and noticed a growing dark spot on the cushion beneath her. She looked down and whispered, "Madre de Dios..."

"We need a code word or a phrase," Tommy said. "Something to say exactly when your water breaks."

"My water just broke," she said with a hint of panic.

"Nah, that's a terrible phrase, too literal."

"No, my water just *broke!*" she emphasized.

He shrugged. "Alright, if you wanna go with that..."

"TOMMY!" she screamed. "My water JUST BROKE!"

He jumped, turned around and yelled, "Holy shit!" Seconds later, he grabbed the phone and started dialing.

Sonyai hung up the phone. The shock on her face was obvious to Ethel and Gerry, who were looking on in the clerical office.

"That... was Thomas," she gasped. "Sarah's gone into labor. They're on their way to the hospital!"

Gerry smiled, "Hot dog!"

"Wasn't she due next week?" Ethel asked.

Sonyai shook her head slowly in disbelief. "When it's time, it's time. That baby is coming! We're going to need some help. He was doing the late night." She picked up the phone and heard it ring till Annabelle Doyle picked up. "Sonny?"

"Doyle, we need some help for the afternoon, do you have a part-timer to spare?"

Gerry scowled and nodded to Ethel. She ignored the look and walked out of the office.

"You've been looking glum all week," Angie said to Heywood upstairs in the staff room. "Want to talk about it?"

"Not really," he replied.

"Okay."

They ate in silence, sitting at the new table for several minutes, then Heywood finally admitted, "You were right. She left to go on a tour."

She nodded. Telling him "I told you so" would only sour the moment.

"So who turned out to be the mysterious...ahem, 'The Man'?"

"You wouldn't believe me if I told you, but I will never look at the film *Purple Rain* the same way again."

She blinked while tilting her head. "Ummm, okay. Cheer up, though... love is a fickle, spiteful bitch. We're destined to live and die alone."

He cringed and dropped his jaw. "Wow, so harsh."

"It's a line from my ex-boyfriend's biggest hit," she said with a grin, followed by a laugh.

He smiled and joined in on the laugh, feeling a lot better.

The Interboro Parkway was a mess. Tommy was driving Sarah's Buick Grand National, easing in and out of lanes heading toward the hospital. Sarah was surprisingly calm in the eyes of his frenzied maneuvers. Her eyes were glazed as she concentrated on breathing.

"We're almost there, hon," he assured her. "Six more exits, just six more exits, you okay? Say something."

"Jussssst. Driiiiive," she panted through her teeth.

They finally arrived. Tommy nearly jumped the curb as he pulled up in front of the entrance.

"Help! Somebody help! My wife's in labor. Somebody get out here!"

Sarah pushed the door open and climbed out. Tommy helped her as he looked around panicking. "Why the hell won't anyone come out?" he yelled.

"Let's just go *in!*" she grunted.

Inside the hospital lobby, people were waiting. The couple walked up to the main desk where a heavyset woman was working on some medical files.

"Uh, hello?! My wife is in labor, can you look up and get us admitted, please?" Tommy asked in his attempt at a pleasant voice.

She finally looked up with a sarcastic glance and produced a clipboard, which she dropped in front of him. "Fill this out and I'll need both of your IDs, along with proof of insurance."

Tommy picked up the clipboard and looked for something to write with. "You gotta pen?" he asked impatiently.

"Pencils are in a box on the counter behind yo—"

Sarah reached down and grabbed the woman behind the desk by her collar, pulling her up off her feet. "Gimme a goddamn pen you hot-air balloon or I'll put you in traction!"

She pulled a pen from her shirt pocket and held it up for Tommy, who started filling out the paperwork.

"Now pick up that phone, and get someone with a wheelchair out here, NOW!" Sarah barked, then let the collar go.

The terrified hospital worker picked up the receiver and started dialing.

"You always had a way with people, hon," Tommy whispered.

It had been a difficult shift during the afternoon rush. Sonyai, Ethel and Gerry worked the first few hours in two-hour stretches. The senior clerk reached out to several branches, but help was unavailable. They were on their own. Robin was scheduled to work a three-to-five day, and Sonyai was feeling pressured to relieve him from his punishment.

The desk schedule was full of revisions that had been scribbled out and written in pencil, with Sonyai stepping in for Tommy doing the late night. She would be working more than ten hours of the day since she arrived at nine this morning, a feat that would test her endurance. Ethel returned from her lunch break as three o'clock was approaching.

A restless Gerry was working with Sonyai as Robin walked in, saying nothing. He checked the desk schedule on the wall, scratched his head, confused by the corrections, then walked inside the office to stamp cards. Gerry walked up to Sonyai. "You have to let him help. We're short-handed today."

"It's slow today. We can make do. The pages can cover us if it gets busy."

"You got me back here working four to six. I've only had my lunch, but not my 30-minute break!"

"Take it in a few minutes at three when Jenkins relieves you."

"This is pushing the limit of..."

"Don't you tell me about limits. I'm facing another five hours here with the last two alone and I've been here since morning!" she snapped.

"You wouldn't have to if you'd just swallow your damn pride and ask the kid to work the late-night instead!"

"You don't tell *me* how to run this branch!"

"Excuse me!"

Gerry and Sonyai turned as Augustus stood in front of the circulation desk. "Is there a problem here?" he asked, folding his arms.

Sonyai's face flushed red, embarrassed by the outburst. She cleared her throat. "No, not at all. We're alright here."

Gerry snorted in protest, which made her eyebrow twitch.

"Very well," the head librarian walked back to the information desk.

"Okay we got a Hispanic female, 26-years-old, seven feet tall, 200 pounds,"

"Ay! 197 Cabron! Don't be rounding up," Sarah protested.

She was in a wheelchair on her way to the maternity ward as the hospital resident doctor addressed the supporting nurses behind him. Tommy was a few steps behind the group, trying to keep up.

"39-weeks-pregnant, experiencing contractions six minutes apart, prep a room...and find an extra-long bed. We got 'The Attack of the 50-foot woman' here!"

Sarah started cursing in Spanish while the nurses confirmed the orders given to them. They arrived in the ward's waiting room when one of the staff turned and stopped Tommy.

"This is as far as you go. We'll get her inside, do some check-ups and then call you."

"What!? I'm her husband, she needs me!" he yelled.

"This is a highly-sterilized sensitive area. You have germs everywhere. We are nowhere near 'showtime' so wait here, call the rest of the family and relax. When it's time, we'll come get you."

The nurse turned around to leave him as his wife disappeared past a set of double doors. Tommy sat in the waiting area staring out into space. It had been three hours since they arrived and the clock on the wall read four twenty-seven. A pair of loud voices was approaching from down the hall, screaming in Spanish. He didn't have to guess when he turned to see Lorenzo and Acindina run in calling for Sarah.

"My baby! Where's my baby?! Who's in charge here? Where's my daughter?"

"Tomas, what are you doing sitting there? Where's Sarah?"

Tommy sighed and stood up. "We've been here since a little before noon. They admitted her at one. I've been here waiting since. All I know is we're nowhere near "the time" yet."

"I want to see her!" Acindina said and headed for the double doors where a security guard stopped her.

"Can't let you through, ma'am."

"You think you can stop me?"

"This gun on my hip makes me think I can," he replied.

After staring him down, she cursed and walked away from the doors. When she was back with the men, she held out her hand and asked Lorenzo for something in Spanish. He rolled his eyes and handed her a bag. She took a seat next to Tommy and pulled out two crochet hooks. Tommy turned to look at Lorenzo questionably.

"It helps her relax," he said with a shrug. "You don't have to worry about hats, socks or blankets for the first five years."

"What's going on?" Lakeshia asked. "Where's Carmichael?"

The pages were near the New Books section as the heated exchange between Sonyai and Gerry cooled down. The tension between the clerks was still visible as they stood in front of the terminals in silence.

"I overheard Miss Yi say his wife is having the baby. It's just the four of them, and Walker is still stamping cards," said Alex.

"So much for Andrew and his help, punk-ass bitch," Tanya whispered.

Alex and Lakeshia exchanged glances. "I guess *she's* moved on," Lakeshia concluded.

"They're going to need help," Alex began. "If one of us gets called, I hope we can still get the shelves done."

They all nodded.

"They should give Robin a chance and let him help."

"Fat chance of that happening, Leelee," Tanya said.

Sonyai pointed in their direction and the trio dispersed after being discovered.

It was almost five when tempers rose between the three clerks. Even Ethel who was usually laid back and level headed was displaying signs of being agitated.

"Okay, I'm getting ready to leave. The two of you will kill each other in the next hour if you don't let Walker work the late night."

"I'm fine Jenkins. Leave it be," Sonyai said, approaching to relieve her.

Gerry was working the returns. He stood with his arms folded, preparing for another hour with the senior clerk.

Ethel was insistent. "Look, I've been humoring this long enough. Yi, this is starting to look *personal*...against our people."

Gerry couldn't believe his ears. *She finally woke up!* he thought with a grin.

Sonyai was used to such accusations from Gerry, but hearing it from Ethel really hurt. "This has nothing—"

"I don't believe that," she interrupted. "Is it true that you objected to him dating your family member?" she asked.

Gerry turned to Ethel and gasped in surprise. "Huh?"

The senior clerk's face flushed red. "How dare you? I don't have to explain myself!"

"Yes you do!" Gerry said, joining the argument.

Their voices started to carry again, attracting the attention of the pages, patrons, and Angie at the information desk. The three were seriously bickering among themselves when someone shouted, "HEY!"

Robin stood behind them at the doorway to the clerical office. "What is wrong with you? You're supposed to be professionals!"

They all looked shocked at the admonishment while he continued.

"This is a library, damnit...people need to read, borrow and return books in a quiet environment."

He gestured toward Ethel and Gerry. "Thank you for sticking up for me, but this is my way of making amends for what was done, and I'm going to do it for as long as it takes to get her respect back! In the meantime, she doesn't need this childish behavior from two grown people who should know better!"

He turned around. "Now I'm going back to stamping cards. Don't nobody worry about me and just get the job done!"

Gerry was furious. "Man, hell with this! I'm taking an hour of comp time. You made this mess, you deal with it yourself!" He stormed around from the desk and out the door.

Sonyai looked at Ethel. She shrugged and said, "I worked my eight hours. I'm gone," then proceeded to leave as well.

The senior clerk stood alone as she faced the vacant work area. *A leader is nothing without their followers.* Sonyai was moved by the part-time clerk stepping in. The *second* time he impressed her. After looking back at the office for a moment, she stepped to the computer terminal on the returns side.

"Miss Stevens," she called out to the page.

Alex popped her head out from the shelves as Sonyai waved her over.

"I believe...it's time for you to learn how to check out materials. Please step around here to the clerical desk."

The page was shocked. She looked at Lakeshia and Tanya, who quietly waved her up with smiles on their faces. Alex walked down the row across the floor and around to the clerical desk. Sonyai walked with her to the checkout side. The page was beaming with excitement as she examined the terminal and arrangement of date due cards. Out among the shelves, her co-workers looked on proudly as the senior clerk showed her the process.

CHAPTER TWENTY FOUR

LAKESHIA AND TANYA LEFT THE BRANCH AT SEVEN, STAYING AN EXTRA hour to help with the shelves while Alex worked the clerical desk with Sonyai.

"You did very well," Sonyai said with praise.

"Thank you, Miss Yi. I can't wait to do this again!"

"Don't get too excited. This was just a one-time thing."

Her face fell with disappointment. "But..."

"In another year, so long as you stay out of trouble, we can start training you for a clerical position. Don't let me down, Miss Stevens. You are dismissed."

She took some books from the shelving cart and went to place them in their appropriate locations.

Augustus walked up to the desk and looked at Sonyai. "You think she's ready?"

"I know you have a valued interest in her or you wouldn't have asked."

The librarian did not reply, so she went on. "She missed a few steps and her speed needs to improve, but for the first time, she did well. I won't encourage her until she's older."

"Fair enough." He looked around and rolled the balls of his feet in an awkward moment of silence. "Um, Zelda spoke to me and I'm sure she's talked to you as well."

"Yes," she answered coldly.

"Alright, let's be honest. We will never agree on policy when it comes to the public, but we have to move past our differences and work together. I admit I was reckless, but there are people plotting against us now." *And I still have dirt on you,* he thought.

She looked at him. He deserved everything he had coming, and she couldn't care less if Baker took him down and placed some stooge in his place. But for now, for the sake of the branch, she was willing to give peace a chance. A quote came to mind for this moment: *Who holds the devil, let him hold him well. He hardly will be caught a second time.*

She held out her hand. *I'll see to it you don't get caught again, so I may take you out myself.*

He accepted her hand and shook it, their fake smiles acknowledging what each of them knew...the truce would only be temporary.

A car drove down the narrow one-way street and stopped in front of the 67th Street Branch at seven-thirty. The rear passenger door opened and Alex stepped out. She crossed the street opposite from the library as the car pulled off. Janelle's school, Julia Richmond had a courtyard right next to Saint Catherine's Park on the street. The page entered the park and found a pair of swings.

Sitting and waiting for her was a stout, white teenager with long blond hair. He had dull blue eyes that followed Alex as she approached. Wearing black sweatpants and a sweatshirt with a picture of Bugs Bunny on the chest, Sean Bailey put on his best smile.

"I was starting to think you weren't going to show," he greeted.

The 67th Street page undressed Alex with his eyes as she took a seat on the swing next to him.

"There was an emergency. I had to stay a little longer. I even got to work the circulation desk doing checkouts for the first time."

"Really? Wow, I've been a page for almost two years and haven't touched a lightpen yet!"

The pair started to swing back and forth slowly.

"So," Alex began. "What information you got for me?"

"Well, I checked with all my people uptown, did some digging, and called in a few favors..."

"Uh-huh?"

"And your Mister, or should I say *Miss* Robin Walker has quite the reputation for himself."

"Miss?" Alex asked. "You sure you checked around the right guy?"

"Page up in Fort Washington? Yeah, that's him. For some weird reason, the Human Resources department has him under as "Ms." Probably some mix up because his name can go both ways."

She shrugged. "Okay, I hope that's not all you found out."

He laughed. "Oh, I got more to tell you." He stared at her bare legs under the flapping green skirt she was wearing. "This guy Robin, was a real bad-ass when he started at Fort Washington. Got into it frequently with this clerk that kept pushing him around for kicks."

"Yeah, I can see that happening," Alex rubbed her neck for a moment. "This clerk got a name?"

"Before I tell you that, how about you make this worth my while? You're getting mighty high on that swing, there... are you even wearing panties?"

She slowed her pace and gave him a coy look. She loved having her way with the anxious page, and wouldn't mind giving him some action. But she was saving herself for someone worth her time. "In your dreams, you horny toad!"

"Every night with the lotion and sock, baby."

She kept on her sly smile, despite being repulsed by the remark. "So nasty, but something tells me you use a nice *big* sock." She threw in a wink to inflate his ego further.

Sean bit his lower lip and let out a lusty laugh. "Guzman, Trevor Guzman. He's a full-time clerk with a serious reputation. How he gets away with stuff is unheard of. He and Robin have had full-on, dragged out fist fights. But as tough as he is, Trevor seems to be the only person that Robin is scared of."

Hearing that made Alex excited. The thought of someone putting the fear of God to Robin. This Trevor person was someone she had to look up. "Anything else?"

"Couple other things, Trevor's beef may be due to a love triangle he got himself in. There was this other page named Comanos that was close to Trevor. Once Robin showed up, she started to get a little friendly with him."

There wasn't anything she could use that information for. She scowled and was about to finish the conversation...

"Then there's this last thing," Sean said. "This is big, the stuff of legends, which makes for most of his notoriety."

That stopped Alex from swinging. "Wouldn't wanna think you were holding out on me, Sean."

She figured it was time to give a dog a bone. She stood up from her seat on the swing and moved to stand in front of him. Looking up to her, the chubby teenager couldn't believe his eyes when she suddenly swung one leg to his left and mounted his lap, hooking her other leg to his right.

"Hmmm, is that a bookmark in your pocket, or are you really *glad* to see me?" she purred, then leaned to start them to swing a little.

Sean started stammering as Alex gyrated her hips to get into a full swing. "L..Last year! Robin and a group of others, including Trevor...they started this...this...thing! This secret...I...I...I don't even know what to call it! But it started to spread throughout other branches in several clusters!"

"Uh-huh...what else?"

"It got a little TOO exciting!" Sean gasped with his voice cracking. "Which I can really, really relate to now!"

"Keep going! What happened next?" She was practically dry humping him at this point as they swung faster.

"The library officials stepped in, warned everyone off from participating! So they negotiated a truce and made a peace treaty!"

"A what!?" she gasped.

"I know, it's crazy, but sooner or later, they believed..." he started panting, with shortness of breath. "...the tension between Robin and Trevor would break the treaty and it would start up again!...Oh my GOD!"

Alex dug her feet down to bring the swing to a skidding stop. "Whooooo!" she let out a breathy sigh.

Sean's mouth was gaping open, making unintelligible sounds. She leaned in, her face inches from his. "And what was this...thing that they were doing...what was it called? Did they give it some kind of name?"

He nodded his head feverishly. "It was...was called...um, it was called *The Game*."

Her head snapped back as she winced. "The Game? That's what they called it? What the hell is up with that?"

She dismounted from the page and adjusted her skirt. Sean's legs were so unsteady, he leaned too far back and wrapped each one on the chains holding the seat. Completely tangled and upside down, he looked back to see Alex making her way out of the park. "Thanks for the information. Hope you had a good time," she giggled.

"Yeah!" he called out. "Anytime."

The page hung, suspended and twisted for over five minutes, lost in his thoughts after she left.

Gerry was still upset, leaving Sonyai to fend for herself just when Ethel was coming around. She was starting to see that the senior clerk was losing it, something he knew the moment he arrived three years ago. He needed to let out some steam and no card game or bar could take his mind off what he was feeling at the moment. He needed to talk to someone.

Denise lived in Park Slope. His sister was probably the only person Gerry could visit unannounced so long as he was bearing spirits. With a bottle of St. Ides in a bag, he approached the door to her brownstone on Garfield Place at eight o'clock.

"Dee!" he knocked several times. "It's me, open up!"

The door sprang open, but only halfway as Denise stuck her head out. "Gerry? What th…"

He pushed in, making her stumble back. "I brought a 40, I need to get drunk. You got cups?" He didn't notice that she was wearing a robe that was tied at the waist as he marched into the living room.

"Gerry! This is not…"

"Why you got it so damn dark in here? Turn on the damn…"

The lamp next to the couch clicked on by the hand of someone who was lying down. The back of the couch was facing Gerry, so he was shocked when a head poked up and turned slowly.

Franklin looked back at Gerry and waved. "Hey, um…what's up?"

Gerry turned back to his sister and noticed the robe. He dropped the bag and the bottle broke, spilling the drink into a messy puddle. "Denise!" he screamed.

"Damn it, Gerry!" she yelled back.

Franklin ran from the couch, picking up his clothes and headed to the kitchen.

Gerry turned around again and yelled, "I'm gonna kill him!"

She moved to cut him off, but he was across the room in a matter of steps. Franklin was already out the kitchen window, jumping down to the alley in the back. He made it back to 7th Avenue and ran twelve blocks north to Flatbush, where he caught the B-train back to the city.

Back at Denise's house, Gerry stormed out of the kitchen. "What the hell were you thinking?" he barked at his sister.

"It's none of your business. Who the hell do you think you are barging in my house like that?"

"He is JUST A KID! You're 32-years-old. Act like the mature woman you're supposed to be!"

"You're drunk. I've seen you like this before, what's wrong?" she asked.

"Don't turn this on me. You're the one moving and grooving with the 'Play that funky Music' white boy! You gonna marry this tenderoni? Take him to Mom and Dad's for Thanksgiving, huh? Guess who's coming to dinner!"

Denise had run out of patience. She punched him across the face with a right cross. His head snapped while his legs gave out and he was on the floor, silent as a mouse instantly.

"What about 'Jose'?" Lorenzo asked.

Sarah's father had been suggesting baby names to Tommy for forty-five minutes straight. Even when he stood up to pace around the area, Lorenzo followed behind, pitching names.

"Reminds me of Conseco, not really a fan," he dismissed.

"Okay then, how about..."

Tommy was about to say something when the doctor stepped out calling their name. "Gonzales! Sarah Gonzales!"

"Carmichael! That's Gonzales-*Carmichael*!" he corrected.

"I apologize, sir. My name is Doctor Gruchala. Your wife is doing fine. She's currently dilating at four centimeters."

"When can we see her?" Acindina asked.

"You each can go in, one at a time. Keep the physical contact to a minimum and you'll have to put on a gown and head cap. Who's first?"

Before both men could speak, Acindina stepped forward. "ME!"

He nodded. "Come with me."

Fifteen minutes later, Sarah's mother walked into the hospital room and did the sign of the cross across her chest. Sarah was sitting up uncomfortably on two hospital beds arranged together horizontally. She had several pillows behind her back and her feet were against the guard rail.

"What is this? You had no beds for taller women?" she hissed.

"Sorry, most extra-long beds were unavailable or broken. We're still searching," Gruchala explained. "Remember, please limit the contact. Any type of infection could be harmful to the baby."

She stepped to the beds and looked at her daughter. "Mija," she smiled and wiped the tears from her eyes.

"Mama, Mama I'm scared."

"I know, I know, you have to be strong. You can do this, look at me, Baby...you can do this."

Sarah looked up at her mother and nodded with reinforced determination.

Acindina knew she only had a moment, so she reached underneath the gown in her purse. "I got you something."

The doctor and nurses tensed up for a moment when she pulled out a group of wooden spoons tied together. "These will help when the contractions get closer and intense. Bite down on them, okay?"

Sarah took them and smiled, "Gracias Mama."

She blew her a kiss which Sarah kissed back and waved as her mother left the room. Lorenzo came later and had a conniption over her treatment. With a brief conversation, he was escorted out of the room. Tommy finally arrived, and the couple comforted each other.

"This is crazy," she whispered.

"I know, hon'. I know. As soon as I can, I'm going to be there by your side. We're in this together."

She smiled. "Yeah, you try pushing this baby through your crotch and we'll talk."

They laughed quietly together.

"I love you, Baby," she said.

"I love you, too, Honey."

He turned and left. The tear came down finally. He had too much pride to let her see him cry.

Ethel knocked on the door. Elisse looked at her after opening. "It's 10 o'clock at night, are you crazy?" She took her sister's question as an invitation and walked in. Elisse closed the door quietly and whispered, "I'm meeting the boys in the morning so..."

Ethel dropped a stack of money on the coffee table. "That's

$1,000.00. I'll get the rest later," she interrupted. Her sister looked down at the money, then back up at her and smiled.

"I want a receipt and a written contract laying out all the details. You ask me for a dime more than the $2,000.00 or disappear into the night, I'll see to it that Deacon and Mac never get this place and are out in the street."

"Ethel Marietta Jenkins," she hissed, "Who the fuck do you think you're talking to?"

"I'm talking to the woman whose husband swindled $5,000.00 from me years ago, and I won't be fooled again."

Elisse looked back at her. "Ex-husband," she corrected. "I knew you'd throw that in my face. Well, I'll have you know, I've drawn up the papers already!" She walked to a bookcase, pulled out a three-ring-binder and opened it. After signing some papers, she held out a payment confirmation slip and three copies of the agreement for each sister.

"Sign each copy and take your voucher, then get the fuck out! I'm making sure our rooms are the farthest away from each other."

Ethel signed the three papers after reading thoroughly. She put the slip in her purse and turned to leave.

"You talking about me, *you* better have the rest by October!" Elisse called out to her back.

Sarah was five spoons in by midnight. She had gotten up to pee at least three times in the last hour due to all the ice chips they were giving her. She was hungry, but felt like she was going to throw-up at the same time. Thankfully, the staff was finally able to find her a regular bed long enough for her as each contraction wreaked havoc on her body.

An hour later, the back pains began. The nurses encouraged her to let out what she was feeling by screaming as loud as she could and not holding back. She bit down on another spoon and did a quick count. There were thirteen still left.

"Okay, we're at 10 centimeters, Miss Gonzales," a nurse announced. "It's showtime."

"No, no, no, no! I'm not ready, no showtime! Not even HBO, Cinemax, The Movie Channel, or MTV!" She started crying, "OH MY GOD! I CAN'T DO THIS!"

"Miss, miss, calm down, I need you to relax, and breathe," the nurse sucked in a breath to show her, "Breathe, in and out, c'mon, you can do this."

She inhaled and focused on ignoring the pain, then let the gasp of air out slowly. The spoon crunched as her jaw bit down, almost breaking. Doctor Gruchala stepped in the room and raised her ankles in the stirrups.

"Okay, I think we're ready. Nurse, keep your eye on her fetal tracing. Miss Gonzales? May I call you Sarah?"

"You can call me The Goodyear Blimp for all I care, pendejo. Just get this kid out!"

"All right, now I'm going to need you to take a deep breath. Suck in as much air as you can and hold it...and now, push!"

Sarah grunted with all her power. The spoon snapped in two as she gripped down on the bed underneath her.

"Keep going, keep going," the doctor coached, "...aaaand stop! Take a breath. Good, you're doing great, we're going to do this a couple of more times."

She started to gasp for air. "So...som...something's wrong! Can't breathe!" she yelled.

"BP's down. Bring in the oxygen!" the nurse ordered.

An orderly brought a tank to the bed and slipped the oxygen mask on her mouth and nose. The blood pressure monitor returned to a steady pace. Gruchala felt Sarah's stomach and looked under the gown. "Something isn't right, let's wait this out a bit, yeah?"

Over the next two hours, several attempts resulted in a serious drop in blood pressure. Sarah was getting weaker with every push. The baby was nowhere near crowning, but there was a severe case of bleeding.

"I think we have a problem," the doctor whispered. "Monitor her vitals. She's gushing like a faucet! Get three pints of O-Negative on standby and somebody bring the father back!"

Acindina was at the vending machine down the hall while Tommy and Lorenzo were sleeping in their chairs. Lorenzo was muttering while he slept, which would occasionally wake up Tommy. A nurse came out and put her hand on his shoulder. He jumped up with a start.

"They need to speak to you," she gestured for him to follow her.

Acindina came back holding three cans of Sprite and looked around, "Enzo!"

"Ay no me joda!" he yelled waking up.

"Where's Tommy?" she asked.

He looked around. "I... I don't know!"

Tommy sensed certain urgency while being led back to Sarah's room. They didn't ask him to put on any protective covering this time. When they got to her door, the doctor was waiting there for him. The look on his face said it all. The nurse left them alone and went back inside.

"Doc?"

"Relax, she's alright, but," he paused as Tommy tensed up. "Okay, here's the situation. We should have had a talk when you first came in for contingency purposes, but we can't look back on that now."

"Okay, okay, I get it, what's wrong?"

He sighed. "Your wife is larger than the average woman, being seven feet and all, so she requires more blood pumping through her heart. But something's gone wrong. Her pressure is very, very low, and she's losing blood as she pushes with every contraction."

Tommy swallowed hard as his eyes began to water. He had no idea what to say. His mouth just hung open.

"From what we can tell, she's suffering from a condition known as Placenta Previa," Gruchala explained.

"Wh..what..?"

"I'll explain. The placenta is like this pouch or sack where the baby gets its nutrients and oxygenated blood from the mother in the womb, attached to the uterine wall. It also takes up the waste..."

"Get to the point Doc, I'm about to puke as it is!"

"Okay, normally it's attached at the top, on the opposite side of the birth canal, but sometimes...it slides down, cutting off the baby as the mother starts to push." He held up his palm, opened and flat. "It's like walking through a real heavy screen door." He pushed his fist against the hand. "The baby can't pass."

"Oh dear God."

"That's only strike one."

"Strike one?"

"As the baby pushes against the placenta, it gets torn, causing it to lose oxygen and possibly asphyxiate. That's called Placental Abruption, aka strike two."

"Tell me there's no..."

"When it's covering the birth canal after sliding, the blood vessels attach back to the uterine wall keeping it in place. In a normal birth it comes out right after the baby, but now it's attached too deep in the wall. Strike three, Placenta Accreta."

"Fucking placenta, damnit! The fuck is with this thing?!"

"I won't lie to you. Something like this is very, very rare. The odds are not that good."

"So, what can you do?"

"We'll have to do a cesarean. A decision needs to be made. You need to make the choice. We have to realize the possibility that either the baby will come out stillborn...or your wife won't survive the surgery. She's in no condition to decide, so it comes down to you. If the worst happens, who do we save? Who is the priority?"

Tommy's head was pounding. This was all too much to take in within a matter of minutes and the clock was still ticking. "I... I can't decide, who can make a choice like that?"

"You need to. Right now... we need an answer."

He weighed the choices in his head. "I... I can't imagine losing her... raising our child alone... we... we can always try again."

"What are you saying? You need to tell me your absolute decision. You can't flip-flop halfway through this, sir."

Tommy looked at the urgency in his eyes. "I... I understand..." he nodded. "Sarah, save Sarah, do what you have to do, no matter what, just please save my wife."

"Okay..." the doctor nodded. "Okay... can you make it back yourself?"

"Yeah."

"Alright." He turned and quickly walked back into the room.

Tommy fell to his knees. "My God, what have I done?" he asked as he leaned against the wall.

Doctor Gruchala called out, "Alright, we're a go for surgery. Prep an operating room for an emergency C-section, call anesthesia and neonatal. Mother is primary, mother is primary, I repeat, MOTHER IS PRIMARY. Time is 3:25 am, make a note of it."

Sarah was stirred awake by all the commotion as the nurse worked quickly following the doctor's order. She pulled the mask off and started to panic. "What's going on? What are you..."

A nurse injected a needle in her behind. She winced, "Ow! Somebody say something to me. What is going on?" Before she could ask another question, nausea hit her like a gust of wind and she suddenly felt sleepy. The last thing she heard before her eyes closed was the nurse telling her to relax.

Tommy came back to the waiting area where Lorenzo and Acindina were waiting. They looked at him with pleading eyes.

"Where were you? What happened?"

Tommy looked at them and simply said, "We need to pray."

Inside the operating room, Sarah was given a spinal epidural to numb her lower half, and a catheter was inserted to collect her urine. Gruchala stepped inside, "Okay, everyone stay sharp. Once the baby's out we have to make sure the placenta hasn't put the mother in jeopardy." He looked at her vital monitor and began the surgery.

After the vertical incision was made, the operation started smoothly. Upon access to the opening, amniotic fluid was sucked out. Then a discovery was made. The sack was found on the baby's crown, covering three-quarters of the baby's head.

"The baby's oxygen may have been limited while bracing, clearing the mouth and nose."

Sarah's blood pressure suddenly dropped. As alarms went off from the monitor, a nurse called out, "Mother's going into arrest!"

"Extracting the baby, prepare to administer infant CPR, then prep the crash cart!" the doctor ordered. Within minutes the baby was in his arms as he quickly handed it over to the nurse.

"Sutures! We got to close her up, she flatlining!"

Everything happened in a matter of seconds. People believe in a near-death experience the consciousness floats above the body and you look down seeing yourself. A light shines from above and you're called to it. That didn't happen with Sarah. It was more of her standing several feet away looking on, similar to that Patrick Swayze film, *Ghost*.

She looked over and saw the nurse administering rescue breaths to her delivered child while others worked furiously over her body. Closing her eyes, she started to experience moments throughout her life. Playing dress-up with her mother, being led around a park by her father in her wagon, first day of school, meeting Tommy in college. Something inside gave her the feeling she was about to die.

A figure appeared before her, as everything suddenly started to fade away. The voices became faint, and the room began to lose focus. An old man stood before her. He had white thinning hair while wearing a sleeveless sweater vest on top of a blue dress shirt. She had never met this man before, but he appeared friendly. *Was this God?*

With a shock of the electric paddles from the defibrillator, the man, her baby and everything she witnessed was gone. Her pulse was back as the rhythmic pattern resumed. "She's back, she's back! Close her up! How's the baby!? How's the baby!?" Gruchala barked.

The infant was pale and not breathing. It may have went without oxygen for approximately ninety seconds, which was a lifetime. After applying pressure on the chest, the nurse patted the child carefully for signs of that first breath. The room was silent in fear. "C'mon..." the doctor whispered.

Tommy and Sarah's parents were all on their knees holding hands. He had no idea if they were praying in Spanish and he should pray in English, but God speaks all languages. The possibility of losing one or both kept creeping in the back of his mind. Would Lorenzo and Acindina forgive him if they ever found out? Would Sarah if the child were lost? He felt both of his hands being squeezed by his in-laws and continued to pray.

Too many minutes had passed. It was time to accept that the child was stillborn...when the baby's cry finally filled the room. "Holy shit!" the nurse yelled. The room erupted with the sounds of joy as everyone cheered. "Oh my God! The angels had slippery hands with this one!" Gruchala exclaimed. "Great job everyone. Check their vitals, have the baby sent to the newborn nursery and the mother back to her room. I'll tell the family the news." *God, I love this job,* he thought as he left the operating room.

Acindina was the first to hear the door open. She sprang up immediately as the doctor walked in. His face showed no emotion. It was impossible to read him. The men rose as he came over to address them.

"Doc?" Tommy's voice cracked, he was on the verge of going hoarse. His eyes were red from crying and exhaustion in the past three hours.

"Your wife and your newborn daughter are fine."

After hearing the sentence, Tommy lost his hearing temporarily as white noise filled his ears. Sarah's parents were screaming at the top of their lungs, overjoyed by the announcement. The doctor finally broke into a smile as Lorenzo shook his hand.

"I need a moment with the father, please excuse us." He put his hand on Tommy's shoulder and they walked down the hall. The new grandparents celebrated, embracing each other, followed by a kiss.

Once they were out of earshot, Doctor Gruchala looked at Tommy seriously. "Buy yourself a lottery ticket. You are the luckiest man on earth today!"

Tommy finally snapped back from his trance as they both began to laugh. "Yeah, oh my God."

"Look," he continued. "I want to tell you this in the strictest of confidence." He checked back up the hall to make sure no one could hear them. "All three of you beat the odds today, and that's good. But look at me, look at me." He pointed to his eyes as Tommy listened attentively.

"Never tell her you and I had that last conversation. Never. Take it to the grave, Son. Never FUCKING tell her you made a choice. She may be thankful you chose her life over the baby at first, but the guilt will eat at both of you slowly as she grows up. In the end, it will tear you two apart. Never. Tell. Her. You understand?"

Tommy swallowed hard and nodded.

"Alright, let's meet your daughter." He waved and called out, "Grandma, Grandpa! Follow me to the nursery, your granddaughter's waiting."

Acindina squealed and trotted down the hallway, followed by Lorenzo.

CHAPTER TWENTY FIVE

ROBIN WAS STARTLED AWAKE BY THE PHONE RINGING. "WHO THE FUCK?" he mumbled as he felt around the nightstand for his cordless phone. "Hello?" he answered.

"Robin, sorry to wake you up man."

"Gerry? What the hell? It's 7:30 in the morning, and you're not even scheduled to work today!"

"Um, I ran into your friend last night. That white boy, Franklin?"

"Okay?"

"Well, he left his wallet at the bar and I'd like to give it back to him. I forgot the name of that clothing store he works at."

"It's Bolton's, located at 51st near 7th, not that far from Radio City. You can't miss it."

"Thanks."

The phone clicked off and Robin scratched his head for a moment, then went back to sleep.

Back in Brooklyn, Gerry hung up the phone in Denise's kitchen. She let him sleep on the couch after socking him with a sucker punch. He woke up at six and ate some breakfast. She wouldn't be up for another hour. Denise worked at a pet store several blocks away and wasn't due until nine.

He took a twenty-dollar-bill from her purse and quietly left the house.

Sonyai walked back in her office at nine after barely getting five hours of sleep. She was looking forward to the weekend after getting clerical help from Yorkville and Webster today. After contemplating going upstairs for a nap, the phone rang at her desk.

"58th Street... ohhh, yes, may I help you?" she asked, fighting a yawn.

"Miss Yi?" Tommy asked.

"OH! Thomas, I'm so sorry, how are you? Is Sarah..."

"It's a girl, ma'am! We had a girl! This night was pure hell. I can make it in tomorrow, but I'm going to need some time."

"That's great, Thomas, congratulations! Oh, take all the time you need. We'll make do! I'm so happy for you! I'll let everyone know, we'll see you tomorrow... goodbye!"

She hung up the phone and sat down. "Ohhh," she sighed, then slowly put her head down on her desk and closed her eyes.

Tommy called his parents after hanging up with Sonyai. He was starting to run out of quarters after making all these phone calls. The phone rang three times before his mother picked up, "Hello?"

"Mom?"

"Tommy!" Maureen gasped.

"It's a girl, Mom. 4:30 this morning, both are fine!" he chuckled while wiping away a tear. Each time he told someone it felt like a new experience.

"Oh my God, Tommy! A granddaughter, we have a granddaughter! I got to tell your father, Jarlath! Wake up! They had the baby!"

Tommy talked to his father and told him an abridged version of the night's ordeal. They planned to visit Queens by Sunday and despite his father's fears, they were excited to see their first grandchild. He hung up the phone and walked back to Sarah's room. The sun came in through the window blinds as Tommy looked at Sarah, Lorenzo, Acindina and his baby girl.

His mind played with the idea of one or the other not there. Sarah holding her stomach with no baby in her arms in tears or her parents holding their grandchild with their daughter in the morgue. Either scenario would have been devastating.

"What are you standing there for, silly?" Acindina waved him over.

"Just, taking this all in," he said, stepping forward. He couldn't stop smiling.

Sarah noticed him staring and smiled as well. "I love you so much," she whispered. "That's why I've come to a decision."

"Okay, we can have another one," he joked. "Just give me a year or two to enjoy her first."

"Ohhh, you'll have more than two years. I'm not going through this again for a long time!"

Everyone shared a quick laugh.

"I'm talking her name, her last name. I want it to be her father's."

Lorenzo understood and looked up at Tommy with a nod, but he was still confused. "What are you saying, hon'?"

"I don't want to be Sarah Gonzales-Carmichael, I want to be Mrs. Sarah *Carmichael*." She then looked down. "And this... is Baby Carmichael."

"A queen," Lorenzo said proudly.

Tommy knelt, looking directly at her eye level. "You sure? It doesn't mean anything."

"It does to me."

"Okay," he nodded.

"What about her first name?" Acindina asked.

"We had a few choices for a girl. We'll pick one," she replied.

Tommy saw a look on her face as she nodded for him to come closer. She whispered to him, "I didn't want to scare Mom and Dad but something happened...something fascinating happened to me."

He chuckled, "What, hon'?"

"Don't freak out, but between you and me...I saw Him, baby."

"Saw him? Saw who?" Tommy asked.

Sarah smiled. "God...I saw God."

He looked at her, trying not to appear skeptical. She looked as certain as if she had just said water was wet. He simply nodded and hoped this wouldn't come up in any future conversations.

Franklin was in the stockroom working. He tried to keep his focus on the job rather than the close escape from Gerry at Denise's place. He wondered if they were still going to New Jersey this weekend. At four, he stepped outside to the back of the store for some air. Despite the heat reaching over 90 degrees in the city, the air conditioning kept the store very cold.

After circling the store for hours, Gerry finally got a glimpse of Franklin while hiding behind a dumpster. He planned to wait until closing time to confront him. There was no way the boy was going to continue to see Denise. Not if he had anything to say about it.

Sonyai informed the entire staff of Tommy's news, which put everyone in a positive mood that Friday afternoon. Ethel had some help from clustering clerks Charlie Maeda and Claude Robinson. Claude and Ethel were working the desk at four-thirty.

"How's your sister, Annie? Over at 96th Street?" she asked.

Claude was just as short as Ethel, with dark skin, cropped hair and a noticeable nose that may have been broken a few times. "She's doing fine, thinking of taking the senior clerk Seminar next year."

"Yeah?"

"Yep, thinking of moving over to Countee Cullen on 136th Street. Heard the senior clerk there is retiring soon."

"That's nice. I can't see myself in charge, giving orders and shit. It's hard enough staying out of trouble as it is."

"Uh huh, is that why I hear what I've been hearing about down here?"

Ethel gave him a side glance. "Whatever you've been hearing, Claude, is just bull. Nothing to concern yourself with. Let's just leave it at that."

There would always be whispers and rumors of what's been going on, but now was time for damage control. Sonyai informed her this morning that she and Augustus were working on being at a good place, so she was determined to smooth out past transgressions like wrinkles on a dress.

Behind them in the clerical office, Robin sat and was still stamping cards. The phone outside for the branch's main line rang and Ethel answered it. After a minute she stepped inside and called to him. "Robin?"

He stopped and looked up quietly, surprised someone was talking to him.

"The phone's for you."

A puzzled look came across his face when he stood and walked over to Sonyai's desk. He picked up the receiver and pressed for the main line. "Uh, hello?"

"Is this Robin?" a woman's voice asked.

There were sounds of crashes and people yelling in the background as he answered, "Yeah this is Robin, who is this? What's all that noise?"

"Franklin told us to call you. Someone's chasing him around the store! A tall black guy with fluffy hair."

He heard a loud crash and Franklin screaming, *"Gerry?! What the hell?"* "Um, tell him I'm coming, please don't call the police! Try to talk some sense to him!"

He ended the call pressing the hang up button, then dialed

Liverty Cab. "Is driver 2Y68 available for a pickup?"

Gerry had good intentions of being civil when he walked into the store, but when he locked eyes with Franklin, his rage took over. Women were screaming as he chased the boy throughout the store. He lost his footing and stumbled into some mannequins, which gave Franklin a moment to catch his breath and talk.

"Dude, I'm sorry you had to find out! Just try to calm down!"

Franklin's co-workers looked on at the carnage. "Sandra's going to be furious when she hears about this!" Shannon said to Tabitha.

"You think that's his um, boyfriend?" Tabitha asked, disappointed.

"It would explain why he turned you down so many times. I almost thought that Robin guy was his boyfriend... maybe Frankie was cheating on him."

Gerry got up and started charging toward Franklin again. "I'm going to kill you if you touched my sister!"

Franklin ran out to the back of the store and grabbed a ladder the painters were using to work on the roof. After scaling up the rungs, he grabbed the ladder and pulled it up on the level with him. Gerry pushed the door open and searched the alley. Franklin dropped down, lying flat and hoping not to be seen.

"Where are you!?" he barked.

Cervantes stopped his cab in front of Bolton's and Robin jumped out. He sprinted inside and called out for both his friends. "Gerry, Franklin! Where are you?!"

"They're out back!" he heard a woman yell.

He ran toward the voice and made it to the stockroom. "Franklin?" He heard Gerry yelling outside at the back alley and ran.

"I know you're up there!" Gerry yelled. He was throwing bottles up on the roof. Franklin rolled to his left while staying low as the glass missed him by inches. Robin finally came out waving his arms. "Whoa, whoa, whoa, Gerry, what the hell you doing, man? I thought you were just giving him his wallet."

Franklin stood up when hearing Robin's voice. "Yo, what the fuck? You told him where I worked?"

"He slept with Denise!" Gerry yelled. "Did you know?" He suddenly advanced on Robin.

"What!?" he turned to the roof. "Are you serious?! She called you four days ago!"

"Hey, she seduced me! Practically ripped the clothes off my innocent, toned body!"

"WHAAAT!" Gerry growled.

"Look, we gotta get out of here!"

"You're goddamn right you do!" a voice called out.

Gerry and Robin turned to look as a woman and a man came out from the stockroom. "I've called the police. You assholes destroyed my store!" the man screamed.

"Mister Pasternak!?" Franklin gasped from the roof. "Ooooooh shit!"

The Jewish store owner stood next to Sandra the manager, as they both looked up to the roof. "What are you doing up there?" Sandra asked.

"Who cares?" Pasternak yelled, pointing up to him. "You are fired! Your last paycheck will cover the cost of the damage you did to my store! Now, if you're not gone by the time the police get here, I'm pressing charges!"

A police siren was approaching from the distance. Franklin lowered the ladder and slid down. Gerry started to move toward him when Robin grabbed his arm. "Cops, man!" He looked to Franklin and nodded, "Go!" then pulled Gerry toward the front of the store. Cervantes was still waiting as they climbed into the cab and took off.

The police arrived seconds behind them.

CHAPTER TWENTY SIX

ANGIE WAS FINISHING HER LATEST NIGHT CLASS AT QUEENS COLLEGE. Her new professor was very impressed with her work and she was certain she would pass. Leaving the campus building at nine o'clock, she gasped as Augustus stood waiting for her on the sidewalk.

"I've been waiting out here for an hour," he began.

She tensed up, frozen stiff and unable to speak.

"At ease, Trueblood. To coin one of your phrases, I come in peace," he said, raising an open palm.

"We did not come up with that!" she snapped and relaxed.

"Very well. I apologize."

"What do you want?"

"I know you've been expecting some sort of retaliation for your part in Yi's plan to have me resign from my position."

"I don't know what you're talking about."

"Don't insult my intelligence, young lady," he said sharply.

She looked down sheepishly as he sighed and continued, "I know she already told you, but I'm here to personally reiterate that you are safe. You've lost my trust. For someone neutral I know where you stand, now."

She tilted her head. "You...you know why I helped Sonyai? I thought she was wrong. I did this to prove you're innocent! I thought after the way you treated Heywood that somehow it was just for show. I never in my life thought you were capable of such deceit. I guess I was wrong."

Augustus was taken aback by her reasoning. He didn't believe her for a second. "If what you say is true, then one day I hope you will trust me again and not question my actions. Then perhaps I may trust *you* again," he walked up and stopped to stare her down. "But rest assured, I will *never* forget this betrayal."

He turned and walked to a parked limousine and got in the backseat. Angie watched the car pull off and pass her, heading up the street. She had no idea he knew where she was attending school. It suddenly felt as if she was under a huge magnifying glass, the watchful eye of Augustus Chavez. A chill went down her spine as she started walking to the nearest bus stop.

For a Friday, today had been a long day. After talking to Gerry over drinks and getting him to forget about Franklin, Robin was bringing a pie from Domino's to Walt's house. He knocked on the door at nine-thirty. Jacques opened the door without a word and let him in. The French roommate then stepped out for a cigarette as Robin closed the door.

Walter was sitting on the floor in the living room watching an episode of *The X-Files*. He looked up when Robin walked in and sighed. "Leave the pizza, turn and walk away."

"This the one about the Jersey Devil? No way am I missing this episode."

He put the pie down on the coffee table and helped himself to a slice. David Duchovny was in the middle of a dialogue with Gillian Anderson on the TV. Walter reached up and grabbed two slices.

"I don't deserve a friend like you," he confessed. "I wasn't there for you when your grandfather died, and you're always there for me."

A commercial came on and Robin asked, "When did Sherry break up with you?"

"Tuesday. She wanted the chance to see other people before things got serious between us."

"Hmm, heard that line before."

"Why do they play with our hearts like this? I mean, I treat them right. I'm not one of these guys trying to fuck every pussy with a pulse... what is wrong with them?"

Robin waited a moment before he asked, "You really wanna know?"

"Please, enlighten the fuck out of me."

"This has been my opinion, Walt, that women date the good guys, but *fuck* the bad ones."

"Huh?"

"You know, those douchebags who are on the team, buy their grades, get drunk and fuck their girlfriend's best friend, sister, mother, and worst enemy? They're getting all the action and good guys like you and me? Who bring flowers on that first date, recite poetry, study with them instead of copying and sharing our homework?" He clicked his tongue. "We just get a pat on the head. We give our shoulder for them to cry on, but we don't get the girl...the girl gets us, and puts us in their pocket."

"That fucking sucks, man," Walter said.

"Yes it does, yes it does. You got anything to drink? This pizza's gonna make me sleepy."

"You're supposed to be my sober companion, remember?" he reached underneath the coffee table and pulled out two bottles of Coors Light.

"It's my night off, give it here," he held out his hand.

They took several sips and ate more pizza.

"You know what? You might be right, Robin. I understand the speeches now. I'm ready to try those 20 push-ups."

"Well, alright. One is a wanderer, two is company!"

They raised their bottles. "No more pats on the head and shoulders to give."

"And here's to not getting put in the pocket!" Robin added.

"Cheers!" they exclaimed.

"So what now, man? Registration is in two weeks, summer's almost over...classes will start in September."

Robin sighed. "About that, I need you to do me a favor, Walt. I need you to tell the others."

"Tell 'em what?"

"I'm...I'm taking a semester off, taking a break."

Walter said nothing and just looked at him. He looked back after a minute and laughed. "Say something man."

"Don't drop out," he whispered.

"I'm not dropping out, I'm just taking a break!"

"That's what everybody says when they leave, then they don't come back!"

"Well I promise, I will come back in the late-fall, early-winter, whatever the hell it is! I'll be back...like The Terminator. Just tell Jarvis, Mouse, Kim, and Gillian. I'd let them know myself, but it'd be better coming from you."

"Robin, man." He got up from the floor and went to hug him.

"Walt, I swear to God, you start crying on me, I will bust your head open with this bottle!"

"I'll miss you, too, man." He patted Robin on his back with a spirited embrace.

"Awww, look at the American Lovers," Jacques said from the back of the room. "Se magnifique!" he added, snapping his fingers.

Jacques quickly ran out of the room down the hallway as Robin and Walter chased after him.

Barbara Schemanske hated the month of July. The summer heat usually peaks, and there was a more personal reason that brought back bitter memories. Holding a single white tulip in her hand she walked through the gates of Saint Raymond's Cemetery.

Robin stood at Jon's gravesite once again. It had been his fifth visit since his burial. This was the first Saturday visit at Schemanske's request since he usually came on Sundays. After he finished a prayer he turned to her as she approached him.

"Good morning. I never thanked you for the card. How did you find out so quickly?"

"You didn't have to thank me. A nurse who works there is a friend of mine. She called that night and told me. I'm just disappointed the staff at your branch failed to give you one."

Robin scoffed. "I'm not."

They started walking together. "I take it your situation hasn't improved?" she asked.

"No, but at least they started getting their act together amongst themselves. Sonyai and Augustus have buried the hatchet."

"How adorable," she dismissed. "Well, after calling in a few favors, I've finally managed to get you a position at Epiphany. You can start in two weeks."

Robin raised his eyebrow and chuckled. "You're kidding."

"That's not the reaction I was looking for," she said with a scowl. "This is the part where you say 'thank you'."

"No offense, ma'am, but..." he looked away. "My grandfather told me a story. It was September 1945, and he had just come home from the war. They dropped him off in Mississippi. Nobody was there to greet him so he walked down the street to a diner. As light-skinned as he was, the owners of the place still looked at him funny when he took a seat at the counter."

She looked on as he continued.

"He was still in uniform with his duffel bag, and he asked for a piece of toast with a glass of water. The man behind the counter looked at him and said, "We don't serve your kind here." So he stayed there and sat. People got up and started pushing him, kicking and screaming for him to leave. A man in uniform, after putting his life on the line for the United States in the name of freedom!"

Robin tried to keep his composure as his outrage was starting to get the best of him.

"After ten minutes of belittling, the mob gave up and he repeated his request, but this time he reached at his hip, pulled out his sidearm and slammed it on the counter for emphasis."

"Wow!" she gasped.

"That...that caused a panic in which the waitress called the police while the man behind the counter pulled a double-barreled shotgun from behind the bar. He pointed both barrels at his face. My grandfather, Jon David Walker, staring death in the face at 28-years-old looked at that man and said, 'Sir, do you know how many japs I've killed with this weapon before me? I am lucky to be stepping back on native soil and I just want something to eat, drink, then I'll be on my merry way. Now, can you do this for me or not?'"

He took a breath and continued, "The sheriff walked in at that moment and everyone in the establishment relaxed. He took one look at my grandfather and yelled, 'Get this man whatever he wants, and charge it to me!' There were sounds of shock and disappointment from everyone as the sheriff then took a seat next to him and asked, 'Sir would you please holster that sidearm and accept my apologies on behalf of the people of this town?' My grandfather did what he asked and when that toast and water arrived, the sheriff shook his hand and said, 'Thank you for your service, welcome home,' then walked out."

"That's a hell of a story," Schemanske remarked.

"Yeah, and it's exactly why I can't transfer."

She blinked in surprise. "I beg your pardon? After everything I just did."

"He didn't give them the satisfaction of leaving. He stood his ground. I need to do the same, no matter how long it takes. I'm staying right there."

She looked at his face. It showed no sign of hesitation. A smile came across her face as she nodded and let out a hoarse laugh. "You're a stubborn man, Robin Walker...and that's what I like about you. Give 'em hell!"

"Yes, ma'am. I gotta go. I'm due at the branch at 12."

"There's an exit to the street over there." She pointed toward the east. Robin walked past her and started on the path she indicated to him. He then stopped and turned back to her. "Oh, one last thing."

The librarian turned to look back at him. "Yes?"

"The card...someone's signature was missing."

She nodded. "Rosana Comanos. Yes, I sent the card to her, but noticed she didn't write anything."

"You have any idea why that would be?" he asked, already knowing the answer.

She sighed. "I don't know why, but from what I understand, for some strange reason...she believes you're dead."

Robin narrowed his eyes at the absurd notion. "That's what I thought." He turned and resumed walking toward the exit.

Schemanske walked several plots over and stopped at a gravesite. She looked down and placed the tulip in front of the headstone, took a moment to reflect and then turned to leave.

On the monument behind the flower, the name engraved read, *Oliver Prince, Beloved Husband, Born July 27th, 1922 - Died October 27th, 1989.* Beneath the inscription, a picture was etched in the gravestone...of a man in a white suit.

It was a grand celebration of life, one that brought together the fractured staff of the 58th Street Branch Library. Except for the three pages, everyone was gathered in a circle at the circulation desk smoking cigars Tommy had brought in. Written in pink letters on the cellophane wrappers was the message, *It's a Girl!*

"Congratulations man!" Gerry said with a playful jab at Tommy's shoulder.

"Here! Here!" Sonyai and Augustus chimed in unison.

"What's her name, what was the weight and all that?" Heywood asked.

"Carridad Angelica...Carmichael."

"Wait... *just* Carmichael?" Gerry asked. "What happened to Gonzales-Carmichael?"

"She decided to drop the hyphenation. We're fixing it with the Department of Vital Records. Tommy, Sarah, and Carrie Carmichael... the Carmichaels," he said with a proud grin.

"That is great! What time was she born?" Angie asked, blowing a perfect circle of smoke in the air.

"Thursday, July 21st, 1994 at 4:35 am. 7 pounds, 6 Ounces. 20.16 inches long! She's going to be a giant like her parents."

Everyone laughed at the joke. Avoiding the smoke for health reasons, Zelda and Ethel sat together at the information desk. Ethel turned the chair next to the desk around so they both faced the group near the entrance.

"It's nice that everyone's back together. You can almost say it's peaceful again," Zelda said.

Ethel nodded. "First time in many years. You'll think it'll last?"

"I have my hopes. They both have their battle scars, but a clean break and retreating to opposite corners... it won't be long before conflict arises again."

"Yes, but let's savor this moment for a bit. Take it all in."

The two shared a quiet moment, watching and listening to the banter.

"Zelda?" Ethel asked.

"Yes?"

"You got $1,000.00 you can lend me?"

"You know, it's a good thing Sarah dropped the double name...and that her last name didn't start with an 'A', like Alverez or Archuleta," Angie said.

Tommy, Heywood, and Gerry all turned their heads.

"Huh? Why not?" Tommy asked.

She smiled. "Because... her initials would have been C-A-C-A...Caca!"

She laughed while everyone else stared blankly.

After an embarrassing moment of awkward silence, she cleared her throat. "Um, you know... we came up with this tradition of celebrating a birth or a great victory with a smoke," she explained while holding up the cigar.

"I don't know, Angie... I think Red Auerbach had something to do with it as well," Tommy said.

Also separated from the group, still at his desk in the clerical office, Robin continued stamping Date Due cards quietly behind a wall of piled up stacks. The top of his head was barely visible, the constant sound of the stamp hitting the table drowned out by idle conversation.

"So how long will Sisyphus push the boulder up the hill?" Augustus asked Sonyai.

"Until I'm satisfied," she replied between puffs on the cigar. She turned to him. "We've made peace with each other. Don't break that up by questioning my authority in this manner."

"I won't interfere," he said, holding both hands up, the cigar in his right hand.

She nodded. "If he's smart he'll just resign and we'll be done with him."

"It would be a shame. Such a waste of potential," Augustus said. He then checked his watch and grabbed his jacket. "Alright, it's 11:30. We'll need to air out the floor before we open. Can't have the public know we've been smoking in here."

The clerks and librarians began to disperse, still in high spirits. There was a sense of true comradery in the air as they prepared to welcome and serve the arriving public, yearning for knowledge.

Gerry Coltraine turned on his terminal at the returns side, then glanced behind him back inside the clerical office. The sound of Robin Walker's endless stamping as he sat in exile echoed throughout the quiet library.

THUMP!...

THUMP!...

THUMP!...

THUMP!...

THE END

Call Numbers continues in Book 3
Date Due: Trial and Redemption

ABOUT THE AUTHOR

Syntell Smith was born and raised in Washington Heights, Upper Manhattan New York City. He graduated from Samuel Gompers High School and began writing while blogging his hectic everyday life experiences in 2004. He loves comic books, video games, and watching reruns of Law and Order. He currently lives in Detroit. "Call Numbers" is his first novel. Syntell is active on Facebook, Twitter and other social media platforms.

Lightning Source UK Ltd.
Milton Keynes UK
UKHW011822091020
371320UK00001B/4